T|

*Also by Christina Jones*

Going the Distance
Running the Risk
Stealing the Show
Jumping to Conclusions
Walking on Air
Nothing to Lose
Tickled Pink
Hubble Bubble
Seeing Stars

# Love Potions

*Christina Jones*

PIATKUS

# Visit the Piatkus website!

Piatkus publishes a wide range of bestselling fiction and non-fiction, including books on health, mind, body & spirit, sex, self-help, cookery, biography and the paranormal.

*If you want to:*
- read descriptions of our popular titles
- buy our books over the internet
- take advantage of our special offers
- enter our monthly competition
- learn more about your favourite Piatkus authors

VI             .co.uk

Copyright © Christina Jones 2006

First published in Great Britain in 2006 by
Judy Piatkus (Publishers) Ltd of
5 Windmill Street, London W1T 2JA
email: info@piatkus.co.uk

**The moral right of the author has been asserted**

*A catalogue record for this book is available from the British Library*

ISBN 0 7499 0835 1

Data manipulation by
Action Publishing Technology Ltd, Gloucester

Printed and bound in Great Britain by
William Clowes Ltd, Beccles, Suffolk

For Nellie Williams
(aka Nellie Pritchard-Gordon) with many thanks for
absolutely everything but especially for allowing me to
*borrow* her gorgeous Milla for this book.

# Chapter One

Okay, so finding a naked man in her bed wasn't *that* unusual. There had been one or two in the past – not at the same time, of course – but Sukie Ambrose had had her moments. Mind you, she had to admit, none of them had managed to look quite so spectacular at this early hour of a grey and chilly March Monday morning.

In fact the only thing wrong with this one, Sukie thought, staring at the lean, tanned torso rising and falling in sleep beneath her dark blue duvet; at the rumpled streaky ash blond hair which looked glorious against her navy pillows; at the superb cheekbones and the curve of long dark eyelashes, was that he was a complete stranger.

The initial terror which had kicked in as she'd switched on the light and found an unknown man sleeping soundly in her bedroom, was tempered by the sheer implausibility of the situation.

All right then, that – and the fact that he was truly beautiful.

Not that that made his presence any less scary, she told herself quickly. Some of the worst villains in history had been extremely attractive, hadn't they? Surely some of those mass murderers of the grim and grimy past had been lady-killers in every sense of the word? And how often had she peered at some serial wrongdoer on the television news thinking guiltily that she'd have fancied him if she'd met him at a party?

So was he a villain? Someone on the run? A fugitive from justice? A crazed killer suddenly overcome by the need to catch up on his beauty sleep?

Sukie shook her head. Doubtful. Not that she'd known any crazed killers, but somehow snuggling under an anonymous duvet simply didn't seem to fit the Tarantino image.

Mentally downgrading the criminality a bit, perhaps he was a burglar? A housebreaker, taking advantage of both her and Milla being away from home for the weekend, and making the most of the facilities before making away with their belongings?

Sukie somehow doubted that too. The sleepy village of Bagley-cum-Russet with its one high-banked main road, cobweb of tiny lanes, and one pub and two shops, was surely never going to be top of any mobster's must-visit list, was it? And she hadn't noticed any sign of a forced entry when she'd opened the cottage's front door. And everything downstairs had seemed untouched and normal . . . but then, exhausted after her journey and simply glad to be home, she hadn't really been looking for indications that they'd been burgled, had she?

She could really, really do without this . . .

Blinking wearily, she stared at the sleeping form again. He was out like a light. Could he possibly be ill? Maybe he'd wandered in from the winding village streets having suffered amnesia? Maybe he thought this was his home? Maybe he'd lived in Bagley at some time in the past and muddled up his cottages? No – Sukie discounted that one straight away. He was probably in his late twenties, as she was, and having been born and bred in Bagley-cum-Russet, she knew everyone who'd ever lived in the village.

He really was very, very pretty. And if he wasn't ill, and was far too clean and classy-looking to be anyone's stereotypical thug, why on earth was he in her bed? Unless . . .

What if he was a *squatter*?

That was it! One of that new breed of upmarket organised squatters reclaiming vacant properties as a protest against homelessness and materialism. Oh dear ... Sukie felt more than a little sympathy with that particular cause, but could also feel a severe case of nimbyism coming on.

Sukie stared at him for a little longer. He really was sensational.

Should she wake him? Ring the police? Scream?

No, too late for screaming, and anyway she'd never been much of a drama queen. And the police would take ages to arrive and then there'd probably be forms to fill in and lots of questions and she was far too tired to even contemplate all that. Maybe she'd just sneak back out of the room, lock the door on the outside and wait for him to regain consciousness and ask questions later.

Dropping her holdall quietly to the bedroom floor and holding her breath while she wriggled the old-fashioned key from the lock, Sukie switched off the light and backed out of the room. Her hands were shaking as she locked the door from the outside. Damn ... Too noisy ... She paused, waiting for the explosion, but there was no angry shout from her bed. She pocketed the key in her jeans and listened again. Still no sound at all from behind the door. Clearly the intruder was exhausted.

Not as exhausted as she was though. Driving back to Berkshire from Newcastle through the night had seemed like a good idea at the time. Her three-day course – 'Advanced Aromatherapy: Essential Oils and Infusions for the 21st Century' – had ended late the previous evening. The delegates had been invited for a night out on the town, sampling every hot venue the Quayside complex had to offer, with the additional tempting promise of spotting premiership footballers and reality TV stars at every turn.

But after three rigorous days of studying, attending lectures, practical sessions and a rather sneaky written exam, and having already spent three evenings of galli-vanting with several like-minded beauticians to make the most of the Newcastle pubs and clubs after classes, all Sukie had wanted to do was go home to Bagley-cum-Russet

3

and crawl into bed and sleep for a week.

Not possible now.

Of course she could sleep in Milla's bed as Milla wasn't due back until later today from her hen-party in Dublin, but maybe this wasn't a great idea with a strange man in the cottage.

Oh, bugger . . .

Feeling bone tired and more irritated than frightened – after all the bedroom door was securely locked and the window, centuries old and much-painted over, opened only a few inches, so the interloper was safely imprisoned for now – Sukie tiptoed downstairs.

The sleeping man upstairs had put a bit of a dampener on the usual sense of euphoria Sukie normally felt on returning to the strangely named Pixies Laughter Cottage. It was her sanctuary, truly her home, a place she loved with all her heart.

She'd always hated having her cherished space invaded, and having it invaded by a naked stranger had thrown her completely. And, she thought with a weary grin, what on earth would her godmother have made of it all?

Cora, Sukie's maternal great-aunt and godmother, had lived all her higgledy-piggledy life in Pixies Laughter. Sukie had adored the elderly, eccentric Cora and spent an idyllic childhood with her in the low-beamed rooms, snuggled up in front of the log fire in the winter, playing wild games in the garden through long hot summers.

When Sukie's aspirational parents, living on the other side of the village in their up-to-the-minute stylised and clinically neat modern estate semi, had inherited the cottage they'd immediately planned to modernise it and sell it at some exorbitant sum to incomers.

Horrified at the thought of losing Cora's home, her happy memories and her childhood bolt hole, Sukie had begged, pleaded and eventually convinced her parents that she'd be the ideal owner for Pixies Laughter. After much wrangling a price had been agreed – nowhere near as high

4

as the Ambroses would have managed to extort from strangers – and Sukie, having convinced the bank that she'd be a great mortgage risk, had moved in. The modernisations – central heating and a bathroom – had eaten into her savings and a further bank loan and more, and her parents had refused to help on the grounds that if Sukie wanted the cottage so badly she took it warts and all and paid dearly for the privilege. So a year previously she'd taken Milla in as a lodger to ease the financial burden.

The whole thing had caused a few ructions at the time, but feathers were now more or less smoothed down... However, Sukie's parents' visits to Pixies Laughter were few and far between despite only living less than a mile away, and Sukie's visits home to the minimalist semi were equally rare.

Sad, really, she thought now, as she ducked under the lowest beam at the foot of the stairs, that she hadn't immediately thought of ringing her parents for advice on the current situation. Apart from the fact that they'd be extremely annoyed at being woken up before dawn, they'd probably feel it was her fault somehow and would trot out trite and irritating lines like 'you made your bed when you took the cottage on – if you've got a problem you've only yourself to blame'.

Nah, she'd deal with sleeping beauty on her own and in her own time, Sukie thought, clattering across the uneven hall floor. The central heating was humming gently, and in the tiny brightly-lit kitchen, Sukie did what any girl would do under the circumstances. She put the kettle on.

She was just scrabbling in the dishwasher for a clean mug when the kitchen door opened.

She screamed and dropped the mug on the ancient quarry tiles. The bits skittered across the floor.

'What the hell are you doing here?' Milla, her cottage-mate, tall, slender and blonde, wearing a very skimpy T-shirt and a black thong, blinked from the doorway.

'I could ask you the same thing,' Sukie snapped, rescuing

the broken mug from under the table and wondering how come Milla always managed to look so perfectly groomed and glamorous even when she'd just woken up. 'Why aren't you in Dublin? I didn't see your car in the lane.'

'Caught an earlier flight. Still a bit tipsy. Didn't want to drive. Left the car at the airport and got a cab.' Milla gave an elegant yawn. 'Collecting it later. Why aren't you in Newcastle?'

'Couldn't stand the pace. And – there's a problem.'

'What?' Milla flicked back her bone-straight silver hair and reached a slender hand into the dishwasher for two mugs. 'What sort of problem?'

'We've got an intruder. Upstairs. In my bed.'

Milla handed her mug to Sukie and laughed. 'He's not an intruder. He's with me.'

Sukie sighed heavily. She really should have guessed. Milla was always careless with her men. She'd once left one at a taxi rank in Reading while she nipped off to find a loo after a night out clubbing and completely forgotten about him. Rumour had it that the poor sap had still been standing there forlornly waiting as dawn broke.

'I should have guessed, I suppose. But couldn't you have labelled him or something? Like Paddington Bear: "Milla's Man – Please Don't Touch"? Anything to indicate that he wasn't a threat? And why—' Sukie wearily spooned granules into the mugs, '—is he in my bed, not yours? And who is he?'

'Whoa! Far too many questions! Anyway, I've no idea about the last one—' Milla perched on the edge of one of the oddment kitchen chairs crossing her long perfectly shaped legs, '—which is the answer to why he's not in my bed. Even I'm not that shallow. I do like to be on least first name terms before I offer B&B. Thanks.' She took the coffee. 'No, honestly, we only met last night. At the airport. Waiting for a taxi. I didn't even see him on the plane. He'd been to Dublin with a stag-party. He was about as hung-over as me so he decided not to drive

6

home either, and while we were chatting in the queue I discovered he came from Winterbrook so we shared a cab.'

Sukie raised her eyebrows. The relief was short-lived. Even for Milla it seemed a bit unlikely, not to mention downright risky.

'And you didn't ask his name? What he does for a living? Like murder, rape, pillage? Chatting up blondes in taxi queues with the intention of relieving them of their worldly goods and their bank accounts and maybe their breathing?'

'Sukie, sweetheart.' Milla shook her head. 'You read far, far too many tabloids. He was just a fellow-traveller in need of a good turn.'

Sukie slid onto the opposite chair. 'Not good enough. Why is he here? Why didn't he stay in the cab and go on to Winterbrook? It's only a few miles away.'

Milla smiled her sleepy-cat green-eyed smile. Sukie, who was of average height, curvy, with short, dark, spiky hair and blue eyes, sighed. She'd kill to look like Milla.

'He was sound asleep by the time we got here,' Milla lit a cigarette. 'Out cold. The taxi driver didn't want the hassle of unloading him single-handed at Winterbrook so he turfed us both out here. Poor bloke was almost asleep on his feet and I knew you wouldn't be back, so I gave him your room.'

'Wasn't that a bit risky? You didn't even know him?'

Milla blew smoke towards the ceiling. 'Like I said, he was practically comatose. And the cab driver legged it. I could hardly leave him outside in the lane, could I? So I woke him up, made him a cup of coffee which he didn't drink, pointed him towards your room and well, that's it really ...' She stubbed out the cigarette. 'And he is rather cute, isn't he?'

'Very.' Sukie sipped her coffee. 'And I should have realised he wasn't one of yours anyway. He's got a chin.'

'Bitchy ...' Milla stretched showing most of her slender toned midriff, then yawned again, still managing to make it look endearingly attractive. 'I don't *always* date chinless wonders.'

'Yeah you do. Well, when you're not dating city traders with sharp suits, sharper tongues and estuary accents.'

'A girl has to maintain her standards,' Milla shrugged. 'You can't support my lifestyle on a labourer's wage packet, sweetie, as I keep pointing out to you.'

Sukie winced. It still didn't solve the problem of the stranger upstairs in her bed and the fact that she had probably never felt so tired in her entire life.

'So – how were you and him going to get back to the airport to collect your cars? Oh no – don't look at me like that. I am not – not – driving you all the way to – good lord!'

A thundering crash from upstairs rocked the cottage to its centuries-old foundations.

'I think he's awake.' Milla frowned at the ceiling. 'Probably needs the loo. He doesn't sound very happy.'

'No.' Sukie bit her lip. 'He wouldn't. I locked him in.'

'You did *what*?' Milla shrieked with laughter. 'Sukes, you're priceless! Then you'd better go and unlock him, hadn't you? And point him in the direction of the bathroom pretty damn quickly.'

By the time Sukie reached the top of the narrow winding staircase, the man was pounding on her bedroom door. She unlocked it and stood back, screwing up her eyes in case he was stark naked.

He wasn't. Well not completely. He'd managed to pull on a pair of faded jeans, which did absolutely nothing to detract from the stunning rest of him.

'Thanks,' he blinked at her through the long strands of ash blond hair. 'Door seemed to have stuck and I walked straight into those bloody beams. Does this place belong to the seven dwarves or something? Er – sorry, but where's the loo? Please?'

'Bathroom's along the passage. End door. And mind the beams.'

'Thanks.' He gave a weary, bleary smile. 'Er – do I know you?'

Sukie shook her head. 'Nope. And I'm not Snow White either. But this is my cottage.'

'Is it?' He looked confused. 'Were you on the plane last night, then? I thought—'

'No, that was my taller, thinner, prettier, blonder friend.'

'Oh, right – sorry – but I must . . .'

Sukie stood aside as he pounded along the passage.

'All okay?' Milla appeared at the top of the stairs. 'Is he in the loo? Good – I'm going back to bed, Sukes. Catch you later . . .'

Sukie sighed as Milla slammed into her bedroom, then casting one last lingering look at the cosy invitation of her own bed, dragged a blanket from the airing cupboard and trudged wearily downstairs to catch up on her beauty sleep on the sofa.

# Chapter Two

'And so you slept on the sofa and he'd gone when you woke up, had he?' Jennifer Blessing raised perfectly arched eyebrows at Sukie later that day in the peaches and cream draped splendour of Beauty's Blessings on Hazy Hassocks High Street. 'And I bet Milla had disappeared too.'

'Yep. Hopefully still living and breathing and not dragged over the quarry tiles to be buried in a shallow grave.' Sukie, struggling untidily into her peach overall, nodded at her boss. 'And I'm still fuzzy-headed from too little sleep, so can we possibly leave the rest of the cross-examination until later, please?'

'Cross-examination? You make me sound like a nosy old bag.' Jennifer frowned but not very fiercely. Botox for Beginners had had a radical effect on her forehead. 'I'm just a concerned employer, that's all.'

Yeah, right, Sukie thought, feeling achy and scratchy and still irritated. She'd had a maximum four uncomfortable and restless hours on the sofa, and hadn't known whether to be pleased, concerned or annoyed that Pixies Laughter Cottage had been empty when she'd woken up.

Still, there'd been no signs of violence, and on the plus side it at least meant Milla and the nameless sex god had made other arrangements about collecting their cars from the airport, and someone – probably not Milla – had stripped her bed, remade it with fresh linen and even put

10

her navy blue duvet cover, sheet and pillowcases into the washing machine.

If Mr Blond and Beautiful was a serial killer, he was a very domesticated one. Which meant, of course, that he could be married. Or seriously attached. Or maybe even . . .

'You did enjoy the aromatherapy course, though?' Jennifer interrupted Sukie's runaway train of thought. 'I realise it pales into insignificance compared with coming home to find a naked man in your bed, but it cost a lot of money and—'

'It was great,' Sukie yawned. 'Oh, sorry. No, I loved it. Learned loads. Until this morning I was bursting with enthusiasm, couldn't wait to put it into practice and I will be again, promise. I just need to sleep for a week and wake up properly first.'

'Good, lovely – I'm really pleased you got such a lot out of it.' Jennifer batted her newly enhanced eyelashes. 'Because you're a natural masseuse and I think offering this mobile service will really put us on the map. No other salons round here do home treatments, and those experimental ones we tried out round the villages last year went down well, didn't they?'

Sukie nodded. They had. Probably because they'd been free. The most unlikely people from Hazy Hassocks, Bagley-cum-Russet and Fiddlesticks had volunteered for lip-filling and head massages and pedicures with the usual rural enthusiasm of getting something for nothing even if they didn't want it.

Jennifer patted her dark red hair in one of the peach-lit mirrors. 'We'll go through the oils and fragrances you'll need later. My suppliers can get hold of any new stuff, then hopefully you'll be out on the road by next week. I've already had several enquiries after that splash in the *Winterbrook Advertiser*.' She stopped patting and preening and peered at Sukie again. 'Oh, sorry to keep on about work. You poor thing – you know I wasn't really expecting you to come in today anyway – and you do look awful . . .'

'Thanks.'

'I'll make some more coffee, shall I? See if that helps?'

Doubting that anything would help apart from sleep, sleep and more sleep, Sukie nodded gratefully as Jennifer whispered away in her own slinky overall towards Beauty's Blessings' tiny kitchenette.

The cold March morning had lengthened into a cold grey afternoon, and not even the warm tones and even warmer scents wafting round the salon could lift Sukie's flagging spirits. Lamps glowed under peach shades, and Classic FM murmured tastefully in the background. Jennifer, Sukie knew, had poured her heart and soul, not to mention a fair whack of her husband Lance's hard-earned money, into the salon which was doing well, but somehow they both doubted if bucolic Berkshire was ever going to be quite ready for eyebrow threading, caviar facials, chocolate body wraps or even chemical derma-peels.

However, since Beauty's Blessings had opened the previous summer, the trade for basic facials and manicures had been steady, and thanks to a concerted leaflet-drop after Christmas, the massages and non-surgical face-lifts were becoming quite popular, but Jennifer was still keen to build the business further, hence the one-to-one home aromatherapy service.

This mobile expansion, Sukie realised, was mainly due to Mitzi, the first Mrs Blessing, having made such a stonking success of her Hubble Bubble Country Cooking outlet at the other end of Hazy Hassocks High Street. Jennifer, the second Mrs Blessing, was nothing if not violently competitive on all fronts.

Beauty's Blessings was housed in a flint and slate ex-cottage next door to Hazy Hassocks Dental Surgery, which had caused a bit of soul-searching for Jennifer as Mitzi's gorgeous, much younger, live-in dentist lover worked there, and this was originally considered a little close for comfort. However, although the location certainly hadn't been Jennifer's first choice, at the moment the relationship

12

between the Mrs Blessings Mark One and Two was reasonably civilised, and as long as no one mentioned Mitzi's entrepreneurial skills on Jennifer's premises the two businesses blossomed in relative harmony.

A couple of hundred years ago Beauty's Blessings had probably housed a family of seventeen, and according to the more elderly residents it had had a chequered history once it had moved into commercialism. It had enjoyed life as a cobbler's early in the twentieth century, then in rapid succession an engraver's, a sweet shop, a dress shop, an estate agent's, a charity shop twice, followed by its most recent incarnation as a juice bar.

Sadly Hazy Hassocks simply hadn't known what to do with a juice bar and it had closed within six months.

As soon as Mitzi had opened, and made a success of, Hubble Bubble at the other end of the High Street, Jennifer had persuaded Lance to back her to fly solo too. Fortunately Lance ran a small building business so the extensive renovations on the defunct Juicy Lucy's hadn't been as costly as they might have been. Before Lance had been allowed to alter anything though, Jennifer had toured various Berkshire salons, attended trade fairs, consulted all the style magazines, checked with colourists, and ordered all the latest equipment, with the result that Beauty's Blessings now offered the most opulent and luxurious and up-to-date surroundings in the area.

Sukie lifted one of the filmy peach drapes and peered out of the window. Everywhere looked very grey and cheerlessly cold. Shoppers hurried past en route to Big Sava, heads down against the wind, their noses the only splash of colour in the uniform beigeness of their bobble-hat-to-bootee attire. Maybe it would snow, Sukie thought. She hoped so. Hazy Hassocks looked much prettier when it snowed.

Hazy Hassocks, with its winding sycamore-lined High Street filled with a mishmash of shops and small businesses, was a large village a few miles away from Sukie's home in Bagley-cum-Russet. It was where the Bagleyites, and the Fiddlestickers from the neighbouring hamlet, did most of their shopping and socialising. Winterbrook, the nearest market town, offered larger supermarkets and banks and other municipal delights, while Reading was regarded as Up Town and reserved for shopping sprees of mega-proportions.

If the Romans had bothered themselves with this part of the county instead of concentrating their efforts on the Ridgeway, then the villages would all be within a few minutes' travelling distance of one another. As it was, the lanes twisted and turned back on themselves in convoluted loops, and while they looked only centimetres apart on the map, the reality was very different.

Jennifer had used the complex local geography to cash in on the beauty business. There were no rival rural establishments for miles.

'Thanks, Jennifer. You're an angel.' Sukie took the coffee gratefully. 'And as the junior here I should be making coffee. And sweeping up and washing the towels and—'

Jennifer laughed as much as her eye-lift would allow. 'If the aromatherapy takes off we'll be able to employ a proper junior for those jobs. I was thinking of asking Winterbrook FE college if they'd like me to take some of their final year beauty students on day-release. And we won't have to pay them much because they'll be gaining invaluable practical experience here, of course.'

Oh, of course. Jennifer could teach Shylock a trick or two. Child labour would be right up her street.

Wandering over to the desk, Sukie sipped her coffee, waiting for the caffeine to kick in, and studied the appointment book. It was reasonably full.

'Shall I go and see to Mrs Fellowes now? She must have been in the cubicle for hours.'

Jennifer shook her head. Her mahogany bob didn't move. 'I'm going to leave her for a few more minutes. The

14

seaweed wrap is good – but not that good. Years of junk food and lager tops have taken their toll there I'm afraid. What she really needs is a body transplant ... You can do Chelsea's nail extensions if you like. She's due in shortly for a complete revamp – I think she wants a hearts and flowers motif this time.'

Sukie groaned. She was so tired, she wasn't sure she could cope with acrylic nails and mini-transfers and glue and clippers and emery boards, not to mention Chelsea's irrepressible non-stop gossiping, without probably doing her some irreversible harm. However, as arguing with Jennifer was never an option, with another yawn, she gathered together the necessary paraphernalia and staggered off to the nail-bar.

Ten minutes later she was half-heartedly buffing away at Chelsea's nails without, so far, having drawn blood.

' ... and then her mum and dad came home and took one look and – Sukie? Are you listening to me?'

'What? Yes, yes of course I am. Fascinating. Really. Try and keep your hand still – I need to get the tweezers just right and these roses are fiddly – oh, sod it!'

Chelsea stared at the tiny rosebud transfer now raggedly adorning her wrist and giggled. 'Mind not on the job, eh, Sukes? Not that I'm surprised ... You look like you haven't slept for days – and who can blame you ... Derry Kavanagh is enough to keep any girl awake.'

'What? Who?' Sukie scraped the escapee rosebud from Chelsea's wrist and tried again. 'What are you talking about?'

'Derry Kavanagh sneaking out of your front door at first light this morning?'

'Who the hell is – oh ...'

Chelsea leaned forward. 'Ah! The all-night passion ration hasn't affected your short-term memory permanently I'm pleased to see. I was just passing the cottage on my way to get the bus to work and almost bumped into him.

15

Ooooh – it was lovely . . . And you're a dark horse – how come we didn't know you and Derry were an item.'

So the sex-god had a name. Derry Kavanagh . . . Sukie nodded. Nice. Suited him.

'We aren't.' She completed the next transfer on the white-tipped talon and sat back. 'He wasn't sneaking out of my bed. Well, actually – no, what I mean is, he was with Milla. Not me.'

'Oh.' Chelsea looked crushed. 'Really? I wouldn't have thought Derry Kavanagh was in her league. Not rich enough, not a fashion victim, not a flashy prat . . . Mind you, I suppose even Milla would forgo all those for a night with someone as lush as Derry. I know I would.'

So would I, Sukie thought suddenly. Then pushed the thought away.

She shrugged and clamped Chelsea's stubby hands more firmly to the table for the final application. 'There. All done. Er, – was Milla with him – Derry – this morning?'

'No,' Chelsea chuckled. 'Stoopid. If she'd been with him then I wouldn't have thought he was your latest, would I?' She held out her hands. 'Lovely, thanks Sukie. Now I'll just need to keep them looking like this until Saturday night.'

'Are you doing something special on Saturday?' Sukie followed Chelsea towards the reception desk.

In Beauty's Blessings' relaxation area Mrs Fellowes had been rescued from the seaweed wrap. Both she and Jennifer were flecked with dark green speckles and looked rather strained.

Chelsea frowned. 'It's Fern's hen-night. In Fiddlesticks. At the Weasel and Bucket – bit of a busman's holiday for her seeing as she works there and practically owns the place, but still – surely you hadn't forgotten?'

Ah, yes – Fern's hen-night. Sukie slid Chelsea's credit card into the machine. Of course she'd forgotten.

Barmaid Fern, who was their age, was soon to marry ancient – well, he must be at least *fifty* – Timmy Pluckrose,

16

landlord of the Weasel and Bucket. Rumour had it that their romance had blossomed the previous summer as the result of someone conjuring up an astral magic spell. Sukie didn't believe a word of it, but the Fiddlestickers swore by their celestial celebrations, and who was she to argue with them?

And just how much did this illustrate the difference between her lifestyle and Milla's? Milla was invited on glamorous hen-nights: long weekends in Dublin, Ibiza and Barcelona – Sukie's invites stretched just as far as a couple of hours in the next village ...

'I might not be able to make it.' She handed Chelsea the card and receipt. 'I'm not sure what I'm doing yet.'

'Get away!' Chelsea laughed. 'Your social diary isn't that full. And if you don't come we'll all know why you want to give Fiddlesticks a wide berth. An ex-boyfriend ring any bells? An ex by the name of Lewis Flanagan?'

Sukie groaned. She really didn't want to be reminded of that mad moment last year when she'd had the briefest romance on record with Lewis Flanagan. Lewis, who looked like some hippie rock god, had asked Sukie out once. They'd had a lovely evening – but Lewis, it was clear, was already mad about Amber, who had recently moved to Fiddlesticks. Under the circumstances, Sukie had known nothing would come of her relationship with Lewis, so they'd called it a day.

'Lewis wasn't my boyfriend,' Sukie said quickly. 'I only went out with him once. Months ago. We – weren't suited. And he's with Amber now and it's all ancient history...'

Well, it was. However much she'd fancied Lewis last summer, it wouldn't have worked out. Not when he was so clearly crazy about Amber. And anyway he wouldn't be at Fern's hen-night would he? Amber would though ... And she liked Amber, honestly she did, but ...

'Course it is.' Chelsea pulled on her padded coat and grinned knowingly. 'Whatever you say – but you'll have to be there – it'll be a laugh. We're all dressing up as fairies.'

Oh God ...

'And you'll be able to tell everyone about Derry and Milla, won't you?' Chelsea tugged her variegated hair from the collar of her coat. 'There hasn't been any decent gossip for ages. And don't forget your present.'

'Present? What present?'

'Fern's wedding shower present. Because we can't go to the wedding, and because they don't need *things*, we're all going to take her something girlie to the hen-night.'

'Oh, right, okay.' Sukie felt this was something she might just be able to cope with. She'd take Fern a selection of Beauty's Blessings' best skin products.

Chelsea grinned. 'I've got her a "grow your own man" kit from Herbie's Healthfoods. Timmy's a nice bloke but he's older than my dad! Right – think I've got everything. Big Sava's checkouts here I come. Thanks again for the nails – and see you tomorrow evening.'

'Tomorrow?' Sukie fought another yawn. She really, really needed to sleep for a week. 'I thought you said the hen-night was on Saturday?'

'It is, dumb-cluck.' Chelsea swung her shoulder-bag in a swashbuckling arc. 'Blimey – you really are fuddled, aren't you? Tomorrow – Tuesday? Hazy Hassocks village hall? Dance practice?'

Oh God times two zillion . . . Sukie groaned. Right now she was too tired to put one foot in front of the other. She'd never cope with *dancing* . . .

'I think I'll give that a miss, too . . .'

'You can't! You're giving me a lift. How am I going to get there without you?'

'It's the next village, not the Outer Hebrides. You could get the bus.'

Chelsea pulled a face. 'I don't think so. Even I draw the line at bussing it after dark. Don't you remember what happened to Sharon Midgely? Caught the bus at the Bagley crossroads, only going to Fiddlesticks, never seen again . . .'

'That,' Sukie stifled another yawn, 'was because she was dumping Mr Midgely for the bus driver and a life of sin in rural France. They found the bus abandoned at the EuroStar terminal if you remember.'

'Yeah, well, okay – but if you don't go Topsy'll have your head on a stick.' Chelsea pushed her hands into Winnie-the-Pooh mittens. 'Death is the only excuse to miss a rehearsal as far as Topsy's concerned. You know what she's like about dancing—'

'Dancing?' Jennifer swept past them, peeling off her seaweed-encrusted latex gloves *en route* to the wash basins. 'Lance and I adore dancing. We're learning to fox-trot.'

Chelsea wrinkled her nose. 'Not that sort of dancing, Jen. Our dancing. The cancan troupe. The one that Mitzi started – ouch!' She glared at Sukie. 'That hurt! What's wrong with mentioning Mitzi? Oh, yeah – right . . .'

Too late. Jennifer had marched off towards the gleaming basins, every inch of her slender back view radiating annoyance.

'Nice one, Chelsea,' Sukie sighed. 'Now she'll be stroppy for the rest of the afternoon. You know how ratty she gets when anyone mentions Mrs Blessing Mark One's ventures – especially in here.'

A couple of years earlier, as well as Hubble Bubble, Mitzi had rejuvenated the Baby Boomers of Hazy Hassocks and surrounding villages by setting-up all manner of activities. The Bagley-cum-Russet cancan troupe had been one of her many triumphs. Six ladies of varying ages, including Chelsea who had replaced her middle-aged mum who was hamstrung after the first session, and varying degrees of expertise had been kicking and screaming with varying measures of success at local events for several months.

At Chelsea's insistence, Sukie had joined the troupe the previous autumn after another of the older originals had done herself irreparable damage during the splits. She'd thought at the time it would get her out a bit, would be more fun than gym membership, and might, just might, make her as toned at Milla.

All she'd achieved so far were calf muscles like a prop

19

forward and more fishnet stockings and suspenders than an Ann Summers catalogue.

'See ya!' With an unrepentant grin, Chelsea clattered out of Beauty's Blessings into the chill bleakness of the High Street.

'Sukie!' Jennifer's voice echoed crossly from the depths of the cloakroom. 'If you've finished chattering about nonsense, these u-bends are all blocked with gunge again! Bring your rubber gloves and the plunger!'

# Chapter Three

'Don't move her!' Topsy screamed above the roar of Offenbach's finest. 'Stand well back and give her some air! Leave her where she is, girls! She'll need intravenous fluids and a spinal board and possibly a neck brace!'

It was halfway through Tuesday evening, halfway through the Bagley-cum-Russet cancan dancers' rehearsal in Hazy Hassocks village hall. Valerie Pridmore had taken a tumble during a particularly energetic kick-and-twist manoeuvre.

The five still-upright members of the troupe stopped staring at Valerie, prone on the stage, and turned their attention to Topsy, excitedly tip-tapping her way from the murky depths of the hall, her eyes wide with vicarious pleasure.

'Stand clear!' Topsy yelled. 'Wait for the crash trolley!'

No one took any notice. Everyone knew Topsy watched far, far too many medical soaps on telly. Topsy could have done *Mastermind* on *ER* or *Holby* and was word-perfect on the early editions of *Emergency Ward 10*.

Sukie, out of breath and aching, looked down anxiously at Valerie. 'Are you okay? You haven't broken anything?'

'Bra strap,' Valerie grimaced. 'Nothing terminal, love. Just give me a sec to get my second wind ...'

'Sukie – leave her!' Topsy, a hundred and ninety-seven if she was a day; small, shrivelled, her hair scraped back into a bun, and fitter than any of them, glared beadily like a bad-tempered tortoise as she reached the foot of the stage. She looked at Valerie and shivered pleasurably. 'You'll probably need CPR, my girl.'

'What I need,' Valerie muttered from her crumpled heap, 'is a safety pin and a double gin and tonic. Help me up, Sukie, there's a good girl. Ooooh, ouch . . .'

'I said don't touch her!' Topsy screeched over Orpheus reaching the seductive bit as she scrambled nimbly on to the stage. 'She might need to get back into sinus rhythm.'

'What I need to get into,' Valerie puffed, 'is a decent pub with—'

'No alcohol!' Topsy shrieked, snapping off the ancient sound system and leaving the gloomy village hall vibrating to silent echoes. 'Nil by mouth!'

Sukie tried hard not to giggle, and hauled Valerie to her feet.

'Thanks love. Ooooh – blimey! I don't think I'll be high-kicking again anytime soon. I reckon I've pulled something.'

'Wish I had,' Chelsea muttered.

'Well . . .' Topsy stood, hands on hips, and stared at her raggle-taggle cancan troupe. 'This is a pretty kettle of fish and no mistake. Can't you give her one of your massages, Sukie, and see if that helps? We can't be a dancer down at this stage – it'll ruin the routines.'

Sukie tried not to smile. To be honest, she felt on a really bad day the Bagley cancanners could ruin the routines quite easily without any help at all. 'Er – well, yes I could massage her leg, but not here. I haven't got any of my stuff and she'd need to be warmer anyway.'

The cancanners might well have been sweating profusely from their recent efforts but the hall itself was subzero. Muscles were stiffening and perspiring bodies growing rapidly chilly.

'Let's get her home, then,' Topsy said, clearly sulking at having been deprived of a fleet of paramedics and an emergency tracheotomy. 'She'll need a comfrey rub.'

'I could do with a comfy rub,' Chelsea grinned, tugging at her sagging leggings. 'But not from Sukie.'

Leaning on Sukie and standing on one leg like a plump stork, Valerie shrugged. 'Maybe my old man was right. Maybe I'm far too old for this game.'

'Nonsense!' Topsy snapped. 'When I taught ballet, my gels were as strong as oxen from cradle to grave. And look at Margot Fonteyn and Dame Nellie Melba – they were still dancing well into their autumn years. And this troupe was your idea, Valerie Pridmore. You were the one who told young Mitzi last year you wanted to be a Bluebell Girl, so don't go all Lib Dem on us now.'

Sukie, despite shivering inside her baggy T-shirt and jogging bottoms, sniggered.

'It's no laughing matter.' Topsy frowned. 'We've got bookings coming up all summer – fêtes and galas and whatnot – not to mention that wedding reception for young Fern and Timmy . . . We've rehearsed with six dancers. We can't rearrange the routines. We're going to need a replacement. Again.'

'Bugger the replacement,' Valerie sniffed, limping heavily and clutching her sagging bosom. 'I'm getting me coat and going home. Anyone else?'

There was a whoop of assent. It was the most animated the cancanners had been all evening.

Pulling on thick jackets and gloves and scarves over their practise clothes, Sukie and Chelsea took charge of Valerie, while the remaining dancers, Betty, Roo and Trace, helped Topsy turn out the lights in the hope that there'd be no short-circuits during the night. Hazy Hassocks village hall was in dire need of re-wiring and re-heating. And probably demolishing. But as it was the only place for miles around that had the room for functions and activities, and Mitzi Blessing had practically sold her soul to the owners for the Baby Boomers to be able to use it at all, no one dared to suggest it should be closed for a refurb lest it never opened again.

'Did you cycle here?' Chelsea looked at Valerie as they emerged into a bitterly cold, black and blustery March night.

Valerie nodded.

'Leave the bike here then, and I'll give you a lift.' Sukie shivered. 'You'll never be able to pedal with that leg.'

'I'll ride her bike home,' Topsy said, emerging from the hall, tying a brown and grey paisley headscarf under her wrinkled chin which only accentuated the tortoise-look. 'I walked over from Bagley.'

Sukie sighed. Topsy walked everywhere. Quickly. It was so irritating to be outpaced on all levels by someone who was so old they instantly equated the name Victoria with Queen rather than Beckham.

Once Valerie was carefully ensconced in the back, and Chelsea'd strapped herself into the passenger seat, Sukie steered the car slowly through Hazy Hassocks' unlit rutted lanes and out on to the Bagley-cum-Russet road.

'Any more news on Milla and Derry Kavanagh?' Chelsea wriggled in anticipation. 'Has he moved in yet?'

'No,' Sukie shook her head. 'Why would he? Milla likes to keep her options open – she'd never have a permanent residential fixture – and he definitely isn't her type. I haven't seen her – or him – since yesterday morning.'

'She's probably moved in with him, then,' Valerie said from behind her. 'I know he wouldn't have to ask me twice. He's bloody gorgeous – only don't tell my old man I said so . . .'

Sukie frowned. Did everyone in the world know every-thing about Derry Kavanagh except her? How come she'd missed him? She really, really hoped that Milla wouldn't go out with him. She couldn't face them being all lovey-dovey in Pixies Laughter's nooks and crannies. Not that she fancied Derry Kavanagh, of course. Definitely not. But even so . . .

'Milla was working late last night and left early this morning.' she slowed down to avoid a couple of teenagers kissing passionately in the middle of the road and sounded the horn. 'Move you silly little sods! Honestly – we were never like that!'

'Yeah, we were.' Chelsea grinned. 'After school . . . on the way home, remember? Along Twisty Lane? Oh, and especially after youth club. You used to drag Barry Lumsden off for a snog at every opportunity.'

'I did not! Barry Lumsden was gross!'

'Good snogger though,' Chelsea said wistfully. 'Blimey, Sukes, that was all so long ago. We had loads of lads back then, didn't we? Spoilt for choice. And here we are now – rushing towards thirty and both blokeless . . .'

Sukie swerved round the still-entwined teenagers who gestured rudely. 'Excuse me – I've had my moments . . .'

'Yeah, but not for a long time,' Chelsea sighed. 'And as you can't count the brief encounter with Lewis Flanagan, you haven't had a steady relationship for well over a year have you?'

'By choice. And you can't talk.'

'I'm picky. Mr Right will have to be Mr Absolutely Perfect . . .'

Valerie giggled. 'You youngsters are so funny. In my day you'd be considered on the shelf if you weren't marching down the aisle on your twenty-first. You didn't play the field back then, you took what was on your doorstep. I was engaged while I was at school, married my old man on my eighteenth birthday, and had all my kids before I was twenty-five . . .'

Sukie and Chelsea exchanged horrified glances. The car jerked a bit.

'Ooops, sorry, Val. You okay? That didn't hurt your leg, did it?'

'No. I'm fine. Look, will you do me a massage though sometime, love?' Valerie leaned forward in the darkness. 'One of your at home ones like you advertised?'

'Yes. Sure. Anytime – but it'll have to go through Jennifer's books. I've agreed not to freelance for the time being.'

'Whatever.' Valerie sank back into her seat with a stifled groan. 'The sooner the better though, love. Before the weekend if poss. I need to be on my feet for work.'

'Okay.' Sukie nodded. Valerie was a dinner lady at Hazy Hassocks Mixed Infants. It wasn't a job you could do sitting down. 'Jennifer says she'll have all the new oils and stuff from the suppliers this week – so as soon as it arrives I'll ring you and we can make an appointment – blimey!'

'What?' Chelsea peered into the darkness. 'What's going on? Oh – how does she do that?'

They'd reached the centre of Bagley-cum-Russet, the bit where the two original villages melded at a zigzag junction marked by a Celtic cross. Topsy, leaning forwards over the handlebars of Valerie's bicycle, was just ahead of them.

Sukie grinned, and indicated left. 'Jet-propelled, I reckon. After years of teaching ballet she must have legs like pistons. Right, Val – shall I drop you off at your bungalow first?'

'Can you take me to the pub, love? My old man's playing darts. I said I'd meet him there after rehearsals – and anyway, I really do need that drink.'

'Me too.' Chelsea nodded. 'I'd rather go to the pub than be at home with my mum and dad arguing over the telly remote and my brothers fighting over the Game Boy and my sisters waging war over their mobiles and— '

Sukie laughed, executed a neat U-turn, and pulled up outside the pub.

'Coming in?' Chelsea asked as she undid her seat belt.

Sukie shook her head. 'No thanks. I want a long hot bath. I'm all sweaty and disgusting – not to mention dressed like a bag-lady.'

'Just about right for the Barmy Cow then, I'd say.'

The pub, a tiny slate-roofed cottage with various bits tacked on in corrugated iron and white-pebbledash, was really called the Barley Mow, but after decades of Berkshire wind and rain sweeping from the Downs and a bit of help from the local yoof, the lettering on the faded sign was sadly defaced. Even the once-yellow illustration of a feathery stook had taken on a strangely bovine appearance.

It had been known as the Barmy Cow for as long as anyone could remember.

It was also not the sort of pub where people went by choice. Most Bagley-cum-Russet residents frequented it only when a trip to Fiddlesticks or Hazy Hassocks was out of the question, so the hard-core of Barmy Cow regulars were either ancient, barking, or both.

Sukie really felt she couldn't spend half an hour listening to the Berkeley Boys, the four ancient brothers who ran the Barmy Cow, yet again guffawing over jokes that had had whiskers in the nineteenth century.

'If you could just give me a hand to get inside before you go, love.' Valerie peered piteously at the shuddery darkness from the back of the car. 'I'd be ever so grateful.'

'Of course . . .'

Heads down against the freezing wind, Chelsea and Sukie helped Valerie hop and hobble into the single low-beamed, fug-filled room of the Barmy Cow. It was all-over nicotine brown and smelled of warm beer and even warmer humanity. But at least, Sukie thought, her teeth chattering, it did have a real fire, even though grey ash spilled untidily on to the sludge-coloured carpet and occasional little puffs of acrid smoke belched out into the bar.

'Ay-oop!' Valerie's husband whooped from the direction of the dartboard. 'Walking wounded alert! What've you done now, you daft bint? Told you you was too old 'n' fat for all that Folly Buggery business! Come over 'ere and let me kiss it better.'

Valerie limped across the tiny bar-room to a ragged cheer from the disparate clientele, and was hugged expansively by her large, scruffy husband.

Chelsea exhaled slowly. 'Oh, gross – still, I guess that's what passes for a romantic encounter in this place.'

Sukie averted her eyes and nodded. 'And I think after

that I really do need a drink. Shall I see what the Boys are offering in lieu of WKD Blue?'

'Yeah, go on then – though I'm not holding out much hope. I'll see if I can find somewhere to sit.'

The Berkeley Boys, all standing in a cramped shoulder-to-shoulder row behind the tiny dull and dusty bar, beamed at Sukie in unison. She smiled back politely, as always trying not to chuckle. The Boys, well over pensionable age and differing wildly in height and girth and facial features, always dressed identically. Sadly, tonight the outfit of choice included fairisle tank-tops and paisley kipper ties.

Behind them, a portrait of their mother, the original landlady of the Barmy Cow, took up most of the space. The woefully inappropriately named Honour Berkeley, looking a bit like Ramsay MacDonald, still held court over the tiny pub years after her demise.

Cora, Sukie's godmother, had regaled her with stories of how the young and skittish Honour had left Bagley-cum-Russet to seek her fortune in London. Taking jobs as a chambermaid in various swish hotels, Honour had eventually returned to the village, her reputation in tatters, her finger devoid of a wedding ring, but with her head held high and the infant Boys in tow. It was rumoured that one of her gentlemen friends had bought the Barmy Cow for her, presumably to remove her – and him – from London and further scandal.

As a mark of her conquests, Honour had named each of her offspring after the hotels in which they were conceived.

Sukie scanned the crowded and disorganised shelves. There didn't seem to be anything even remotely drinkable on display. The Barmy Cow specialised – if that was the right word – in real ale for real drinkers; girlie drinks never featured strongly.

It looked, Sukie thought, squinting at the shelves of faded bottles, to be a choice between Cherry B or something called Pony.

'What would you like, my dear? Something feminine, I'll be bound? Can't see a pretty little thing like you with a pint glass somehow.' Savoy leaned forward from the Berkeley Boys line-up. 'Tell you what – Claridge found some Babycham in the kitchen yesterday. And we've got cherries left over from Christmas and some tooth picks somewhere. All the ladies love a Babycham, don't they?'

Sukie grinned at him. Maybe halfway through the last century they did. Oh, why not? 'Okay. Thank you. Can you make it two, please?' Well, she wasn't going to suffer alone.

With an imperious click of his fingers Savoy had Dorchester and Hilton galvanised into action.

While bottles and glasses were dusted and cherries impaled, Sukie stared at herself in the flyblown mirror behind the bar. God – she looked a wreck: her spiky hair was in clumpy tufts, her make-up had all disappeared during the cancan routines, and her warm padded jacket, which had once been Cora's gardening coat, made her look like a rough sleeper. Still, at least there was no one remotely impressible in the Barmy Cow. In fact she looked quite band-boxy compared to the rest of the punters.

Putting an abrupt end to any misplaced thoughts of vanity, Dorchester and Hilton plonked two Babychams, heavily spiked with faded cherries, on the counter in front of her.

'We haven't got a set price for them,' Dorchester beamed. 'What do you reckon?'

Sukie looked down doubtfully. 'A pound?'

'Each?'

'Well – no . . . Oh, go on then . . .'

Transaction completed, Sukie manoeuvred her way towards Chelsea.

'Don't ask.' She pushed one of the glasses across the rickety sticky tabletop. 'It was this or warm beer.'

Chelsea took a tentative sip. Grimaced. Took a gulp. Grinned. 'Bloody awful.'

29

'Mmm.' Sukie rolled some on her tongue and pulled a face. 'Wonder why it's got bits in it?'

'Mine hasn't. Oooh look – your cocktail stick's disintegrated and all the cherries have fallen off and – why are you going purple?'

Suddenly unable to breathe, Sukie gave a panic-stricken choke. 'I-think-I've-got-a-cherry-stuck-in-my-throat . . .'

'Not surprised.' Chelsea bounced hers across the table. 'They're as solid as ball bearings . . . Sukes? Are you okay?'

Shaking her head, gasping for breath, Sukie stumbled towards the door.

Chelsea downed the rest of her Babycham in one and rushed after Sukie into the bitterly cold car park. Yanking at the sleeve of the disgusting padded jacket until Sukie, still coughing and gasping, was standing beneath the illuminated Barmy Cow sign, Chelsea looked terrified.

'Okay, Sukes . . . Now I'm going to try and get it out. Stand there while I get behind you and press on your breastbone – or maybe it's your windpipe . . .? I've done this Heimlich thingy at first aid – now hang on while I just grab you and press and shove – press and shove . . .'

'Don't tell me!' An expensive voice echoed through the swirl of the wind. 'Let me guess – it's some sort of lesbian chav mating ritual . . .'

As the cherry shot disgustingly out on to the car park, Sukie jerked away from Chelsea and stared at the long, low silver car, which had pulled up alongside the pub. She groaned. Milla, all immaculate power suit and glossy hair, was laughing from the driving seat.

'She got a cherry stuck,' Chelsea snapped.

'I'm not even going to ask where or why – nothing surprises me any more,' Milla chuckled, rolling up the electric window. 'Oh, and as we're going into Reading tonight I'll probably be late home, Sukes, if at all. 'Bye. Have fun.'

*We?* Just too late Sukie realised that Milla wasn't alone.

Derry Kavanagh, his ash blond hair striking against a dark top, was in the passenger seat. Looking gorgeous. Looking at her. And laughing.

# Chapter Four

'Valerie Pridmore had to be carried up the path last night!'
Marvin Benson's voice rang from the depths of the bungalow's dinette. 'Nearly midnight it was. And that oafish
husband of hers was laughing. Laughing – I ask you! I'm
ashamed to say we live next door to the likes of them. They
lower the whole tone of this Close. The woman's practically an alcoholic. Jocelyn! Are you listening to me? Did
you hear what I said?'

In the kitchen, Joss Benson stared out of the window at
the grey and drooping March garden. What a dismally
disappointing month March was: too late for significant and
lasting snowfalls to transform the visual boredom into a
winter wonderland, and too early for sensual days filled
with glorious sunshine and birdsong and hot flowers.

And how wonderful it would be to be carried home.
Roaring drunk. Laughing.

Oh, lucky, lucky Valerie Pridmore ...

'Jocelyn!'

Joss dragged herself back from fantasies of riotous
drunkenness and laughter. There were far more important
things to concentrate on. Things like Marvin's breakfast
and getting him off to work, and because it was Wednesday
morning, the bedrooms to clean, the floors to polish, the
paths to sweep, and the recycling bins to be organised – and
then her own work, of course.

Not that her own work was work, or even hers, as such, but—

'Jocelyn!' Marvin's voice had raised a tone and reached peevish. 'It's seven forty-three!'

'And my breakfast needs to be on the table by seven forty-five if I'm to catch the eight forty-five,' Joss mouthed in synchro as she picked up the tray. 'Coming, Marv.'

She backed into the dinette, smiling. Marvin hated the diminutive with a passion.

'I've told you before, don't call me Marv – and did you hear what I said about Valerie Pridmore?' Marvin arranged his boiled egg, toast, coffee pot, butter and marmalade into the pattern he'd used for the last thirty years of breakfasts. 'And this toast is burnt.'

Joss shrugged. 'No it isn't. Just a bit more well done than usual. And yes, I heard what you said about Val. Were you spying on the Pridmores again last night?'

'I don't spy, Jocelyn. I merely observe. And this toast is definitely burnt.'

Marvin seemed to spend an awful lot of time twitching the net curtains, watching the comings and goings in The Close. Especially when he had to get up for a late-night pee. He always said it was because of his role as Neighbourhood Watch co-ordinator; that he had to keep his finger on the Bagley-cum-Russet pulse so to speak.

Joss knew it was because he was nosy and small-minded and conservative and a killjoy.

She sat opposite him, as she always did, eating nothing, pouring a cup of coffee, trying not to let her irritation show. She really should have got used to Marvin's break-fast rituals by now: the scraping of the butter to every corner of the toast until the coverage was even, the align-ing of his knife and spoon, the smoothing of the non-existent wrinkles in the tablecloth, the nodding of his head as he took his first mouthful of coffee.

Breakfasts were always silent affairs – apart from Marvin's crunching and gulping of course. It was the only

33

time of the day Marvin didn't hold court. Joss welcomed the silence although the tinkle of the radio would be nice – or even a bit of breakfast telly in the background like the Pridmores had.

Oh – how wonderful it would be to be like Valerie Pridmore – noisy, disorganised, always cheerful, never knowing what was going to happen from one minute to the next. And madly in love – still – with her large, untidy, happy-go-lucky husband ...

'Right, I'm off.' Marvin said eventually, as he always did, dabbing, as he always did, at his moist lips with his napkin. 'Make sure you finish those notes by this evening, won't you?'

Joss nodded, as she always did, and continued to nurse her coffee cup. They'd long given up the pretence of the goodbye peck. She only had five more minutes to go. Five minutes while Marvin collected his briefcase and his coat and his car keys and set out, as he always did, in his beige car to join the late-commuters at Reading station.

It was one of the perks, Marvin always said, of climbing the corporate ladder within the same company, man and boy. He was part of the highly-prized furniture. He had earned his position and his colleagues' respect through years of dedication and loyalty to the firm. And it meant he didn't have to be at his city desk until ten o'clock.

Joss had survived and supported the man and boy tribulations of Marvin's scramble up said ladder for the last thirty years, from lowly clerk-of-all-trades in the basement post room, to something huge in HR up on the glass-walled fifteenth floor. This had been Personnel in the old days, of course, and Joss really couldn't help thinking that HR sounded too much like something to do with hormone replacement therapy. And that there was a cruel irony in putting the intransigent Marvin in charge of sensitive employees' deepest problems and anxieties.

The front door snapped closed. The beige car purred into life and out of the drive.

Joss exhaled.

The routine chores took very little time, accompanied as they were, by mindlessly cheerful radio music. Needless to say, Marvin didn't like radio music. If Marvin switched the radio on at all it was for the more sombre programmes on Radio Four. Marvin liked to argue loudly with the presenters.

Joss, shivering as she returned to the kitchen from the back garden and the sorting of the recycling bins, caught sight of her reflection in the window. Goodness! Her short fair hair was blown all anyhow, her unmade-up face looked pale and pasty, and her beige cotton trousers and sweater seemed to mould her into a thin pale toneless sausage.

I look like an uncooked chipolata, Joss thought sadly. Beige, pale, cold, uninteresting . . .

Still, she did match the rest of the bungalow. Currently, Marvin was an Ikea junkie. Marvin, a Sunday supplement style victim, had fallen in love with the clean lines and blond furniture and no clutter. Even at the beginning of their marriage Marvin had eschewed the then-popular dark, rich colours and painted the bungalow an all-over cream. The young Joss, simply happy to have her own home and a husband with ambitions and a car and job in London, had sighed a bit, and yearned silently for an orange and gold living-room, a raspberry pink bathroom, and a sultry bedroom in purple and turquoise, and then accepted the blandness.

Big mistake, she thought now as she whizzed the all-purpose mop across the all-purpose pale laminated floors. She really should have been more assertive earlier on. The acquiescence had become a habit. As had staying married to Marvin and everything else . . .

Only the bedrooms to do now. Well, only their bedroom really – the other two were never used. Not any more. They never had guests and the children, grown and flown, never came home to stay. Which was a blessing in a way. Joss sighed again. It was surely wicked and unnatural not

35

to like your own children much? Not – she thought, as she straightened the cream linen duvets on her bed and Marvin's: a double bed with separate linen; a double bed in which they slept, side-by-side but a million miles apart – that they seemed to like her much, either.

Maybe that was harsh. They were affectionate in their distant way, and never forgot birthdays or Christmases, but they led such busy corporate lives with their busy upwardly mobile partners. Maybe if they had children . . . Joss shook her head. She doubted that either of her offspring would halt their careers to breed.

Ossie and Tilly had always been mini-Marvins – probably because he'd been the strong, dominant parent, while she'd been the cipher in the background, the one handing out love and cuddles and encouragement to a son and daughter who, from childhood, had never seemed to need any of them.

Too late to change things now, Joss thought, casting a final eye round the barren bedroom and closing the door. Far too bloody late.

'Yoo-hoo!' A cheerful shout from the kitchen interrupted her melancholy. 'Joss?'

'Through here.' Joss hurried across the now-gleaming hall towards the kitchen, grinning at the welcome sound of Valerie's cheery Berkshire growl. 'Just coming – and why aren't you at work? Oh . . .'

'Done me leg in tripping the light fantastic,' Valerie said happily. 'Last night. So I thought you might to like to pop round for a cuppa and a natter?'

'Love to.' Joss hurled the cleaning paraphernalia unto the kitchen cupboard. 'Shall I bring biscuits?'

'Only if you've got them posh Marks and Sparks ones,' Valerie chuckled over her shoulder as she hobbled towards the back door. 'They're such a treat after our Big Sava specials.'

This was Joss's one big vice; a secret that Marvin knew nothing about. Illicit coffee and gossip with Valerie

Pridmore in the next-door bungalow. A deep friendship forged over the years between two women with nothing in common except their age and the proximity of their homes.

They'd got to the elbows-on-table-amongst-tea-mugs-and-biscuit-crumbs stage in Valerie's cluttered, warm and hectically-hued kitchen.

Joss now knew all about the disastrous fall while cancanning and the resultant visit to the Barmy Cow and the amazing effect several gins had when added to a handful of assorted painkillers supplied by the rest of the troupe. She really wished she had similar raucous stories to add, but as usual, there was nothing of interest going on in her life.

'I've got to get back to work soon as,' Valerie said, pushing her mop of untidy dark hair away from her face. 'I can't bear being at home all day. Don't know how you stand it.'

'Oh, believe me, I've often thought about going back to work – but Marvin still won't hear of it. He says I have more than enough to do. Anyway, I'm probably unemployable now. I was a shorthand-typist before we married.'

'Blimey!' Valerie spluttered bits of Marks and Spencer's best across the table. 'You don't get them any more! It's all computers and things these days. You'd have to retrain. They do back-to-work courses at Winterbrook college.'

'Yes, I've looked at them – but they're scary – even if Marvin agreed.'

'Listen to yourself!' Valerie leaned across the table. 'This is the twenty-first century! Your Marv doesn't have to agree or disagree. You've got your own bloody life!'

'Oh, I know ... I don't want to make him sound like some Victorian ogre – but, well, we know where we are. The boundaries. He goes out to work, I stay at home and make things nice. We sort of rub along and it's comfortable and undemanding and—'

'Sodding boring?'

'Well ...' Joss smiled. 'Yes.'

'Then do something about it.'

37

'Too late. I've got no confidence at all. I'd be petrified in the workplace. I wanted to be at home when the children were small and I've just got used to it, I suppose,' Joss gathered biscuit crumbs into a little pyramid. 'It's my life, right back from being there when the children were young, and then even when they went to school Marvin preferring me to be a housewife, not wanting me to work . . .'

'Yeah, well, with his salary I suppose there was no financial need, was there? My old man's been in and out of work all our married life, love him. One of us had to knuckle down and bring home the bacon. Still, working at the school means I've always been here for the kids.'

Joss nodded. Valerie had five children, all married, all living locally, all with at least two children of their own, all returning to the Pridmore's bungalow all the time with whoops of laughter and expansive hugs and kisses.

Marvin always closed the windows and tutted a lot when the Pridmores were visiting *en masse*. Joss simply ached with jealousy.

Anyway, she did sort of work: she had her typing to do – she typed Marvin's Neighbourhood Watch notes every Wednesday afternoon on her ancient portable typewriter with three carbons, and two mornings a week she collated the articles for the current month's *Bagley Bugle*.

The *Bagley Bugle* was the village news-sheet and Marvin was the editor – not that he did a lot of editing. Once Joss had checked through the pieces and discarded the more inflammatory ones, and proof-read the advertisements, and banked the cheques on Fridays – Marvin charged quite a lot, she thought, for local adverts – Marvin took the whole kit and caboodle off to London where his secretary, Anneka, used scanners and computers and laser printers and binders and all manner of hi-tech gadgetry to produce the six hundred and seventy-two monthly copies of the *Bagley Bugle*.

Maybe she'd suggest to Marvin that she had a word processor or a computer at home. Then Anneka needn't be involved and it would give Joss time to practise just in case she was ever brave enough to approach an employer.

'Young Sukie's going to give me a massage on me leg to get me up and running,' Valerie's voice cut through this burgeoning media mini-plan. 'You know, she's in the cancan troupe? Lives in Cora's cottage on the other side of Bagley? Works for Jennifer Blessing?'

'What?' Joss, lost in a world of screens and no Tippex, frowned. 'Sukie? Oh yes. Pretty dark girl? Looks Irish? The cottage used to belong to that really weird elderly lady who talked to birds and animals ... Was she called Cora? Yes, of course, I'd forgotten,' Joss smiled. 'We had several flyers about the mobile beauty therapy thing delivered – I thought the at-home massage sounded wonderful – but Marvin threw them all in the bin and said they were nonsense, of course.'

'Of course.' Valerie poured more tea. 'Tell you what, if I arrange for Sukie to do my massage while your Marv's at work, why don't you come round and have a de-stressing one here? At the same time. He'd never know would he? And I'm sure Sukie'd be glad of the business as she's just trying to get this off the ground for Jennifer Blessing.'

Joss grinned. Why not? What harm could it do? She'd pay for it out of her housekeeping by decanting Big Sava's cheap own-brand goodies into labelled jars in the cupboard. It was the way she'd financed her little treats for years. What Marvin didn't know couldn't possibly hurt him, could it? And a de-stressing massage would be another wonderful sinful secret luxury ...

'Okay.' Joss nodded, absent-mindedly reaching for the last biscuit. 'You're on. Just let me know when – oh, looks like you've got another visitor.'

Valerie squinted through the window. 'Bugger, just when we've eaten all the biscuits – oh, it's okay. It's only Topsy. She'll have brought me bike back. She don't eat anything at all.'

Topsy, still muffled in a mass of grey and brown, poked

her elderly wrinkled face round the back door. 'I've propped your bike up against the lean-to, Valerie. Oh, hello Joss – goodness me! Look at the pair of you. Sitting around scoffing carbohydrates and sugar – deadly combination. If you don't get an embolism your arteries'll be furred to buggery. You'll need Warfarin to get any blood through all that cholesterol – and probably a heart-by-pass, if not an angiogram.'

'Thanks, Topsy.' Val grinned. 'Guaranteed to cheer us up, you are. And thanks for returning the bike. Lord knows when I'll be able to ride it again, though.'

Topsy made a sort of snorting noise. 'Don't know what we're going to do about replacing you in the line-up, neither. We took ages to get young Sukie in last year.' She turned her brown-beady eyes to Joss. 'You wouldn't be no good at a bit of kicking and screaming along to Offenbach I suppose?'

Joss shook her head quickly. 'Two left feet, I'm afraid. Never even mastered the Valeta at school. And I'm far too old.'

'Stuff and nonsense!' Topsy tightened her headscarf under her skinny wrinkled chin. 'You're the same age as Valerie here and the majority of my gels, and as I always say, there's no such thing as too old. It's all in the mind. Still, I suppose I'll have to start advertising for a half-decent replacement, but she'll have to be a quick learner – we're already into the routines and rehearsals and—'

'Get Joss's Marv to put an advert in the *Bugle*,' Valerie cut in. 'It goes to every house in Bagley-cum-Russet. You might be able to find someone.'

'Good idea – you never cease to amaze me Valerie Pridmore! There's a brain in there somewhere!' Topsy nodded towards Joss. 'Can you do me a good rate for an advert as soon as possible, then?'

'I'll do better than that,' Joss said quickly, fired by a sudden burst of enthusiasm. 'I'll write an article about the cancan troupe – and say that you're looking for new blood. Well, not blood as such,but . . .'

It was probably the mention of blood, but Topsy gave one of her rare smiles. It crinkled her from forehead to chin making her face look like quarter pound of haslet. 'Ah, I like it! An article ... hmmm. That way there won't be a fee for an advert, will there? Good thinking my girl.'

Joss beamed back. Marvin wouldn't like it. Marvin never liked it when she wrote pieces for the *Bugle*. Not that he knew they were hers now. He long since thought he'd put an end to all that nonsense. She'd become very adept with *noms-de-plume*. Again, what he didn't know wouldn't hurt him.

'And I can ask Sukie all about the cancan thing when she does our massages, can't I? It'll be like a proper investigative journalist gleaning all the snippets of insider gossip,' Joss continued happily, having a vision of becoming Bagley's answer to Ephraim Hardcastle.

'Lovely.' Topsy clapped her hands. 'Oh! That reminds me! I've got to go and see young Sukie about them at-home massage things, as well. I need to put her straight on one or two things before she's let loose. I'm not sure she's got the full picture about what she's playing with. Not sure at all. There's a lot of folklore history in this village that she should be aware of before she starts rubbing lord knows what into people. Could all go very wrong if she ain't careful. Look what happened to young Mitzi Blessing when she first started concocting her Hubble Bubble recipes. Surprised no one died. Ah well, – no rest for the wicked ... No, don't get up – I'll see meself out.'

They watched Topsy's skinny, multi-wrapped figure stride off into The Close, then looked at one another.

'Barking,' Valerie said fondly. 'But good for her age.'

'How old do you reckon she is?'

'Eighty-five or thereabouts – wonder what she meant about needing to speak to Sukie?'

Joss shrugged. 'No idea. Probably something to do with magic and witchcraft and flower power ... She and Cora were always cackling over herbs and nature's medicinal powers, weren't they?'

'Blimey, yes.' Valerie wriggled more comfortably in her chair. 'A pair of old hags and no mistake. Mind you, I suppose we shouldn't knock all that stuff. Whatever Topsy says, Mitzi Blessing's had a fair bit of success with her herbal cooking and folksy recipes, hasn't she?'

'But Mitzi Blessing is one of us,' Joss said. 'Normal. No one could ever say Topsy was that. Now, are you desperate to get on with anything or will you make a fresh pot of tea while I go and get the blueberry cheesecake I was saving for Marvin's supper?'

'Oooh, tough one,' Valerie chuckled hauling herself up and hobbling towards the kettle. 'You've got a wicked streak in you, Jocelyn Benson. You want to be careful – you're in danger of becoming a bit of a devil on the quiet.'

# Chapter Five

'Quick! Before we have to open up, come and have a look at these.' Jennifer Blessing beckoned Sukie towards a spare cubicle. 'They've just arrived. Aren't they simply too lovely for words?'

At half-past eight on a grey, wet, cold Saturday Sukie felt that nothing could be *that* lovely – except maybe an extra hour in bed. She really wasn't a morning person, especially on Saturdays when it appeared the rest of the world was allowed to slumber. And the soporific, warm, sensuously-scented salon only served to enervate her further. Sleepily, she squinted at the peach leather cases displayed across the massage table in front of Jennifer.

In an instant her lethargy was forgotten as her fingers itched to touch and stroke.

Rows of pretty little faceted glass bottles with gorgeous multicoloured gemstone stoppers nestled in the folds of cream silk lining, and glowed like dozens of glittering jewels. Even the more prosaic pale apricot plastic containers of base oils and various synthetic essences seemed alluring in such a sumptuous setting. The essential oils, the essentials of her business, displayed like this, were just so pretty, and colourful and *girlie*.

Etched in italic gold on the tiny black labels, the names – juniper, eucalyptus, bergamot, lavender, clary sage, geranium – which she knew as well as her own, seemed

43

to ring with a new magical mysticism.

'Oh, Jennifer – they're absolutely, absolutely—' she searched for a fulsome enough word. 'Absolutely ravishing. Wonderful. Fabulous. Look at them ... there's a really comprehensive stock here, something for everything I reckon, and they look so beautiful and – well – almost too pretty to use. Thank you so much.'

'You're welcome, although of course it's as much for my benefit as yours. Probably more as I'll be taking a cut of the profits,' Jennifer said with her usual candour. 'But I agree, the suppliers have come up trumps this time. Look, they've even tooled "Beauty's Blessings" in gold leaf on the cases. Very professional. I knew you'd love them.'

'Oh, I do. Now I can't wait for Monday morning – which will be a first – to get started. And I've been thinking, I might even set up a massage table in the back parlour of Pixies Laughter. It's supposed to be our dining room but we never use it, and it might be nicer for people who don't want all my stuff spread all over their living rooms or who prefer a bit of privacy. What do you reckon?'

'That's not a bad idea – and if you take on the massages away from here it'll give me space to install that spray-tan booth I've always wanted. I'll check with the powers-that-be about inspection and home licensing and what have you for your cottage, although as you're a qualified practitioner I don't think you'll have a problem there to be honest – and add it to the next lot of adverts and – damn! Is that my phone?'

'No, mine.' Sukie scrabbled in the pocket of her overall for her mobile. 'Sorry, Jennifer – oh, it's a text from Topsy. She keeps trying to contact me about something which is apparently vitally important. We keep missing one another.'

'Is it to do with the dancing?' Jennifer pouted her glossy lips.

'Don't think so. Something to do with my aromatherapy I think. She keeps saying I mustn't start my massages

44

without talking to her first – or I'll be sorry.'

'Crikey – sounds a bit strange. Although maybe she just wants a cut-price massage,' Jennifer smiled. 'If so, I think you ought to decline, kindly of course, and recommend a tannery – her skin looks like leather. No, sorry, cruel of me – but she is a weird old bat, isn't she?'

'Very. But an ace dancer even now. She must have been a veritable Ginger Rogers in her heyday. And, of course, a frustrated nurse on the quiet.'

'Oh, I know!' Jennifer laughed. 'She's mad on medical stuff, isn't she? She wanted to give the kiss of life to my Lance once when he choked on a pickled gherkin in the Faery Glen. Had his head yanked back against the wall and his tie off and her fingers down his throat before you could say Hamlet manoeuvre.'

Sukie started to snigger at the malapropism then stopped quickly. Jennifer hailed from Essex. Sometimes there were language difficulties. And the memories of her own close-encounter with Heimlich were still very raw – and definitely no laughing matter.

She turned the snigger into a little cough. 'Blimey. What did you do?'

'Wrestled her off before she throttled him. She clung on like a bloody limpet. I practically had to beat her off with a stick.'

Sukie winced at the picture. Fortunately her phone chirruped again before she could say anything else.

'Topsy again? She's very persistent, I'll give her that.' Jennifer applied a further coat of gloss to her high-shine lips. 'And is it just me, or do you always find it sort of strange that old people have mobiles and *text* ?'

Sukie nodded. Actually, she did. But Topsy seemed quite adept at it, using all the correct abbreviations. Maybe she'd chivvied some hoodied child from the Bath Road estate to give her lessons.

'She says she'll be waiting for me at Pixies Laughter when I get home at lunchtime.' Sukie squinted at the hieroglyphics. 'Says again it's imperative that I don't do anything until she's spoken to me.'

'Poor old thing. Clearly going to give you some pearls of wisdom circa 1920. So sad when the mind starts to go and you cling to the past and can only see danger in change. Topsy probably thinks massage is seedy and you're going to turn Bagley-cum-Russet into a sort of rural Reeperbahn Strasse. She's probably got so little going on her life that everything becomes a matter of national security ...' Jennifer giggled with as much animation as much as her recent non-surgical chin-lift would allow. 'Right, well, as soon as you've finished making your assignations with the geriatric double-oh-seven, I suppose we better get ourselves ready to beautify Berkshire.'

And still chuckling, Jennifer swished off to open up the salon for her always-busy Saturday morning trade.

Having texted an affirmative reply to Topsy, Sukie smiled a last soppy smile at the cases and their contents as she clicked the locks shut. The massage oils had totally lifted her spirits – which was just as well. They'd been lurking somewhere just south of despondent ever since Tuesday evening.

Of course it had been humiliating in the extreme for Milla and Derry to see her jigging around with her mouth wide open and Chelsea clinging to her back outside the Barmy Cow, but that was just Sod's Law. No, the worst thing was Derry, who she'd secretly turned into some perfect love god, laughing at her for doing so.

Face of an angel, heart of a bastard, feet of clay, Sukie had decided. He and Milla deserved one another. Definitely.

And she hadn't even been able to escape him. Milla had arrived home, fortunately alone, on Wednesday morning, refusing to answer questions, beaming from ear to ear and singing in the bathroom which clearly indicated a night of unbridled passion, and had been out with Derry every evening since.

46

It was so unfair.

And on each occasion when Derry had arrived at Pixies Laughter to collect Milla he'd looked gorgeous – Sukie wondered if he had a live-in stylist to advise him on the best clothes to wear with that stunning layered ice-blond hair and dark blue eyes – and smiled at her and said polite hellos in the nanosecond that Milla allowed them to be alone together, but had made no apology at all for laughing at her discomfort.

Ah, well ... Fortunately today was going to be pretty hectic so there'd be no time to fester about the vagaries of beautiful men with no manners: work until midday, the mysterious meeting with Topsy, then the joys of dressing up like a fairy with Chelsea for what would probably be a truly dire hen-night.

She checked her appearance in one of the peach-lit mirrors and struck a self-deprecating pose. 'Ooh, Sukie Ambrose, you lucky, lucky girl. Bet Paris Hilton'd kill for a social diary like yours.'

Then she straightened her slinky overall, checked that her hair was at its spiky best and her eyes perfectly kohled, and prepared to join Jennifer to do battle with Beauty's Blessings' Saturday morning clientele.

By lunchtime the weather was still grey, cold and drizzly. With the peach leather cases ensconced in the boot of her nondescript hatchback, Sukie made short work of the journey between Hazy Hassocks and Bagley-cum-Russet.

Topsy, wearing a long grey mac and a fawn headscarf which made her merge with the murky surroundings, was waiting by the cottage gate. There was no sign of Milla's silver car or Derry's always-dirty jeep, which hopefully meant they weren't in the cottage.

'Sorry I'm a bit late,' Sukie apologised, hefting the cases from the car. 'Everyone seemed to want nail extensions or facials for their Saturday night out. No – I can manage these, thanks – go on indoors, it's so cold and you've probably been waiting ages and ...'

'Stop babbling,' Topsy said sharply. 'And stop treating me like I'm an old lady. Age,' she tapped the headscarf, 'is all up here, my girl. And up here I'm still in my prime.'

'Of course, yes sorry – go through into the living room.' Chastened, Sukie motioned with her head as she piled the cases on to the hall table, praying that the living room was reasonably tidy and that Milla and Derry hadn't abandoned their cars and their inhibitions somewhere and weren't currently indulging in sexual athletics on the sofa. 'Would you like a cup of tea?'

'No thank you,' Topsy looked round the room, which was fortunately Milla and Derry free, and agilely skirted the clutch of fat cushiony non-matching armchairs to stand in front of the black grate where gas-logs burned now rather than the real thing. 'You've kept it much as Cora had it, then?'

'I didn't want to change it. I loved it. It's always been my home. Even when I'd had the central heating installed I put everything back as it was because that's how Cora always had it and ... okay, I guess you don't want to talk to me about Cora, do you?'

'Actually I do. No – I'm not going to go all maudlin on you – and we're both busy people so I'll cut to the chase. I could have spoken to you at rehearsals – but this is a delicate subject and there are far too many wagging ears there.'

Sukie was intrigued now. Was Topsy going to tell her some alleged dark secret about Cora? Had her scatty godmother, in Topsy's fertile imagination, been a Cold War double-agent, or a cross-dresser, or a secret dope peddler?

'You want to tell me something about Cora? But there's nothing I don't know about her.'

'I think there probably is.' Topsy released the headscarf. Her hair was scraped back into its bun and pressed tightly to her skull. She looked even more tortoise-like. 'Me and Cora were friends from the cradle. We shared a good many things. Things that youngsters like you have probably never got wind of. As soon as Valerie Pridmore mentioned you were going to make a business of these flower power massages I knew I had to put you straight.'

Sukie bit her lips. If she wasn't harping on about the latest lifesaving surgery as employed in the medical soaps, Topsy was inventing Bagley-cum-Russet folklore. Sukie had no doubt she was just about to find out that Cora had been a Grade A witch and spent her free time in levitation and flying too close to the moon. She sighed.

'And don't sigh, my girl. I've got hearing like a weasel I'll have you know. Now, look at this ...' Topsy marched across to the window, her back straight as a ramrod under the mac. 'What do you see out there?'

Sukie joined her in peering through the tiny leaded panes at the back garden. 'A sort of dripping, damp, tangled mangle of weeds. It's on my to-do list for the summer but—'

'Not weeds,' Topsy interrupted. 'Raw materials.'

'Sorry?'

'Raw materials. The raw materials for your craft. Cora's garden is, and always has been, a veritable storehouse of natural energy.'

Sukie laughed, but kindly. 'Topsy – is that honestly what this is all about? Cora's garden? All those strange old plants that used to be in my adventure playground which I've shamefully neglected and will restore to their former glory as soon as the weather warms up a bit?'

'Those plants,' Topsy said sternly, 'aren't there by accident. Don't think, young lady, with the usual arrogance of youth, that you're the first person in this cottage to work with infusions and oils.'

'What? You mean—? Cora ...? No, you're wrong. I spent all my life with Cora. She never so much as used a sprig of lavender in the airing cupboard.'

'And why, when she has a garden full of it, do you think that was?'

'I honestly don't know. But I do know that I have a

49

whole case filled with synthetic oils and essences – I certainly won't need to wade around out there in all that weedy mess to find the perfect plant for my massages. Look, Topsy, I'm sure this is very interesting but please don't try to involve Cora in some imagined practical magic rubbish.'

'Rubbish?' The beady eyes glittered. *'Rubbish?* You can't have lived here all your life and not known that things – unexplained and inexplicable things – have happened here in Bagley and the surrounding villages. You know fullwell that Mitzi Blessing didn't stumble on her Hubble Bubble kitchen-witch recipes by accident in Hazy Hassocks, or that those star-ceremonies in Fiddlesticks don't produce results that no earthly reasoning can explain?'

Sukie shook her head. 'Herbal cooking might just make susceptible people believe that there's magic afoot if they want to believe it – and the Fiddlestickers are all crazy anyway and their star things are just an excuse for a party . . . But Bagley isn't like that.'

'Yes it is.' Topsy turned away from the window. 'And it always has been. Maybe in your lifetime these powers have been left undisturbed, but way back, when me and Cora were gels together, and long, long before that even, Bagley-cum-Russet had more magic than Hazy Hassocks and Fiddlesticks put together. And Pixies Laughter Cottage was always at the root. Cora knew only too well about the power of her garden. She wouldn't have used her plants while you were around, that's for sure. In fact after all the trouble, she left it well alone. That's why she didn't as much as pick a sprig of rosemary for her lamb roast.'

'Trouble? What trouble?'

'My lips are sealed.' Topsy clamped her mouth shut to illustrate the point. It looked like a ruckled grey zipper. Then she opened it again. 'Let's just say, Honour Berkeley wasn't the only woman in Bagley to rue the amount of time she spent in this garden. No, as soon as I knew you were going to be dabbling in perfumery and oils and rubs and

50

balms here, I had to warn you what you might be unleashing.'

Sukie tried really hard not to laugh. Topsy was clearly insane. It was all too Harry Potter meets Winnie the Witch to be true.

'No.' Sukie frowned. 'Sorry. I simply don't buy it. I don't want to be rude, but Honour Berkeley – if the Boys and the gossip are to be believed – was a whole generation ahead of you and Cora, and a bit of a flapper-slapper to boot, so how could you know anything about her? And what on earth does the cottage have to do with Honour Berkeley's – or anyone else's – *troubles* ? I've never heard so much nonsense in my life. And honestly, Topsy, you – well, everyone knows about your dreams, the dancing or the medical profession that simply didn't happen for you – and so, well, maybe ... '

She stopped and stared at Topsy. Topsy stared defiantly back.

Sukie shrugged, not wanting to hurt Topsy's feelings. 'Look, the whole village knows that you have a very vivid imagination. It must be hard sometimes to remember what's real and what isn't. I don't blame you for making things up. But please don't drag Cora into your fantasies. Cora was—'

'Cora was a matchmaker.'

# Chapter Six

Sukie hooted with laughter. 'A matchmaker? Oh, pul-lease! Come on, Topsy, pull the other one. Crikey, I've heard some nonsense in my time, but—'

'It's far from nonsense,' Topsy said quietly. 'Cora was the best in the business.'

Actually, Sukie wasn't a hundred per cent certain what a matchmaker was. She vaguely remembered that old Barbra Streisand film, of course, but surely Cora had never been one of *those*?

Aware that Topsy was still watching her carefully, she knew she'd have to be very kind and gently disabuse Topsy of this latest fanciful notion before it, like the medical terminology and wanting to turn the entire village into Bluebell Girls, got completely out of hand.

Using the voice she used for Beauty's Blessings' clients when a facial hadn't quite cut the mustard, she smiled at Topsy. 'Look, it's pretty chilly in here. Why don't we sit by the fire and talk about this – and are you quite sure you wouldn't like a cup of tea?'

'Don't treat me like some geriatric imbecile,' Topsy snorted, her eyes narrowing. 'I've still got all me marbles! This is for your own good. And while we're on the subject, there's another thing – have you never questioned why this cottage is called Pixies Laughter?'

'No – but why would I?' Sukie walked quickly across to

the fireplace. 'Because it always has been for the last two hundred years, I suppose. It's just an ancient version of Dunroamin', isn't it? I've never thought about it – although I do know my parents wanted to change the name to Rose Cottage when they inherited it because they thought Pixies Laughter was too twee for words. Thankfully they didn't get round to making the change – and I certainly won't – and what's that got to do with Cora being a matchmaker anyway? You're just confusing me now.'

Topsy turned away from the window. 'The cottage is called Pixies Laughter because that's exactly what happened here. According to local folklore, hundreds of years ago, probably before the hamlets of Bagley or Russet existed and certainly before they joined together as one village, this site was a hidden meadow, an enchanted place filled with magical plants, a place where illicit lovers met in secret and drank petal wine and where pixie's laughter could be heard on the night air ...'

Sukie valiantly tried to disguise her sniggers as she bent down to switch on the gas logs. 'Oh, of course! Silly me! Why didn't I think of that? This whole place is awash with sprites and elves all the time! Sometimes you can't even get into the bathroom because it's full of goblins!'

Topsy tutted at such levity. 'This isn't a joke, Sukie. There are things that have happened here that no one could ever explain. Cora could hear the pixies' laughter. That's how she knew she had the power. She knew she was in tune with a magical world. You've never heard them, have you? The pixies laughing?'

'No!' Sukie frowned. Was Topsy actually safe to be allowed out alone? 'Of course not. I don't believe in fairies ...'

'I'm glad you haven't heard them. It probably means you're not blessed with the gift.'

Sukie wasn't sure whether she was supposed to be pleased or disappointed by this. All she knew was that she really, really mustn't hurt Topsy's feelings. This poppycock was clearly very important to her. As real to her as her medical obsession and her frustrated dancing dreams. 'Ah, well – we can't have everything, can we? I'll just have to learn to live with being out of tune with the little people. But do you think, seriously, if there was anything like that here – if Pixies Laughter was haunted in any way – that Cora would have allowed me to live here without warning me?'

Topsy hadn't moved from the window. 'One it isn't haunted. And two, Cora didn't give the cottage to you, did she? She left it to your parents – who, if you'll forgive me saying, are the most unimaginative, stolid, uninspiring couple I've ever met. There was no danger of them being touched by the magic, or having the least curiosity about the cottage or its past. I'm sure Cora willed it to them, knowing that they'd probably sell it and that you'd never live here, never have to find out about its history.'

'But my parents must have *known* the cottage was okay and that Cora wasn't a-a matchmaker . . .' Sukie sank into her favourite deep-cushioned armchair, still stumbling over the word. 'They let her be my godmother, for heaven's sake. They wouldn't have done that if they'd thought she was a witch.'

'Cora wasn't a damn witch! She was your mother's aunt. An aunt, I must say, who your mother shamefully ignored because she refused to conform. Asking her to be your godmother was simply paying lip-service to the family. They wouldn't have known anything about the matchmaking. I doubt if your parents knew, or cared, very much about Cora at all.'

Sukie nodded. That much was probably true. Cora and her parents had always been light-years apart. It was however unpleasant to hear this from Topsy.

She really wished she could rush to her parents' defence. Or even wanted to.

Tempted at last by the warmth, Topsy crossed the room and held out wrinkled brown hands towards the fire. She watched the blue and red and yellow flames dancing. 'All her life, all your mother has cared about has been her social climbing and the latest must haves. Heavens – I've never known a more self-obsessed person than your mother, even as a little girl. She should have married that awful pompous prig Marvin Benson.' She stared at the fire for a moment longer, then smiled at Sukie. 'Oh, did I tell you I asked his wife, Jocelyn, if she'd like to join the cancanners? She said no but she's going to do an interview with you about the troupe for the *Bagley Bugle*. Won't that be nice?'

'Sod the Bensons and the cancanners and the bloody *Bagley Bugle*,' Sukie snapped. 'Don't start back-pedalling now, Topsy. You started telling me this nonsense about Cora – so you just carry on. Go on. You were saying that Cora left Pixies Laughter to Mum and Dad because she knew they weren't into Saturday Night Satanism and therefore wouldn't have any sixth sense about sacrificial altars in the garden shed or recognising a ducking stool in the outside privy? Is that right?'

'Don't mock, Sukie, dear. Please don't mock. This is nothing to do with devil-worship or black magic or witchcraft. I know Cora really wanted you to live in this cottage because you loved it and she loved you very much – we discussed it a lot – but she knew it might be too dangerous. She always felt you were a little fey ...'

'Fey? Bloody fey? I'm not fey! I'm not a bloody hobgoblin! This is real life! I'm an aromatherapist, working with synthetic oils and fragrances. I'm hardly likely to go ripping up clumps of nettles from the garden at dawn when I've got all those gorgeous little bottles of – what – what have I said now?'

'Nettles. Dawn. There you are you see, you automatically mentioned the most magical time of day for herbal-gathering and nettles in one breath. Nettles are one of the most potent ingredients of any love potion.'

'Bollocks! I just said dawn because it's what fairy-tales are all about, and because nettles are the most boring plants

55

ever and they grow everywhere and the garden is full of them and – and *what*? *Love potions?* What love potions?'

Topsy turned away from the gas logs and perched on the edge of one of the cushiony chairs opposite Sukie. 'You really haven't been listening have you? Cora made love potions. Haven't I already explained?'

'You said she was a matchmaker. Even if I believed that bit, which I don't, I thought you meant she was a sort of pre-computer Dateline-dot-com or something. You know, got her mates together, sorted out which blokes they fancied, had a word in a few ears, that sort of thing. You mean she concocted mixtures from plants – like dandelion and burdock for beginners – and forced them down people's throats?'

Topsy sighed. 'The drinking potions were her main stock in trade, yes, but Cora worked with infusions and oils as well – which is why I needed to tell you just in case—'

'I suddenly got the urge to go skipping round the garden pulling up weeds, boiling them, mashing them down, straining them into bottles and rubbing them into unsuspecting people? Yeah right – very likely when I have all the twenty-first century fragrances and essences and oils I need out there in those cases; oils and infusions which will help my clients and enrich their lives – not bloody poison them!'

Topsy said nothing. Just perched on the edge of the big fat chair still looking sad.

Sukie sighed. She really didn't need this. She had enough silly things to occupy her waking moments. She looked across the room, through the window at the darkening steel-grey sky and the scudding charcoal clouds, then back at Topsy. 'Okay, so if she was so bloody good at being a matchmaker – how come she never married? And what about you? Did you get the late Mr Turvey to propose by chucking one of Cora's bottles over his head and chanting – *love divine, Algernon Turvey be mine* – or some such nonsense?'

Topsy winced. 'That's rather insensitive of you, dear.

56

But since you ask, then yes I used Cora's special skills – but it wasn't quite as blatant as your version. I wasn't in love with Algernon Turvey, but he was with me. He was never the love of my life – but I asked Cora to make him my husband ...' Topsy smiled, clearly in some far-off place. 'Look, dear, I can understand why you're angry and confused. I just wish I hadn't needed to tell you any of this – but I promised Cora, promised her, that I'd always keep an eye on you – and if there was any danger at all that you might find out about the flower magic—'

'Which I wouldn't have done if you hadn't told me, would I?'

'But you might have done. With your chosen trade and working from home ... I couldn't risk it. I'd never forgive myself. Look, I've probably said enough for now. Just be careful, Sukie, that's all.'

'No, it's not all. Tell me all of it. Everything.' Sukie leaned back in her chair. 'I still don't believe any of this – but you can't stop now. So – go on – tell me the rest. Please, Topsy. I promise I won't mock.'

Topsy stared deep into the fire. 'There's not much to tell. Me and Cora, we were friends like you and young Chelsea – just as giggly and giddy. Hard for you to believe, I'm sure, but I haven't always been an old lady, and nothing much changes. When Cora and me and all the other village girls were your age and younger – and like you, had rampaging emotions and needed love, all the young men had gone to war. All of them. Well, most. There were some who weren't fit enough, or in reserved occupations, or pacifists – but the majority of boys our age, boys who we yearned for just as much as you youngsters do today, were suddenly taken away. Gone. To fight. And probably die. Gone to who knew where, for who knew how long ... Imagine it, how you'd feel, if that happened today.'

Sukie stared at the dancing flames of the gas logs. How would it be? Just awful ... Too awful to contemplate if young men like Lewis Flanagan and Derry Kavanagh and

57

all the other gorgeous boys were suddenly taken away from the village to fight and possibly die ...

'So do you mean, once all the boys had gone to war, if the girls couldn't have their first choice, then Cora concocted something from weeds to make them fall in love with whoever was available? The old men or the invalids? Any port in a storm? That's disgusting ...'

'It's very easy to be prim about it now, Sukie, but it wasn't like that at all. It was just that some girls, left alone in these villages, lonely, scared, bored – whatever – needed love. There were other boys stationed near here, or visiting foreign servicemen, who were also desperately lonely and homesick and separated from the ones they loved. Goodness, you know how these things happen? Cora mixed potions for them because she had the gift. She saw it as a service for the lovelorn and lonely. Just as a short-term thing, of course, but some of the relationships developed into more than that.'

'What was wrong with that? The war lasted years and years. I suppose the women at home would have had to move on, and if they found happiness with strangers ...'

'All very well for the single girls, but when the local boys came back after the war there were some pretty serious liaisons in place. Do you understand? Married women, fiancées, madly in love with Other People? Not all down to Cora of course, but scores of desperate women, who had taken her elixirs to start with, begged her to make them fall in love with their men again – men who had been away for five or six years and who were virtual strangers. It all got a bit unpleasant in some cases. Cora never forgave herself for some of the more unfortunate pairings or marriage break-ups ... it wasn't what she'd intended. That's what I meant by troubles – and that's why she stopped matchmaking.'

Even if it had happened – which Sukie still doubted – it was all ancient history. Maybe just maybe, Cora had discovered some sort of herbal mind-altering plants ... and maybe, just maybe, there were enough lonely and gullible women in the village to believe it would work. But that was then – this was now, real-time, and simply not relevant. It was, as so many of Topsy's stories were, simply a rural myth writ large.

'Okay, if I buy that much of the story, it still doesn't explain why Cora never managed to make her love potions work for herself or why you ended up with Non Turvey who you didn't love.'

Topsy seemed to withdraw into the collar of her mac, like a tortoise disappearing into its shell. Her voice was very faint. 'Cora and I were in love with two village lads ... very much in love. When it was obvious that the war was about to start they were all fired up with patriotic zeal and enlisted. They said that way they'd get the pick of the fighting jobs rather than waiting for compulsory call-up and becoming cannon-fodder ...'

Sukie started into the flames again. How strange to think Topsy and Cora had been like her and Chelsea ... They'd done World War II at school. She knew all about it. It just hadn't seemed to have involved real people ... Real girls in love with real boys ...

'And what happened to them? The boys you loved?'

'Cora's boyfriend was blown to bits in the back of a Lancaster bomber, mine was killed in the Western Desert ...'

Sukie swallowed. She wasn't sure where the Western Desert was but it didn't matter, she couldn't look at Topsy.

'Cora certainly wouldn't have looked at anyone else. Her heart was broken for ever.' Topsy's voice was still quiet. 'Me? I probably shouldn't have done it, but I didn't want to be Miss Jean Millett for the rest of my life.'

Jean Millett? Sukie frowned and opened her mouth then shut it again. Of course, Topsy must have been saddled with the nickname the minute she married Algernon. It was like her geography teacher; Miss Black one term, married to a Mr Crawley in the holidays, and forever

59

after known to the entire school as Creepy.

Topsy plucked at the folds of her mac with skinny wizened fingers. 'Non Turvey was a farm-hand. He didn't go to war. He had flat feet and a dicky ticker to boot. He was here and he was a man and he was young and he liked me. It probably sounds odd to you, but I really wanted to be married, so I asked Cora to make a potion for me to take ...'

'And it worked?'

'Yes. We married and were happy enough until the dicky ticker did for him. I never stopped loving my first beau. And I knew I didn't love Non like he loved me, but Cora kept giving me top-ups, and me and Non bumbled along together for the next thirty odd years. And no I don't regret it. It was still better than being alone.'

Sukie said nothing. For a moment she could see herself as Cora and Topsy and the other girls must have been back all those years ago. And she could understand how, without the freedoms and diversions of twenty-first century life, they must have been desperate enough to grab at anything. But even so ...

Topsy leaned forward in the big fat chair. 'Sukie, all I wanted to do was warn you that things can happen here. The gentle magical power of plants has been used for thousands of years – and especially plants grown in places like Pixies Laughter. Cora knew how to engage earth energies – no, don't laugh at me. I told her she should have let you know what went on here – but she said it wasn't necessary because you'd got your heart set on being a beautician and that this place would never be your home and that you'd never be tempted to use the garden ... I think she thought that you'd be standing behind a counter in a department store with your face plastered in make up ... She clearly had no idea that it would eventually involve these flower potions and massages or that you'd be living here.'

Surely it was all far too bizarre to be true? But, what

60

if it wasn't? What if Cora really did have some sort of gift? What if the tangled garden of Pixies Laughter really was a storehouse of *magic* plants? Sukie listened to the March wind buffeting round the cottage making the gas logs sing.

'So did Cora write all this down? All her potions? Did she have an ancient recipe book like the one Mitzi Blessing found for her herbal cookery?'

'No.'

Sukie stared at Topsy. The denial had been too quick. Far, far too quick.

'I don't believe you. She did, didn't she? It's here some-where, isn't it? Still in the cottage?'

'No,' Topsy said again. 'There was no book. Nothing written down.'

'You know there was!' Sukie struggled from the depths of the fat cushions. 'Topsy – you *know*! And you hoped that it would have been chucked out when mum and dad cleared the paperwork out of the cottage after Cora died – but you can't be sure, can you? There's still a lot of her stuff every-where – so it could well be here, couldn't it?'

Topsy stood up in one graceful movement, straightened her mac and headed for the hallway. 'There is no book. No papers. No recipes. Cora had it all in her head. Everything died with her. Sukie, I'm sorry if I've upset you with any of this – but I don't regret telling you. You have the information now. What you do with it is up to you. Now, if you'll excuse me, I really do have to go. I like to be snugged in early of a Saturday night ready for *Casualty* . . .'

From the window, Sukie watched Topsy stride down the garden path and disappear into the grey gathering March gloom.

The cottage suddenly seemed strangely silent. Lonely. Despite the cheery gas logs she shivered. She wished Milla was home. She wished Chelsea would turn up and fill the cottage with giggles and scurrilous gossip as they prepared

61

# Chapter Seven

Saturday evening in the Bensons' bungalow was as ritualistic as the rest of the week. In fact the whole day was organised with almost military precision: in the morning Marvin washed the car or played nine holes of golf while Joss shopped – food shopping only – in Hazy Hassocks; lunch was at one on the dot and something light on toast; in the afternoon Marvin dozed in front of the sports channels, and Joss gardened if the weather was fine and read if it wasn't.

And then in the evening ... Well, Saturday evenings were the worst of all.

Joss, sitting in front of the dressing table mirror, staring wistfully at her reflection, as always hoping that someone sensuous and wanton would smoulder back at her, wondered why no one had ever warned her that vowing 'until death do us part' would mean that on Saturdays she really, really wished it would be sooner rather than later.

She and Marvin always 'did something' on a Saturday evening. It was as much of a ritual as the rest of the day and far less enjoyable. If they went out it was never to dances or concerts or the theatre or the cinema, all of which Joss would have loved. Especially dancing. She wondered why she'd told Topsy Turvey that she couldn't dance – years of denial probably. Marvin loathed dancing and it simply seemed easier to say she was useless at it. She probably was now anyway. Use it or lose it, as everyone kept saying . . .

No, there was no Saturday night dancing because they always went out to eat. Usually to supper parties with Marvin's Rotary or cricket club chums, or at the Golf Club in Winterbrook, or to restaurants recommended by the Sunday supplements which served tiny, pretty meals which never, ever lived up to Joss's expectations or satisfied her apparently unfashionably healthy appetite.

Slowly, she fixed her pearl ear-studs: pale, safe jewellery to match her pale, safe face and cream silk sweater. So bland . . . What would Marvin say, she often wondered, if she shimmied downstairs with more make-up than Danny La Rue and a flamboyant outfit in scarlet and orange? What would Marvin say if she suggested they did something impromptu and daring? What would Marvin say if she told him how she hated Saturday evenings more than any other time of the week?

Occasionally on Saturday evenings they stayed in and invited people to dinner parties at the bungalow. These were the worst ones of all. If they could have invited people she knew and felt at home with it would have been fine, but Marvin had, over the years, actively discouraged Joss's friends from visiting The Close, and eventually even the more determined ones had drifted away.

So they entertained Marvin's cronies and Joss loathed the bitchy, snobbish small-talk with people she hardly knew and with whom she had nothing in common, and always felt under pressure to produce the latest designer meals which would pass muster with Marvin's pals and their squeaky-voiced well-bred wives.

Joss had always felt she was what was known as a good plain cook – well, good plain everything really – and longed to dish up hearty stews and pies and casseroles and steamed puddings. But Marvin wouldn't have any of that. No, she had to sweat over arty-farty cookery books and

64

create drizzled things in stacks, and remember if pomegranate or blueberry was the latest culinary fad.

At least tonight wasn't going to be one of those, although where they were going remained, as ever, a mystery. Marvin made those decisions.

Standing up, straightening her neat taupe skirt, Joss wished that she was accompanying Valerie Pridmore and her husband to the Barmy Cow for a riotous night of drinking, darts, and laughter.

Marvin, of course, never set foot in the Barmy Cow; and, to be honest, it was a dive – but it was a dive filled with people who were happy with their lot, who enjoyed what they had and didn't spoil the here-and-now by yearning for the what-may-be. People who knew how to laugh and sing and have a damn good time. People like Valerie Pridmore and her husband who still made love . . .

Even the Berkeley Boys amused her. Marvin, who had never shed his ancestors' Victorian Values, would go all prim when they were mentioned and call them the Berkeley Bastards. Marvin, who knew foul language was the verbal currency of the underclasses, always felt he could use the world bastard in its correct context without the sky falling in.

'Jocelyn!' Marvin's voice rang through the bungalow. 'Are you ready? It's nearly seven!'

Joss dragged her beige raincoat from the wardrobe – it was still grey and cold and drizzly outside – and slid her feet into her sensible low-heeled courts which she always wore because she always drove on Saturdays so that Marvin could drink, then walked across the hall into the living-room with her usual sense of death-row dread.

'Ready . . . Who are we eating with tonight?'

Marvin, polished and poised for the off, gave her a cursory glance. 'That skirt looks a bit snug. You could do with losing a couple of pounds – oh, we're meeting Simon and Sonia. You like them, don't you?'

Joss, who always felt she'd like Simon and Sonia a lot

more if they'd do something interesting like spontaneously combust, said nothing.

'Old Simon has got the needle because I beat him hollow at golf last week,' Marvin guffawed, straightening his cricket club tie. 'Sonia says I owe her a decent dinner because he's been unbearable to live with ever since.'

Someone owes me about thirty years' worth of decent dinners then, Joss thought, as she removed the car keys from their hook by the front door. 'And where are we eating?'

Please, please not somewhere minimalist and *nouveau* with food she didn't recognise.

Marvin pushed past her through the door and shivered in the damp onslaught. 'Damn chilly tonight! Oh, a chap on the train the other morning said he'd had the best meal ever at a little local hostelry. Can't think why we've never tried it before.'

Joss could. Little local hostelries were, according to Marvin, filled with feral yobs, chavs, scum and inbreds.

'Not far for you to drive tonight,' Marvin sounded as though he was handing her the moon wrapped in silk. 'We're going to Fiddlesticks. To the Weasel and Bucket.'

'What the hell are you doing down there in that cupboard?' Chelsea shrieked at Sukie's rear view. 'And why are you still in your dressing gown? Haven't you showered yet? It's nearly seven o'clock!'

'Ow!' Sukie, startled by Chelsea's sudden appearance, leapt up, cracking her head on the open drawer above her. 'Ouch ... that hurts ... don't laugh ... And how did you get in?'

'The front door was unlocked. I let myself in. Why the hell are you spring cleaning now?'

'I'm not spring cleaning ... I'm – er – looking for something. And I showered ages ago and ... and – good God!' Sukie blinked, focusing on Chelsea properly for the first time. 'What on earth have you come as?'

'I'm a fairy.' Chelsea, her painted face covered in silver glitter, pirouetted, waving a pink and silver flashing wand above her head. 'Nice, innit?'

Sukie blinked some more. The brief pink net tutu barely covered Chelsea's brief pink knickers; the white satin bodice looked suspiciously like something from a porn shop; the pink fishnet tights and ballet pumps were – well – odd; but the most amazing thing was the fluffy flashing candyfloss pink tiara sitting atop Chelsea's variegated hair.

'You didn't walk through the village like that?' Sukie giggled. 'Please tell me you didn't . . .'

'Nah, it's far too cold. Dad dropped me off. He'll be back to pick us up in fifteen minutes and take us to Fiddlesticks. We'll have to get a taxi back, mind. Er – I don't suppose the love god is here, is he?'

'Who?'

'Derry Kavanagh, of course.' Chelsea frowned, her tiara winking and blinking. 'I'd love to flash me wand at him.'

'Sad.' Sukie grinned. 'So sad. And no he isn't here. Neither is Milla so he won't even be dropping in to collect her. You'll have to go and do your Fairy Vamp act on someone else tonight.'

'Bugger,' Chelsea said good-naturedly. 'And as the pub is going to be filled with women it'll all go to waste. We could always hang around for a bit and see if Derry turns up I suppose . . .'

No we couldn't, Sukie thought. Derry Kavanagh had laughed at her once – he'd never get the chance to do it again. 'Oh, I doubt if Milla will bring him back here anytime soon. She's probably got him shacked up in some five-star boudoir as we speak.'

'Lucky cow,' Chelsea sighed. 'Oh well, in that case you'd better get a move on before my dad arrives. Yours is in one of these carrier bags.'

'My what?'

'Outfit. Fairy stuff.'

'I'm not dressing up.'

'You bloody well are. We all are. It's what Fern wanted and it's her hen-night so you have to. Now go and do your slap and get dressed – and I'll look for whatever it was you've lost in that cupboard.'

No, Sukie shook her head. No way was she dressing up – and definitely no way was she telling Chelsea that she'd spent the last hours driving herself crazy thinking about Topsy's ill-timed revelations and subsequently scouring Pixies Laughter for Cora's allegedly non-existent love potion recipes.

'I'm just wearing a pink T-shirt with my jeans and a bit of body glitter.'

'You are not! Everyone's dressing up. And you're wearing this,' Chelsea thrust a Big Sava carrier bag towards Sukie. 'Same as me. Ronald made them specially.'

'Would that be Ronald of Bagley-cum-Russet? Couturier to the stars?'

'Ronald from Hazy Hassocks,' Chelsea sighed. 'You know Ronnie? That odd one of Mitzi Blessing's Baby Boomers who Topsy got to make our cancan dresses. He's great on show-bizzy outfits. Loves the glitz and sequins. You can pay me later.'

Sukie peered into the carrier bag. 'And this is the same as yours, is it?'

'Exactly,' Chelsea said proudly. 'We'll look like twins.'

'I'll look like a fat tart. And as my legs look like raw sausages at this time of year – pink fishnets will really look good on them.'

'Duh!' Chelsea struck a pose, wand above her head. 'And what does Topsy always say about fishnets? "Make sure you're wearing a pair of tan tights or stockings under-neath, gels, and the fishnets will work wonders on *any* legs."'

Sukie giggled again. 'Yeah, well maybe she was right about that – but I'm still not being seen in public in the rest of it.'

'Of course you bloody are.' Chelsea shoved Sukie

towards the twisty staircase. 'Go and get dressed – and you have remembered Fern's present, haven't you?'

'Yes, the bottles are on the hall table – if you grab them while I'm upstairs and put them with yours I won't forget them, but—' she squinted again at the fairy outfit, '—I'm really not sure about this . . .'

'Blimey, Sukes – it's no more revealing than the cancan dresses – they're all basques and suspenders and stockings and petticoats and stuff – and you don't mind that, do you?'

'That's different.'

Well, it was, Sukie thought as she marched upstairs clutching the Big Sava bag. As they had so far cancanned only to various audiences in care homes or at school fêtes, Ronnie's interpretation of the Moulin Rouge costume seemed glamorous and exciting and well, appropriate. Sukie had never thought of it as arousing in any way. Whereas this skimpy fairy stuff – she shook the Big Sava bag – was downright inflammatory.

Still, she thought as she grabbed her can of glitter spray, as Chelsea had pointed out, at least the Weasel and Bucket would be a man-free zone tonight. It would be full of Fern's Fairies. No one would be even slightly interested in her curves spilling out of a costume that really belonged in the Mixed Infants Christmas play, would they?

The Weasel and Bucket was everything the Barmy Cow wasn't, Joss thought, looking round in delight at the highly polished surfaces, the twinkling brasses, the original low black beams, the crackling log fire. A real country pub. Cosy, friendly, warm – and, for a Saturday evening, surprisingly empty.

'Oh, isn't it lovely?' Joss turned to Marvin in delight. 'Why on earth have we never been here before?'

'You know my feelings on local pubs.' Marvin was already powering his way to the far end of the Weasel and Bucket's long bar. 'Although this one appears passable at least – but I'm always wary of this village – you know what goes on here, don't you?'

Joss did. Fiddlesticks believed in astral magic. They had the wildest outdoor parties because the villagers believed that the moon and the stars controlled their destiny. Well, they probably didn't believe that these days, of course, but they still held the parties.

Joss thought it was wonderful. Marvin, naturally, didn't.

'Look – old Simon and Sonia have beaten us to it – trust them to have bagged a table by the fire.' Marvin was rubbing his hands together. It was really irritating. Joss always longed to add superglue to his Atrixo. 'You'd better get the drinks in, then.'

Joss stared at his retreating tweed-jacketed back. Drinks for all of them? What on earth did Simon and Sonia drink? Could she remember? Did it matter? Did she care?

'Um – a large glass of dry white, please.' She smiled at the elderly woman behind the bar. 'And a large spritzer for me, please. And refills of whatever they . . .' Joss motioned towards Sonia and Simon at the fireside table, 'are having? Thank you.'

'They're having the same as you,' the woman told her. 'Except they didn't say please and thank you.'

Joss smiled in sympathy. They wouldn't. 'It's very quiet in here tonight.'

The woman paused in pouring the wine. 'Lull before the storm. There's a hen-night booked. We're just relief bar staff for the evening because the landlord and his girlfriend are getting married. He's gone off to Blackpool with the lads but she's having her do here – pink fairies is the theme, apparently. She's a lovely girl, young Fern, but fairy-like she ain't. It'll be bedlam later, you mark my words.'

Joss smiled in delight. A hen-night! Not only would that drive Marvin completely insane, it would liven up her Saturday evening no end.

'Maybe I'd better take a few bottles of wine and some

70

soda then – if it's going to be crowded later on.'

'Good thinking. I'll get you a big bucket,' the barmaid chuckled. 'Not to drink out of, mind, dear. Just to keep your Chardonnay cool.'

Joss chuckled back, pushing away the superb mental picture of Marvin slurping from a bucket, took the wine and the ice bucket, arranged the glasses on a tray and paid.

'Lovely. Thanks. Oh, we're planning on eating here tonight, too. So did the other couple ask for a menu?'

'No – but it wouldn't have mattered if they had. Timmy Pluckrose does a super spread usually, but like I said, we're only relief for the weekend. And I only do the basics. So, if you want to eat, dear, you'll have to order early because of the party – and it's steak and kidney pie or my special stew – either beef or veggie – with herb dumplings. And there's just spotted dick and custard for pud.'

Joss could have capered on the spot. This was getting better and better.

'That sounds perfect. I'll go and let the others know and be back in a second ...'

Carefully carrying the loaded tray, Joss made her way to the fireside table. Marvin didn't even look up.

Simon and Sonia, gym-honed and Next-dressed, skimmed vague smiles in her direction and didn't say thank you for their drinks. They were clearly deep in conversation with Marvin about the delights on the extensive menu arrayed on blackboards around the pub's nubbly walls.

'Er—' Joss sat down, '—there's no point in choosing from there. The landlord isn't—'

They all stopped talking for a moment, looked at her as if she were some irritating insect, and then continued.

'Marv ...'

Sonia tittered. 'Marv? *Marv?* She makes you sound like some ancient soul singer! Goodness, Simon would want an instant divorce if I called him Si ...'

If only it were that simple, Joss thought viciously.

'Jocelyn knows that I loathe being called Marv,' Marvin

71

growled. 'She must have forgotten.'

Joss took a deep breath, ignoring Marvin's thunderous expression. It was his purple one with the little pulsing neck veins. 'The lady behind the bar has just said that she only has a reduced menu tonight ...' and she reeled off the delights.

'Damn typical! School dinner stodge!' Marvin sniffed. 'Well, I don't know about you two but I vote we go somewhere else.'

Sonia and Simon exchanged a long look. Joss was pretty sure she'd kill all of them if they wanted to make a move to some faux-rustic eatery.

'I don't know – it might be fun in a retro sort of way,' Simon said with an air of desperate jollity. 'It's years since I had a decent steak and kidney pie. Old Sonia is a bit of a demon on the low-fat malarkey.'

Sonia winced and looked as if she was just about to list the amount of saturated fats and cholesterol-inducers in pastry, not to mention the statistical likelihood of heart attacks caused by the trans-fat in dumplings.

'Whatever you think, Simon,' she said, inverting her lips. 'But don't come to me for sympathy if you're up all night with raging indigestion.'

Marvin, still looking mauve, nodded slowly. 'Probably inedible – after all, who eats that sort of stuff these days? Pastry, for heaven's sake! But still, if you're willing to take the risk ...'

They were staying! Yessss! Joss had a little moment of mental elation. Then, taking a gulp of her spritzer, she stood up. 'So? Everyone for steak and kidney? And four spotted dicks? Lovely – I'll go and order.'

'Steady on. What's the rush?' Marvin frowned. 'You're being very bossy tonight, old girl.'

'I'm starving,' Joss said happily, knowing they had to have their food on the table before the hen-night started. Marvin was far too tight to leave food untouched when it had been paid for, but she knew he'd be out of the Weasel and Bucket like a greased gannet if he got wind of the upcoming party.

She could, she thought as she hurried back to the bar, even forgive him for calling her 'old girl'. It was worth it to be able to watch him become apoplectic later.

The food, huge heaped platters and various tureens of fresh vegetables which looked as if they really had come from someone's garden rather than the local cash-and-carry, arrived remarkably swiftly. Joss, piling her plate with carrots and purple sprouting, noticed that Simon was already wolfing back his pie crust like a man desperate for a carb fix.

'I say. What's going on over there?' Sonia piped up through a chunky mouthful. 'What are all those old ladies doing?'

Joss kept her eyes on her plate. She'd seen the twinkly banners and dozens of pink balloons and sparkly tinsel streamers stacked behind the bar when she'd ordered the food.

Everyone else stared across the pub to where a clutch of less-than-young ladies were scrambling on to chairs and small step ladders, fixing the decorations.

'Oh, Simon – look! Isn't that Gwyneth Wilkins and that huge woman she's friends with?' Sonia's voice was still muffled by a mouth filled with forbidden delights. 'Ida Something? It is! We've seen them at our Slim'n'Slender Salsa class in Winterbrook, haven't we? Fit for their age of course, but both very strange old ladies. They dance in panne velvet catsuits and plimsolls.'

'And there're those Motion women – the undertakers! Thank the lord they haven't brought their weird brother. And that cantankerous old Mona Jupp from the village shop here,' Simon added, taking the opportunity to reach across for more gravy-mopping bread. 'What on earth are they doing? And why are they all dressed up like Barbara Cartland?'

Joss dared to look then. And tried not to hoot with

73

laughter. The more senior hen-nighters had chosen varying degrees of floor-length pink tulle, feather boas and glittery pink headgear.

They looked like the Billy and Freda Watkins Formation Ballroom Team gone mad.

'What on earth is going on here?' Marvin asked.

Joss was delighted to notice he had purple sprouting broccoli caught in his teeth.

'I think it must be some sort of party,' Sonia, clearly forgetting that she never touched steak and kidney pie, had cleared her plate and was squinting across the pub. 'What do the banners say? Happy Hen-Night? Congratulations to Fern and Timmy? Goodness me – I think we may have clashed with a bit of a do.'

'In that case we're definitely leaving,' Marvin snorted. 'We certainly don't want to get involved with any village goings-on, do we?'

'But we haven't had our spotted dicks yet,' Simon said plaintively.

'And the barmaid is just bringing them over – and you've paid for them – and all these drinks,' Joss added, saying thank you for all of them as four huge steaming bowls were placed on the table. 'Er – is the party about to start?'

'Yep. Young Fern's just come downstairs in her regalia so the countdown's started,' the woman beamed. 'That's why I thought I'd better get your puds dished up. You won't be able to move in a minute. Ah – here we go!'

Like the first day of the Harrods' sale, the Weasel and Bucket's door flew open and a tidal wave torrent of pink-and-sparkly women poured in, filling the pub with wands and wings. The noise was incredible.

With a further huge roar and a blast of the Dixie Cups 'Going To The Chapel' from the jukebox, which clearly had nothing much prior to 1985 in its musical selection, Fern – the bride-to-be if the skin-tight skimpy pink bridal outfit and adorning L plates was anything to go by – shimmied out from behind the bar on stilt-heels.

'Bugger me,' Simon spluttered through a mouthful of spotted dick and custard. 'Look at the tits on that.'

# Chapter Eight

Pushing into the Weasel and Bucket behind Chelsea, Sukie immediately felt better. The pub was heaving with pink fairies of varying ages all wearing similar revealing outfits. She'd had an awful feeling, in the back of Chelsea's dad's car, that Chelsea might have got the dressing up bit very wrong indeed.

And true, her fairy costume was skimpy, but some of the others were positively indecent. And she needn't have worried about not knowing Fern very well; clearly every female from the surrounding villages had been invited tonight. It was going to be okay.

'Hiya!' Fern shrieked from the bar. 'I'm the Sugar Plump Fairy!'

And with every inch of her curves on display and a snazzy little veil pinned on to her curls, she bounced over to them in time to the strains of Chas and Dave belting out 'I'm Getting Married In The Morning'.

There was a sparkly moment of hugging and kissing and shared body-glitter. Followed by an almost identical twinkly moment of hugging and kissing and thank yous as Chelsea handed over the bag of presents.

'Great to see you both!' Fern yelled. 'Drinks are all free. We've put bottles on the tables but just go to the bar for refills when they run out – I think there's some nibbles to soak up the alcohol somewhere – and there's a space for dancing over by the loos. We're having pink champagne later! Don't you both look lovely? I'm sure you know everyone – just mingle and find a table – if you can!'

'Thanks,' Sukie roared back. 'And congratulations. When's the wedding?'

'End of April! In the Maldives! Just me and Timmy! We're doing the parties before and after, and having the wedding – and the honeymoon – to ourselves!'

'We're doing some of the entertainment for the after-party,' Chelsea screamed. 'Cancanning? Remember?'

Sukie nodded. Fern hugged them again, and leaving a shower of multicoloured dust shimmering behind her, powered off to greet another group.

'Look there's Phoebe and Clemmie!' Chelsea tugged at Sukie's wings. 'They're waving! They must have saved us a space!'

Phoebe and Clemmie, girls they'd been to school with, were indicating with flashing wands that there was room at their table. Sukie, feeling her spirits soar – there was nothing like a girls' night out to make you forget all the gloom and doom – clutched her flashing tiara and waved her wand back in reply. It was like silver semaphore.

All talking at once, they crammed round the table, pouring wine, shrieking over the costumes, catching up on gossip. Sukie took a slug of Chardonnay and felt the tension ebb miraculously away.

The sadness and anger she'd felt after Topsy's revelations were no more than a twinge now. And whatever Cora had or hadn't concocted in Pixies Laughter, and her reasons for doing so, were best left as ancient history. Although, looking around her now, at all these women having a good time, she couldn't help feeling a little pang for the other women who must have sat in the Weasel and Bucket, generations before, in far less happy circumstances.

She had toyed with the idea of telling Chelsea about Topsy and Cora, but decided against it. Chelsea was lovely, but had little imagination and lived happily in the present.

77

Chelsea probably would never understand how the women of Cora and Topsy's generation had suffered; would never be able to picture them as young girls, madly in love, grieving for the boys who never came home.

No, it was all best left well alone. As was her search for the love potions. Maybe they existed, probably they didn't. It was all in the past. And that was where it must stay.

'... and what he sees in her is anyone's guess ...'

'... she's such a miserable cow ...'

'Her dad owns a Porsche dealership.'

'Ah ...'

Sukie, relaxing, easily slipped back into the current girlie-chat.

Chelsea suddenly grabbed her arm. 'Blimey! Look at them! Just come in ... Look! Who are they?'

Obediently, Sukie looked at the newcomers: four stunning girls straight out of *Footballers' Wives*, all tall, slim, glossy and slinky, their micro-skirted pink fairy dresses showing acres of sun-tanned legs, and diamanté tiaras reflecting in their super-shiny hair.

'Blimey! Who are *they*?'

'They're with Amber,' Clemmie hissed. 'Her mates from Oop North. They're down here to stay with her especially for this. They were in here last night – er – Emma and Jemma, Kelly and Bex, I think – and they're really, really nice too. Like Amber. Beautiful and lovely. Not fair. It's so annoying, you'd really like to hate them for being so foxy, wouldn't you?'

Sukie grinned. She'd really wanted to dislike Amber when they'd first met, but found it impossible. No one could ever hate Amber. And, apart from their friendship, she and Amber had a lot in common as they both worked for a Mrs Blessing: Amber as Mitzi's assistant in her catering business, Hubble Bubble, and Sukie, of course, with Jennifer. The rivalry between the past and present title holders had made Sukie and Amber close allies.

Clemmie refilled the glasses again. 'Talk of the devil –

here's Amber now. Oh, doesn't she look gorgeous in that little pink fairy dress? And so happy.'

She did, Sukie had to admit. And so she should. She'd been living with Lewis Flanagan for the last six months. That was enough to put a smile on anyone's face.

'Didn't you have a thing with her Lewis, Sukie, before she did?' Phoebe asked.

'Oh, it was only a one-night stand,' Chelsea said. 'Poor old Sukes – there was never any contest there, was there?'

Sukie shook her head amiably. 'They were made for each other. My turn will come – but not with Lewis. That was a non-starter. Oh, hi . . .'

Amber and her girlfriends had stopped at their table. There was another round of introductions and squeals of excitement over the outfits, and speculation about what Timmy and his stags were getting up to in Blackpool.

'Has Jem gone to Blackpool too?' Sukie asked.

'Too right,' Amber chuckled. 'He wouldn't have missed out on a weekend of big dippers and casinos – although he was a bit miffed that the boys weren't dressing up too. You know what a show-off he is?'

Sukie laughed. Jem was Lewis's best friend and very special. A young-old man with cerebral palsy, a vibrant personality and a wicked sense of humour, he lived on a one-to-one basis with Lewis as his carer. Sukie had always found it hard to believe that the rock-star-looking Lewis was really a social worker – but he and Jem were inseparable. It also said a lot about Amber that she had fitted so happily into the set-up.

'And,' Amber moved a bit closer, 'I've heard on the Mona Jupp gossip grapevine that you've been entertaining our Jem's boss at your cottage. Lucky you. He's pretty bloody gorgeous, isn't he?'

'What?' Sukie was relieved that Chelsea, Clemmie and Phoebe were more interested in discussing the joys of celeb-spotting in Manchester with Amber's friends than listening-in. 'I think you've got the wrong end of the stick.

I haven't been out with anyone for ages. Who the heck is Jem's boss anyway?'

'Derry Kavanagh,' Amber sighed the words. 'Not as beautiful as Lewis of course, in my opinion, but pretty damn close.'

'Derry Kavanagh ...' Sukie shook her head. 'Oh yes, he's sensational, but I'm not going out with him – more's the pity. He's seeing Milla ... you know? She shares my cottage? And I didn't know he was Jem's boss.'

'Jem does a couple of days' work placement every week at Winterbrook Joinery. Derry runs it.'

Ah, Sukie thought. So that explained a lot. Derry was a carpenter; one of those superbly-toned young men you saw on summer building sites, stripped to the waist and all muscles and suntan. It would certainly explain the body – but why on earth would Milla be going out with a labourer?

'He's brilliant with wood – Derry, I mean. He's a bespoke joiner – designs and makes fabulous one-off pieces of furniture and spiral staircases and all sorts of amazingly clever things – all for the disgustingly wealthy, of course.'

Sukie nodded. That made even more sense. Derry wasn't strictly a labourer, then. He was not only a talented crafts-man but also the owner of a clearly expensive business – Milla would certainly love all that.

'I really don't see much of him,' she said, deciding not to say that she'd seen practically all of him fairly recently and still remembered every glorious inch. 'Milla seems to keep him out of the way. Mind you, he'll probably soon be history. They only met last week but Milla dumps blokes like other people dump used chewing gum.'

'No one would dump Derry though,' Amber's eyes were huge. 'They'd have to be crazy. Maybe Derry'll turn out to be her Mr Right and we'll have another wedding on our hands.'

Sukie really, really hoped not.

'Amber! Oh, you look so cool! Isn't this the greatest hen-night ever?' Fern, who everyone knew was Amber's best friend in Fiddlesticks, suddenly swooped down on her and they disappeared in a massive squealing hug, tiaras and wings entangled. 'Come and dance over here – they're going to play "Crying in the Chapel"!'

'See you later,' Amber giggled as Fern dragged her away from the table. 'And don't forget to say hi to Derry for me next time you see him.'

Across at the fireside table the silence was cutting. After Simon's outburst, Sonia had rapped him smartly across the knuckles with her pudding spoon. The custard had landed on Marvin. Joss, having the best Saturday night she could ever remember, hadn't helped to scrape it off.

The landlady had been right. The whole pub was in uproar. It was fantastic. There were women of every age, shape and size, cavorting around in the most amazing interpretations of fairy costumes. And loud music. And laughter.

'Looks like we're here for the duration,' Joss yelled cheerfully to no one in particular. 'We'll never get out through that lot. Still, it's like a floorshow, isn't it? And all for free. Shall I pour more drinks?'

Still no one spoke. Marvin was thunder-faced. Sonia simply looked prim and pious. Simon's eyes were out on stalks, leering at so much female flesh. Joss took this general silence as an acceptance and happily refilled the glasses. She simply couldn't wait to tell Valerie all about it.

Settling back in her chair, her knees nicely warmed by the fire glow, her toes tapping out of sight under the table, Joss scanned the riotous crowd. Despite the disguise of the pink and sparkling costumes, she thought she recognised most of the partygoers. Oh, how she longed to be part of that colourful, noisy bunch. If only she could get up and join in and shimmy across the floor clutching her glass above her head, giggling as her wings became entangled with someone else's tiara.

Still, she thought contentedly, simply being an observer was a million times better than her usual Saturday night boredom, and even more so as Marvin had chosen the Weasel and Bucket and therefore couldn't blame her for this fiasco later.

And people-watching was such fun. All the old ladies from Fiddlesticks were doing the hokey-cokey and Fern was dancing on top of the bar with one of her friends – oh, and wasn't that Sukie with that laughing crowd round the table by the door?

Such a pretty girl with that lovely curvy figure and her dark hair and blue eyed Irish colouring, Joss always thought, and probably more so because she always seemed totally unaware of it. And so clever, with her aromatherapy. Had Valerie arranged the illicit massage session with her yet? Joss was really looking forward to being pampered in secret. If only there was some way of having a quick word with Sukie, just to make sure she'd got them pencilled in . . .

'Sorry.' She leaned towards Marvin who was glaring at the fire. 'I'm going to have to make a dash for the loo. Far too much soda in my spritzer.'

Marvin tutted and frowned a bit more. He prided himself on never needing to use public conveniences and always became quite critical of Joss's need to find a ladies wherever they went.

Sonia raised skinny eyebrows. 'You need to practise bladder control at your age, Jocelyn, or you'll be a martyr to Tena Lady. I personally never go a day without exercising my pelvic floor.'

Joss felt there was no suitable response to this, so she pushed her chair back, stood up and without meeting Marvin's eyes dived across the pub into the fairy fray.

It was like being swallowed up by a twinkling cloud of sensuous scents. Joss felt she was already getting high on the heady mix of Chanel and Jean-Paul Gaultier and J-Lo's finest.

82

Having 'sorry'd' and 'excuse me'd' her way into the lavatory, and waited for a while listening to some frankly wonderful scurrilous gossip in the queue, she emerged again into the mêlée.

Elbowing her way through acres of net and tulle and diaphanous dresses, she reached Sukie's table.

Clemmie Coddle from the Bagley-cum-Russet Post Office Stores was holding court.

'... and then he said his other one was yellow and he'd bring it with him next time!'

Everyone exploded with laughter. Joss, not having a clue what was going on, joined in.

Sukie, wiping mascara from under her eyes, looked up. 'Oh, hello ... Er – Mrs Benson?'

'Jocelyn, Joss, please ... Sorry to interrupt you, and I'm sure you don't want to talk about work, but I just wondered if Valerie – Mrs Pridmore – had mentioned to you about booking us in for a massage at her place?'

'Valerie? Oh, cancan Val? Yes, she did – and I think we arranged it for two-ish on Friday afternoon, but I was going to ring her anyway because I'm going to set up a room at home and I wondered if you'd prefer that?'

'Oh, yes – definitely,' Joss said quickly. It was far, far better for her to have her massage as far away from The Close as possible. 'I'll tell her shall I? Friday ... lovely ... thank you.'

Feeling deliciously wicked at her planned deception, she turned away, hoping that Marvin hadn't spotted her detour, and found herself grabbed round the waist and dragged back towards the loos.

'C'mon!' A large woman in what looked like a fluorescent nightie yelled in her ear. 'Fern's pouring the pink plonk! And we're all dancing! Mind, you haven't made much effort with yer outfit, have you, duck?'

'I'm not with the hen-night—' Joss started to pull away. 'I was just ...'

But the scrum simply surrounded her and swept her

along. She could see Sukie and several other familiar faces, all giggling, all being manhandled on to the minuscule dance floor.

Oh, what the heck, Joss thought, refusing the champagne because she was driving and still had some sense of responsibility, I might as well be hung for a sheep as a lamb.

And with a sense of giddy excitement, she whooped her way through Dave Edmunds claiming that he Knew The Bride When She Used To Rock'n'Roll, Sir Elton's suggesting that everyone should Kiss the Bride, and even something sassy about a teenage wedding by Chuck Berry. On and on she danced, pinned in on all sides by pink fairies.

It was just fantastic.

But as with all good things, it had to come to an end. Fern and Amber, whirling dizzily, collapsed in a heap. Several other fairies had lost their wings and looked rather green. Joss, still laughing and very out of breath, panted her way out of the madness.

The fireside table was empty.

'Jocelyn!' Marvin's voice bellowed from the inglenook's dark recess. 'I've got your coat! We're going home!'

'Sonia and Simon already gone, have they?' Joss grabbed her coat, avoiding looking at Marvin. She knew that his expression would be the puce one with the petulant lower lip and the tom-tom pulse in the temples. 'I must have missed them.'

'They escaped as soon as there was a gap in that – that moronic rabble. I was ready to go too. In fact I've been waiting for ages. Where the hell have you been?'

'There was a queue for the ladies.' Well, that was true. 'Anyway, I'm here now so shall we go? And—' she smiled happily up as Marvin as they picked their way through the Weasel and Bucket's debris, '—hasn't this been a simply wonderful night?'

Marvin shuddered his way out of the door. 'Are you

insane, woman? It's been bloody hell on earth.'

Sukie, still reeling giddily from the frantic dancing, flopped down at her table again. Wow! What a fantastic night! And to think she hadn't been looking forward to this! She grinned at Chelsea, Phoebe and Clemmie who had now been joined by Amber's girlfriends. They looked, as she did, distinctly dishevelled and dishabilled. There was probably more flesh on display at their table than on an average night in the Spearmint Rhino.

Sukie, relaxed and happy, pushed her chair away from the table, and slumped inelegantly amidst the froth of her skimpy skirt.

The door flew open, allowing a blast of welcome cold damp air to waft over the acres of hot bodies.

'Jesus!' Milla, looking superb in a little black something which definitely hadn't come from Primark, stared around her in amazement. 'What the hell is going on in here?'

Sukie tried to sink beneath the table.

'You can't hide, Sukes!' Milla gurgled. 'You never said you were coming here tonight. Are you the entertainment? I mean, I knew you danced the cancan – but that outfit must be strictly for poles.'

'Oh, ha-ha-ha,' Sukie said, still feeling slightly squiffy and trying to tug her bodice up over her escaping chest and her tutu down over her knickers. 'And why are you here anyway? You're a bit late for the hen-night.'

'Is that what this is? *Really*? How fascinating.' Milla surveyed the scene with some amusement. 'Must say it's not like any hen-night I've ever known.'

Well it wouldn't be, would it, Sukie thought. This is hardly Barcelona or Rome.

Milla flicked back her hair. 'Actually, we're on our way to a club in town. I thought we should pop in for a quiet rural drink first, somewhere we could be alone, but clearly that wasn't the best idea I've ever had. I guess we'll just have to head for somewhere a little more secluded, won't we?'

85

We, Sukie thought. The dreaded *we*.

On cue, Derry appeared behind Milla in the doorway. 'Couldn't get the jeep into the car park, so I've left it out on the road. Oh, hi . . .'

'Hi . . .' Sukie said shortly, still disliking him for laughing before and knowing she'd dislike him even more now if he as much as sniggered.

He didn't. Well, not quite. True, his mouth wasn't even slightly grinning, but his eyes were. A lot.

'We're not stopping.' Milla had already turned round and was trying to shove Derry out through the door.

Too late. Amber's friends had spotted him and were whooping and wolf-whistling with gusto. Chelsea, preening madly, flapped her wand at him in excitement. Clemmie and Phoebe joined in.

Derry grinned in delight. Sukie's stomach did somersaults. God – he had a gorgeous smile . . .

'Down boy,' Milla said, turning on her designer heels. 'We'll find somewhere else to drink. Somewhere you won't get eaten alive.'

'Shame,' Derry said cheerfully. Then looked at Sukie, his lips not quite steady. 'Bye, then. See you again, no doubt?'

'No doubt. Have a nice time.'

Pig! Sukie thought as the door closed behind them. He was probably rolling around the crowded car park right now in paroxysms of hysteria. Why, oh why, did he always catch her at the worst possible moments?

'C'mon, Sukes!' Chelsea yelled in her ear. 'The love-god's gone and I've just poured out the antidote. Drown your sorrows with the rest of us! What you need is one of these.'

Sukie squinted down at the masses of tiny shot glasses, all brimful with brightly coloured liquid, on the table. Vodka Shots always gave her a mega-hangover. Oh, what the hell . . .

They all picked up their first glass and started the countdown.

'One-two-three,' Phoebe laughed. 'Now!'

Sukie swallowed and pulled a face. It was very strong.

'No wimping out!' Clemmie spluttered. 'Next one! One-two-three ...'

By the time the glasses were empty, Sukie felt pretty inebriated. Everyone was shrieking with unnecessary laughter.

Fern, her eyes crossed, wobbled from the throng and threw her arms round Sukie's neck. 'Thanks so much for the fab present, Sukie. I don't know what to say – it was the loveliest thing I've ever had.'

Was it? Sukie wondered just how much Fern had had to drink. True, the sun-blocking skin cream and moisturising lotion were certainly from Beauty's Blessings' top range, but they weren't anything that special.

'I'm so pleased you like them. I thought you'd be able to use them on honeymoon.'

'Oh, I will,' Fern gurgled sexily as she undulated away from their table. 'Believe me – me and Timmy will make full use of them ...'

'Fern must be well gone—' Sukie squinted at Chelsea, '—to get that excited about a couple of pots of nourishing cream.'

'Crikey,' Chelsea slurred. 'And you must be more drunk than she is if you can't remember what present you gave her. I put those all those little bottles in my bag while you were getting dressed, remember?'

'All what little bottles? I bought her skin cream. What are you talking about?'

'Skin cream? Nah – you gave her all those little bottles of exotic massage oils. Loads of them. Nice present, Sukes – no wonder she was so excited. They'll spice her and Timmy up no end.'

Holy shit!

'Chelsea! You didn't take them out of my aromatherapy case? Tell me you didn't.'

'Well, yes. Grab the present, you said. On the hall table,

you said. So I did – all those little bottles of – er – geranium and jasmine and lavender and rose ... Oh, bugger ...'

Oh bugger, indeed. She'd just given away her entire exclusive and highly expensive aromatherapy stock.

'You can't ask for them back can you?' Chelsea whimpered. 'It's a present and she was so excited. Sorry, Sukes. Are you going to kill me?'

'Not me,' Sukie said, thinking of the almighty wrath of Jennifer Blessing. 'But I know someone who will ...'

# Chapter Nine

The following morning, there was a series of increasingly apologetic texts from Chelsea, but Sukie, nursing a thumping hangover, curled in Cora's favourite chair in front of the fire, clutching her umpteenth mug of black coffee, with the rain lashing down outside, wasn't mollified.

The peach leather cases were sadly depleted. It was fortunate that Chelsea hadn't taken any of the base oils or the tiny empty replacement bottles with their flowery labels and gemstone stoppers, but even so most of the essential oils, the essences, the tools of her trade, had gone.

She only hoped Fern and Timmy would put them to good use on their Seychelles honeymoon.

But what on earth was she going to do? These were no ordinary massage oils: these had been special blends, organically nurtured, wildly expensive. Sukie knew she couldn't just nip off to the nearest Holland and Barrett for replacements, she had no reserve stocks of her own, and purloining refills from Beauty's Blessings was out of the question. One, Jennifer would notice before she'd even started decanting, and two, the supplies at the salon were only very, very basic – certainly not comprehensive enough to replace the dozens of specially ordered, probably-made-by-monks-in-a-dew-soaked-meadow, eye-wateringly costly, missing essences.

Oh, bugger with bells on.

Dreary grey Sunday mornings in March were probably a prime time for suicides, Sukie thought. Add Jennifer Blessing's incandescent fury at the loss of what was probably hundreds and hundreds of pounds worth of stock before the mobile massages had even started, and Sukie could see the appeal of taking the easy way out.

'Is the kettle hot, Sukes?' Milla breezed into the living room, tucking a lemon silk scarf into perfect loops in that irritating way people who knew exactly what to do with scarves always did. 'I'm running late so I can't wait to boil it up again but I'm dying for a shot of caffeine. Sweetheart – you do look rough. Mind you, having seen you in action last night I'm not surprised.'

Sukie, wearing comfort clothes – her scruffiest jeans and an ancient baggy sweater washed second-skin-soft – glared at Milla who was naturally all band-box-fresh in designer jeans and tan leather jacket and boots and of course the perfectly looped scarf.

'You could always make the trek to the kitchen and check the kettle for yourself,' Sukie grumbled, uncurling herself from the chair. 'I know you're probably used to having people dance to your every whim but—'

She headed for the kitchen anyway. It was easier to bury her head in coffee-making than face Derry emerging any minute from the twisty staircase looking all gorgeously tousled and sexually fulfilled.

'There.' She pushed the mug into Milla's hands. 'I didn't bother making one for Derry. He can get his own when he gets up. I'm not everyone's slave.'

'Clearly a bad, bad hangover.' Milla smiled. 'And coffee would have been wasted on Derry anyway. He's not here.'

Despite feeling awful, Sukie brightened a bit as she scuttled back to Cora's chair. 'Oh, right ... Did you have a row?'

'Derry and I don't do rows.' Milla flicked at her already perfect hair in the mirror. 'No, the club was pretty disappointing, so we called it a day – anyway, I'm off for

90

Sunday lunch at the parental pile, so I needed an early night. Alone.' She perched on the arm of Cora's chair. 'You know how Mummy and Daddy always look for signs of debauchery.'

Sukie's momentary uplifted spirits plunged again. Milla was taking Derry Home To Meet The Parents. Already. It must be serious.

'And will they approve? I mean, I know Derry is – er – very attractive, but he's not your usual type, is he?'

'After my broken engagement, I no longer have a type, as you well know.' Milla sipped her coffee. 'And why shouldn't Derry be the Right One? Okay, he might not be a trader or an analyst or my usual city slicker as you so sharply pointed out, but look at us, Sukes. Chalk and cheese – but we get on well living together, don't we?'

Sukie nodded. They did.

'I mean, when you needed a lodger, everyone thought you'd share Pixies Laughter with Chelsea, didn't they? You've been friends since infants' school. It would have made sense.'

Sukie shuddered. 'Chelsea couldn't have afforded the rent I needed to keep this place going. Big Sava only pays the minimum wage. And although we're lifelong best friends, we'd have probably killed one another before the first month was up.'

But it was true. Bagley-cum-Russet simply couldn't understand why city-girl Milla had become Sukie's lodger rather than Chelsea. Sukie had let them wonder. She knew from Milla that her advert in the lettings papers had been exactly what Metro Milla had been looking for when she needed to escape from city living after the sudden and painful break-up of a long engagement with someone implausibly called Bo-Bo.

Bo-Bo, it transpired, had been some sort of embryo Sir Alan Sugar figure, and if the much-kissed and cried-over photo in Milla's bedroom was anything to go by, resembled an early Bryan Ferry: all gorgeously dark and dangerous and lounge lizardy. Bo-Bo had suddenly got cold feet, merely weeks before the wedding of the century. It had broken Milla's heart.

Post-Bo-Bo, Milla had embarked on a series of mad one-night stands with posh blokes in a futile attempt to heal the pain – and then she'd met Derry ...

'So, if you and I can happily make a go of house-sharing, I don't see why Derry should be any different. Right,' Milla stood up, 'now I must fly. Mummy will have probably invited the neighbours in for pre-lunch drinks and she hates anyone being late. Thanks for the coffee, Sukes. I may stay overnight with the parents so don't worry if I don't come home. Bye, then ...'

After the front door had slammed, Sukie stared into the gas flames again. Alone on a wet Sunday. Super ...

'Get a grip,' she muttered to herself. 'You've got less than twenty-four hours to salvage the massage oil situation – sitting around here feeling sorry for yourself isn't going to solve anything.'

So, what were the options?

Well, she could be honest with Jennifer. No – Jennifer would probably scream and yell and then sack her and replace her with a trainee from the FE college who'd work for pocket money and wouldn't allow her chums to give away the essences.

She could possibly fill the bottles with a few drops of synthetic fragrances from the basic oils she kept in the bathroom, top them up with water and cheat. No – absolutely not – she was very proud of her aromatherapy skills and her reputation as a masseuse and her integrity.

Or she could raid her overdraft and drive to Reading and see if she could find an organic, exclusive aromatherapy supplier open and ready to replace her stocks. No – definitely not – even if such a shop existed and was open on a Sunday, her overdraft was already a no-go area.

'Oh Cora.' Sukie uncurled herself and wandered to the window, wincing as the headache thumped again. 'Why aren't you here to give me advice like you used to? What on earth am I going to do?'

Staring bleary-eyed out over the rain-washed garden, at the weeds all bowed and tangled and dripping, something penetrated the buzzing fuzz in her brain. Something half-remembered. Something she'd laughed about.

Topsy's words . . .

'. . . the garden is a veritable storehouse of natural energy . . . out there you have all the raw materials for your craft . . . Cora knew the power of the garden plants . . .'

Sukie bit her lip. What if? Just what if? What if Topsy had been telling the truth – what if Cora had made potions from garden flowers? What if Pixies Laughter really could give her what she needed? She'd be able to replace everything and save money at the same time. The perfect solution.

Then she sighed. Okay, so she might just have the right flowers and herbs growing out there in the back garden's soggy wilderness, but how was she supposed to turn them into the essences she needed? It wasn't something they'd covered on her course in Newcastle. They hadn't even touched on going down the Grow Your Own route.

Oh, sod it! If only there was someone who could give her some sort of instructions on what to look for and what to do with it when she found it.

If only she could find Cora's flowery recipe book – not that she believed it actually existed, of course – but hey, what else did she have to do with a long, wet, lonely Sunday?

Two hours later the cottage was in a state of chaos. Sukie had turned out boxes and suitcases, and drawers and cupboards. She'd even – remembering what Doll and Lulu Blessing had told her about Mitzi's discovery of the herbal cookery book – ventured into the attic.

She'd found hundreds of old photographs, and had cried fat tears over pictures of a very much younger Cora in the

93

arms of a handsome young man who must have been the one who died in the war; and old address books and strange shopping lists and embroidery and knitting patterns – but nothing at all that resembled How To Turn Weeds Into Essences In Time To Save Sukie's Life.

She was sitting amidst a heap of papers on the living-room floor when someone knocked on the front door.

No doubt it was Chelsea escaping Sunday with her huge, boisterous family. Sukie wasn't sure she wanted to spend the rest of Sunday with Chelsea, but neither did she really want to be alone. Sighing, scrubbing the worst of the dust and cobwebs from her face and clothes, she padded to open the door.

A huge bunch of flowers greeted her.

'Hi.' Derry Kavanagh grinned from behind the flowers.

Sukie groaned. Par for the course. She must look like some sort of filthy dirty, wild-haired vagrant. No doubt the remnant of last night's mascara was still clogging her eyelashes and she'd probably got congealed egg-yolk on her sweater. He'd laugh at her at any minute.

'Lovely flowers, but Milla isn't in,' she said round the bouquet. 'She left ages ago. Was she supposed to meet you here?'

'No.' Derry shook his head. 'She's gone to see her parents, I know. I wasn't invited. The flowers are for you.'

'Me? Why?'

'To say a very belated thank you for letting me use your bed – and for not kicking me out of it when you must have been exhausted. It was very generous of you – and I really should have said thanks before ... Oh, have I interrupted a spring clean?'

Sukie shook her head. She couldn't remember the last time a man had bought her flowers. And Derry still hadn't laughed at her. 'Er – well, thank you. They're lovely. Um – do you want to come in? Have a coffee?'

Derry Kavanagh was bound to say thanks but no thanks.

'Great – yes, thanks – if you're sure I'm not interrupting

anything.' Derry stepped into the hall and glanced into the living-room. 'Good God! Have you been burgled?'

'No.' Sukie smiled. 'I was – um –looking for something. Shall I take the flowers?'

The bouquet was huge, and not a petrol station or supermarket special. She smiled at him again through the profusion of pastel blooms. 'These are wonderful –but there was no need . . .'

'Yes, there was. I should have done this straight away. And I certainly should have said how grateful I was sooner – not that I've seen you for more than a split second. If Milla had decided to stop in the pub last night I could have spoken to you then. I'd have liked that – it looked like a lot of fun.'

'It was. But strictly girls only. Anyway, it was as well Milla had somewhere else in mind. You'd have probably been torn limb from limb.'

'A bloke lives in hope. You all looked very – um – fairy-dollish.'

'We probably looked terrible, but we had a great time . . .' Sukie hid her embarrassment by inhaling the glorious spring fragrances. 'These really are gorgeous. Thank you so much. Look, sit down if you can – I'll put these in water. Oh, just chuck that lot on to the floor . . .'

Grinning to herself, Sukie managed to find the flowers a suitable home, make coffee, spike up her hair and scrape the worst of the grime off her face in less time than it took Milla to apply lip gloss.

Walking back into the living room with the coffee, she allowed herself a moment of sheer pleasure, staring at Derry, in his faded jeans and navy sweater, sprawled in Cora's favourite chair. The ice-blond hair was in the sort of textured layers you ached to touch, and his profile, as he stared into the gas flames, was almost sculpted.

She exhaled. He truly was sensational. And, of course, off limits and not even slightly interested in her.

Ah, well . . .

'Coffee up. I'll just clear a space ... er – well if there's anywhere left to clear a space to.'

'Thanks.' Derry took the mug. 'What exactly are you looking for?'

Sukie perched on the edge of the opposite chair. Should she tell him? No, of course she shouldn't. He'd laughed at her before – he'd probably choke himself if she told him the truth. And she reminded herself, she might fancy him like mad, but she didn't *like* him, did she? Because of the laughing.

'Nothing much.'

'Really?' Derry raised his eyebrows.

God he was gorgeous, Sukie thought as she drooled over his blue, blue eyes. 'No, nothing – well, actually, yes – something vitally important ...'

And she told him. All of it. And she'd kill him if he laughed.

He didn't. Well, only at the amusing bits where it was okay to. And he was very quiet and turned away to stare into the fire when she told him about Cora and Topsy and the boys they'd loved and lost. Derry Kavanagh earned himself quite a few brownie points on that score.

'So—' she finished, '—that's it really. I was looking for something that probably doesn't exist to make something that probably won't work.'

'Quite a challenge. Want some help?'

'No! I mean – well, no thanks – I mean – you must have far more interesting things to do with your Sunday.'

'I live alone. Milla is in her stockbroker belt homeland. My mates are all playing happy families. There's no football on the telly.'

'Well, if you put it like that ...'

They grinned at one another.

'So – where do we start?' Derry drained his coffee. 'Shall we look for the – um – recipes first? Or the plants?'

'That's the dilemma,' Sukie sighed. 'Chicken or the egg?'

96

'Maybe if we cleared some of this stuff up first? Make a bit of space? Get organised?'

Sukie, who rarely did organised, was impressed. A man who could tidy up. Of course, he probably had to be organised in his job, and he lived alone so didn't have anyone to come along behind him picking up debris.

She nodded. 'Okay. We'll just put stuff into piles for now.'

After a further half an hour and more coffee and an unhealthy but hangover-curing lunch of crisps and a whole packet of chocolate digestives, the living-room looked less of a disaster area.

'What about these?' Derry held up a pile of age-bleached squares of canvas. 'Are they yours? Which heap do they go in?'

Sukie looked up from the sideboard. 'Oh, no – they belong in Cora's needlework-basket. That big wicker thing behind the sofa. They're Cora's tapestries. Well, I think people call them cross-stitches these days. She always did them while she listened to *The Archers*. I kept them because they were so much part of her.'

'They're very intricate.' Derry shook out the first square. 'Oh, yes – my nan had loads of these, too. Little embroidered pictures with quotations under them. Home is where the heart is and all that. She used to frame hers.' He gently unfolded several others. 'Your Cora was very clever – look at all these tiny flowers ... really intricate work – and they all seem to have little poems underneath them.'

Sukie nodded. 'They were a huge part of my childhood. I used to play with them. Make up stories round them, use them for my dolls' dresses ...'

She stopped and turned her head away. A nasty lump of tearful nostalgia had lodged in her throat.

'Sukie? Are you okay?'

'Fine – look, just put them in the work-basket for now.'

Derry said nothing. Sukie, wiping the tears away before they fell, prayed that he wasn't laughing at her. She took a

97

deep breath and looked across the room. He was smiling. Damn him.

'Sukie . . .?'

'I said I'm okay.'

'Yes, but – look. Have you ever read the poems on these tapestries?'

'As a child I knew them off by heart. They were like my nursery rhymes. There was one about roses and honeysuckle. And one about herbs . . . oh, yes, basil and coriander because I used to think they were people – and something about cowslips and daisies . . . and – holy shit!'

'Couldn't have put it better myself.' Derry grinned at her. 'First part of the puzzle solved. We've found Cora's recipes.'

# Chapter Ten

'You think I'm crazy, don't you?' Sukie, muffled unflatteringly in her mac, peered at Derry through the slanting rain. 'You think all this is a load of hokum, don't you? Be honest – you're only humouring me.'

The wind whipped through the slate-grey gloom of Pixies Laughter garden, slapping wet brambles and nettles and fat fleshy dock leaves against their legs.

Derry, wearing Cora's ancient gardening coat and still managing to look sexy, grinned through the raindrops. 'No, I don't think you're crazy – if I did I wouldn't be humouring you I'd be running a mile and be sitting somewhere warm and dry with a pint. No, honestly, I'm intrigued. I'm always open to new ideas. I'd never discount anything simply because it seemed a bit – well – odd. And let's face it, you don't get much odder than this. So – now, what are we looking for?'

They'd copied out the rhymes from Cora's tapestries although Sukie, once reminded, could probably recite them all off by heart. She'd never thought of them as anything other than Cora's poems. Never thought they were strange in any way. Never thought about the meaning behind the familiar and oft-repeated words. And certainly never connected her childhood playthings, always to hand in Cora's work-basket, with the elusive recipes she'd been searching for.

'Do we need myrtle?' Derry crouched down over a particularly nasty heap of vegetation. 'Because if we do, I think this might be it.'

'Honestly? Fantastic. Yes ... yes, I know myrtle is mentioned in one of the rhymes,' Sukie squinted at the damp pieces of paper in her hand. 'Something to do with bridal bunches – along with rosemary. I remember not understanding the rhyme because I thought they must both be bridesmaids at a wedding so I asked Cora about them ...' She stopped, instantly whisked back to her happy childhood, remembering Cora's sweet smile and hearing her gentle Berkshire voice. She swallowed. 'Er – but Cora pointed out that myrtle was linked with fertile in the poem which meant she was the bride.'

'Myrtle and fertile? Jesus! We're not talking Wordsworth here, are we?' Derry laughed. 'Okay, so we've got poor old myrtle and I'm sure I can find rosemary the bridesmaid, so who else are we looking for? A whole churchful of guests?'

'Are you mocking me?' She looked at him quickly. 'Because if you are—'

'No, honestly.' He shook more raindrops from his hair which was now streaked dark-blond. 'My nan taught me all sorts of nursery rhymes and things, too. I could probably do all the actions if pressed – and no I'm not going to, so don't look at me like that. So – what else do we need?'

'Um – in no particular order, violas ... sweet briar ... hawthorn ... nettles ... wild rocket ... borage ... cowslips ... daises ... wild thyme ... basil ... oh, there are so many.' She sighed. 'Even if they exist in this wilderness how on earth do we recognise them?'

'Well, I'm no Alan Titchmarsh, but my nan was a keen cottage gardener and she did teach me a bit about wild flowers and herbs and things like that. She always had a patch of wilderness garden long before it was trendy. I knew most of the plants that grew there.'

Sukie looked at him in surprise. A man of many talents.

100

And who had clearly adored his grandmother as she'd adored Cora. And, of course, firmly attached to Milla. Sod it. 'Really? Okay – so are we likely to find any of these in March?'

'Possibly. Probably in some cases. I guess that Cora wrote different verses and made different potions for each season depending on what was available out here. We'll just have to go with the late winter and early spring ones for now. If this works you'll be spoilt for choice in a few months. Hey – look, this is definitely rocket. And under this lot—' Derry heaved at an upturned wheelbarrow and several chunks of stone which squelched unpleasantly in the mud, '—I reckon this could be borage. And these—' he squatted down in the soggy, cold mass of weeds, '—are definitely violas.'

Sukie beamed at him in sheer admiration. And quite a lot of lust. What a man!

'Don't just stand there, woman.' He grinned at her. 'Grab your trowel and start digging.'

A soggy hour later, having sluiced the mud from their hands and taken turns with the hair dryer, they surveyed their harvest in Pixies Laughter kitchen. Having washed the heap of plants, Derry had sorted them into relevant clumps to match Cora's verses.

'The next problem,' Derry said, flicking his dampish hair away from his face, 'is how we change them from their raw state into what you need.'

Sukie, making restorative coffee, frowned. 'When I was taking my first aromatherapy courses we did touch briefly on the history of the science. I didn't take a lot of notice, I'm afraid. It didn't seem relevant. So my methods may not be accurate, but we know we need to extract the essences, and get them into the bottles – sort of like cooking really. Er – I don't suppose you're a secret Jamie Oliver, too, are you?'

'Nah, strictly a pierce-and-ping man I'm afraid.'

'Me too,' Sukie shrugged. 'So – we'll need something to grind them with. Then something to mix them with. And in. And something to strain them through, and then something to get them into the little bottles ...'

'No problem there, then.' Derry leaned against the kitchen table. 'Any chance of finding anything useful in these cupboards? Cora's stuff? My nan keeps all sorts of ancient things that looked like they belonged in an operating theatre in her kitchen cupboards. Lovely old bits and pieces. Have you still got Cora's things here?'

Sukie nodded. Good thinking. Cora had also hoarded enamel dishes and stoneware crockery bowls and battered spoons and masses of other weird paraphernalia in the cupboards under the sink. They should still be there unless her parents had junked them in the early days of their inheritance blitz.

She knelt down and peered into the musty darkness, then pushed her hand into the recesses. Yes! Her fingers clanged against enamel and earthenware. Fantastic! Noisily, she turfed out enough late nineteenth and early twentieth century kitchen utensils to have the entire *Antiques Roadshow* team salivating.

'I reckon ladies of your Cora and my nan's generation all read the same How To Be Domestic Goddesses manual.' Derry knelt beside her on the uneven quarry tiles, sorting the spoils. 'This is wonderful – here's a pestle and mortar ... and a big cake mixing bowl ... and loads of little funnels ... and what's this funny stuff? I don't recognise this?'

Sukie emerged backwards from the cupboard. Derry was very, very close.

'Er ...' She shuffled away slightly and hoped he wouldn't realise she was blushing. 'I've no idea – it looks like dress material ... oh, yes I know what it is! It's buttermuslin! Cora used it to strain her ginger beer and all sorts of things – that's brilliant – I think we've got everything we need. Right – let's get cracking.'

102

They stood up at the same time, almost colliding, both moving away at the last minute. Sukie sighed. Damn.

Clearing the table and the work surfaces, they organised themselves into a kitchen production line.

'Do you think we need to say incantations or something?' Derry looked up from squidging a massive handful of basil and coriander into the mortar. 'After all, Topsy Turvey said your Cora's lotions and potions were magical.'

Sukie paused in checking a heap of pastel violas – their pink, white, pale mauve petals looking like confetti strewn across the table – for livestock. 'Yes, but – we've decided that's all rubbish, haven't we?'

'Have we? I don't think you have and I'm not so sure. Like I said, I always keep an open mind on everything until I'm convinced differently. Still, we'll leave that for the moment. Pass the pestle, please.'

'There you are – and no incantations,' Sukie said firmly, trying not to look at his muscles moving sensuously under the thin sweater as he got to work with the pestle. 'Whatever Cora did or didn't do with her potions doesn't concern us right now. This performance is simply to refill the bottles to save my skin and my money and my whole career. Ooooh – that one smells lovely . . .'

In fact, by the time they'd finished pulverising and filtering and mixing and decanting, the whole cottage wafted with glorious scents. A heady, sensuous mixture of herbs and flowers and the fresh tang of rainwater drifted beneath the beams.

In fact, Sukie thought dreamily, if she closed her eyes she could imagine the kitchen being filled with tiny floating multicoloured stars and flowers and butterflies . . .

'Don't think we need any magic,' Derry grinned, sprawled on one of the mismatched kitchen chairs. 'I'm as high as a kite simply inhaling the fumes . . . and they—' he nodded towards Jennifer Blessing's little gemstone-stoppered bottles once more filled to the brim, and neatly

103

relabelled, standing in rows on the table, '—look the business.'

Sukie, tired, dishevelled, but triumphant, grinned back at him. 'They do, don't they? Thank you so much. I'd never have managed this without you. Literally.'

'My pleasure. This was far more fun than doing the joinery accounts or waiting for one of my mates to get fed up with playing happy Sunday families and need to make a dash for the pub.' Derry stretched. It was almost unbearably exciting. 'Shall we start to clear up, then?'

'Oh, we'll just shove all the mess into the bin and the crocks into the dishwasher ...' Sukie dragged her eyes away from his body. 'And I'll whizz a cloth over everything else. It'll only take five minutes.'

'And the rest of the cottage?'

'I'll sort that out later – before Milla gets back. The whole place needed a spring clean anyway – and I need to clear out the dining-room because I'm setting up a massage table in there so that I can start working from home this week.'

'With these?' Derry indicated the fruits of their labours.

'Yes. Why?'

'Because I think you might have missed something.'

Sukie, who'd been wondering if inviting Derry to share a pierce-and-ping microwaved supper would be a step too far, peered at him from beneath her spiky fringe. 'What? We've finished haven't we? What have we left out?'

'Nothing from the bottles – but how do you know they'll work? We need a guinea pig.'

Trying really, really hard not to think lustful thoughts of pinning Derry down on the kitchen table and massaging that gorgeously tanned, muscled body with one of the new unguents, Sukie attempted to look intelligently alert. Sadly, an even more treacherously delicious fantasy – him massaging her with those beautiful long, strong fingers – rapidly overtook the first one.

Sukie made a valiant effort to reinin the mental pictures,

knowing she was failing miserably.

'Guinea pigs?' Her voice came out all squeaky, so she coughed and tried again. 'Um – surely you're not suggesting that we should test drive these on each other?'

'Not a chance!' Derry laughed.

Oh, bugger. The death of two fantasies in a single stroke. And he'd laughed ... Again.

Derry stretched. 'I just think it might be an idea to find someone who knows you well, who needs a massage and who isn't likely to sue you – or Jennifer Blessing – should it go wrong.'

'Er – were you thinking of Milla?'

'No way! I may not know that much about Milla, but I'd guess she goes to discreet little beauty salons in London where she pays a fortune to someone called Camilla or Sophie to sort out her executive stresses. I also have a feeling she wouldn't take kindly to being rubbed up the wrong way with a few weeds from the garden. Especially by you – er – us.'

He was right, of course. So – who? Well, of course Chelsea would be the ideal choice, but Sukie definitely, definitely, definitely didn't want Chelsea muscling in on the rest of the afternoon and the pierce-and-ping supper.

Then again, there was Valerie Pridmore who was already booked in for a massage – but Valerie Pridmore was such a terrible gossip, and if she got even a whiff of an idea that this test-drive wasn't exactly kosher it'd be all over the village in no time.

'Topsy!'

Topsy would be perfect. Topsy who was fanatic about all things medical. Topsy who must never, ever know that the massage oil she was testing was created from Cora's recipes.

'Topsy Turvey?' Derry looked perplexed. 'Are you sure?'

'Positive. I'll just blend one of these new essences with my base oil and we'll—' Sukie stopped. She was presuming an

105

awful lot here. 'Er – sorry. I mean, I'm sure you've had enough of all this by now and want to go home.'

'I'm not going anywhere – I'm pretty curious to see what happens – but *Topsy*? Won't she wonder why we've suddenly barged into her living room on a Sunday afternoon brandishing massage oils?'

Sukie was carefully measuring almond oil into one of the tiny bottles. 'Oh, she won't be in her living room. She'll be in the pub. She always is on a Sunday afternoon – like all us singletons of any age, sometimes any company is better than being alone.'

'So you're going to massage some poor unsuspecting old lady in the middle of a busy pub on a Sunday afternoon?'

'Yep. That's about it. Are you up for it?'

'Wouldn't miss it for the world.'

# Chapter Eleven

The lopsided pebbledash and corrugated iron exterior of the Barmy Cow looked even more disreputable than usual in the chilly grey murk of early evening.

Sukie scrambled inelegantly from the passenger seat of Derry's scruffy jeep. She'd offered to drive the short distance – after they'd both agreed walking was out of the question because they couldn't stand getting wet again – but Derry wouldn't hear of it. This had delighted her because it meant, hopefully, that he'd drive her back to Pixies Laughter afterwards, so the pierce-and-ping could still be a possibility.

She looked at the grime-streaked, run-down, ramshackle pub with severe misgivings. 'Are you quite sure you want to do this? Have you ever been in here before?'

Derry shook his head. 'No, but the other night, when I saw you outside here I thought it looked – er – rather more interesting than Milla's choice of the wine bar in Winterbrook.'

'Oh, yes,' Sukie said coldly. 'Of course. The other night. When you were laughing at me.'

'I wasn't!' Derry tried not to smile.

'You were,' Sukie said crossly. 'You were sitting in Milla's flashy car, laughing at me.'

'Laughing, yes. But not *at* you. Absolutely not at you. Oh, God – is that what you thought?'

'Thought? No. Knew? Yes.' Clutching her handbag containing the massage oil against her chest, Sukie marched towards the Barmy Cow's battered door. 'I know what I saw – and you were laughing! Don't try to deny it – and anyway, it's too cold to stand out here arguing.'

Derry moved in front of her. 'I'm not denying it and I'm certainly not arguing. Goodness, you're prickly sometimes, aren't you? Do you want to know the truth? I saw you and your friend messing around out here, acting like kids – and I thought you looked like an uninhibited, happy girl who knew how to enjoy herself. I laughed *with* you, because whatever you were doing looked fun. I had no idea that you'd seen me – and even less that it would offend you if you had. Weren't you just messing around? Wasn't it some sort of game?'

'I'd got a very ancient glacé cherry stuck in my throat. Chelsea was getting it out.'

Derry laughed. 'Oh – sorry . . . no, really . . . I'm sorry – but why the hell did you swallow a whole cherry? No – okay . . . Maybe I shouldn't have laughed. Oh, sod it – yes, I should.'

'Pig!' Sukie shook her head, trying to hide her smile. 'Just one word of warning – don't drink anything in here that contains a cocktail stick, okay?'

'You ate a cocktail stick as *well*?'

'Forget it.' Sukie grinned, skipping inside the pub.

He hadn't laughed at her. He wasn't the nasty mean-minded bastard she'd thought he was. He wasn't such a bad bloke after all. In fact . . . No – whoa, girl. Remember Milla.

She took a deep breath. 'And I hope you're prepared for this . . .'

Sadly, no one could really be prepared for a Sunday in the Barmy Cow.

Dim, damp, smoky from the grey ash of the fire, and smelling strangely of brilliantine and mould, it was filled with morose customers hunched over cloudy drinks.

The Berkeley Boys were, as always, arrayed neatly behind the bar. Their Sunday Best involved once-white dress shirts with unironed frills and doubtful stains, drooping polka dot bow ties and lovat cardigans with most of the buttons missing. It wasn't a good look.

'Sukie!' Valerie Pridmore, surrounded by her huge family, waved enthusiastically from the dartboard side of the pub. 'Hiya!'

Sukie waved back. So did Derry. Val blew him a kiss.

'Do you know Val?' Sukie asked as they reached the bar.

'No. Never seen her before in my life. Just being friendly.' Derry gazed round the pub with something like disbelief in his eyes. 'Well – this is – um – unusual . . . And—' he caught his first glimpse of the ancient Boys, '—bloody hell!'

Smothering her giggles, Sukie beamed at Dorchester Berkeley. 'Hello, you look really smart. Can we have a pint and a half of whichever beer you recommend today, please?'

Derry looked impressed. 'That was extremely AA Gill of you. How did you know I was a beer drinker?'

'What? Oh, there's no choice here. It's just whichever beer hasn't gone rancid in the cask on the day. They've never heard of lager or anything brewed much after nineteen fifty-five.' Sukie peered through the gloomy fug at the hunched punters, trying to spot Topsy. 'Ah – there she is. Over there. She hasn't seen us yet.'

Savoy and Hilton, jostling to pour a pint each, smiled beatifically at Derry. To give him credit he smiled bravely back.

'Haven't seen you here before, have we?' Claridge leaned across the bar. 'Are you Sukie's young man?'

'No, he's not,' Sukie said quickly, pushing the money across the counter before Derry could pay. 'He's just a friend.'

'Am I?' Derry took his pint. 'Oh, good. Thanks, Sukie. And this,' he grinned at Hilton, 'looks like a great pint.'

'It is, young man,' Hilton wheezed joyously. 'A perfect mix of hops, yeast and downland water. Nice to see someone of the younger age group who knows what's what.'

'Smoothie,' Sukie hissed as they made their way towards an empty table. 'It looks like sludge. And it'll taste like nothing on earth.'

'Heavenly?'

'Whatever.'

If you could ignore the aura of dust and grime, the Barmy Cow wasn't too awful, Sukie thought. At least clearly not for the various lonely Bagleyites who sought refuge there. Topsy, sitting with several other elderly people, was playing cards with deft animation. She still hadn't seen them, and Sukie decided to leave her in happy ignorance for a little longer.

How awful it would be, Sukie suddenly realised, to be that old and for all the people you knew and loved to be dead and to have to make do with whoever was left for company.

'Are you okay?' Derry leaned towards her.

'Yes ... yes, fine, thanks. I was just thinking about growing old and being alone.'

'Well, there's nice and cheerful for a Sunday.' Derry sipped his pint and swallowed bravely. 'Um – you're right about the beer. It's probably an acquired taste. So, are you going to march straight over to Topsy and demand she allows you to massage her, or what? We didn't really discuss the plan of action, did we?'

'There was no need.' Sukie watched the tiny head on her beer disappear in little pools of grease. 'Topsy will be up for anything medical – you'll see. I thought we ought to let her finish her card game first though. She looks really happy.'

Derry nodded. 'She probably is. Is that what bothered you? Topsy being alone?'

'Yes ... and the fact that because we're young, we're so

sure we're immortal, aren't we? I mean to us they're just old people who have always been old people. We don't think we'll be like that – but we will.'

'Yes, we will. But inside we'll still be young, like they are. We'll still be us, like they are. The only difference will be that we'll have a lifetime of memories and experience to draw on – like they have. And there will still be new things to look forward to. Different things, but there will still be a point to being alive even when we're very old.' Derry swirled the beer in his glass. It stuck to the sides. 'Finding Cora's stuff has really affected you, hasn't it?'

'Sort of. It's made me realise how many things I didn't know about her and now it's too late to ask. And that she had a life – apart from just being Cora and being old and being the person I loved most in the whole world.'

Derry pushed his hair away from his eyes. 'You're nothing like I thought you were. You're not at all like Milla, are you? I thought— '

But whatever Derry thought – be it good or bad – Sukie wasn't destined to discover as Valerie Pridmore chose that moment to hobble nosily up to their table.

'Sorry to interrupt,' she gurgled throatily, looking anything but and staring at Derry with lust-filled eyes. 'I just wanted to make sure we're still on for Friday. Me and Joss. The massages at Pixies Laughter? Only I won't be at rehearsals on Tuesday, will I? So I might not see you before, and I thought . . .'

Sukie sighed. 'Yes, everything's lined up. I told Joss last night. She was dancing with us in the Weasel and Bucket. She was brilliant – we might have to persuade her to take your place in the troupe.'

'Her old man won't allow it,' Val laughed. 'Topsy's already asked her, remember – and she said she couldn't dance.'

'Well she can,' Sukie said. 'Very well indeed. And surely no one is ruled by their partner these days, are they? I'll talk to her on Friday. She might change her mind.'

'You can try.' Val raised her eyebrows. 'But you'll be wasting your time. Her Marvin's a complete bastard. He stops her doing anything he doesn't approve of. And he sure as hell won't approve of his Jocelyn kicking and screaming and showing her knickers. Anyway, sweeties, I'm clearly interrupting – so I'll love yer and leave yer and see you on Friday for me rub-a-dub-dub.' She chortled lasciviously in Derry's ear before limping away. 'While the posh cat's away, eh, duck? Don't blame yer! Young Sukie's got magic fingers.'

Ooooh! Sukie wanted to sink her head onto the grubby tabletop and scream.

'If I wasn't pretty sure that this was Bagley-cum-Russet, on a Sunday in March, in the twenty-first century,' Derry grinned, 'I'd be convinced I was in some parallel universe. I didn't understand one word of that conversation.'

'Good,' Sukie said shortly. 'Oh –look! Topsy's just finished her card game! Shall we—?'

'Well, that was the object of this exercise, but—' Derry was still grinning, '—just explain some of that stuff. Rehearsals? Troupe? Dancing? Are you – do you—?'

'Dance? Yes – and not round poles or on laps before you start heading down that route. We – me and Valerie and Chelsea and a few others – are the Bagley-cum-Russet cancan troupe. And,' she glared at him, 'if you as much as snigger I will empty that beer glass over your head.'

'God forbid,' Derry said straight-faced. 'It'd probably skin me alive. But – I'm impressed. Do you mean you do high-kicks and the splits and all that Nicole Kidman Moulin Rouge stuff?'

'Well, we're hardly that standard and we mainly wear more clothes, but we try – and stop leering.'

'I never leer.'

'Good. Are you ready for this?'

'Pouncing on an old lady and massaging her with – what? Which oil did you choose, by the way?'

112

'Viola . . . it seemed the most gentle and the least likely to cause any problems.'

'Okay, yes then, I'm up for mugging some poor unsuspecting soul and turning her into a lab rat in the weirdest pub I've ever been in. It's always my occupation of choice on a wet Sunday.'

'Sarcasm is not allowed.' Gathering up her bag but leaving her beer, Sukie headed across the Barmy Cow towards Topsy. 'Neither is laughing or wincing or feeling obliged to tell anyone what we're really doing. Okay?'

'Okay.' Derry laughed anyway. 'Lead on.'

Having introduced Derry, Sukie hoped her acting skills would be good enough not to let Topsy know that, despite the denials, she now knew Cora's recipes not only existed but had also been discovered and resurrected.

Topsy beamed at them, as did the half a dozen elderly members of the card school who, clearly tired of blackjack, sat back in their chairs waiting for further entertainment.

'I'm so pleased to see you, dear,' Topsy smiled. 'I hoped we hadn't parted on bad terms.'

'No of course not. Er – did you get home in time to watch *Casualty*?'

'I did, dear, thank you. It was a lovely episode. Someone was impaled on a spiked fence. They had to carry out a roadside operation by torch light. They had to cut through the spike without damaging the vital organs. Mind you, I wouldn't have given the tracheotomy so early on and as for the sloppy use of the intravenous fluids—'

'Mmm, fascinating . . . oh, er – that medical stuff reminds me – you know how, during our can-can warm-ups, you're always stressing that if we look after our leg muscles they'll never let us down and how yours are as strong as pistons but that you sometimes get twinges in your fingers and—'

'Cut to the chase, dear, please. We've got a few hands of whist planned before closing time or death whichever comes first.'

'Sorry – okay, well as you know, I'm starting up the at-home massages this week, and I wondered if you'd be interested in being a bit of a guinea pig for me. I just want to make sure I'm doing things right.'

Topsy cocked her thin grey head to one side. 'You've been giving massages for years. Why would you need to practice?'

Sukie groaned inwardly. Bugger Topsy for being as sharp as a tack.

'Oh – er – these new oils that Jennifer Blessing has supplied – they might not be the same as the old ones and – um . . .'

Oh, lordy! Even to her, it sounded really, really feeble.

Topsy patted Sukie's hand. 'Look, if it's some sort of *medical* thing then I'm definitely your woman. Look no further. Do you want me to call into the cottage sometime?'

'No need!' Sukie exclaimed brightly, delving into her bag. 'Just by chance I happen to have one of the new massage oils here! If you'd like to put your hands on the table, I'll just . . .'

There was a bit of a delay while the card school spat on hankies and scrubbed the muck from the table top and then polished the result with their sleeves.

Sukie, not daring to look at Derry, unstoppered the bottle.

The aroma from the violas was certainly wonderful: the heady, garden-fresh scent of the oil wreathed and wafted into the Barmy Cow's fug. The release of the fragrance was almost a physical thing – like the genie escaping from the lamp in Aladdin – deliciously swirling and growing and engulfing.

The smoky, mildewy atmosphere was suddenly transformed into a summer meadow with sunshine and butterflies and vibrant flowers and birdsong.

Topsy sniffed. 'That smells very – oh . . . I don't know – sort of familiar . . . lovely scent, dear. So clever, these synthetic perfumes – it's almost like being outside in the

114

garden – like being young again. Synthetic, did you say? Hmmm – they smell real enough to me . . .'

'Yes, they do,' Sukie said quickly. 'Amazing what they can do in the lab, isn't it? Right . . .'

Warming her hands, Sukie then applied the oil in smooth practised movements across Topsy's skinny, gnarled hand and fingers, gently stroking in the direction of the heart, rhythmically massaging the joints and pulse points, feeling the energy flow.

A sizeable crowd, including Valerie Pridmore and her entire family, had gathered, watching intently. Even the Berkeley Boys had emerged from behind the bar and were leaning over the table in a matching row.

'We've got some terrible aches and pains, young Sukie,' Claridge said gruffly. 'Specially in our feet. What with all that standing behind the bar. If this works on Topsy here, maybe we could all come along to Pixies Laughter for a bit of treatment?'

'Well – yes, of course,' Sukie said bravely, trying not to think of the collective disgusting state of the Berkeley feet. 'I'll leave you my card.'

'That's lovely, Sukie,' Topsy smiled sleepily. 'Really lovely. I've got a pre-med sensation of floating and my hands feel like they've been amputated.'

Phew – Sukie thought. High praise indeed. It was going to be okay . . .

Topsy gave a little sigh. 'These oils of Mrs Blessing's are wonderful. You must tell her. Oooh my heart's fluttering like a defibrillator.'

Oh, God, please don't let her be going to have a heart attack, Sukie thought, wondering if she should stop. 'Topsy? Are you feeling okay?'

'Wonderful, dear. I can feel the tension and the knots just sliding away. My fingers are unfurling like little flowers. It's better than being on steroids. What's this one got in it?'

'Violas.'

Topsy's head jerked up. Her beady eyes glittered into Sukie's. 'Violas?'

'Yes,' Sukie continued massaging, frantically improvising. 'It's – um – one of the new wildflower aromatherapy range.'

'Violas?' Topsy gave Sukie a calculating look. 'You know the stories behind violas, don't you?'

Still stroking and circling, Sukie shook her head. She didn't – but she had a horrible feeling she soon would. However, what she did know was Cora's cross-stitched verse, which had just popped unbidden into her head.

Ooooh nooooo ...

*Pretty violas so sweet and shy*
*Can cure a maiden's lonely cry*
*Can soothe and smooth an aching heart*
*Can make a lovers' meeting start*

Oh dear, oh dear ...

Topsy stared at her. 'According to legend, they were the flowers created by Zeus to seduce his bride. And they're also known colloquially as Loving Idols or Kiss Me At The Garden Gate – with very good reason. They're used in love potions.'

'Really?'

'Yes, really.'

'But that would only be the *real* flowers, wouldn't it?' Sukie said, her heart sinking. 'Not these synthetic fragrances?'

'Oh yes – the real plants are very powerful indeed. No one should mess around with the real ones. Oh ...'

Topsy suddenly seemed to have lost all interest in the ins and outs of violas. She was gazing dreamily across Sukie's shoulder.

Sukie turned her head. 'Oh, sorry Dorchester – were you wanting to clear this table – we won't be a moment. Nearly finished.'

Dorchester Berkeley had moved in really close. He simpered – there really was no other word for it – at Sukie. 'No, no my dear. I just wondered if I could touch Topsy's hand. It looks like silk.'

He stretched out his knobbly brown fingers and slowly caressed Topsy's hand.

Fully expecting Topsy to shriek like a banshee and wallop him smartly, Sukie held her breath.

Topsy, however, just smiled sweetly and allowed her fingers to be linked with Dorchester's.

'All we need now,' Derry whispered, 'is a crescendo of violins and an angelic choir.'

Sukie swallowed. 'Quick – grab the stuff and let's get out of here. Er – Topsy – if that feels okay, I'll leave you now. Thank you very much for—'

'No, thank *you*.' Topsy was still staring soppily at Dorchester. 'I feel wonderful. Simply wonderful. In fact I haven't felt like this since my Eddie left Bagley in nineteen thirty-nine . . .'

# Chapter Twelve

Without doubt, it had been one of the most wonderful weeks she could ever remember, Joss thought on Friday, as she sang her way, accompanied by Radio 2, through the last of the ironing.

It was certainly one of the best weeks she'd had since being married long enough to realise she and Marvin were never going to be happy-ever-after; and one of the best since finally accepting that the children she'd conceived, carried, delivered and nurtured, weren't anything like she'd imagined they'd be.

Ever since the fabulous Saturday evening in the Weasel and Bucket, Marvin had been in a foul mood and hardly spoken. He'd been up and down all Saturday night, knocking back Andrews Liver Salts and groaning. Joss, knowing the indigestion was due to Marvin's temper rather than the Weasel and Bucket's superb food, had snuggled under her single duvet and smiled to herself. As Marvin's internal explosions reached a crescendo to rival the Trumpet Voluntary, Joss had closed her eyes and ears, running through the dancing and the laughter and the sheer giddy happiness of the night out in her head.

And on Sunday, Simon had phoned and Marvin had sunk even deeper into growling sulkiness. Apparently Simon and Sonia were sleeping in separate rooms; Sonia had banned Simon from playing golf with Marvin ever again; they'd resigned from the Saturday evening supper circuit clique; and they were both blaming Marvin, loudly and publicly, for such an appallingly *common* choice of venue.

Marvin had thrown all of the *Sunday Telegraph* across the dinette in a fit of pique and locked himself in the bathroom.

Marvin's week-long foul-tempered grouchiness had given Joss loads of time to get on quietly with her own life. She'd gone through the ritual routines with Marvin, of course. They'd just been carried out in relative silence, and the lack of grizzles and censure which could in no way be directed at her for once, had been blissful.

The housework had been a breeze, and Marvin didn't even want to talk enough to complain about burned toast, overdone eggs or anything at all she'd cooked for supper. She'd typed the Neighbourhood Watch notes with an unusual flourish, and had even taken the opportunity to write an article for the *Bagley Bugle* about the possibility of resurrecting the Russet Revels on August Bank Holiday Monday, using the nom-de-plume Maggie Mettle. And Marvin hadn't even glanced at it, but carried it off with the rest of the copy for the secretarial Anneka to print and bind.

Not that Joss had any interest at all in reviving the Russet Revels, but she loved writing these anonymous bits and pieces for the *Bugle* to liven up the rather dull content, and was really, really looking forward to interviewing young Sukie Ambrose later on about the cancan troupe, and maybe even about the link with the at-home aromatherapy sessions. She'd probably choose an exotic French-sounding pseudonym for that one – something outrageous like Fi-Fi Lamour? She giggled to herself.

Even more, she thought happily as she placed Marvin's white shirts on hangers, and folded his Y-fronts and socks – Marvin always insisted on having his smalls ironed – into their respective drawers, she was looking forward to having a massage. Today's appointment had been another deliciously thrilling secret to spice up her week.

And Valerie had said, during one of their illicit coffee morning chats, that Sukie had massaged Topsy Turvey in the Barmy Cow last Sunday and that it had been *wonderful*. Valerie had actually claimed that something rather strange and magical had happened between Topsy and the equally elderly Dorchester Berkeley – but Joss put that down to Val having supped far too much of the Barmy Cow's doubtful beverages.

Right – Joss looked round the bungalow's neat and pristine sterility – everything was done. All that she needed to do now was grab the car keys, as Valerie's cancan injury meant they couldn't walk through the village to Pixies Laughter, and go.

'Ready for this, are you?' Val puffed as she eased herself into the passenger seat. 'Prepared to bare all?'

'Absolutely,' Joss said happily as they swung out of the neatly-manicured Close and into the tangled, tree-lined village streets. 'I can't remember when I last had any of what the magazines call "me-time".'

'You poor cow,' Valerie said kindly. 'And it's a lovely day for it, innit?'

Joss nodded. It was. It was as if the weather had been arranged specially to match her mood. The gloom and darkness and rain and biting winds had suddenly disappeared this week and Springtime had arrived in Bagley-cum-Russet.

Today the sun shone in a pellucid sky, drying out the soggy ground, wreathing the village in a warm, milky, earthy haze. Flowers had appeared, as if by magic, from the ground's grim grey morass and tiny green shoots unfurled everywhere.

Spring was bringing new life, Joss thought cheerfully as they approached the Bagley and Russet junction and stopped at the Celtic cross; bringing new experiences, new opportunities. Spring never failed to make her optimism soar, and she always thought the Pagans had it right –

celebrating Springtime as their new year. It made sense.

Valerie wriggled down in her seat, waving regally to any Bagleyites they passed. 'I'm looking forward to this massage too – not only to get me back on me feet, but there's loads of gossip to catch up on. Not only old Topsy and Dorchester acting like Charles and Camilla on Sunday, but young Sukie turned up with Derry Kavanagh. You know Derry? Runs Winterbrook Joinery? Sex on legs?'

'Mmm, yes ...' Joss nodded, trying to recall what Val had told her about Derry Kavanagh during their coffee morning chats. 'Oh, yes – didn't you say he was going out with Sukie's house-sharer?'

'Exactly!' Val said triumphantly, sketching a royal acknowledgement to the knot of gossiping villagers dawdling in the sunshine outside Coddles Post Office Stores. 'So if he's dating that swanky Milla, why was he with Sukie then? That's what I want to know.'

Joss slowed down to concentrate as they approached the narrow lane leading to Pixies Laughter. She really didn't care about why Derry and Sukie were seen together, but it was simply lovely to indulge in mindless tittle-tattle.

'Watch out!' Valerie shrieked suddenly, grabbing Joss's arm. 'That car's not going to stop!'

Joss stood on the brakes as the car roared towards them head-on then swept past them, missing them by a hair's-breadth.

'Stupid sod!' Joss's heart was pounding, her mouth dry as the fight-or-flight adrenaline pulsed through her body. 'He must have come straight off the Hassocks road and been doing well over seventy! Are you okay, Val?'

Valerie nodded, wriggling round in her seat belt, peering over her shoulder. 'Yeah – but ... did you get a look at the driver? I could've sworn it was your Marv ...'

'No, it couldn't possibly have been,' Joss drove on carefully, still feeling incredibly shaky from the very near miss. 'He's in London. At work. And there are millions of cars like his – and Marvin never, never breaks the speed limits.

Oh, I really need that massage now – my heart's going mad. Are you sure you're all right?'

'Yes, yes I'm fine, love. But—' Valerie settled back in her seat, frowning, '—you know, I still think that was Marv.'

'Definitely not.' Joss managed a shaky smile at the very idea. 'Believe me, Marvin never does anything out of character or out of routine. Marvin would never be home at this time on a Friday. Marvin's miles away, thank goodness. Ah – here we are . . .'

Sukie, preparing for her first ever at-home massage session, gazed round the dining room with a feeling of pride. With flickering banks of little rose-scented candles, the rows of essence bottles, base oils and copper blending bowls on the shelves, and all her aromatherapy and massage certificates framed on the walls, it looked every inch the exclusive private beauty salon. Cora's green and gold flocked wallpaper and bottle green velvet curtains had scrubbed up well and gave it a dark, sumptuous air, and the massage table supplied by Beauty's Blessings fitted in perfectly.

Jennifer had been wonderful this week, supplying piles of big white fluffy bath sheets and matching robes as well as the table, and moving mountains to make sure Sukie had all the right health and safety checks, and employment law and insurance paperwork in place to work from home.

Of course the fact that Sukie had been frantically busy since Monday with the mobile massages had delighted Jennifer, too. They'd quickly organised a routine, Sukie calling into the Hazy Hassocks' salon each morning to collect her appointments, and popping back there in between to help Jennifer out with nail extensions and facials.

'We're really going to have to get some help from the students at the FE college,' Jennifer had said excitedly, trying to chip away a face mask from the worst crevasses of an elderly sun-worshipper from Fritton Magna. 'The bookings for mobile massages are coming in thick and fast. I can see you're going to be out of Beauty's Blessings more than you're going to be in it and I can't keep up with it all on my own. It'll be like running two businesses in one. Think of all that lovely money rolling in, Sukie.'

And Sukie had smiled and nodded and thanked her lucky stars that, thanks to Cora's cross-stitch tapestries and Pixies Laughter garden and, of course, Derry Kavanagh, Jennifer would never, ever need to know about the depletion of the essential oils, then set off again to ease and pamper.

Being busy with the massages each day and de-cluttering the dining room every evening had had other advantages too: it had prevented Sukie having to think about things. Things like Topsy and Dorchester. Things like Cora's concoctions. Things like love potions.

And especially things like Derry.

The hoped-for pierce-and-ping hadn't come to fruition. They'd arrived back at Pixies Laughter from the Barmy Cow, chuckling like children, still stunned by Dorchester and Topsy's inexplicable flirtatious behaviour after the massage – and both trying really hard not to think of the implications – to find Milla's car outside, and Milla pacing around the cottage in a tearing rage.

'My bloody mother!' Milla had screamed at them. 'My bloody mother had invited A Man to lunch! A Man who is supposed to be Suitable Husband Material! A Man who is not only three hundred years old with four wives already under his belt, but a man who doesn't even have his own teeth or hair! But of course, he's a baronet, so that's okay according to my bloody mother! And she was sooo un-subtle! Mrs Bennet could take lessons from my bloody mother!'

Trying not to laugh, Sukie had rushed to the kitchen to make coffee, leaving Derry to placate the enraged Milla. Then there'd been a bit of fudging over the messed-up state of the cottage and where the bouquet of flowers had come from, and why Derry and Sukie had been out together.

Fortunately, Milla was far too obsessed with her bloody mother's attempts to replace Bo-Bo in her daughter's life, to dwell too long on anything else.

Derry had left soon after the coffee, kissing Milla and grinning at Sukie, and as she'd been so frantically busy she hadn't seen him since.

Ah well ... Dragging herself back to the here and now, Sukie took a last look out of the dining-room window before pulling the velvet curtains to ensure total privacy and the right intimate and relaxing ambience. She leaned her hands flat on the sill, drinking it in. The garden looked so different in the sunshine. Nature was truly amazing. All those dreary, dripping, sinister heaps of plants had somehow dried out and disentangled themselves and were forming riotous tumbled clumps of glossy leaves with dozens of little flowers, making it look like a real cottage garden again.

If she was going to continue the pick-your-own aromatherapy system, she'd have to ask Derry to identify the burgeoning blooms for her, wouldn't she? Just so she didn't make any mistakes, of course. It would be the death knell of the business if she garnered the wrong plants and gave all her clients galloping urticaria, wouldn't it? Any excuse to keep in touch, really.

'Oh, face it,' she said to herself, closing the curtains, 'you just want to recreate last Sunday, don't you? And you can't and mustn't because he-belongs-to-Milla-and-isn't-remotely-interested-in-you – okay?'

Not waiting for an answer – because she knew what it would be – she padded out of the dining room to welcome her first paying customers.

Val and Joss, talking excitedly at the same time about their near-miss with the maniac driver, oohed and aahed over the interior of Pixies Laughter, and even more over the rejuvenated dining room.

'If you'd like to undress through there—' Sukie said,

indicating a tiny dark green curtained-off area, '—and wrap yourself in one of those towels – they're warm enough, I hope – then we can decide how to do this. Do you each want to have your massage privately? Or are you okay with being in together and being an audience for each other?'

'Together!' Joss and Val chorused, already unbuttoning and unzipping and giggling.

Once Val had stretched out face down on the table and Joss had snuggled in her robe on a chair, Sukie's professionalism kicked in. This was something she knew she excelled at. And she enjoyed it. Nothing else mattered while she was working. Not even Derry Kavanagh. Not really.

'I'll do your leg first, Val, before I do the full body massage, if that's okay? Just hitch the towel up a bit. Lovely. Thanks. So – toes to knee, is it?'

'Mmm, please love. And especially round the ankle. The doctor checked it out and said it was just a bit of muscle strain – but it's still giving me gyp when I put any weight on it.'

'Not for much longer ...' Sukie unstoppered one of the little gemstone bottles, carefully measuring six drops from the pipette into the almond base oil. She'd selected the home-made rosemary and lavender blend as both had wonderful healing properties.

'Oh, that smells lovely, Sukie, love.' Valerie wriggled in anticipation. 'It's like the garden has suddenly come indoors, innit?'

'Beautiful,' Joss mumbled sleepily, inhaling deeply from her chair. 'I can almost reach out and touch the flowers ... Oh, I could get used to this ...'

The scent escaping from the bottle was, Sukie had to admit, far more powerful than any synthetic oil she'd ever used. She'd noticed this phenomenon all week while doing her mobile massages. All her clients had commented on the 'bringing the outdoors indoors' effect the moment the bottles were uncorked. Sukie'd agreed that the fragrances magically melted away the surroundings, conjuring up almost tangible images of perfect cottage gardens, gravelled pathways, hidden arbours, cascading roses, warm sunshine, butterflies and birdsong.

Having convinced herself that the Topsy – Dorchester thing was nothing more than a coincidence, Sukie had chosen not to dwell on Cora's recipes being aphrodisiacs or on the meaning behind the poems or the likelihood of her massages being the cause of unsuitable pairings across Berkshire. She was simply grateful that she now had an entire garden of raw materials to work with, and her natural ingredients were clearly far, far superior to anything concocted in a laboratory.

'Oooooh – that's bloody wonderful,' Val groaned with pleasure as Sukie gently kneaded and stroked and circled. 'I can feel the tension just dissolving – and that's the first time for ages that my muscles haven't been knotted up. I can feel the pain melting away. You've definitely got the gift, my love, I'll give you that.'

Joss, who'd been watching avidly, looked at Sukie. 'Is it okay if I write something about the cancan dancing and about your massages for the *Bagley Bugle*? I know Topsy's looking for a replacement for Val in the troupe, and it seemed like a good idea to write a story combining the two – it'll make a nice change from the usual tripe we have in there.'

'Yeah – it's mostly what do to with leftover lemon curd and how to make a montage of the Hanging Gardens of Babylon with grains and pulses, isn't it?' Sukie concentrated on Valerie's ankle tendons. 'I'd be delighted. So, do you want to do a proper interview, or what?'

'I've got a really good memory.' Joss smiled. 'So if you just chat, I'll remember most of it – and I can ask you about the specific massage oils and things like that later – then I'll show you the copy before Marvin whisks it off to be printed so that you can make sure there are no mistakes.'

'Sounds great.' Sukie nodded. 'And I still don't know

why you don't join the cancan troupe yourself. You danced wonderfully last Saturday and you obviously love it.'

'Oh, I just couldn't ...' Joss sighed. 'No, don't even bother to try to persuade me – but I'm sure you'll get loads of applicants once the article is in.'

'Speaking of which,' Val opened one eye. 'When you went to rehearsals on Tuesday, did Topsy say anything more to you about the how-you-do in the pub with old Dorchester?'

Sukie felt herself blushing, and quickly concentrated on the long sweeping strokes along Val's plump calf. She'd had a brief conversation with Topsy as they'd all been leaving the village hall, but she certainly wasn't going to share it with Valerie – or anyone else for that matter.

'Hang fire, young Sukie,' Topsy had nabbed her in the vestibule. 'Before you go belting off – I'd like a word about last Sunday. My massage. You used viola oil just by happenstance, did you?'

'Er – yes,' Sukie had nodded. 'It's a light, floral oil and beneficial for the skin as well as unknotting muscles and relaxing joints and—'

'Poppycock! Don't try to fob me off with all that promotional gobbledegook! It might all be true, but violas aren't commonly used in aromatherapy circles, I'll be bound.' Topsy's beady eyes had glittered in the darkness. 'Being more of a *natural* remedy.'

'Yes, well – maybe ...'

'No maybe about it. Just remember – I *know*. And now the card school – all being in their September years – were very impressed with the demonstration and my renewed flexibility and wondered if you could pop in some other Sunday and do them all – to help with their shuffling and dealing.'

'I'd be delighted,' Sukie had said, relieved that this was the point of the conversation and making a move towards her car. 'Anytime, you know that.'

'Not so fast, young lady.' Topsy had fastened her now-supple fingers round Sukie's wrist. 'I'll tell the others that you'll come along to the Barmy Cow and sort 'em out – but no more violas though. Not even *synthetic* ones. Understood?'

'Yes, okay. But the viola oil worked, didn't it? On your hands and fingers I mean?'

'Oh, it worked all right my girl.' Topsy had released her grip and tied her headscarf tightly beneath her wrinkled chin. 'As you well know.'

And Sukie had said good, and there you are then, and made her excuses and left.

Now she realised Valerie was still waiting for some sort of reply.

She shrugged. 'No – not really. Er – Topsy said the massage worked well and her fingers were still really flexible and that she'd have to make it a regular thing for the card players. Chelsea had got wind of the gossip, of course, and was sort of teasing her about Dorchester. But Topsy said she and all the Berkeley Boys had been friends for ever – and changed the subject to some new heart by-pass system she'd seen on *Holby*.'

'Hmmm,' Val chuckled. 'The pub was a right den of iniquity Sunday, wasn't it? Topsy and Dorchester – and you being out with Derry.'

'There!' Sukie said brightly, 'that's you done! Now I'll just sprinkle some more lavender and rosemary on this warm towel and wrap it loosely round your leg, and if you'd like to slip the robe on to make sure you don't get cold, I'll start on Joss.'

As they swapped places and Sukie decanted the relaxing camomile and winter jasmine into the base oil, Joss watched with interest and asked various questions, both about the aromatherapy and cancanning.

'Oh, that's superb.' Joss broke off from her investigative journalism and sighed pleasurably as Sukie's fingers kneaded the tightly-knotted shoulder muscles and circled on her rigid spine. 'I can feel all my angst sort of floating

128

away. And I don't even feel guilty about enjoying this. And I know you'll think this is completely insane, but I can practically see little jasmine flowers tumbling out of the wallpaper and the floor turning into a camomile carpet – and the scent is simply delicious. Oh, I'm going to give you a sensational write-up and tell everyone I know that you are absolutely brilliant.'

Sukie smiled happily and said a silent thank-you to Cora.

Half an hour later, with Joss and Val both glowing, and relaxing sleepily in their warmed robes and sipping tea and chatting idly, Sukie washed her hands then skipped upstairs to her bedroom.

'There!' She grinned at Joss on her return, hauling armfuls of vibrantly coloured frou-frou satin and net behind her. 'I thought you might like to see this. My cancan dress – I didn't know if you'd seen one close up. I thought it might help with your article. Give it a bit more colour so to speak.'

Joss simply stared, saying nothing.

'Sorry.' Sukie frowned. 'Is there something wrong?'

Joss shook her head, sensuously stroking the satin of the black and scarlet basque and circular multi-frilled skirt, running her fingers greedily through the miles and miles of hot pink, purple, orange and crimson net petticoats.

'It's the most glorious thing I've ever seen . . . Incredible . . . oh, these colours! Like – like a fallen rainbow. Oh, I've always longed to wear something as sumptuous and wanton as this . . .'

'You could wear mine,' Val chuckled from the depths of her robe. 'If you'd join the troupe. Old Ronnie'd take it in a couple of hundred yards to fit you.'

'Don't!' Joss's voice was anguished. 'I *can't*, Val! You know I just can't! But—' she looked at Sukie, '—thank you so much for letting me see this. It's put the icing on my cake today. I'll probably dream about it . . .'

Valerie and Sukie exchanged disbelieving glances.

It wasn't until about twenty minutes later, after a very

happy Joss and Valerie had left, while Sukie was clearing away the remnants of the massages and replacing the essence bottles back on the shelf, that it hit her.

Rosemary and lavender!

Sukie didn't even need to look at Cora's cross-stitch rhymes ...

*Lavender and rosemary, pretty in the sun*
*But beware the perfume when they become one*
*Apart, so innocent like a child*
*Joined, make passion's fires burn wild.*

Oh – lordy! And she'd smothered Val with it! Mind you, Valerie and her large scruffy husband were always very touchy-feely, so maybe no one would notice.

Oh, and blimey – she looked at the second gemstone bottle; the one she'd used on Joss.

Camomile and jasmine ...

*Camomile the perfume for a lost sweetheart*
*Jasmine the scent for lovers torn apart*
*Infused together make a magic blend*
*And broken hearts will forever mend*

Eeek! Sukie winced. Still, hopefully Joss didn't have a broken heart and surely, after what Val had told her, the ghastly Marvin couldn't possibly be anyone's lost sweetheart, could he? Hopefully, this one wouldn't be applicable either. No, of course not. Neither of them had any bearing on Val and Joss, did they? It was all hokum, wasn't it? Wasn't it ...?

'Well!' Val said as they approached The Close, 'I don't know about you, but I feel right peculiar ...'

'Me too.' Joss wriggled under the seat belt. 'Lovely, though – sort of floating and a bit – well, squiffy, I suppose.'

'That's it exactly,' Val giggled. 'Like I've had just that

bit too much to drink and feel frisky and ready for a bit of slap and tickle, know what I mean?'

'Yes,' said Joss, who didn't, but could imagine.

'I hope me old man's in when I get home. I'll treat him to a bit of afternoon delight!'

'Oh, yes,' Joss said wistfully. 'That would be lovely. I mean – not for me with your husband, of course.'

'Or with yours!' Valerie snorted. 'Wouldn't touch yours with the proverbial barge pole!'

'Marvin used to be – different ...' Joss said wistfully, still not quite recognising the strange feelings inside her. The massage had been a revelation. Her body felt young and supple for the first time in years; all her stresses had simply melted away. It had been a truly magical experience – unlike anything she'd ever experienced. And she felt – well, *frisky*? She sighed. 'When we were young, when we first met – Marvin was rather dashing.'

'Dashing?' Val snorted as they pulled up outside the Pridmores' bungalow. 'Can't imagine it meself – and who wants bloody dashing? What you wants is downright bloody sexy! Ooooh – I feel proper perky if you get my drift.' She scrambled from the car, her leg now bearing its not-inconsiderable load with ease. 'Thanks, Joss – see you for coffee. Now let me get me hands on that hubby of mine!'

Valerie darted through her front door, and Joss laughed to herself as she reversed into her own drive. She felt a bit 'proper perky' too. She hadn't felt like this for – oh for goodness knows how many years – if ever. Maybe, she thought, she'd *never* felt quite like this.

It took her several seconds to realise that there was another car in the drive. A beige car. Marvin's car. But, why on earth would Marvin be home so early on a Friday afternoon?

Joss was still frowning as she unlocked the front door. Was that Marvin who had almost driven into them as Valerie had thought? No, surely not ... Although, she grinned to herself, if it was, perhaps the Pridmores

131

wouldn't be the only ones indulging in a little afternoon delight ...?

For some unknown reason she felt wickedly daring and crept into the living room. Marvin was standing, his back to her, gazing out of the window. Just for a second, Joss remembered how it had been once upon a time in another lifetime, when she and Marvin had first met.

He'd been her first, her only, boyfriend, and occasionally she'd felt ripples of what she'd imagined was lust when he kissed her, a wild desire for something more when he held her.

Oh, how she wanted that now ...

Tiptoeing up behind him, she slid her arms round his waist.

'What the hell are you doing?' Marvin swung round, managing to shake her off at the same time. 'Have you gone mad, woman?'

Joss, still feeling the ripples of something exciting and unknown, smiled at him. 'Sorry to make you jump. It's lovely to have you home so early.'

'*Lovely*? Buggering *lovely*?' Marvin roared. 'Are you buggering *insane*?'

Aware that her lusty ripples were definitely not being reciprocated, Joss backed away from his rage. 'Marvin – dear, what on earth is wrong?'

'Wrong? I'll tell you what's buggering wrong! I've been buggering sacked – that's what's buggering wrong!'

# Chapter Thirteen

You can keep April in Paris, Sukie thought, driving cheerfully through the bosky lanes on Tuesday morning; springtime in Bagley-cum-Russet is as near to perfect as it gets.

The sunshine bounced from the whitewashed walls of the pretty cottages, gardens flounced with daffodils and crocuses, and the shaggy verges were studded with cowslips, celandines and early daisies. Funny, she thought, how she was suddenly noticing flowers more; actually looking at them, recognising some, wondering about others. Strange, in fact, how many things had changed since she'd discovered Cora's recipes.

Halting for a moment at the Celtic cross, squinting into the sun, Sukie then headed towards the Hassocks road and sang along with some la-la-la-la-la 70s hit on the radio. Her mood, her energy levels, her optimism, had soared with the lighter evenings and warmer days. March had given way to a balmy April, and all round her life was emerging from the winter doldrums, sap was rising and love was in the air.

Hah! Sukie thought, hold that last bit – well on a personal level at least. Maybe it was true that this was the season for young men's fancy to lightly turn to thoughts of love – or whatever that quotation was that had made her and Chelsea giggle in Eng Lit lessons at school – but no man, young or otherwise, seemed to have any sort of romantic thoughts about her at all.

Then, of course, there was only one man who she'd really want to have flighty springtime daydreams about her, wasn't there?

Oh, sod it!

Maybe she'd just concentrate on becoming a career woman and climbing the highly-scented aromatherapy ladder and retire in a million years time and grow roses and keep hens and lots of cats. Yep, she nodded as she reached Hazy Hassocks High Street and negotiated the bottleneck by the library and Mitzi's Hubble Bubble outlet, far better to think about work.

Work, in the ten days since she'd massaged Valerie Pridmore and Jocelyn Benson, had been incredibly busy with bookings and the coming weeks were no exception. Maybe, if things continued the way they were going, she'd one day be able to make a break away from Jennifer and become self-employed. Hmmm, she smiled to herself. Now, there was something to really think about ...

She was still smiling as she parked behind the dental surgery and scurried into Beauty's Blessings, determined to hurl herself body and soul into work and empire-building and be far, far too exhausted to entertain non-reciprocated thoughts about Derry Kavanagh.

'Sukie! Sweetheart!' Jennifer emerged from a peaches and cream cubicle followed closely by a dowdy woman who had either just had a lip-fill or who'd been in a brawl the previous evening. 'It's so exciting! You're going to be so busy! I've had loads of bookings – nearly all for massages at Pixies Laughter. Is that okay with you?'

'Wonderful, thanks Jennifer – you've helped so much. I really do appreciate it.'

'No probs.' Jennifer whizzed the trout-pout's chip and pin through the machine and beamed her farewells as she thudded out of Beauty's Blessings' peach-shaded door. 'Sad case. Discovered her husband's got a blow-up doll in the wardrobe. Wants to compete. Right – to business. How are the oil and essence stocks going? Will you need me to order any replacements this week?'

'Er – no.' Sukie didn't quite meet Jennifer's eyes. 'I've – um – found them really economical. In fact, I think they'll last for ages.'

'Good,' Jennifer beamed. 'Because they were awfully expensive. Still, you're potentially earning so much money for the company now, you mustn't skimp on them.'

'I won't be doing that,' Sukie smiled, delving into her bag and withdrawing a folder. 'And before I forget – here're the cheques and cash from last week's at-homers. And the invoices and copy receipts.'

'Thank you. Oh – lovely.' Jennifer's eyes sparkled as her fingers rifled through the paperwork and her brain worked out the profits for Beauty's Blessings. 'Do you know, Lance, silly boy, has suggested that you should take a bigger cut of the massage money as it's exceeded all expectations. I said you probably wouldn't want to, but—'

'Yes I would, actually. Thank you,' Sukie interrupted. 'All contributions gratefully received. I'll just collect this week's appointments then – oh, what's going on in there?'

'Ah!' Jennifer seemed to have recovered reasonably well from the fiscal blow. 'I've set our new girls an easy little lower leg wax. You haven't met them yet, have you?'

Sukie hadn't. She'd heard that Jennifer's sorties into Winterbrook FE college had come up with a couple of likely students to help out in Beauty's Blessings, but she didn't know they'd actually started.

'They had their first day yesterday, a sort of induction, learning the ropes, finding their way round, that sort of thing,' Jennifer said, whispering silkily towards the cubicle. 'I didn't let them touch anyone, of course, but they're nice girls. Recommended by their tutors. Keen to learn. Sadly, they're both called Kylie,' she swished back the curtain, 'but they're very good at – oh, my God!'

Peering over Jennifer's shoulder, Sukie giggled.

The two Kylies seemed to have made one of the basic

errors of waxing: never allow the bodies of the waxer and the waxee to come into close proximity whilst the latter is still sticky.

The Kylies were both welded by the overall to the chunky calves of a hockey player from Winterbrook.

Moving quickly into damage limitation mode, Jennifer grabbed the larger Kylie round the waist, easing her gently to one side, and indicated that Sukie should do the same with the smaller version, all the while murmuring professional and soothing remarks to the unfortunate victim.

'Grab a spatula,' Jennifer hissed at Sukie. 'Pull your Kylie's overall taut, slide the spatula under and – oooh, sorry Beryl – no, no – nothing wrong at all. Four of us? Um, yes – we do encourage a sort of *en masse* approach for our very special clients . . . right, and ease away!'

Still trying really, really hard not to laugh, Sukie wriggled the spatula between her Kylie's overall and Beryl's calf. Fortunately the wax was still pliable, and Beryl's skin appeared to be more or less intact.

'Don't say anything,' Sukie hissed in the skinny Kylie's much-ringed ear. 'Whatever you say now will be wrong, believe me. Just smile and look like this is meant to happen. Now brace yourself.'

Kylie braced, Sukie eased, and Beryl winced.

After a bit more gentle manoeuvring and a sort of unpleasant sucking noise, Beryl's calf and the smaller Kylie parted company.

Jennifer was having a slightly tougher job with the larger version and was audibly panting. With her tongue protruding from the corner of her mouth, she sounded a bit like a Sumo wrestler as she eased and tugged.

'Ah! Gotcha!'

Jennifer and the larger Kylie shot backwards.

Both Kylies gave a little whimper and disappeared through the curtains.

'There!' Jennifer said brightly. 'A superb wax, Beryl. Not a follicle left standing. Now, I'll leave you with Sukie,

136

our senior beautician, and she'll finish you off with our special vitamin-enriched emollients and moisturisers – what? Oh – sorry, no, Beryl. No! When I say finish you off, I'm speaking professionally of course . . .'

Sukie, chewing the inside of her cheeks to prevent herself from sniggering in a most unprofessional manner, reached for the jars of scented soothers and soakers and set to work.

By the time Beryl had left Beauty's Blessings – with Sukie agreeing that the leg wax should be free of charge, much to Jennifer's chagrin – and been further placated with the promise of a free facial, Jennifer had clearly finished her dressing down of the Kylies.

Now both out of their waxy peach overalls and with identical Croydon-face-lifts scraped-back pony tails, belly-flaunting T-shirts and cargo pants, they cowered in a corner, looking tearful and absolutely terrified.

'No harm done,' Sukie said kindly. 'We all make mistakes when we're learning – and that's one you won't make again. Jennifer is a very kind boss, really. Oh, I do like your tattoos – er – big, aren't they?'

The Kylies nodded. Some sort of wishy-washy denim-blue Eastern hieroglyphics stretched licking tongues round their protruding stomachs from, presumably, the small of their backs.

'Tatty Spry did them, in Steeple Fritton,' the smaller Kylie confided proudly. 'She's ever so good. They mean good luck and health and happiness in something foreign.'

What they also meant, Sukie thought, was that in about fifty years' time there'd be an entire generation of OAPs queuing for their pensions and shuffling on their zimmers with wrinkly, indecipherable tattoos sagging beneath their Damarts.

'Mmmm, lovely.' She smiled at them both. 'My friend Chelsea has had tattoos done by Tatty Spry, too. She tried to persuade me to have one but I'm too much of a wimp. Now – I've got to fly, but if you just do exactly what

Jennifer says and ask if you don't understand, you'll be fine. Trust me.'

The Kylies gave her tremulous smiles and said thank you. She suddenly felt quite grown-up.

Jennifer, perched behind the reception desk watching, beamed at her. 'You're a very sweet girl, Sukie. Very kind. And patient. I'm not a kiddie-person, as you know. Never been maternal. But you'll make a lovely mother one day.'

'Oh, pul-lease!' Sukie pulled a face. 'Let me find The Man and have the Big Romance first. Followed by the Big Wedding. Followed by a bit of a life.'

'Well, you want to get a move on,' Jennifer said. 'You haven't got that many decent baby-making years left, have you, and you're not even seeing anyone, are you?'

Sukie now not only felt grown-up, but positively past-it. Wasn't that exactly what Valerie Pridmore had told her, too?

'I'm in my prime, if you don't mind, and happy being single – and certainly not quite ready to slap a "desperate – apply within" sign on my forehead.' She decided muttering that she also wasn't ready to stoop to Jennifer's remedy for manlessness by nicking someone else's husband to fill the gap, might not be a good move career-wise. 'Anyway, if you could just let me have a list of the appointments for the rest of this week, I'll have to dash.'

Jennifer printed off two closely typed sheets of paper. It would, Sukie knew, be just as easy for Jennifer to e-mail her the list of massage appointments that came in via the salon, but she also knew that Jennifer always wanted to be in control and continue to have a manicured fingernail in the pie, so to speak. One day soon, though, Sukie thought, she'd sound out Jennifer on the possibility of setting up her own business – but not just yet.

'Thanks.' She skimmed the lists. 'Oh, we've got several repeats here, that's good – and several "recommended by a friend" ones.' She pushed the papers into her bag. 'It's going well, isn't it?'

'Very,' Jennifer whispered from behind the desk to attend to a couple of pedicures. 'Oh, and I knew there was something I had to tell you! You know how everyone gossips while they're having treatments? How they confide in you because you're sort of anonymous? Well, it's rather curious, but some of the people who've asked for second massages have made really funny remarks.'

'Have they? What, like stand-up comedians?'

'No,' Jennifer, who was a very literal person without a fully developed sense of humour, looked momentarily irritated. 'I was going to tell you this straight away, but then we had the Kylie problem which put it right out of my head ... Anyway, they've said that after they've had their massages at Pixies Laughter, they've gone home and felt – well – a bit frisky, I suppose.'

Sukie held her breath.

Jennifer smiled. 'Ever so enthusiastic, they were. Several of them have hinted that the massages have spiced up their love life no end. And, more than that, some of them said that afterwards they felt tempted to make *improper suggestions* to complete strangers!'

'You're kidding?' Sukie asked hopefully. 'Aren't you?'

'No, I'm not. They said they felt so – well – full of oomph, that it was like being a teenager again! And that miserable old Mrs Dowding – the one who always says we don't do her corns justice when she has her nails clipped and polished – she said she went straight home and fancied the pants off the insurance man.'

'Really?' Sukie reverted to the cheek-chewing. 'She said *that*?'

'Well, not in so many words, no, but that was the gist. You don't think those new essences I bought could possibly have *aphrodisiac* properties, do you?'

'No, definitely not,' Sukie said truthfully, concentrating fiercely on the floor of the salon. 'Absolutely not. No way. Your new essences were – um – are as pure as the driven snow. It's – er – probably just the relaxing effect of the massage in the privacy of the cottage that makes them feel more – um – responsive, don't you think?'

'Maybe ...' Jennifer paused for a moment, then nodded. 'Yes, you're probably right. Good – I wouldn't have wanted us to get a *reputation* for anything smutty, if you get my drift, even if it does bring in the punters. But if it's just the general ambience of the surroundings, that's fine.'

'And they weren't angry about – about feeling – um – frisky?'

'Oh no, far from it. They all sounded delighted. So whatever you're doing, you carry on. They'll tell their friends, and it all means more money coming in, doesn't it?'

Sukie nodded. Did that make it okay? She could be turning the entire area into Sodom and Gomorrah and Jennifer wouldn't care as long as the shekels kept rolling in? Yeah, knowing Jennifer, it probably did.

'Right, then,' Jennifer switched into pedicure mode. 'You'd better scoot. You've got your first massage booked in an hour.'

Waving goodbye to the Kylies, Sukie scooted out of Beauty's Blessings and into her car.

Blimey ... Who had she massaged at Pixies Laughter during the last week? Several elderly ladies from Hazy Hassocks including the miserable Mrs Dowding and her corns, a couple from Fiddlesticks and two or three from Winterbrook –all on the pensioners' special. None of them had been under seventy, had they? None of them, surely, could have been affected by her potions? But as none of them were from Bagley-cum-Russet, she wouldn't have heard any gossip even if they had, would she?

She started the car. She'd been so careful, using a basic herbal mix for all of them – a blend for relaxing muscles and energising the spirits – basil and coriander with a dash of dill. A mixture of herbs sorted from the handfuls she and Derry had rescued from Cora's overgrown kitchen garden.

What on earth was Cora's herby rhyme? The one with

basil in it . . .? Sukie furrowed her brow, trying to remember the exact cross-stitched words.

'Ooooh – noooo!' The poem filtered through just as the lights turned red at the Winterbook junction. She stood on the brakes and thumped the steering wheel. A youth in a back-to-front baseball cap in the white van alongside her leered. She ignored him. 'Oh, bloody, bloody hell!'

*When Basil and Coriander meet*
*A meal can be a tasty treat*
*But add to Dill and there's a danger*
*Even the faithful will kiss a stranger*

'Damn!' Sukie groaned, roaring away as soon as the lights turned green, leaving the white van standing. 'Damn and blast it!'

That evening, in the chill, dim mustiness of Hazy Hassocks village hall, the cancanners were halfway through their rehearsal. Topsy was Not Happy.

'That, girls,' she snapped, 'was bloody awful! I've seen patients on trolleys on *ER* with more animation than you lot!'

'Give us a break,' Chelsea groaned, sitting on the stage and rubbing her ankles. 'We're still trying to do the same routines with one less person. We get confused.'

'Confused?' Topsy's little eyes glittered beneath her headscarf. 'Confused? You have a senility problem, do you? How difficult can it be?'

Bet, Roo and Trace, the other dancers, huddled together, muttering mutinously.

'There being five of you instead of six only becomes awkward in the set pieces! And surely you've got enough intelligence to work things out between you? The crossovers, and the lines and circles should present no problems whatsoever! And there's no excuse at all for you to lumber about like hippos! I'm surprised the stage is still

141

intact!' Topsy shook her head. 'It doesn't matter how many of you there are! The lack of numbers doesn't make any difference to your suppleness and agility for heaven's sake!'

Sukie, still out breath, sat on the edge of the stage with Chelsea and puffed out her cheeks.

'You're a disgrace!' Topsy, despite her long mac, executed a perfect high-kick from a standing start. 'There! I'm old enough to be your mother – and grandmother in some cases – and I can out-dance the lot of you! Anyway – what's happening with the replacement? Or are we getting Valerie Pridmore back again?'

'Val's back at work,' Sukie said, brushing dust from her leggings, 'but she won't be able to dance for ages. She says her leg is okay for standing and walking for little bursts, but she can't dance.'

'She never could,' Topsy spat. 'So, have we advertised – or is that being left to me, too?'

Sukie sighed, and explained about Joss Benson and her piece about the aromatherapy and cancanning for the *Bagley Bugle*, in which she'd mention they were looking for a new dancer, and which should appear at the end of the week.

'Hmmm,' Topsy pursed the thin lips, 'that's still on, is it? Well, let's hope someone with a bit of verve reads the damn thing and gets in touch soon as. Mind you, most of the *Bugles* just get dumped in the bin, so I ain't holding out a lot of hope. Right,' she clapped her hands. 'One more time!'

There was a universal groan, but everyone hauled themselves to their feet.

Sukie, who had been massaging elderly backs and legs and shoulders all day having abandoned the old herby mixture for a new one with juniper and sage which only had a poem linked to happiness and age so it must be okay, helped Chelsea to her feet.

'Jesus! You smell like an old person!' Chelsea wrinkled

her nose. 'You know, when you stand behind them in the chemist and they reek of TCP? Why do they do that? Where do they put it? Is that what you've used?'

'No.' Sukie grinned. 'It's one of my new oils. It lingers.'

'You can say that again,' Chelsea held her nose. 'No wonder Derry Kavanagh has vanished into the ether. Even if he wasn't gooey-eyed over Milla, he'd run a mile from you ponging like that. You're hardly alluring, are you? Is that why we haven't seen him or heard about him all week? Or has Milla eaten him?'

'Derry has apparently had an urgent commission from one of his best clients,' Sukie said, reporting Milla, and trying to sound disinterested as they shuffled into some sort of order. 'From some theatrical couple who own a manor house on the outskirts of Winterbrook. Derry's already rebuilt their kitchen and drawing room and they pay a fortune for craftsmanship and won't have anyone else to work on their house – so he's been there all hours, building a spiral staircase for one of the upper storeys.'

'A likely story,' Chelsea chuckled, straightening her T-shirt. 'Oh, bugger, Topsy's cranking up the stereo and counting us in . . . Is this the bit where we go in on the skip or the run?'

'. . . and two and three and . . .' Topsy stopped, looking furious. 'Stop! Is that someone's phone ringing?'

Sukie groaned and broke formation. 'Sorry, Topsy. Mine. I'll have to answer it – it's not on message service and it might be work.' She scrabbled in her bag at the side of the stage. 'Hello?'

'Sukes!' Milla's voice screamed happily in her ear. 'Where are you?'

'Hassocks village hall. Cancan rehearsals. Milla, I can't chat . . .'

'I'm not calling for a chat, Sukes. Look at the phone! You've got the wrong one. You've picked up mine. Yours is here and I've spent all evening taking weirdo messages about things that I don't understand from people who sound

143

like they think they're calling a massage parlour. And now I need mine because I'm going out and not coming home tonight and I'll go straight to work tomorrow and—'

'Sukie!' Topsy howled. 'Put that bloody thing down! Now!'

'Crikey,' Milla sounded shocked. 'I heard that. She's in a temper, isn't she? Okay, Sukes – look, I'm on my way now – I'll just pop in with your phone and we'll do a swap, okay?'

'Okay. See you in a minute.' Sukie clicked the mobile off and pulled a face at Topsy. 'Sorry. I've picked up Milla's phone – we've got the same ones. She needs hers and—'

'I'm not interested!' Topsy snapped. 'Now – ladies, let's get ourselves back into the Miss Bluebell mindset. Listen to the music ... Listen ... Let the music seep into you, fire you, inspire you. Let the music carry you away to gay Paree ... And one and two and – go!'

Off they went again with the roar of Offenbach filling the village hall. The Bagley-cum-Russet dancers whooped and linked and ran and slid and kicked like billy-oh.

'Better, gels!' Topsy shrieked, doing an impromptu floor-to-knee-to-shoulder kick in her excitement. 'Much better! And one more time – right – off we go!'

And off they went.

Sukie, who really loved the music and the routines, and the sheer sexy glamour of the dance, hurled herself into it with renewed vigour. It was a shame, she thought giddily, as she and Chelsea linked arms, circled wildly, grabbed their right ankles and hauled their legs up alongside their ears, that Joss Benson couldn't join the troupe. Poor woman. She'd have so much fun. And she obviously loved the costume and the idea of exotic dressing-up too, not to mention her being a great dancer. She'd be perfect.

The troupe separated, screaming, high-kicking. Chelsea and Sukie pranced to opposite sides of the stage, then flouncing imaginary skirts, hurled themselves into whoop-

144

ing diagonal cartwheels. Perfect, Sukie thought, dizzily, it's going really well. Back into line – one more set of high-kicks – then leap and scream and into the splits and finish . . .

'Superb!' Topsy shouted as Orpheus's seduction faded. 'Superb! Just like the Moulin Rouge, gels!'

'Couldn't have put it better myself.' Derry Kavanagh, grinning, the ice blond hair looking divine against the softness of his ancient leather jacket, appeared from the hall's dark recesses. 'Er – sorry to interrupt but I just have to collect a mobile phone.'

Topsy beamed at him. 'Yes, yes, of course. We've finished now. Did you enjoy that?'

Derry's eyebrows rose. 'You could say . . . Um – Sukie, did Milla ring?'

Sweating, out of breath, desperately embarrassed, Sukie nodded and staggered to the corner of the stage. Chelsea, damn her, was laughing. Everyone else, including Topsy, was staring at Derry with lascivious eyes.

She grabbed Milla's phone from her bag, and held it out to Derry. 'She said she'd come and get it. I wasn't expecting to see you.'

'No – I think she was scared she'd be roped in if she set foot in here.' Derry's gorgeous eyes crinkled. 'That was very – um – impressive.'

God! Sukie sighed heavily. Now he'd seen her lumbering about like a baby elephant in her truly, truly unflattering practise clothes and reeking of the residue of the massage oil which probably smelled like disinfectant and second-hand gin by now.

'Glad you liked it,' she said shortly, still holding out Milla's phone. 'Er – how long were you watching for?'

Derry's fingers briefly brushed hers during the handover. It was like a fizz of electricity. He moved away. 'Oh, long enough to know you can touch your ear with your foot, and do perfect cartwheels, and do things with your legs a bloke can only dream about – oh, and do the splits from a run and jump.'

145

Bugger. Bugger. Bugger.

'Far too much then,' Sukie tried joking to cover her embarrassment. 'It'll probably give you nightmares. Er – thanks for the phone. Um – how's the staircase going?'

'Great, thank you. Milla's coming to see the progress tonight and meet my clients. You know what she's like about celebs – even minor ones. What about the aromatherapy? Do the new oils work well?'

'Yes, fantastically. I'm busy all the time, like you.'

They stared at one another for a second.

'Yes, I suppose I shouldn't keep Milla or my clients waiting,' Derry said softly. 'Lovely to see you again. We never seem to meet under normal circumstances, do we?'

'What's normal?' Sukie asked, knowing that her mascara was smudged under her eyes and her face was shiny and her hair probably looked like Don King's best.

'Not you.' Derry grinned at her. 'Thank goodness. Bye then . . .'

'Whooo!' Chelsea sighed as Derry disappeared. 'He is *divine* . . . Sukes? Sukie? Ohmigod! Look at you . . . You are sooo smitten, aren't you? It's written all over your face. Oh, dear – it cancan only end in tears.'

# Chapter Fourteen

'Joss!' Valerie Pridmore yelled delightedly. 'Hiya, stranger! I'm so glad I've caught you. I was getting really worried, love. I haven't seen you for – what – it must be a couple of weeks? What the hell is going on? Are you avoiding me? Have we fallen out or summat?'

Joss, trying to make the early-morning back garden sorting of the recycling last forever, looked across the fence at Val and lowered her voice. 'Oh, Val – I've been meaning to come round and ask about your leg and catch up with things, but—' she cast an anguished look over her shoulder towards the bungalow, '—Marvin's been here all day every day. It's difficult.'

'Is he off sick?' Valerie laughed. 'Nothing trivial, I trust? I'd noticed his car was in the drive – thought he might be having a bit of a holiday. And my leg's hunky-dory, thanks to young Sukie. I'm not up to dancing the cancan, but I can stand on it for hours at work now without a twinge.'

'Good. I'm really pleased you're better.'

'So am I – but – look at you ... you look terrible, if you don't mind me saying. Are you okay?'

'No.' Joss shook her head, knowing she was probably going to cry. 'I don't think I'll ever be okay again.'

'Jocelyn!' Marvin's voice roared from inside the bungalow. 'What are you doing out there? You've been ages with that rubbish!'

Valerie chuckled. 'He must have seen me, bless him. Look, love, I know you can't come round if he's got you under lock and key, but surely he couldn't stop you taking a little walk down to Coddles? To post a letter or buy some sugar or something? In about ten minutes or so? Okay?'

'Okay.' Joss nodded. 'Ten minutes. Thanks.'

She trudged wearily back into the bungalow.

She'd probably end up in prison, Joss thought, if she had to spend one more day – all day – in the house with Marvin. His ongoing anger was only now surpassed by his sense of injustice and self-pity. It seemed a lifetime since she'd come home from her massage feeling renewed and energised, her body tingling – was it really only two weeks ago? It might as well have been two years.

'Now what are you doing?' Marvin looked up from his chair in front of the television. 'It's nearly ten o'clock. You haven't cleared away the breakfast things.'

'You could do that.'

'What?' Marvin's teeth clenched. 'Women's work? I don't think so. I do have my standards. Why are you changing your shoes? You're not going out?'

'Just down to Coddles. We're running low on – er – tea.'

'I don't like their tea. Cheap rubbish.'

'They do have named brands, too.'

'Which we can't afford.' Marvin dragged his eyes from the television again. 'It's all spend, spend, spend with you isn't it? Are you too stupid to understand that we're having to count every penny now?'

Ignoring him, Joss flicked at her hair in the mirror and groaned inwardly. Valerie was right, she did look terrible: washed-out, wrinkled, defeated, old. She picked up her handbag. 'I won't be long. Is there anything else you want?'

'Nothing we can afford,' Marvin hissed, tapping his fingers on the arm of his chair. 'And don't forget there's no more monthly allowance for you, so don't buy yourself

148

some silly little frippery like shampoo or bath foam. You can use washing up liquid.'

Joss took a deep breath and had a silent scream.

Marvin continued the irritating tapping. 'Don't be gone long – and bring a receipt back for the tea. I don't want you overspending. And don't take the car.'

'I wasn't going to. See you later.'

Marvin grunted, his eyes already back on some programme about the erosion of the coastline of some third world country.

Joss stepped out into The Close, her eyes dazzled by the glorious sunlight, which failed to warm her body or lift her spirits. She had a permanent headache and a tight knot of dread deeply embedded in her stomach. Oh, what had she done so very wrong in a previous life to deserve this? Still, it'd be wonderful to unburden herself on Valerie. She'd never needed a friend more than she did right now.

Every step through the high-banked, sweet-smelling lanes towards Coddles Post Office Stores and away from the bungalow was like a glorious step to freedom. Joss felt as though she was on autopilot. If only she could go on walking away for ever . . .

Val was waiting outside Coddles, sitting on the rustic bench in the sun. 'I bought us a sticky bun each,' she grinned up at Joss. 'You looked like you could do with a sugar rush. Oh, blimey love, it's only a cake . . . don't cry . . .'

Joss sniffed back her tears, said thank you as she squeezed alongside Val on the bench, and finally exhaled.

'Talk if you want to,' Val said comfortably, 'and don't if you don't.'

Joss sat in silence for a while, eating the sticky bun without really tasting it, only vaguely thinking that Marvin would have a purple fit if he knew she was eating in public. She watched the Bagleyites drifting in and out of the shop as if she were watching a film. It was all unreal. But the sun was beginning to warm her, and the colours – the acid green shoots unfurling on the overhanging lime trees, and the mauves and yellows and reds of the spring flowers in tubs outside the shop – began to filter slowly through her permanently-sepia-hued brain.

'Marvin's lost his job.' Wiping sugar and crumbs from her lips, she finally looked at Val. 'He's not taking it well.'

'Oh, love.' Valerie patted Joss's hand. 'What a bugger. I know what it's like – my old man is in and out of work like a yo-yo. But, I thought your Marv was one of the high-ups? Untouchable? And surely he can get another job? He's not that old . . . So – what happened?'

Joss, lifting her face to the sun, took a deep breath. 'Are you sure you want to hear it?'

'What I want ain't important,' Val shifted her bulk more comfortably on the bench. 'But I think you need to talk about it, love, so I'm all ears. Ain't got to be at work for an hour or so, so I'm listening.'

'Well,' Joss sighed, 'it was the day we had our massage. You were right – it was Marvin's car that nearly hit us, and when I got home . . .'

Leaving out the cringingly humiliating bit about her half-hearted attempt to seduce Marvin, Joss started to tell the whole sorry story. It was like being there all over again. Like some horrific *Groundhog Day*.

Despite Marvin's initial outburst that he'd been sacked, the reality was very different.

'I'm redundant! No longer needed! Buggering useless! The place has been taken over!' he'd stormed. 'The whole company, all the divisions, all the outlets! Taken over. A boardroom coup! There'd been rumours of foreign interest and whispers of possible outside corporate investment for ages, but we'd been told they'd be putting money in and expanding us maybe overseas – not buggering this!'

It transpired the take-over had been from an Asian-based conglomerate. Marvin had sworn to never, ever eat at another curry house. Joss had been secretly relieved at that point that the taking-over company hadn't been

Scandinavian; Marvin would have probably stripped the whole bungalow of the Ikea furniture and set fire to it in The Close.

'But surely,' Joss had said, trying to grasp the implications, 'surely you must have had some inkling?'

'If I'd had a buggering inkling,' Marvin had snarled, 'I'd have buggering done something about it, wouldn't I, woman? All I got this morning was a "you're surplus to requirements, thanks for your years and years and years of work but we don't need you any more, buggering clear your desk, and buggering bugger off"!'

Joss, shell-shocked, had clasped her hands together and walked to the window. She'd wished she could comfort Marvin, say something useful and positive, but all she could think of was that he'd be at home. Always. Those awful Saturdays and Sundays would be seven days long.

'Okay, but once you've got over this initial shock,' she'd said encouragingly, 'you can look for something else, can't you? You'll be snapped up. And they must have given you a nice golden handshake so we'll be okay ...'

Marvin had gone into his white-lipped, temple-pulsing mode. 'Are you mad, woman? Listen to me! I've been in the same job, man and boy, all my buggering life! I'm clearly considered a buggering dinosaur! I'm ten years off retiring – and thanks to the general mismanagement of funds in this country there'll be no early pension for me! And we were given statutory redundancy payments! Peanuts! Buggering peanuts! We're on the breadline, Jocelyn! Paupers!'

Joss had thought this probably wasn't quite true. And the bungalow was paid for. But she could see that without Marvin's more than generous salary there'd have to be some drastic tightening of belts.

'So what's happening to everyone else?' She'd turned from the window. 'Has the company suggested anything? Courses for retraining? Help to find other posts? Relocation?'

151

Marvin had turned magenta. His cheeks had gone shiny. 'You know nothing about the business world, Jocelyn, so stop making ridiculously feeble remarks! The company doesn't give a buggering toss! The company has shed those posts the new bastards feel unnecessary. The company forgot about me the minute I walked through the buggering revolving doors!'

Joss had turned to the window again and read between the lines. So it hadn't been a full-on coup, then. Not everyone had been 'surplus to requirements'. Just Marvin and possibly several others who had been there from school, who thought the company owed them a cradle-to-grave living; Marvin and the others who turned up at the office each day but who probably didn't do an awful lot of productive work; who, by dint of their length of service, now probably cost more than they earned; who could be replaced by bright young things willing to start on a basic salary and work their way up the corporate ladder.

It was the way of the business world.

'I know this has come as a blow to you,' Joss had said, trying to stop the panic rising, 'but you could look on it as a brand new start. You've got years yet to share your – um – expertise with another company. Maybe not in London, but there are masses of firms in Reading and other places all around here that would surely be glad to give you a job.'

'I don't want another buggering job!' Marvin had roared. 'I had a buggering *career*! The only buggering career I've ever wanted or ever needed! I don't want to work anywhere else. No, this is the end of my life! The buggering end!'

And then it had got even worse.

Marvin had phoned Tilly and Ossie, blustering and exploding down the phone, slandering his old company and the new owners with every expletive-laden breath. And the children had turned up for the first time in – oh, it seemed like years, with their snooty corporate-minded partners and they'd all treated Joss like a skivvy and had closeted themselves in the dinette with Marvin while she'd fetched and carried.

Joss had stood in the doorway, staring at the husband she really couldn't even feel sorry for, and her son and daughter who barely acknowledged her, and wondered if her spirits had ever been at a lower ebb.

Then Tilly and Ossie and their partners had left, briefly kissing Joss's cheek as an afterthought, with vague promises to 'be down again soon', and as they'd been unable to suggest any even remotely suitable employment for Marvin within their own companies, he'd sunk ever deeper into smouldering gloom.

Joss took a deep breath, back again in the present, outside Coddles, with the village coming and going around her on a glorious spring morning. Oh, how she wished she'd never have to go home.

'. . . and that's it really.' Joss looked at Valerie. 'The whole sorry story.'

Val reached out a pudgy hand and closed it round Joss's. 'Poor, poor you. So, doesn't he ever leave the house? Play golf? See his cronies?'

'He says he can't afford golf any more.' Joss shook her head. 'And his so-called friends haven't even phoned. They don't care, Val. I doubt if they even liked him. They probably just think "there but for the grace of God . . ." and thank their lucky stars they're still working.'

'And money?' Val asked. 'Look, tell me to mind my own business, but I know when my old man's been unemployed, my money's been vital. Are you really broke? I haven't got much, but if you're short . . . oh, blimey, don't cry again.'

Joss squeezed the pudgy hand. 'You're such a good friend. Thank you . . . it's so kind of you, but I wouldn't dream of borrowing money.'

'Borrowing? It'd be a gift, love. For you, mind. Not him.'

'Oh, Val – thanks. You're brilliant, but we're not quite bankrupt. We've got some savings, and we've cashed in a couple of insurances and we've got our investment income – but, unless Marvin finds another job, it means we'll be living in reduced circumstances until we reach pension age, that's for sure.'

'Well, if he won't get up off his silly self-centred lazy arse and look for work, then you can, can't you?' Val grinned. 'It'd be the making of you, Joss, love. You'd be out of the sodding bungalow and have a bit of independence to boot.'

'But I can't do anything!' Joss shook her head. 'We've already discussed this, haven't we? I can only do touch typing and shorthand – and no one needs those skills nowadays, do they?'

'I'm not suggesting you try for something highfalutin'. But there's loads of stuff you could do. Work in a shop, a pub, a café, cleaning . . .'

'Marvin wouldn't let me do anything menial—'

'Now you listen to yourself!' Valerie looked stern. 'One, this isn't anything to do with Marv, and two, there's nothing menial about jobs what don't need a string of letters after your name just to walk through the door. And you need a regular income, don't you? A bit of money of your own?'

'Yes, but – oh God, Val – I can't go out to work! I wouldn't know where to start! I've got no confidence at all. I haven't worked outside the home for decades . . .'

'Neither have a lot of women, but they gets themselves little jobs easy enough.'

Joss traced a pattern in the gravel with the toe of her shoe. The sun glinted on the millions of tiny fragments, making them glitter like a scatter of precious stones. 'Actually, if you promise not to laugh, I've been thinking of starting a bit of a career in freelance journalism.'

Valerie shook her head. 'What? On the strength of a few things in the *Bagley Bugle*? Look, I'm the last person to piddle on your parade, love, and I don't know a lot about the media world, but I can't see any of the tabloids beating a path to your door because you've written a couple of articles about the Russet Revels for a local freesheet.'

Of course, the *Bagley Bugle* had now also bitten the dust – or at least, Marvin's involvement in it had. Joss had rather foolishly, with hindsight, suggested that he'd have far more time to concentrate on the *Bugle* and the Neighbourhood Watch now. He'd hurled the files and folders and templates across the dinette and snarled that some other soft sod could take over the buggering thankless tasks. Joss had assumed this must have a lot to do with the secretarial Anneka no longer being available to do the *Bugle's* scanning and printing and binding.

'I sent the article about Sukie's aromatherapy and the cancan dancers to the *Winterbrook Advertiser*.'

'Did you?' Val said admiringly. 'That was a bit daring. I thought it was for the *Bugle*?'

Joss explained about the Bugle's demise. 'So, I thought the *Advertiser* might be interested in the article anyway, and any other little bits I could write for them. It's a start . . .'

Val nodded. 'If you say so, love. It's not the *Daily Mail* though, is it? Personally, I'd be looking for something in Big Sava. Has the *Advertiser* got back to you?'

'Not yet.'

Val patted her hand. 'Never mind, love. Maybe they'll be on the phone when you get home offering you a regular slot or whatever they call it – but I wouldn't hold yer breath. In the meantime, do you want me to pick up an application form from Big Sava when I'm next in Hazy Hassocks?'

Joss smiled as she stood up. 'Maybe that'd be a good idea, just in case I don't turn into an investigative journalist overnight. Yes, please do. I mean, surely even I could stack shelves – even if I couldn't work those computerised cash register machine till things.'

'Blimey, love.' Valerie puffed to her feet too. 'If a scatterbrain like young Chelsea can cope with them, then you'll be able to do it with yer eyes shut. Look, until things sort themselves out, we'd better meet here for our chats. Ten tomorrow okay?'

'Yes, lovely.' Joss smiled. 'Thanks, Val.'

They walked back through the village together, but Joss went on ahead when they reached The Close. She knew it was feeble, but she really, really didn't want to antagonise Marvin any further.

He didn't look up from the television. The third world country's coastal erosion had been succeeded by something about the development of the jet engine. It was very noisy.

'You had a phone call,' he said. 'And where's the receipt?'

Bugger, Joss thought, she'd make a lousy secret agent. 'Oh, er – I didn't buy any tea after all. There was only the expensive loose sort. We'll have to make do ... Who was the phone call from?'

'No idea,' Marvin yawned. 'I'm not your secretary, Jocelyn. I said you weren't in and hung up.'

Thanks, Joss thought, kicking off her outdoor shoes and sliding her feet into her slippers. In the dinette, the breakfast things were untouched. She sighed, grabbed a tray and started another day of tedium.

The phone rang as she was scraping eggshells into the bin. Marvin didn't move.

'Hello?' She said tentatively. It was probably someone selling something. They didn't get many personal calls. 'Yes, this is Jocelyn Benson ... oh, hello ... yes, oh you liked it? Wonderful! You're running it? In this week's edition? Out tomorrow. Fantastic! What? Oh, yes – the invoice ... Yes, I included it because – what? What do you mean you don't *pay*? You mean you expect people to write for you for nothing? What? What's a by-line? Oh – is it? Well a by-line won't pay the bills, will it? Yes, of course I'm pleased that you liked it enough to use it but – no, I don't think there'll be more of the same without remuneration. Yes, I'm sorry too ...'

156

She replaced the receiver with a sigh and a feeling of ever-deepening gloom. That was the end of the brief sortie into journalism, then. It looked like Big Sava was her only salvation.

'Jocelyn!' Marvin shouted. 'Have you made my coffee yet?'

On the other hand, Joss thought, kicking viciously at the dinette's door and heading for the kettle, ten hours a day on a supermarket checkout was beginning to look pretty alluring.

'Coming, Marvin,' she muttered under her breath. 'Coffee and cyanide coming up . . .'

# Chapter Fifteen

There was quite a queue in Pixies Laughter's living room the following morning – and it wasn't yet eight o'clock.

'Bloody hell,' Milla grumbled through her cigarette while making coffee in the kitchen, 'it's like a doctor's waiting-room out there. I keep being ogled by geriatrics.'

'Get dressed then.' Sukie grinned. 'Those old boys probably haven't seen so much flesh on display since the days of Jayne Mansfield.'

Milla yawned, pushing her blonde hair away from her eyes. It fell straight back down again. Silkily. Just like Derry's, Sukie thought. They really were an impossibly glamorous match. Damn it.

'Who?'

'Jayne Mansfield – old-time film star, beautiful, bosomy, great legs. Hot pin-up babe of a couple of generations ago. Actually, Cora loved her films – she used to take me to see them when they were on in Winterbrook.' Sukie continued decanting the almond and apricot base oils from their containers into smaller plastic bottles which were easier to deal with in the dining-room-cum-massage parlour. 'And sorry if I'm in your way. When I booked the early morning sessions, I thought you either would be already at work or staying at Derry's.'

'I'm on flexitime – going in this afternoon – and Derry's too knackered from working on his spiralling staircase deadline to be much fun at the moment.' Milla grabbed her mug of coffee. 'Is the bathroom safe? You haven't got eighteen people waiting in there, too, have you?'

Sukie laughed. 'Nope. Just that lot out there – Topsy's card school. I couldn't do them all at the Barmy Cow, which was their venue of choice, so I arranged for them to pop in *en masse* this morning. They only want hand and finger massages so it shouldn't take long.'

'No sweat.' Milla sniffed at the base oil. 'Ooh, that smells nice ... you know, I do envy you this – and everything else, really. You've got this lovely rounded rooted life here in the village, with the aromatherapy business and your friends – not to mention the cancan dancing.'

Sukie smiled. 'It's okay as lives go, I suppose. It could be a hell of lot worse.' Well, it could. It could be like Jocelyn Benson's. 'Er – did Derry say anything about the other night, by the way? About the dancing, I mean? He looked a bit shocked ...'

Hopefully, Sukie prayed silently, he'd simply been shocked at the sight of women of various sizes doing acrobatic things and yelping rather than being shocked rigid by realising, as Chelsea had, that she'd got a mega-sized stupid school-girly crush on him – and it showed.

'Shocked? I'll say he was shocked! He couldn't get over it! I've no idea what he thought dancing the cancan actually entailed – but it certainly opened his eyes. But blimey, Sukes, even I didn't know you could do the splits. How amazing!'

Sukie exhaled. 'Oh, it's easy when you get the hang of it. Anyone can do it with the right exercises and a bit of practice. Although I did gymnastics at school which helps. And – um – that's all he said about it, was it?'

'No – believe me, it was the main topic of conversation until we met up with his clients – oh, and they were a major disappointment, let me tell you. Took themselves sooo seriously. Proper Ac-Tors, don't you know, luvvie?' Milla giggled. 'Anyway, once we arrived we had to talk a boring mix of woodwork and repertory theatre for the rest of the evening – but on the way home he kept saying I should have a go – oh, not just at doing the splits, God forbid, but at joining the cancan troupe.'

Sukie thanked her lucky stars that Derry clearly hadn't read the give-away signs. Phew! And she could just see Milla in the gorgeous frou-frou costume, prancing and high-kicking with those endless legs – sod her. 'Well, why don't you come along? We still need someone to replace Val – you'd look ace in the frock, and you've been living here for some time without really joining in on the villagey stuff. You're always saying you need a new hobby.'

Milla shook her head. 'No way! That's *not* my idea of fun! And while playing at being a rustic suits me at the moment, I'm a city girl at heart and always will be. My hobbies involve buying shoes and handbags and lunching in European capitals – not thundering around in some draughty village hall being barracked by an ancient madwoman who thinks she's the love-child of Anna Pavlova and Christiaan Barnard.'

'Yeah, well, put like that I can see it possibly wouldn't have a lot of allure.' Feeling guilty about the wave of relief that immediately swamped her, Sukie concentrated on wiping down the oily work surfaces. 'I seem to have made one heck of a mess in here – hope you weren't wanting breakfast any time soon. Still, once I've done the card players I've got an appointment with one of my regulars in Winterbrook at eleven, so I'll be out of your way.'

'Fine by me.' Milla hugged her coffee mug. 'Take as long as you like. This is your home. Your business. I've got no rights to grizzle about what goes on here. What? Don't look at me like that. I can be a nice person when I want to. I'm not always a Princess Mi-Mi-Mi, you know.'

'I know,' Sukie grinned, tightly stoppering the bottles. 'You're okay, really. Derry thinks so, obviously.'

Milla smiled. 'Ummm. We do get on well. He's such a

lovely straight bloke. Gorgeous. Funny. Decent. Honest. And amazingly bloody sexy. But—'

'But?' Sukie paused in deciding which essence would be safe to use on Topsy's card-players without causing an OAP orgy. 'There's a "but" after that roll call of perfection?'

'Oh, not a huge but ... But a but, yes ...'

Sukie held her breath. 'Milla, you're not thinking of dumping him are you?'

'Goodness, no! Do you think I'm mad?'

Sukie hoped that her groan wasn't audible. 'So – what's the problem? Is it because he's not a wheeler-dealer with a seven-figure bank balance, a Coutts cheque book and his own island somewhere in the Indian ocean?'

Milla perched on the edge of the table, sipping her coffee. 'No, of course not. I've put all that shallowness behind me, I hope, and as well as all his previously listed attributes, Derry's also supremely talented. God, Sukes, you don't think I'm that much of a materialistic snob, do you?'

Sukie nudged round Milla's long bare legs, trying and failing to shut the kitchen door with her elbow to prevent the elderly poker players from having a joint apoplexy.

'I thought you were a rich, very beautiful, scarily efficient business woman when you came here to look at the cottage. I still do, because you are. But no, I don't think you're a gold-digger or a complete snob.'

'Thanks.'

'You're welcome. So, if Derry being a joiner isn't the problem, what on earth is?'

Milla shrugged. Her T-shirt slipped from her shoulder. There was a mass intake of breath from the living room. 'It's just – I feel we kind of drifted into this relationship. Both of us. The way we met, the way we were thrown together – it was just so easy to carry on seeing one another. But if we'd met at a party or in a club or at work, we'd have probably found each other attractive and enjoyed

161

one another's company for a little while – but that's as far as it would have gone. For him as well as me. I just get the feeling that we're only going through the motions because neither of us can find a really good reason not to. Does that make sense?'

'Sort of.' Sukie decanted her essences, trying to look noncommittal. 'Yes, I suppose so. So, you're not in love with him?'

'God! I don't know! I don't think so. But I'm so useless with men. There've been so many since Bo-Bo, and they've all been lovely but they haven't been—'

'Bo-Bo?'

'Exactly.'

'And you know you're in love with him? Still?'

Milla shrugged. The T-shirt slipped further. 'Yes, still. Sad cow that I am. I know I'll always love him – but I also know I'll never get him back. He made that perfectly clear by jilting me – and my parents will never, never forgive him for ducking out just before the wedding. It almost ruined them socially.'

Sukie gathered up her bottles. 'Whoever you end up with though, it's got to be your choice, Milla. Not your parents'. Wouldn't they approve of Derry?'

'Probably not. Oh, they'd probably love him to craft them some bespoke furniture – and they'd boast about it and tell their chums that they've got this "brilliant little man in" – but not as son-in-law material. The bloody balding toothless baronet was definitely what they think I should be aiming for.'

'Shouldn't every girl?' Sukie teased, wondering if the healing properties of the buttercups she'd picked from the garden at the weekend would mingle with those of the daises already in the essence bottle for the cardsharps' shuffling fingers.

'You wouldn't, would you? Marry for money?'

'Not unless there was a lot of reciprocal love involved too, no.'

162

'Ah, love and money ...' Milla stubbed out her cigarette, slid from the table and decorously rearranged her T-shirt. There was a universal groan from the living room. 'I had both with Bo-Bo. We had the same backgrounds, same income bracket families, same lifestyles, same social circle ... We understood and enjoyed all the same things. It would have been perfect.'

'If only he hadn't buggered off at the eleventh hour,' Sukie said, feeling brutality was needed here to defend Derry's social, professional and financial standing. 'I can't imagine Derry doing that.'

'Neither can I.' Milla stretched. 'He's possibly far too good for me. Why on earth can't this lurve thing be more simple? Why does everyone always seem to fancy the wrong person?'

Sukie shrugged. It was something she and Chelsea had discussed over many a bottle of WKD Blue. 'Life, I guess?'

Milla swept her hair behind her ears. 'Did you do *A Midsummer Night's Dream* at school? Hermia and Lysander? Helena and Demetrius? Everyone fancying the person who fancied someone else? All in love with the wrong partner? That's what my love life seems to have been. A compete mix-up and a huge mistake. If only there was some sort of magic pill you could get on the NHS to sort it all out ... Oh, this is all too much for me. I think I'm going back to bed for a couple of hours.'

The living room fell into an awed silence as Milla undulated through and disappeared up the twisty staircase.

Sukie exhaled, a dozen possibilities whirring round her brain.

What if? Just, what if?

Is this how Cora had felt, knowing as she did, that her herbal potions could work romantic magic? That by the judicious use of a few garden plants and oils she could match suitable couples, bring happiness to people who deserved not to be lost and lonely? Where was the harm in it, really?

163

Sukie sighed heavily. It was pretty tempting to try a little love potion experiment on Milla. Without her knowledge, of course. The absence of Bo-Bo the runaway bridegroom might throw a bit of a spanner in the works, and then, even if by some miracle she did reunite Milla and Bo-Bo, who was to say that a dumped Derry would immediately fall in love with her anyway? The chances of that happening were slim to not-at-all, weren't they?

It was always so different in fiction, wasn't it? Shakespeare managed to handle his star-crossed lovers and his love potions with remarkable confidence. And Puck, with his fairy magic, had been the troublemaker, hadn't he? Maybe she should have concentrated more on the ins and outs of *A Midsummer Night's Dream* at school. She and Chelsea had nodded wisely at the 'course of true love never runs smooth' bit – and scoffed at the gullibility of the star-crossed lovers and laughed at the Happy Ever After ending which they'd felt was pretty contrived. Real Love, they'd declared with all the arrogance of youth, couldn't possibly be that easy – could it?

No, she thought now as she had then, it couldn't. Not even with Cora's elixirs. And this was Real Life, too, not fiction. And she couldn't possibly play Puck and *dabble* in Milla's love life, could she? It wouldn't be fair or moral or ethical or . . .

'Are you ready for us yet, Sukie, duck?' Tom, one of the card players, called through from the living-room. 'Only some of us is taking root here.'

'Yes, sorry.' Sukie dragged herself back from mulling over love potions and half-remembered Shakespearean text and gathered her bottles together on a tray. 'If you'd like to follow me.'

The card school, groaning and stretching, creaked after her into the dining-room. She'd dragged half a dozen odd chairs from all over the cottage so they could all sit round the massage table for the joint session.

'Eeeh, it looks like we're going to be dealing blackjack,'

Edie chuckled, squeezing her chair a bit closer to Tom's. 'Are you licensed for gambling, Sukie?'

'Never mind the gambling,' Bert snuffled, 'I liked the floor show. That young lady in the T-shirt can come and shuffle my pack any time she likes.'

Tom and Ken snorted with wheezy laughter. Edie and Rita didn't.

As she worked the buttercups and daisies into the gnarled and knotty fingers, the card school chattered happily about village gossip and rumours and supposed scandals.

'That's a nice smell, young Sukie,' Ken interrupted, sniffing noisily. 'Reminds me of summer meadows when I was a lad. Buttercups and daisies, is it? Smells like being a kiddie again – off across the fields on a hot July day with a bottle of pop and a bit of bread and cheese. Happy as larks we was then.'

'Ah.' Rita nodded. 'Playing out from dawn 'til dusk. No worries in them days. Funny, I can almost see the flowers growing in here. Feel the sun. Hear the birds. It's like being in a dream. I'm not sure what's real and what isn't – but I could swear there's grass growing under this table. Proper makes you want to take your shoes and socks off and run barefoot it does.'

The others muttered rather stunned agreement. Sukie, also aware of the swirling lush bosky ambience but no longer surprised by it, smiled happily to herself.

'We used to hold buttercups under our chin to see if they reflected golden – and if they did it meant you liked butter.' Edie's voice was decades away. 'Course, they reflected gold on everyone, every time, but we still did it.'

'And daisy chains?' Ken said. 'Remember making daisy chains? No one thought it was sissy, did they? Kept us quiet for hours.'

The card school started reminiscing about long-ago hot summer childhood days.

Sukie, concentrating on the massages, didn't really listen, merely continued to smile her professional smile and nodded and murmured in what she hoped were the right places.

'... mind you, I've heard the gossip, but I reckons Topsy's had her eye on old Dorchester for some time. I don't hold with none of that old love potion nonsense, whatever she says.'

'Ooooh – sorry, Edie. Did I slip there?' Sukie pulled an apologetic face. When had the conversation shifted from summer flower nostalgia to Topsy and Dorchester? 'Sorry, look I'll just work this a bit deeper into the knuckles ... Are – um – Topsy and Dorchester – er – seeing one another, then?'

The card school chuckled.

'Oh, you know the Berkeley Boys! They don't never *see* anyone as such. Their old mum put 'em off getting involved – and who could blame 'em? But—' Bert nodded, '— strange as it seems, I reckon Topsy and Dorchester might be courting on the quiet.'

'Really?' Sukie moved on to Ken's hands, hoping no one could hear her heart thundering. 'Courting?'

'Ah,' Tom nodded, 'she reckons – after she'd had a fair few of what the Berkeleys pass off as milk stout, mind you – it's because she'd been dabbling with love potions. I reckon that was just to throw us off the scent.'

'More like to put us off who's holding all the trumps ...' Ken inhaled the buttercups and daisies infusion. 'All the old Bagley love potion nonsense died out years ago – after the war – didn't it? Cora used to be the queen of the funny mixtures, or so the story goes. Don't hold with it meself, but my sister swore by 'er – Cora got our Freda out of a proper pickle with a Yank, so she reckons. Hope you don't take after her, young Sukie?'

They all laughed.

Sukie tried hard to remember the exact wording of Cora's buttercups and daises rhyme. What on earth was it? Ah, yes ...

166

*Buttercups with golden glow*
*Hearts desires and needs do know*
*Mix with daisies white and pure*
*And love forever will endure*

Hmmm, fairly safe as Cora's potions went. Possibly room for misinterpretation there, but surely nothing too risky?

It was only slightly worrying, Sukie thought, that Tom and Ken, having inhaled deeply and somehow accidentally touched one another across the table's close environs, were now eyeing one another in a slightly speculative manner.

'There!' she said brightly, pushing the verse to the back of her mind. 'That should have you all as nifty as a set of Las Vegas croupiers.'

They all happily flexed their fingers in unison and proclaimed they'd been rejuvenated.

'Well, if this buttercups and daisies stuff is one of Cora's love potions I reckon I'll go and set me cap at Savoy, then,' Rita chortled. 'And Edie here's had her eye on Claridge since nineteen fifty-four ...'

'What about poor old Hilton?' Sukie asked, joining in the gaiety. 'Doesn't anyone fancy him?'

'Ah, Hilton's a different kettle of fish altogether,' Bert said. 'We all reckons Hilton's carried a torch for someone in Bagley-cum-Russet since he was a nipper. We don't know who, mind. But he wears a little locket under his singlet. Says it was an heirloom from his old mum, but I don't believe it. I think his heart was broke many moons since.'

'Oh, how sad.' Sukie collected the money from the still-flexing card school. 'Poor Hilton.'

And how weird, she thought. How odd to think someone as ancient as Hilton could be in love. And even more weird, that Topsy and Dorchester were an item. Not to mention pretty scary that Topsy had obviously mentioned *love potions* in the Barmy Cow.

Deciding to tidy up the massage table later, she waited

patiently until the card school had gathered together various bags and coats and sticks, then waved them goodbye from the front door of Pixies Laughter.

'Have they gone?' Milla peered down from the twisty staircase. 'Is it safe to come down again for a coffee refill?'

'Perfectly,' Sukie laughed. 'Although Bert will have been bitterly disappointed to have missed you.'

'Which one was Bert? Not the one with the comb-over and the layers of clashing jumpers?'

'Yep.'

'Definitely the man of my dreams ... Oh, the papers came while you were in there massaging the wrinklies. I took them up to bed—' Milla giggled, '—the papers, that is, not the wrinklies. Hope you don't mind?'

'Course not.' Sukie bustled round, collecting a clean overall and making sure the peach leather cases were fully stocked and reaching for her car keys. 'I've got to dash off for my eleven o'clock appointment now. I won't have time to read the papers until tonight at least.'

Milla headed towards the kitchen. 'Whatever – but you really ought to see the *Winterbrook Advertiser* ...'

# Chapter Sixteen

'Jocelyn!' Marvin's voice rang irritably over the drone of *Model Maniacs*, his latest morning must-view television programme. 'Have you seen the *Winterbrook Advertiser*?'

In the kitchen where she was chewing the end of her pen and wondering if RSA touch typing stages I, II and III and first-class Pitman's shorthand counted as suitable qualifications for checkout work, Joss frowned and slid the half-completed Big Sava application form under a tea towel.

'Jocelyn!'

She'd taken the newspapers through and put them beside Marvin's chair an hour or so ago when they'd first arrived. Of course she knew they were on his list of 'things we can do without' along with her car, and her monthly allowance, and her hair appointments, and a million other things which didn't impinge one iota on his comfort, but somehow she couldn't bring herself to make that final cancellation. How else would she have any sort of contact with the outside world?

'It's by your chair, Marvin! With the other papers.'

'I know where it is! I asked you if you'd seen it!'

This is it, Joss thought, he's flipped. The last couple of weeks have finally taken their toll. He's lost his grip on reality. He's joined all those other sad and deluded people with too much time on their hands without whom the daytime-television schedules would be bereft. People who not only watched the brain-numbing stuff but also featured in Marvin's now-favourite all-day viewing; people who spent their lives worrying about crop circles, or alien invasions, or having trans-gender realignments, or their neighbours building nuclear warheads in the spare bedroom.

Making sure her application form was well hidden, Joss walked warily towards the living room.

Marvin was hunched, as always, his hands bunched into fists on his knees, slightly leaning forward towards the ever-flickering screen. He didn't look up.

The programme, as far as Joss could tell from the constantly repeated updates for those viewers with less attention span than a gnat, seemed to involve Russell, an ex-policeman, who'd spent five years painstakingly building an extremely large scale model of a Nautilus submarine from egg boxes and matchsticks in his garden shed and then discovered he couldn't get it out through the door. A crane and three fat people in fluorescent jackets were currently removing the shed's roof as the presenter kept up a bouncily unintelligent commentary, Russell supervised nervously, and a grey-faced women – presumably Russell's wife – stood looking woebegone in the background.

Marvin was riveted.

'There!' Joss said with as much false gaiety as the telly presenter. 'There's the *Winterbrook Advertiser*! By your chair!'

'I know where it is,' Marvin growled, still watching Russell's discomfiture with some sort of grim satisfaction, 'I just wanted to know if you'd read it.'

Oh, right. 'No.' Joss shook her head. 'No time yet. What with breakfast and the washing and everything. I was going to glance at it over a cup of coffee later.'

Marvin lost interest in Russell and his submarine for a moment and looked at her. His eyes were cold. 'You're in it.'

170

'Am I? What on earth have I done to be— Oh! You mean the article about the aromatherapy and the cancan dancing! Of course!'

'It's got your name on it and it's utter buggering bilge.' Marvin continued to stare at her. 'We'll be even more of a laughing stock than we already are. What gave you the buggering idea that you could write for the local rag? Those ridiculous bits you slipped into the *Bugle* when you thought I didn't know were bad enough but at least they weren't under your own name! Are you mad, woman?'

Probably, Joss thought, recoiling from the verbal onslaught, which hurt far more than any physical abuse. Mad to have married you, mad to have stayed, mad to still be here ...

'I don't suppose anyone will actually look at my name,' she said defensively. 'I never take any notice of who's written what, do you?' She picked up the paper. 'And anyway, it can't be that bad otherwise they wouldn't have printed it.'

'They'll print any old rubbish to fill up space in that two-bit tat.' Marvin resumed gawping at Russell and his problems. 'Especially if they get it for free. And while you're not doing anything, I want more coffee.'

'Oh, get it yourself,' Joss muttered. 'I'm far too busy.'

She walked into the kitchen, holding her breath, waiting for the explosion. She didn't have to wait long.

'Jocelyn! I said—'

'I know what you said!' She marched back into the living room and stared at Marvin. 'And I said I was too busy. Which actually is a lie. I'm only going through the motions of the housework – but you are doing absolutely nothing – and don't—' she held up her hands, '—don't start telling me, yet again, that I don't understand how you feel or how you're suffering.'

'Of course you don't understand,' Marvin said coldly. 'How could you possibly understand what this has done to me? You have no comprehension of my situation. You're not only unemployable but you've also been a kept woman for years. You've never had any standing or importance in the greater scheme of things. Whereas I – who had it all – have lost everything. With one stroke I've lost not only my self-respect, but my very reason for living. And has there been one word of sympathy from you? One word? No! Not one!'

Biting back tears and the bitter words which so often almost, but never quite, escaped, Joss swallowed. 'That's unfair, Marvin. I've been sympathetic and I've tried to talk to you. To suggest things. This happens – it happens to lots of people. They don't simply wallow – they're shocked of course, and they reel a bit, then they shake themselves down and get on with the rest of their lives.'

'What life do I have left? Eh? Answer me that?'

'Probably about another thirty or forty years – at least half of which could be spent working,' Joss tried hard to keep her voice steady. 'You really ought to find another job. There are plenty of opportunities out there for someone like you. But they won't come to you. You have to go and look for them.'

'And you're the expert in employment matters, are you?'

'Actually,' Joss said, glancing at the television screen and willing Russell's wife to run at her stupid husband with a machete in a gesture of solidarity, 'no, I'm not. But I intend to be. If you won't get another job then I'm going to. I'm going to go out to work, Marvin.'

He laughed. A lot. Without humour.

'And who in God's name do you think will employ you? Someone who had the minimum qualifications thirty years ago and who hasn't been employed outside the home since? The world has moved on, Jocelyn, while you've been living in your ivory tower being spoilt rotten. You won't ever find a job. No one in their right mind would want you!'

Digging her nails into her palms, Joss managed not to explode until she'd reached the sanctuary of the kitchen.

172

Then through a blur of angry and impotent tears, she slammed doors, kicked cupboards and hurled knives into the sink.

Feeling slightly better, she poured herself a cup of coffee hoping Marvin would smell it and recognise the defiance, then she spread the *Winterbrook Advertiser* across the table and, her hands still shaking slightly, flicked through it until she reached her article.

It looked really good: a whole page, with a couple of library photographs – one of the cancanners performing energetically at a local Christmas show, and a second of Sukie with Jennifer Blessing on the day Beauty's Blessings had opened in Hazy Hassocks – and with her own name printed boldly under the rather cringe-worthy but typical title: Cancan Girl's Sweet Smell of Success.

Joss skimmed though it, reading her words, and gradually feeling inordinately proud of herself. The *Winterbrook Advertiser's* editor seemed to have left her original article pretty much as it was. There didn't seem to be too many embellishments and very few additions, corrections or errors. Sukie should be really pleased with the coverage for her aromatherapy business – and there surely would be several applications for the vacant cancan post too.

Joss glanced through the kitchen window. It was a shame Valerie had already left for work – she'd have loved to share this moment of mini-triumph with her. With someone. She shook her head quickly. It wouldn't do to dwell on the fact that she actually had no one else to share this with. No one who cared.

Still, staying positive, she'd had something published. Her name was in print. She'd achieved something, hadn't she? All on her own. She sipped her coffee and relished the thought, trying hard not let Marvin's sneering reaction take root in her brain and her heart. No, damn Marvin to hell! He wasn't the only one with a life to live. He was probably madly jealous that she'd written

173

something worth publishing – it was more than he ever had. Ha! That was it! He was jealous! Unwittingly, she'd made Marvin jealous. It was a soul-stirring moment.

And this was just the start. The world was her oyster. The sky was the limit. And every other cliché she could think of.

Buoyed up by this small success, and because she, at this moment, loathed Marvin more than she could ever remember, she removed the Big Sava application form from beneath the tea towel and pondered on the possibilities of fictionally tweaking her entries in the 'Previous Experience' section.

She'd just reached the bit about 'what I hope the company can do for me' when the phone rang. And rang. As Marvin would probably sulk for the rest of the day and was no doubt far too involved with Russell and his almost-roofless shed to answer it, she pushed the application form under the paper, and padded into the hall.

'Hello? Yes, this is Jocelyn Benson … Sorry? Who?' Joss frowned. The name was familiar. Oh, yes, the editor of the *Winterbrook Advertiser*. 'Oh, hello … yes, I've seen it. Lovely, yes thank you – what? Yes, even without payment … Sorry? For me? Are you sure? Oh, right … Yes, oh no … no – I'll come into Winterbrook and sort it out. Yes, I'm sure it's not a problem. Yes, thank you for letting me know.'

She replaced the receiver with a smile.

'Who was that?' Marvin barked from the living room above something that sounded like feral screams emanating from Russell as the crane dropped the shed roof on to his submarine. 'Some captain of industry offering you a six figure salary?'

'Just someone selling double glazing,' Joss said, kicking off her slippers and delving into the coats cupboard for her shoes. 'And I'm going out.'

'Don't take the car.'

'Sorry, have to. I'm going into Winterbrook.'

'Catch the bus.'

'No.' She jangled the car keys. 'I've just missed one and there won't be another for three hours.'

'You'll have to wait then, won't you? And why are you going into Winterbrook?' Marvin yelled. 'Jocelyn! I said why—?'

Joss slammed the front door and raising her face to the glorious April sun, practically skipped towards the car.

'How does that feel?' Sukie stood back as Ellen, her Winterbrook appointment, gingerly slid her frail legs to the floor. 'Better?'

'Superb.' Ellen stood upright and took a few steps. 'Cheers, Sukie. That's miraculous – as always. Carry on like this and I'll be running the marathon next year.'

Sukie grinned. Ellen was in her late thirties and had been diagnosed with MS a couple of years before. She swore that Sukie's weekly massages and a fair amount of cannabis worked far better than all the beta-blockers and steroids under the sun.

While she'd been massaging Ellen, they'd gossiped about Sukie's splash in the *Winterbrook Advertiser*, and Sukie had told her all about having to replace the synthetic essences and why, and the love potions thing, and the rumours that her clients had been reporting rejuvenated lust-lives and fancying mostly the wrong people ever since.

Ellen had laughed a lot and said she was okay in that department, thanks. Her bloke, a rock since her diagnosis, still had the hots for her big-time, and they had no need of any outside help from Sukie's potions.

'I'm using the ginger and sweet nettle on you anyway,' Sukie had said, working the oils deeply into Ellen's disappearing muscles. 'You've always had that one. It's just this is the home-made version.'

'And did your Auntie Cora have a poem for it?'

'Mmmm, yes – let me think – oooh!'

175

*Nettle sweet and ginger hot*
*Can reach a lover's lonely spot*
*Pain they'll quench with natural fire*
*And light the way to true desire*

'Wow!' Ellen had pulled on her jogging pants. 'Maybe I'd better ring my bloke right now after all. He'd be right dogged off to have wasted that.'

They laughed together and Sukie declined the offer of a shared spliff to celebrate, and said she'd see Ellen again same time, same place, next week.

Then she packed her cases into the boot of her car, and drove away from the crescent of Victorian terraced houses and towards Winterbrook's town centre. She had no more appointments until the afternoon, and wondered idly if it was worth ringing Chelsea and meeting her for lunch in Hazy Hassocks. The Faery Glen did great bar snacks, and Patsy's Pantry literally oozed cream cakes and sticky buns.

On the other hand, if she was in Hassocks, it'd be sod's law for Jennifer to spot her, and as she really didn't want to get roped into working for a couple of hours in Beauty's Blessings while hearing about the further shortcomings of the Kylies, maybe it wasn't such a good idea.

Mind you, Jennifer would be delighted with Beauty's Blessings name-check in the *Winterbrook Advertiser.* Jennifer loved something for nothing, especially publicity. Joss Benson had done a great job. Even the photographs were okay and that, considering the varying ages, shapes and sizes of the cancanners, was nothing short of miraculous.

So, Sukie pondered at the first set of traffic lights – to lunch in Hassocks with Chelsea or not? Probably not, she decided, moving slowly through the congested market-town main roads. Not only did she not want to be cornered by Jennifer, but there was also the drawback of the fancying-Derry-thing with Chelsea.

Chelsea's texts on the subject had been more than

enough; face-to-face, she'd go on and on and on about it. As best friends had a right to do really, Sukie thought. If the Mukluk was on the other foot, she knew she'd be just as dogged.

So – no to Hazy Hassocks on both counts then. She'd go home for lunch and tidy up after the card school and prepare for this afternoon's clients at Pixies Laughter and possibly pick some more flowers from the garden to replenish her stocks. She'd noticed celandines and periwinkles growing in one of the borders – and maybe arrange to meet Chelsea in the Barmy Cow tonight.

Goodness, the traffic was awful, nose to tail, crawling along ... Sukie rolled down the window, allowing the warm air to billow into the car. The sun was really strong, and it wasn't yet Easter. Hopefully it'd be another scorching summer like last year. She inched into the right-hand lane alongside Winterbrook's municipal park where the flowering cherry trees frothed pastel pink and white, like giant sticks of candyfloss, against the eggshell blue of the sky.

It truly was turning out to be a gorgeous spring.

Oh, sod this, Sukie thought a second later, all bucolic reverie squashed flat by the sheer volume of traffic and bad-tempered drivers. There now seemed to be a massive traffic jam right into the town centre. She'd be here for ever. The diversion through the trading estate would surely be less congested than this ... if she could just squeeze into the other lane ... Indicating left, she infuriated an entire line of traffic by changing lanes and heading away from the town.

Winterbrook Trading Estate had grown, like a small dormitory town, over the years. From its early beginnings in the Thatcherite eighties, when a few brave entrepreneurial souls risked renting the half-a-dozen Portakabins, to the current flourishing Village of Industry as the signboards proclaimed. Much as the trading estaters hated it, the mesh of narrow roads had turned into a bit of a rat run for those

177

locals anxious to escape Winterbrook and head for the neighbouring hamlets.

Sukie, singing along with the radio, turned a sharp bend and observing the walking-pace speed limit drove slowly through the trading estates main gates. There were masses of different businesses here, and all doing very nicely, if their brightly coloured exteriors and full car parks were anything to go by. Even the *Winterbrook Advertiser* had moved from its high street premises and now filled two single storey buildings. Slowing even more to take the bend by the newspaper's car park, Sukie came to a rapid halt.

A vibrant green van with dayglo pink lettering was practically blocking the road ahead of her. A girl with long blonde hair and a very short black skirt, and a tiny, shock-headed man were attempting to change a tyre.

Sukie sighed. So much for her short-cut.

She leaned from the window. 'Do you need a hand? Is there anything I can do? Oh – Amber – and Jem! I didn't realise – hang on! What happened?'

Sukie pulled her car on to the verge and scrambled out.

Jem, young-old, bird-boned and pixie-faced, was squatting beside Amber, and fixed Sukie with a challenging stare.

Sukie, aware that the previous year when she'd had her mini fling with Lewis Flanagan that Jem, who had adored Amber from the start, had been less than friendly towards her, smiled at him. 'Hi, Jem. Great to see you again. What's going on here?'

In his trademark sign language and with extremely mobile facial expressions, Jem explained about the burst tyre and the need to change the wheel.

'Blimey.' Sukie shook her head. 'That's a bummer.'

Jem's eye's danced wickedly and he gave her a double thumbs up.

Phew, Sukie thought, I think I've been forgiven.

'Sorry if I'm in your way,' Amber, dexterously removing the Hubble Bubble van's ragged tyre, pulled a face.

178

'Bloody thing! It went with an almighty bang. Scared me to death – mind you, Jem loved it.'

Jem grinned and nodded.

'Are you both okay?' Sukie asked. 'Have you got a spare? Can I ring anyone?'

'We're both fine, thanks.' Amber straightened up. 'And I can handle this easily enough. I've surprised myself with the stuff I can do since I've lived in Fiddlesticks. I've learned all sorts of new skills – so yes, I can change a wheel. And—' she chuckled, '—I can even milk a goat.'

Sukie frowned. 'Er – can you? Why would you need to?'

'Gwyneth and Big Ida's latest rescue mission. Goats. Allegedly destined for the curry market,' Amber pulled a face. 'Now all named after characters in *Coronation Street* and living in luxury on Fiddlesticks village green and providing everyone with milk and cheese.'

'Aaah, sweet. I'm so glad they're okay. I do love a happy ending – but are you sure you're all right here? You don't want a hand?'

'Well, actually,' Amber wiped her hands down her skirt, 'there is something you could do for me – if you're not in a tearing hurry, that is.'

'Anything. I'm only going home – I haven't got any appointments until later this afternoon. What do you need?'

Amber, aided by Jem, gave the wheel another yank. It clattered on to the road. 'I'm on my way to do a kiddies' party at the trading estate crèche – got all the food in the back – as Mitzi's tied up with a funeral wake with the Motions. And Lewis is driving Fern and Timmy to the airport for their island wedding trip and—'

Jem made rapid wind-up movements with his hands and pulled a face at Amber.

'Yeah, okay – cutting to the chase. If you could just drop Jem off at work for me while I fix this. He hates being late for his shift and—'

'Of course,' Sukie said, giving Jem a wary look. 'As long as it's okay with Jem?'

Jem winked and nodded.

'Oh, great.' Amber straightened up and lifted the spare wheel from the back of the van. 'You're a lifesaver. I'll pick him up later, of course, but—'

'Where do we have to go?' Sukie asked Jem. 'Is it far?'

Jem shook his head, gave a few extravagant gestures and then jerked his head further into the depths of the trading estate.

Amber laughed and looked at Sukie, her eyes glinting. 'Surely you haven't forgotten? Jem does his work placement a couple of blocks away. At Winterbrook Joinery . . .'

# Chapter Seventeen

Joss took a deep breath and walked into the *Winterbrook Advertiser*'s chrome, glass and fleshy-plant reception area. She'd driven round and round the trading estate's narrow roads for what seemed like hours, putting off this moment, alternately feeling sick then immediately furious with herself for the feeling.

How pathetic was she? No, correction, how pathetic had Marvin made her?

Why should doing something as simple as this make her feel so inadequate? So damn ill?

She had to keep reminding herself that if she gave in to her nerves at this point, she'd have simply let herself down. No one else. There was no one else in the equation – just her and her self-worth. If she turned tail, Marvin and his years of domineering and vicious barbs would have won.

This may be the biggest wild goose chase in the world, but she'd stood up to Marvin and on her own feet at least twice already this morning – might as well go for the hat-trick. And to the majority of women, women with normal lives and confidence and a grip on reality, this would be absolutely nothing, wouldn't it? Walking into a strange office and asking to see someone? Other women did this sort of thing all the time without even thinking about it.

Well then, so could she ... couldn't she?

Glimpsing herself in the plate glass she nodded with

some small satisfaction. She didn't look cowed or bowed or some sort of sad cipher. She looked exactly what she was this morning: a middle-aged woman, neatly groomed and safely dressed, if a bit pale and rather insignificant.

The reception area was empty. Nowhere to hide. Joss swallowed.

'Good morning. Can I help you?' A woman of about her own age, wearing a light blue cardigan and a tweed skirt, smiled kindly from behind the sleek beech and silver desk. 'Do you have an appointment?'

No time to turn and walk away now.

'No, not really.' Joss returned the smile. This was a good sign. The receptionist wasn't intimidating or ultra-glossy or about twelve or glottal-stop-challenged. Just normal. 'The editor – er, Mr Brewster – rang me earlier. I said I'd pop in and see him. My name's Jocelyn Benson. I-I wrote an article for this week's paper.'

If she'd expected the receptionist to leap to her feet, grab her from across the desk and hug her with screams of adulation normally reserved for the name of the winner of the Nobel Prize for Literature, she'd have been very disappointed.

'Did you? How nice. Rang you, did he? Benson? Hmmm – can't see anything mentioned in the diary here. Just hang on and I'll give him a buzz.'

Joss hung on and the receptionist buzzed.

'You're in luck. He'll be free in about five minutes. He'll buzz down. Would you like to take a seat?'

'Thank you.' Joss retired to some rather strangely shaped beechwood chairs, which were surprisingly comfortable, and while awaiting the further buzzing gazed at the ranks of silver-framed photos on the wall.

She'd expected a newspaper office to be more – well –gritty and exciting. All whirring machines and constantly ringing phones and masses of people rushing about shouting a lot. Maybe all that went on somewhere else unseen. This was like being in the foyer of an anonymous well-appointed company anywhere.

The photos weren't even culled from the *Advertiser*. They seemed to be of the staff, like they were in Hazy Hassocks Health Centre, all taken at the same time, with the same lighting and the same background and the same coy smiles.

The photo of Mr Brewster, the editor, who had sounded like Jeremy Paxman on the phone, looked exactly like one of those interchangeable politicians who used to want be in charge of the Conservative party: pleasant, pale and slightly balding.

Joss thought it was all most unsatisfactory.

And now her nerves were starting to get the better of her again. Her palms were sweating and her mouth was dry. She'd never done anything like this before. Her life was so regulated – what on earth was she doing here anyway? It wouldn't matter what Mr Brewster said to her, she'd still have to go home and live her sad life with Marvin, wouldn't she? In fact, she might as well do it right now.

She made her way across to the reception desk. 'Er – I'm sorry. I don't think I'll wait—'

The receptionist was on the phone and waved her fingers. 'Right – yes, she's here now. I'll send her through.' She put the phone down. 'Mr Brewster is free for you now. Were you saying something?'

'No, not really.' Joss felt sick to her stomach. 'No – thank you. Where do I go?'

Following the directions, she walked slowly along a couple of cloned glass and chrome corridors, past closed doors which may or may not have housed the whirring, mad, newspaper offices she'd expected. There was certainly no sign of anyone shouting 'hold the front page! ' or enthusiastic cub reporters tearing off with a coffee in one hand and a notebook in the other to capture the latest local scoop.

Mr Brewster's office was, as the receptionist had said, at the end of the second corridor. He answered her knock with a Jeremy Paxman bark.

Joss walked in and almost smiled. This was more like it. Well, almost. Piles of newspapers, albeit very neat and orderly looking piles, covered every surface; cuttings bulged out of files on the shelves; two computers whirled with *Winterbrook Advertiser* screen savers, and three spiked note-holders labelled 'leads: current', 'possibles' and 'dead' bristled with pieces of paper like miniature Christmas trees.

The pleasant, pale and balding Mr Brewster sketched a smile and indicated that she should take a chair. 'Mrs Benson. Nice to meet you. Nice article. But I must say, there was absolutely no need for you to come in to see me.'

'Yes there was.' Joss smiled back at him. 'For various reasons I didn't want to discuss whatever you wanted to talk to me about at home.'

Mr Brewster raised sandy eyebrows but made no comment on her personal circumstances. 'I actually didn't want to talk to you about anything.'

Joss's spirits plunged.

'No,' he continued, 'I'm sorry if you thought I'd reconsidered giving you a regular job as a freelance – although of course I'll happily look at anything you care to send in ad hoc, but I have salaried journalists to cover everything I need on a weekly basis.'

'Yes, of course.' Joss fiddled with her fingers, twisting Marvin's wedding ring round and round as she always did when she was nervous. 'And I didn't expect . . . but you did say . . .'

'That I had a query for you, yes.' Mr Brewster flicked on one of the computers and expertly scrolled through various screens. 'Ah, here we are. Now – someone rang me about your article this morning. Asked if we could put you in touch. Because of the Data Protection Act naturally I couldn't give the caller your contact details. All I am allowed to do is pass their details on to you and allow you to make the next move – or not.'

Joss sighed. 'Oh, right. Is that all? It's probably someone

wanting to join the cancan troupe – in which case they'd have to contact Topsy – er – Mrs Turvey in Bagley-cum-Russet. Or if it was to do with the aromatherapy massages then Sukie Ambrose would be able to help them. I don't think they want to contact me at all.'

A phone rang somewhere. In one of the other offices someone shouted and someone laughed.

'Maybe not.' Mr Brewster looked kindly at her. 'They certainly didn't tell me what they wanted. Just asked if you could contact them – as the author of the article. You never know, they might run some little county magazine or something and be looking for someone to fill a local correspondent role. As I say, we could have discussed this on the phone.'

'No.' Joss shook her head. 'Believe me, we couldn't. And I needed to come into Winterbrook anyway.' Well, she had. Just to escape. 'Look, if you just pass the details to me I'll ring the person and see what they want, then make sure either Topsy or Sukie gets them – and thank you anyway. This has helped me a lot.'

'Has it? Really?' Mr Brewster looked a bit bewildered, but printed off the details from his screen. 'There we are. Just a name and a couple of phone numbers. No e-mail address. Apparently the caller doesn't have internet communication.'

'Neither do I.' Joss took the piece of paper. The name – Mr F Fabian – meant absolutely nothing to her. She'd somehow expected it to be a woman. 'Oh, the first number's local and the other I presume is a mobile. I don't have one of those, either.'

Mr Brewster looked as if this was inconceivable but said nothing.

'I wonder,' Joss leaned forward slightly, 'if I might make the call from here? Only – well – making it from home would pose all sorts of difficulties.'

Mr Brewster sighed. 'Well, yes . . .' he pushed one of the desk phones towards her. 'Yes, of course.'

185

'I'll pay, naturally.' Joss punched in the local landline number with shaking fingers. She never liked ringing people's mobiles in case she was interrupting them doing something vital. It rang out continuously. 'Oh ... I don't think there's anyone there ...'

'Try the mobile, then,' Mr Brewster sighed again. 'But please make it snappy.'

It took Joss three attempts to get the sequence of numbers right. Then there was a silence. Should she hang up? Had she got it wrong – again? Then the ringing began. On and on and on.

She was about to put the phone down for the second time when a voice answered.

'Hello?'

'Um,' Joss started, but her mouth was too dry to speak properly. She tried again. 'Er – hello. Is that – um – Mr Fabian?'

'Speaking. And who are you, duck?'

Joss felt a bit better. The voice was warm and full-on Berkshire.

'Jocelyn Benson. I'm at the offices of the *Winterbrook Advertiser*. I wrote the article about the cancan dancing and the aromatherapy and—'

'Bingo!' The voice burred happily. 'Thanks for ringing back so quick, duck. Lovely bit of writing by the way. Right – when can we meet?'

'Er – well, I mean ... I don't think you want to meet me, actually. Maybe you need to talk to someone who can help you more with the details of the dancing or the massages.'

'Maybe, duck. Maybe. But first I'd like to meet you to get the bigger picture. You free tomorrow? About two or thereabouts?'

'Yes, but can't we do this on the phone?'

'Not my way of doing business, duck. I likes face-to-face hands-on if you see what I mean.' The Berkshire burr dissolved into throaty laughter. 'So – we on for two tomorrow, then?'

'Oh ... I don't know ...' Joss looked down at her wedding ring, then heard Marvin's voice in her head. She swallowed. 'Yes. Yes, two o'clock tomorrow will be perfect.'

'Lovely, duck. You know Winterbrook okay, do you? My office is right next to the bank on the High Street. Green door. Got a name-plate. You can't miss it.'

Joss hesitated for a moment. Mr Brewster was looking as if he wanted her to finish the call and leave. Quickly. And at least Mr Fabian – even if he was some sort of closet Lionel Blair or had got completely the wrong idea about the massages – hadn't suggested that she should come to his home, had he? An office meeting was surely safe, wasn't it? And Marvin would absolutely forbid it.

'Very well, yes. Tomorrow at two.'

'Smashing, duck. Look forward to it. Bye.'

Joss put the phone down feeling – goodness – what did she feel? Scared? Excited? Daring? Sick?

All those. And more.

She stood up and held out her hand. 'Thank you. I'm very grateful to you.'

'Are you?' Mr Brewster, still looking perplexed, shook her hand. 'Well, good. Good. I hope everything goes well with your meeting. And glad to have helped. And don't forget what I said about sending in more articles.'

'For no money?' Joss almost grinned as she reached the door. 'Just a by-line – isn't that what you called it? We'll see ... And thank you again.'

And beaming at the receptionist, she walked out into the trading estate's balmy golden glow.

On the other side of the estate, Sukie pulled up outside Winterbrook Joinery and stared at the three sprawling buildings with interest. Nice. Very nice. Prosperous looking, spacious, well-kept units, several cars parked in the vast yard area outside, including Derry's mucky jeep, and a very impressively liveried name plate. The two larger units had their roller doors open and it appeared one was a workshop, while the other was a showroom of sorts. The third smaller unit must be the office.

Helping a bouncing Jem unfasten his seat belt and open the car door, Sukie grinned at him. 'Do you want me to come in with you? Or are you okay on your own? Help me here, Jem – I'm not Amber. I don't want to insult you – or do the wrong thing.'

He winked at her and held out his hand, cocking his head towards the workshop area.

'Okay,' she took his hand. 'I'll walk in with you, deliver you safely and – oh . . . hi . . .'

She blinked as Derry appeared in the workshop doorway. Oh, God – her heart went into overdrive. He was wearing age-bleached jeans and a black T-shirt with a faded logo. His blond hair was untidy and multi-streaked in the sun. He was truly the most beautiful man she had ever seen.

'Hi.' He grinned at them both. 'Amber just rang to say you were on your way. I'd have driven round the estate to collect Jem myself but she said you'd already left.' He looked at Jem. 'Lucky sod. Two gorgeous women performing escort duty today.'

Jem said something in sign language and gave Derry the thumbs up.

'Yeah – right.' Derry grinned. 'No chance. Okay, you go in with Pauly—' he indicated a sturdy elderly man walking towards them from the workshop, '—and make a start. I'll be along in a minute. You know what you're doing today, don't you?'

Jem nodded.

'Tell Sukie.'

Jem made flapping movements with his elbows, then linked his twisted fingers together.

Sukie frowned. 'No, sorry Jem, I'm no good at this. Try me again, please?'

Jem repeated the performance, this time flapping his arms behind his back.

188

'Wings? Tails?' Sukie hazarded. 'Birds? Flying?'

Jem shook his head, going through the routine more slowly. Twice. Sukie, dredging up everything she knew about woodwork, suddenly had a light-bulb moment.

'Dovetails! You're doing dovetail joints!'

Jem punched the air, capered on the spot, threw his arms round Sukie and kissed her, then holding Pauly's hand, walked slowly and carefully across the yard.

'Nice one.' Derry smiled at her. 'You'll have made his day.'

'I'd've felt terrible if I'd got it wrong,' she admitted. 'And this—' she looked round the units, '—is very impressive.'

'Thanks. Are you in a hurry or would you like a quick guided tour?'

Even if she'd had half the royal family and the entire England football squad waiting impatiently for massages at Pixies Laughter, Sukie knew her reply would have been the same.

'No – I'm not in any rush at all.'

'Right answer.' Derry said. 'So, how are things going?'

'With the aromatherapy stuff? Brilliantly, thanks.' She walked beside him, hotly aware of his body, the way he moved, the clean, warm, working-man smell of him. 'Fully booked for weeks ahead. Or did you mean the dancing?'

'That blew me away,' Derry laughed. 'If that was a rehearsal – I can't wait to see it for real.'

'Same as all blokes – just in it for a glimpse of stocking tops and suspenders.'

'Yep. What else?'

They grinned at one another. Oh, help . . . Sukie thought. This is so, so wrong.

'And no more trouble with Aunt Cora's love potions?'

'Not what you'd call trouble, no. Although everyone has said that they've felt something has happened to them after they've had a massage. And there have been a few reported – um – unlikely liaisons.'

'Really?' Derry chuckled. 'Good old Cora.'

They'd reached the doorway of the workshop and Sukie inhaled the gorgeous scent of sawdust and raw, fresh timber. Several men were working at massive benches with what looked like terrifying circular saws and other whining, screaming machinery, sending showers of what she imagined must be chips of oak and ash and cherry and walnut skittering into the air like a manic sweet-smelling snowstorm.

'We're really busy at the moment,' Derry shouted above the noise. 'Tons of orders. I'll have to take on more carpenters – and I'll need a couple of good lads as apprentices this year, too.'

Sukie, suddenly wishing she'd done woodwork at school, watched the craftsmen somehow manoeuvring the great hulks of wood, checking drawings, measuring, slicing the finest sliver off, planing, sanding.

'It must be wonderful – starting with well, trees, and, through age-old skills, ending up with something handmade and beautiful – oh, not that trees aren't beautiful, of course – but—'

'You don't have to come over all environmentally friendly here,' Derry said, his mouth close – too close – to her ear. 'And we only use sustainable timber. Come and have a look at the samples.'

Jem, sitting at a bench with the ever-watchful Pauly, glanced up at her and blew her a kiss. She blew one back.

'I'm glad Jem's so happy here.'

'He's got a natural talent,' Derry said as they moved along the yard to the next unit. 'He loves working with wood and he has infinite patience. And despite his co-ordination being not great when it comes to walking, and his hands maybe not functioning in quite the normal way, he'll sit for hours and produce the most amazingly delicate stuff – better than I ever could.'

'It was kind of you to take the time to find out, though.'

'Not kind at all,' Derry grinned. 'It wasn't an act of

190

charity – although I hope I'm a nice enough person – but we're bloody lucky to have him. He came here initially because Lewis is a mate of mine and Jem needed a work placement, but he's on the payroll now. The blokes love him as much as I do, and we couldn't do without him.'

Lucky, lucky Jem, Sukie thought.

They'd walked along to the next unit. The shingle scrunched under their feet, and the sun was increasingly warm, and the sky was a glorious pale and cloudless blue. Sukie gave a little shiver of enjoyment: it was almost like being at the seaside.

'In here,' Derry said, standing back to let her into the showroom area first, 'I keep all the catalogued pictures and photos of stuff we've produced, and samples of wood, and some mock-up furniture and of course, the apprentice cabinets.'

'The what?'

'Apprentice cabinets.' He said. 'No, they're not some-where we lock away our NVQ kids at night. They're considered old-fashioned now I think, but I still like the newcomers to make them because there's no better way to learn. They're small scaled-down items of furniture and boxes and stairs – practice runs for every woodworking skill. But they also come in handy to give potential customers some idea of what we can do.'

Sukie moved round the showroom, still inhaling sawdust and the fabulously natural smell of sap and fresh-cut wood, admiring the beautifully enhanced grains, and the colours and textures of the exquisitely crafted pieces.

'Wow.' She looked at the catalogue of photos on the wall. 'These are absolutely amazing. Did you really make all these?'

'With a little help from my friends.' Derry did the stand-ing-close thing again. 'Yep. Most of these are my designs, but I'm always open to suggestions from potential clients – and most of them know more or less what they want. I'll just advise and then translate their ideas, hopefully, into something that pleases us both.'

'You're brilliant.' Sukie shook her head. 'Do you know, I had no idea ... I'm really sorry but I thought that you went out on to building sites and probably nailed bits of wood together to make door frames or ceiling joists or something like that.'

'Oh, I'll do that too,' Derry said cheerfully. 'No job too big or too small. I just love working with wood and creating things.'

'And I thought there'd be a plate over the workshop door saying "established eighteen-oh-four" or something.' Sukie moved a little bit away from him, afraid that he'd hear her heart thundering under her T-shirt. 'But this is all yours, isn't it? Not inherited?'

'All mine. Risky to set up at first, and we flew very close to the wind to start with.' Derry ran his long slender fingers lovingly across a small table with criss-crossed veneers in several different types of wood. 'Of course, when I started, most people were setting up small businesses in technology and IT – the safe way forwards in the twenty-first century. My bank manager nearly had a fit when I told him I wanted to set up my own company using traditional skills from over a thousand years ago.'

'But he believed in you and backed you? Eventually?'

'Eventually, yes. With a million get-out clauses for the bank, and even more millions of dire warnings of what would happen if I failed. The first couple of years we made no profit at all and only just broke even. After that, well, by word of mouth, things just grew ... and now—' he smiled at her, '—now the bank manager sends me a Christmas card and invites me to his parties.'

'Great stuff,' Sukie laughed. 'So, in a way, I suppose we're both working with ancient wisdoms, aren't we?'

He nodded, pushing his hair away from his eyes with the unselfconscious gesture that had started to haunt her dreams. 'I'd say we've got a lot in common, yes. We're very hands-on, working closely with our customers, creating magic from nature.'

They looked at each for a fraction too long.

'Er . . .' Sukie swallowed, 'Milla must love all this.'

'Milla's never been here. She's not really interested. This isn't her sort of thing. Any more than corporate wheeling and dealing is mine.'

'Still,' Sukie said, breaking her own heart, 'you know what they say about opposites attracting and all that.'

'Yeah.' Derry nodded. 'And you don't get more opposite than Milla and me. Sorry to cut this short, but I really ought to be getting back to make sure Pauly and Jem are okay . . .'

'Yes, of course – I shouldn't have kept you so long. Although I could spend ages in here.'

'So could I.' Derry smiled, 'but we both have businesses to run, don't we?'

They walked back in the sun, across the beach-like shingle, towards the workshop.

Above the scream and whine of the machinery, Jem waved at them and winked.

'Thanks again,' Sukie said, fishing her car keys from her bag. 'For taking time to show me all this. I've loved it.'

'Me too.' Derry nodded. 'Look, Sukie—'

'Derry!' Pauly had walked to the workshop door. 'Sorry to interrupt, mate! We need your input here!'

'I'll have to go.' Derry turned away from her. 'See you soon?'

'No doubt. And thanks again.'

She slid into her car, started the engine and turned slowly in the yard. The last view she had of Derry was through the open workshop doorway. He was sitting next to Jem at the bench, leaning close to him, explaining something, making him laugh, guiding his hands with infinite patience.

Ooooh, Sukie groaned, racheting up the plinketty-plonk radio music to teeth-vibrating levels. Oooh, damn and bloody sod it!

By the time she'd turned on to the trading estate's exit road, she still felt dazed and confused and irrationally restless. The current accompanying blast of the Bay City Rollers' 'Summer Love Sensation' made her feel even worse. And now there was a bloody beige hatchback dithering in front of her, signalling to turn out of the *Winterbrook Advertiser*'s car park across her path.

Sukie, furious with herself for being silly enough to fall head-over-heels for someone who not only could never, ever love her in return but was also forbidden fruit, fought the urge to give a sharp blast of her horn. No point in taking it out on other people. Instead, she slowed and flashed her lights.

The driver of the hatchback raised her hand in acknowledgement, then to Sukie's surprise, changed the gesture to a wave, stopped her car and rolled down the window.

'Sukie!' Joss Benson called across to her. 'How fortuitous! The very person! Have you got a moment?'

Sukie pulled over and switched off her engine. This must be her day for rescuing damsels in distress. 'Hi, Joss. Are you okay?'

Joss looked, Sukie thought, rather flushed and flustered.

'Well, yes . . .' Joss slid from her car and walked across to Sukie. 'At least I think so. I've just done something rather daring.'

Sukie listened, smiling despite herself, at Joss's enthusiastic retelling of the whole story; reminding herself that for someone as browbeaten as Jocelyn this was indeed a hugely brave step to have taken.

'. . . and—' Joss finished, '—I was going to ring and ask you if there was any chance of a massage to relax my stupid nerves and give me, well, maybe a bit of confidence for this meeting with Mr Fabian tomorrow? Oh, I know it must sound really silly to you, and it's probably a wild goose chase anyway, but I really need something to make me feel – well – less petrified and—'

Sukie smiled and nodded. 'I understand, believe me. And

I've got the very thing you need. It's not a massage as such, but some oils absolutely guaranteed to give empowerment and confidence. Hang on . . .'

Sukie climbed out of the car into the sunshine and carried her aromatherapy cases from the boot, opening them on the back seat, watched by several passing motorists who no doubt thought they were witnessing some sort of desperate housewives' drug deal.

'Here we are – these essences will do the trick, I promise you. Now, really this should be ylang-ylang – but I've got a jasmine substitute which is just as good – and this one is lavender – and the rose here is actually hawthorn which is basically the same thing only at a different stage.'

'And I can use these myself?' Joss took the tiny gemstone-stoppered bottles. 'Are you sure?'

'Absolutely,' Sukie agreed. 'They're all used in massage oils, but in this case all you need is to add them to a warm bath just before you leave for your meeting. Four drops of the jasmine, three of the lavender, and one of the hawthorn. Okay? Relax in the bath, close your eyes, inhale the fragrances as they blend in the steam, imagine yourself being confident when you meet this – er, Mr Fabian – and you will be everything you want to be. Honestly.'

Joss beamed. 'Fabulous! Thank you – and I'll let you know how it goes. I mean – I expect it'll be you he wants to talk to really, but I'm sure this will make me feel so much better.' She slipped the tiny bottles into her bag. 'Four drops of this one, then three of that, and one of this – I'll remember that. Thank you – oh, how much do I owe you?'

'Nothing at all.' Sukie grinned. 'Honestly, Joss I'm just delighted to be able to help. And don't forget to let me know how it goes. Good luck.'

Joss hugged Sukie. 'You're wonderful. Thank you. And of course I'll let you know what happens.'

Sukie watched Joss practically skip back into her car and drive away with a huge smile.

Ah well, at least with her lotions and potions she'd solved poor Jocelyn Benson's problem today. And the card school's. And Ellen's. And indirectly Amber's. And Jem's.

If only she could concoct something which would deal so easily with her own ...

# Chapter Eighteen

Having spent the rest of the afternoon daydreaming about Derry in particular and pondering on star-crossed lovers in general, Sukie ate a late-lunch-early-tea pot noodle, cleared up the dining-room-cum-massage parlour and carried out her final at-home appointments for the day.

Given the successes of the home-grown remedies so far, Sukie was sure – absolutely positive – that Cora must have had some sort of recipe for this long-distance lonely hearts problem, given her alleged wartime matchmaking skills.

In fact, Sukie was sure she half-remembered a verse, a longer verse than the love potion ones, which Cora would sometimes unfurl and read softly, almost to herself. The poem had always made Sukie sad in childhood, even though she hadn't understood its implications. The words – involving loss and loneliness – had always made Cora stare into the far distance and stop smiling, and the young Sukie had shared her great-aunt's sorrow without knowing why.

So far, this particular piece of cross-stitch hadn't emerged with the others, probably, she decided now, because it didn't involve a massage potion. But it might be just what she was looking for and it must be somewhere . . . And she knew she wouldn't rest until she'd found it.

So, breaking off only to answer several congratulatory phone calls about Joss's article, including one from her mother who became very chatty and said they really must see one another for a meal or shopping or something soon; a mickey-taking text from Chelsea; a lengthy gush from Jennifer to say the publicity for Beauty's Blessings was fab and the Kylies were settling in and shaping up nicely; and a text from Derry – which she'd clicked through with stupidly trembling fingers – to say that the blokes in the workshop had cut out the cancan picture and pinned it on the wall alongside Jordan and Jodie Marsh, Sukie delved once more into the darkest recesses of the work-basket.

As the afternoon melted into evening, right at the bottom of the pile of faded cross-stitched embroidered verses, she found what she was looking for, wrapped in brittle-with-age tissue paper:

*So many lonely people*
*So many broken hearts*
*So many lovers torn apart*
*So much loss and so much sorrow*
*Can be cured maybe tomorrow*
*No matter how many miles away*
*Love can be brought home to stay*
*Belief in the herbal powers*
*Belief in the scented flowers*
*Will bring true lovers back together*
*To be in love for ever and ever*
*With no more tears and no more pain*
*Together, never to part again*

Sukie read and reread the verse. Okay, it probably wouldn't pass muster with the literati, but the meaning and the emotion was surely raw enough for anyone. Now Topsy had told her about Cora's lost love, no wonder the words had made her cry. Sukie sniffed back a tear of her own, wishing she'd known then, been old enough to understand and sympathise.

Still, she thought as she folded the piece of cross-stitch and slid it carefully back into its tissue paper, the poem was one thing – but without a potion recipe it was totally useless. So near and yet so far . . . Damn it. She tried to ease the tapestry back into the tissue. For some reason it didn't quite fit . . . Sukie peered into the folds. Ah! There was another piece of paper tucked inside, yellowing and crackly. Intrigued, Sukie pulled it out, opened it and read it.

Her mouth was dry. This was it, then. This was what she had been looking for . . . Cora's familiar writing blurred in front of her:

*Distance love potions are very effective but are considered powerful earth magic and should only be undertaken as a last resort to bring lovers together.*

*They should be used only if you are absolutely sure that the outcome is what you want because they may not be reversed.*

*To make: 3 drops ginger, 2 drops rosemary, 2 drops jasmine, 1 drop clove, 1 drop cinnamon, 1 pinch powdered mandrake root, mixed with almond oil. The potion should be rubbed on a pulse point, preferably the left wrist as this will take the infusion straight to the heart of one of the parted lovers while they visualise their beloved. They will, in every case, be united in everlasting love.*

Sukie sat back on her heels and exhaled, then pushed the piece of paper carefully into her pocket, and put the cross-stitch back into Cora's work-basket and closed the lid. The essences were easy to find. The potion simple to concoct. She even knew that at the back of the store cupboard Cora had kept a jar of powdered mandrake root. There was nothing stopping her from making it, but would she – should she – use it?

Two hours later, she'd finally reached a decision. It was, she conceded, probably the wrong one and – as it was going to involve sharing stuff with Chelsea – it was almost bound to end in tears.

At nearly nine o'clock, the balmy faux-summer day had darkened into a typically chill April evening and Sukie, shivering slightly inside her second best jeans and third best sweater, hurried through the door of the Barmy Cow.

Seemingly untouched by the Rites of Spring, the pub remained grey, smoky, grubby, and was also practically empty.

'Hello, young Sukie!' Hilton Berkeley, clearly dying for someone to talk to, hailed her garrulously from behind the bar. 'Lovely pic of you in the *Advertiser* today, and Mrs Benson from The Close wrote nicely about them massages, too. And Topsy was cock-a-hoop over the cancan bit. She reckons she'll have more applications for the vacancy than that Factor-X programme. I hope it does you both a power of good.'

'Thank you.' She leaned her elbows on the bar top, belatedly remembering the ongoing stickiness and quickly stood up straight. 'It's very quiet in here tonight – and I think there's something else strange as well but I can't quite put my finger on it.'

'Is there?' Hilton beamed at her. 'That's nice. Mind, we're often quiet in the week these days. People seem to prefer the telly to the pub – can't think why.'

Sukie could but was far too polite to say so. 'Oh – I know what's odd! It's you! You're on your own! I don't think I've ever seen any of you working solo before.'

'It happens occasionally.' Hilton inclined his grizzled grey head kindly towards her. 'Not often, I'll admit, but it does occur sometimes when one or other of us is unwell, or is invited out. What would you like, my dear?'

'Oh, two halves of shandy please.' Sukie went for the safest option. 'Chelsea should be here shortly. So, where are the other Boys tonight, then? Not ill, I hope?'

'No, thank the Lord.' Hilton mixed two shaky half pints. 'Dorchester is upstairs with young Topsy. He's bought her a boxed set of *Dr Kildare* but she don't have a DVD whatsit

200

so they're having a pizza and film night in his room.'

On a school night? Sukie thought, trying not to giggle. Without parental supervision? And clever old Dorchester – the entire set of *Dr Kildare* would make Topsy putty in his blue-veined hands. The viola massage mixture was clearly still working its magic there.

'This – um – thing with Topsy and Dorchester. Being friends, I mean. You don't mind? I know how close you and the Boys are ...'

'Bless you, no!' Hilton beamed. 'Between ourselves, I think Dorchester has had his eye on Topsy for several years. And what's the point of people being alone when they don't have to be? Especially at our age. We've all steered clear of affairs of the heart because they never did our beloved mother any good,' he inclined his head towards the awful picture of Honour Berkeley above the bar. 'But, tell the truth, it makes me rightly glad to see our Dorchester so happy.'

Sukie offered up a silent prayer of thanks. Maybe the viola massage had done some good, then? Maybe her plans for this evening weren't so risky after all? Then again ...

'And Claridge and Savoy?' She paid for her drink. 'Are they upstairs too?'

Hilton shook his head. 'That was a very funny thing, Sukie my duck. The card players came in at six, like they always do, for their apéritifs, and Edie and Rita were behaving really oddly.'

Sukie took a sip of her shandy. It was strangely thick and tasted neither of beer nor lemonade. She wasn't sure she wanted to hear the rest of the story. 'Oddly?'

'Ah,' Hilton leaned across the bar, clearly oblivious to the residue that was now clinging to his lovat sleeves, 'flirty and that. You know, all coy and giggling? They were done up to the nines, the pair of 'em too, and well, they made a fair old play for Claridge and Savoy. Upshot being, as we're quiet tonight, they've all four of 'em gone off to the flicks in Winterbrook.'

201

Oh, dear ... Sukie thought. Oh dear ... Less than twelve hours after the buttercups and daisies rub ... Less than twelve hours after using the potion that Cora had sworn *'hearts desires and needs do know'* and that having used it *'love forever will endure'*.

Oh, dear ... The folded, yellowing paper and the little glass phial in her bag felt almost incendiary now. She really, really shouldn't even consider doing this, should she?

'Er – I thought they'd closed the cinema in Winterbrook? Turned it into a rabbit hutch housing estate for singletons called Alhambra Meadows or something?'

'Ah.' Hilton tapped the side of his nose. 'That they did, duck. But they'm showing films at the Corn Exchange now three nights a week. The boys and Edie and Rita have gorn to see *Revenge Massacre of the Zombie Flesh Eaters*.'

'Oh, lovely.' Sukie tried not to look too appalled. 'And – um – what about the others in the card school? Tom and Bert and Ken? Did they all go home?'

Hilton unpeeled himself from the bar top and chuckled. 'Well, call me a silly old duffer if you likes, but I'd stake me cellar full of best bitter that Tom and Ken went off *together* if you get my drift. Chummy as anything they were. Tom was saying that Ken ought to come back to his place and look at his curly kale.'

Sukie inhaled her shandy. There was a prolonged moment of spluttering and mopping.

Oh, dear.

Still, at least Bert was untouched ... so far.

'Bert seemed at a bit of a loss.' Hilton looked sad. 'All his pals gorn off like that. Said he was going home to have a cheese and chutney sandwich and watch *Men and Motors*.'

Phew – well, at least she couldn't be blamed for that, could she?

Fortunately Chelsea arrived at that moment and her denim mini skirt and tight jumper seemed to take Hilton's

202

mind off the defection of his brothers and the majority of his regulars.

There was a lot of girlie giggling over the *Winterbrook Advertiser* article as they crammed into a clean settle, and shared a bit of a catch-up generally: Sukie filled Chelsea in on an expurgated version of the events of her day, and Chelsea told a funny-in-retrospect Big Sava story about a man with a hairpiece and the faulty door on the upright chiller cabinet.

'So—' Chelsea peered at Sukie through her shandy, '— what's all this stuff you have to talk to me about? Is it to do with Derry? Now we both know that you fancy him like crazy, are you going to pinch him from Milla and be labelled The Man-Stealing Bitch From Hell?'

'Nooo, of course not.' Sukie hoped she wasn't blushing. 'But I have got something a bit – well – tricky in mind and I'll need your help.'

'Really?' Chelsea's eyes widened. 'No – let me guess. Does it involve me acting as a decoy and dressing up and pretending to be seducing him while you come to the rescue and Milla sees me as the villain of the piece and—?'

'You read far too many Real Life magazines.' Sukie grinned at her. 'No, what I've been wondering about is whether it would be possible to reunite Milla and Bo-Bo.'

'Whoa!' Chelsea slammed her glass down. 'Stop right there! How the hell do you think you can do that? I was only joking about the tabloid mag stuff – but you mean it, don't you? And didn't you say he'd practically left her at the altar? He must be a right bastard. And just suppose you could get them back together, what if Derry loves Milla to bits, and his heart is broken – he'd hate you for splitting them up, wouldn't he? You'd be the last person he'd want to be with after that! Good God, Sukie – have you lost all your marbles?'

Sukie raised her eyebrows. Whatever reaction she'd expected from Chelsea, it certainly hadn't involved moral outrage. 'Look, I know it all sounds devious ...'

'Too right it does! I'm shocked. Really. There is a Girl Code, you know. Sisters together and all that.'

'Yes, okay – just listen . . .'

And giving the carefully edited version, leaving out Cora's love potions and the reuniting elixir for the moment – because Chelsea would never understand or accept any of that in her current high-ground mode, Sukie outlined her plan.

'Crap,' Chelsea said at the end. 'You're going to turn yourself into some sort of witch, are you? Just like that. And somehow magic – bloody *magic* – up something that will make Milla and this Bo-Bo bloke fall into each other's arms and live happily ever after?'

'That's more or less it,' Sukie agreed, realising that without sharing Pixies Laughter's secrets with Chelsea, the scheme wouldn't seem at all viable. 'Although I probably wouldn't have used quite such pagan language.'

'Of course it's pagan! What else can you call it? And all this old hokum rampaging round the village, started by mad Topsy, about love potions has finally gone to your head, has it?' Chelsea was scathing. 'Get real, Sukes. You know what happens to people who start believing in their own hype? They come crashing down in flames and look like prats.'

Sukie drained her glass. There was sediment at the bottom. 'Okay, but just suppose I could do it – could find something to bring Milla and Bo-Bo back together – because she really does love him you know, and she'll always be miserable without him, would that still be so wrong?'

'Of course it would! It would be meddling! And it still wouldn't mean you'd get your carefully manicured Beauty's Blessings nails into Derry, would it? Or are you planning to use voodoo on him, too?'

'No, of course not. But Milla and Bo-Bo—'

'Stop! First stumbling block – how the hell would you find this Bo-Bo? None of us knows what his real name is, do we? Milla is hardly likely to tell you without wanting to know why, and I can just see Companies House, or wherever it is you'd need to go, being able to give you a life-file on someone who sounds like a cartoon rabbit.'

'Yeah, I've thought about that. Now, suppose again that I didn't need to find Bo-Bo – suppose all I needed was Milla – and suppose all she needed to do was think about being with him again for ever and ever.'

'You,' Chelsea said, standing up and collecting the empty glasses, 'are getting seriously unhinged. You scare me sometimes, Sukes, do you know that? Same again?'

'Please . . .'

Sukie sighed and slumped back in her settle. Maybe she should have considered that Chelsea wouldn't jump at this once in a lifetime opportunity to test drive a love potion. Maybe she'd have to tell her the truth about Cora and the verses and the discovery of earth magic in Pixies Laughter's cottage garden.

No – she simply couldn't. If Chelsea was sceptical now, she'd run a mile after hearing all that wouldn't she? Bugger.

'Thanks.' She took her second shandy. 'Oh nice – it's got crumbs in it.'

'Hilton was eating crisps.' Chelsea sat down. 'Probably best to scoop them out with a beer mat.'

'Look at this another way.' Sukie tried again. 'You know when we fancied boys at school and we did the Truth, Dare, Kiss, Promise thing? And we all thought it worked because we absolutely believed in it? And remember that time at Phoebe's birthday party when you got Nicky Hambly's name up three times on a promise to love for ever, and you went after him like a starving dog after a bowl of raw liver?'

'I never remember it being *quite* so romantic, but yes.' Chelsea stared at her. 'Go on.'

'Well, what if we could do a grown-up version? What if there's a grown-up version of Nicky Hambly – the love of your life – out there, just waiting for you? What if you could meet and fall in love and be together for ever and ever?'

'What if you got a grip?'

'Oh, come on, Chelsea, join in here – you're always the first up for party games and pretend spooky stuff. You're always saying you hate being single and still being at home with your mum and dad and all your brothers and sisters, aren't you? You're the one who says they want to be married to Mr Absolutely Perfect and have kids and a semi. Wouldn't it be wonderful to be in love with this man who's – well – perfect for you, who loves you just as much in return, for always? Who would you like to be with for the rest of your life? Who's your secret heart's desire? Not some film star or footballer or anything – but a real man. Who's your grown-up Nicky Hambly?'

'Nicky Hambly.'

'No, I mean . . . What? *Really*? How come I didn't know that?'

'Because.' Chelsea pushed a beer mat across the table in a circular motion. It got stuck and puckered. 'Because he told me to push off when we were sixteen and broke my heart. He didn't fancy me then, and he wouldn't fancy me now – even assuming he's still single, and straight, and alive.'

'Didn't he join the RAF?'

'Yep. Haven't seen or heard of him for over ten years.'

'And no one has come close to taking his place?'

'No.'

'And when you've gone on and on about your Mr Absolutely Perfect – you've meant *Nicky Hambly*?'

'Yes, okay?' Chelsea was suddenly defensive. 'And don't look at me in that "I'm your best and oldest friend – why didn't you tell me?" way.'

'No, but why didn't you?'

'Because you never had any trouble getting boyfriends, and it just seemed easier to be known as your happy-go-

206

lucky mate who played the field, rather than the sad one who listened to heartbreaking songs and wrote Chelsea Hambly over anything that didn't move and dreamed hopelessly about our wedding and our house and our babies.'

'Blimey.' Sukie was genuinely shocked. 'Chelsea, I never had an inkling. And you still – er – fancy him?'

'Love him. Love him truly, madly, deeply. Love him so much that any other bloke is measured on my Nicky Hambly scale and never gets past halfway. Hopelessly unrequited love for some skinny kid who is now a grown-up stranger and probably happily married with umpteen children and wouldn't even remember my name.' Chelsea stared at her. 'So, what are you going to do about that, then?'

Sukie looked down into her shandy glass. The little phial was practically bubbling its way out of her handbag. 'God, Chelsea – I am sorry – really. I had no idea. You should have told me.'

'There was nothing to tell, was there? Stop looking so guilty, Sukes. It was my secret. How sad would it have been if you'd *known*? And, who knows, maybe one day someone else will come along and knock Nicky into second place.'

Sukie gave Chelsea a quick hug across the table. They had to peel themselves off the beer mats.

'Do you know the thing I find funny about all this?' Sukie swirled the remains of her cloudy shandy. 'The fact that you – the original Miss Trippy Lips – have managed to keep it a secret for years and years. I didn't think you could ever keep quiet about anything.'

'Spoken like a true best friend.' Chelsea grinned. 'And just goes to show that you don't know everything about me, doesn't it?'

Sukie nodded. It did. It also meant that Chelsea might, just might, be able to be trusted with the secret of Pixies Laughter. 'Well, look if we did a little experiment—'

207

'Oh!' Chelsea sighed. 'You're not back on that again, are you? The witchcraft stuff.'

'It's not witchcraft. It's earth magic – no, listen – please Chelsea – and don't tell anyone else what I'm going to tell you. Just listen . . .'

Chelsea listened. Occasionally she laughed; once or twice she snorted derisively; several times she shook her head in mocking disbelief; but she listened.

'. . . so—' Sukie finished, '—that's why I thought you might be up for a bit of a trial run. I thought if you gave it a blast before I did it for real on Milla and Bo-Bo . . .'

'I certainly won't be telling anyone that load of trash,' Chelsea shrugged. 'Your secret is safe with me – the whole thing is bloody insane, you know that. Look, I'm really happy for you that Pixies Laughter's garden provides you with real essences – but you're just imagining that Cora's flower power love potions have worked, because Topsy told you they would. And don't tell me about Mitzi Blessing's herbal cookery magic – or even about Fiddlesticks and the star-wishing – I don't believe in any of that either.'

'Okay, so as a total disbeliever, where's the harm in test-driving this for me? What's the worst that can happen? Nicky Hambly appears like magic and makes all your dreams come true?'

'It won't happen. You know it and I know it. And I still think it would be wrong to try it out on Milla without her knowing – just in case. And I also still reckon it's a really bad idea to think that by splitting her and Derry up you'll be in with a shout. That's still man-stealing in my book – whether it's by fairy means or foul.'

Sukie was beginning to waver. Chelsea was right. 'Oh, God – don't make me worry about ethics now. Okay, if I promise to sound out Milla before I do anything, will you still give this a go? And if it works can I be bridesmaid?'

'No.'

'Oh, come on Chelsea – after all, this is all your fault, really. If you hadn't nicked most of Jennifer's madly-expensive synthetic floral essences and given them to Fern, then I wouldn't have had to look for replacements and I wouldn't have used the plants from the cottage garden and none of this would have happened.'

'That's blackmail!'

'Yep. So – give me your left wrist and close your eyes and start thinking about Nicky Hambly.'

'As I rarely stop, that won't be a hardship.' Chelsea pulled up her sleeve and closed her eyes. 'And I must be bloody mad to even think about doing this. Oh, and I'm really, really sorry Mrs Hambly, if you're listening, and all the little Hambly kiddies who may be out there, for even thinking that this might work and robbing you of your husband and father.'

Quickly, before either of them could change their minds, Sukie scrabbled in her bag and removed the potion. She glanced round the pub, making sure no one was watching, but Hilton was busy making snowballs for an elderly couple. All three of them were spattered with yellow froth and the remaining handful of customers were watching the advocaat manoeuvres with rapt attention.

Easing the stopper from the phial, Sukie turned Chelsea's left wrist face-up on the table.

'You don't have to dance around me and chant, do you?' Chelsea muttered. 'And – actually, that smells lovely ... all herby and sweet ... like being in Pizza Hut with flowers on the table.'

'Stop talking and start visualising Nicky Hambly running towards you through a summer glade, all diffused sunlight and flowers and butterflies, his arms outstretched, ready to hold you and love you for ever and ever.'

Chelsea smiled to herself, and Sukie, her hands shaking, allowed a few drops of the elixir to fall on to the pulse point. Quickly, she massaged them into Chelsea's wrist as the glorious aroma wafted into the murk of the Barmy Cow, engulfing the grey smokiness with the essence of sun-kissed gardens and honey-sweet blossoms.

209

'Do you know,' Chelsea said dreamily, 'I can almost see that summer meadow and hear the birds ... And as for Nicky – he's still really hot ... You know, Sukes, it might be all baloney but it's very relaxing and rather lovely. Can I open my eyes now?'

'Yes, and thanks.' Sukie pushed the phial back into her bag. 'Really. I'm very grateful.'

'Hmmm, so you should be.' Chelsea sniffed her wrist. 'Well, at least it still smells nice and my skin hasn't fallen off. And I'll have what passes for a double vodka and lemonade as payment, thanks. So, what happens now?'

'Haven't got a clue.' Sukie grinned, standing up to make her way to the bar. 'I suppose we just sit back and wait for Nicky Hambly to come charging through the door – blimey! That was quick!'

Startled, they both stared as the Barmy Cow's door flew open. Sukie realised she was holding her breath.

'Hiya!' Valerie Pridmore bundled inside, followed by her large, untidy husband and several of her grown-up children. 'Jeeze! Dead as the grave in here tonight, innit? Smells funny an' all ... you been using a new disinfectant in the lavs, Hilton? And who's up for a game of darts?'

Chelsea snorted. 'So much for bloody earth magic. Ah well, back to reality. Nice try, Sukes – and you nearly had me believing in your hocus-pocus there. You might as well go ahead and try it on Milla and Bo-Bo – we both know it'll never work, don't we?'

# Chapter Nineteen

'Jocelyn!' Marvin thundered on the bathroom door. 'What the hell are you doing in there?'

'Having a bath.'

'It's midday! No one has a buggering bath at midday! Midday is when you get my lunch. And did you use the immersion heater? We can't afford to run the immersion heater! You know we can't afford—'

Joss turned the taps on full, the thundering roar drowning out Marvin's latest fiscal drone.

If she thought she'd been nervous yesterday braving Mr Brewster at the *Winterbrook Advertiser*, this afternoon's meeting with Mr Fabian was such a step into the unknown that her teeth were chattering.

Clutching her towelling bathrobe more tightly round her, Joss fumbled in the pocket for the little bottles of calming essences. She'd been repeating the dosage in her sleep like a mantra: four drops of jasmine; three of lavender; one of hawthorn. Opening the bottles with trembling fingers, she carefully counted them out now, dripping them slowly into the hot water.

There! She re-stoppered the bottles and returned them to her pocket, then slid off her robe and swished the water with her hand.

'Oh, glorious ...' She inhaled the rich, evocative fragrance rising in the clouds of steam. 'Wonderful ...

211

Oh, Sukie, you clever, clever girl ...'

'Jocelyn!' Marvin hammered on the door again. 'Come out! Now!'

'I'm in the bath,' Joss fibbed happily, swooshing the water around again, feeling oddly calm. 'I'll be out in a little while. I've made some sandwiches for lunch – they're in the kitchen. Save one for me. Now please go away.'

She smiled. This standing up for herself was becoming quite a habit these days. Why on earth hadn't she done it years ago? Well, she knew the answer to that, of course – but things were going to be slightly different now, weren't they? In fact, ever since the day she'd had her first-ever massage at Pixies Laughter, she'd felt bolder and slightly less intimidated. Sukie had already worked miracles on her self-esteem. Who knew what might happen in the future – especially after this self-affirming aromatherapy bath?

While Joss wasn't expecting miraculous changes in the bungalow's balance of power, she was damned if Marvin's self-pity was going to drag her down even further. She still had some small sense of self-preservation, and if Sukie's magic worked again, she may even become assertive – or something very close.

Waiting until she heard Marvin stamp off back to the television via the kitchen, Joss stepped into the bath and lowered herself luxuriously into the silky scented water. What had Sukie said she should do? Ah, yes – relax, inhale the exotic steam and imagine herself facing the unknown Mr Fabian with confidence. Okay, then ...

Leaning her head back, closing her eyes, she did just that, and could feel herself instantly floating, drifting away. It was a slightly strange out-of-body feeling – like having a pre-med – but not unpleasant. Far from it. She felt warm, weightless, carefree; and as the perfumes from the essences engulfed her, lulling her senses, she drifted drowsily into another world ...

Joss opened her eyes. And blinked. Surely she hadn't fallen asleep? She must have done ... But for how long?

212

And was she still dreaming? No – she was definitely awake, but . . .

The billows of steam swirled and dipped, forming and reforming like summer morning mist, masking the harsh edges of the austere beige and chrome bathroom in a fragrant pastel haze. And the bath was no longer a bath: it was a pool, a warm sweet-scented tree-shaded woodland pool. Joss sleepily turned her head in wonderment. The utilitarian shower had become a trickling, twinkling, dancing waterfall, and vibrantly-coloured flowers twined and blossomed down the walls, cascading rainbow petals into the water.

It was, Joss thought, just like one of those highly-imaginative television adverts for organic bath foam – only a million times better because this was *real*.

Now almost sure that the dozens of radiant jewel-coloured butterflies fluttering in and out of the green fronds surrounding her were alive, Joss was surprised that it didn't seem strange at all. Not even slightly alarming. Just simply wonderful. She tipped her head back, certain that she could see the blue of a summer sky where the ceiling should be, knowing she could hear bees buzzing in and out of the outrageous blooms just beyond her reach.

She felt so calm, so happy, so relaxed. Had Sukie added something hallucinogenic to the floral essences? Possibly – that must be the only explanation. Joss simply didn't care, because now she could, she knew, face anything. Anything at all.

'Jocelyn!' Marvin's voice outside the door sounded cruelly harsh amid all this lush glory. 'You've used piccalilli in the sandwiches! They're ham! You know I like chutney with ham!'

The woodland fantasy dissolved.

Joss looked around her with a feeling of acute loss. She was back in their normal cream plastic bath, the water growing cold, the decor pale and safe.

'Jocelyn!'

'Just coming.' She hauled herself out of the bath, delighted that even if the gorgeous surroundings had disappeared, the feeling of calm confidence hadn't. And she still had the little bottles in her pocket, didn't she? She could sneak off to her fantasy woodland pool anytime she wanted.

Sukie had handed her bliss on a plate.

By the time she was dry and moisturised and made-up and dressed – black skirt to the knee, flesh-coloured tights, cream shirt, black jacket – it was past one o'clock and Marvin had eaten all the sandwiches despite his pickle peccadillo.

'Where are you off to?' He looked up from a television programme about getting the best from your organic allotment. 'Someone's funeral?'

'An interview,' Joss said, gathering bag and keys and black court shoes. 'Like yesterday.'

Marvin had sulked mightily when she'd returned home from the *Winterbrook Advertiser*, especially as she'd interrupted a graphic programme about Holiday Romances From Hell. And then, as she'd been very noncommittal about the details of her excursion, he'd sneered a lot and repeated his homily about no one wanting to employ someone who was without even the basic skills and how she was wasting her time and that they'd have to sell the bungalow and down-size and that would put paid to her gallivanting. And Joss had said that down-sizing from the bungalow would clearly mean living in a shed, and Marvin had blustered and gone purple and said buggering every second word and thrown the *Winterbrook Advertiser* at the television.

Now Marvin looked up from 'how to mulch your bean trenches with fresh animal manure', and drew his lips back from his teeth in what passed for a smile. 'If you think you're going to work in that supermarket in Hassocks, you can think again, my lady. I found the application form yesterday while you were out – it's now shredded at the bottom of the recycling box.'

Joss stared at him, determined not to let her anger show, wishing she'd hidden the Big Sava form more carefully. 'And you think that will stop me, do you? I can get plenty of application forms. What on earth is wrong with you, Marvin? All I'm trying to do is find a little job so that we don't have to scrimp and scrape quite so much ... something to tide us over until you find another post, something to help out.'

'I don't want your buggering help! I don't want you getting a job that an imbecilic monkey could do better than you! I do not want to be kept by a woman!'

'I'd hardly be keeping you—'

'Not by stacking supermarket shelves, no! Which is all you can possibly do – and probably not even that with any degree of success! You're useless, Jocelyn! Useless!'

Joss stared at him again. The really weird thing was that although his words hurt her as much as ever, she wasn't crumbling inside. Even if she tried really hard, she failed to feel intimidated, and there was none of her usual need to immediately apologise for her stupidity.

'Right – I must be off or I'll be late. We'll talk about this later, Marvin. Maybe you'd like to wash up the lunch stuff? I've no idea how long I'll be ... Good bye.'

The feeling of calm, quiet confidence stayed with her all the way to Winterbrook. It could only be as a result of Sukie's oils, couldn't it? Joss simply didn't care – she was delighted with herself. And what on earth would Valerie make of it all when they met, as they did now twice a week, outside Coddles? She couldn't wait to share this with Val.

Having parked in the Corn Exchange and averted her eyes from the gory posters outside the new 'cinerama' for some horror film, Joss took a deep breath and headed for the High Street.

The sun was strong, and the black jacket may have been

215

a mistake, she thought, as she pushed her way through the shopping crowds. She really hoped she wouldn't look flustered and shiny when she arrived.

Now what had Mr Fabian said? Next to the bank? Joss stopped outside the bank ... okay, well as it possibly wasn't the Oxfam shop because he'd have said so, it must be the other side: the rather dingy green door, firmly shut, with a bank of faded name cards and little push-buttons.

Joss squinted at the names – ah, yes, there it was – Mr F Fabian – with something else underneath it which was too faint to read. Taking a deep breath, she pushed the intercom button.

'Yup?' A voice crackled cheerfully in her ear.

Joss, who'd never used an intercom before, jumped, then put her mouth very close to it. 'Mr Fabian? I'm Mrs Benson. We arranged to meet. About my piece in the *Winterbrook Advertiser*.'

'Gawd blimey, duck!' The Berkshire voice chuckled. 'There's no need to shout. You've all but deafened me! Come along up!'

The green door clicked open and Joss made her way gingerly up several dingy wooden staircases, past closed doors which according to their name plates housed debt collectors, private investigators, recruitment consultants and financial advisors.

Mr Fabian's office was right at the top.

Puffing slightly, Joss tapped on a strangely painted door – faded silver with stick-on gold stars – and wondered belatedly if Mr Fabian had something to do with the sex trade.

'Come in, duck!' Mr Fabian shouted. 'Straight through! There ain't no one in reception!'

Joss, still feeling slightly out-of-body and more curious than nervous, closed the silver door behind her. The small and airless reception area was covered, floor to ceiling, with show-biz posters and faded photos of old-time film and music stars. Joss recognised Marilyn Monroe and John

Wayne and Humphrey Bogart and Elvis and Jimi Hendrix.

'Straight through, duck!' Mr Fabian called from an archway through to the next room. 'We don't stand on ceremony here!'

Now more bemused than ever, Joss crossed the tiny cluttered reception area and into a second office, decorated in a similar vein with decades-old posters from cinemas and music halls and concerts – here she could just pick out the Rolling Stones, Cliff Richard, Bill Haley and the Comets.

'Lovely to meet you, duck.' Mr Fabian rose from behind a piled-high desk, knocking over several piles of correspondence and held out his hand. 'Freddo Fabian. Agent to the stars.'

Smiling, because she simply couldn't help it, Joss shook hands with the cheerful, fake-tanned, leathery 60s throwback with his dyed yellow Peter Stringfellow hair and huge friendly grin.

Marvin, she knew, would insist that Mr Fabian should be locked up and the key thrown away.

'Sit down, duck. Sorry about the mess. Paperwork's never been my forte. Can I get you anything? Coffee? Tea?'

'Coffee would be lovely, thank you,' Joss amazed herself by answering calmly, clearing a pile of music papers from the chair in front of his desk. 'I meant to have some before leaving home but ...' She stopped. There was a very thin line between confidence and being over-chatty. Mr Fabian really wouldn't want to know why she'd missed her lunch. 'Yes, coffee, thank you.'

She watched as Freddo Fabian shimmied sure-footed around his untidy office, pouring two cups of coffee from a bubbling pot. He was wearing the sort of torn and faded jeans that Marvin always went puce over on anyone – especially anyone over sixteen – and a baggy collarless pink shirt, and a lot of bling bracelets.

'There,' he handed her a rather prettily delicate porcelain mug and sat down again. 'Biscuit?'

Joss, who was terrified that her stomach was going to

rumble at any minute nodded. 'Please – thank you – oh, lovely. Chocolate digestives. My favourites.'

Crikey, she thought, helping herself from the packet, where had that come from?

Chummily, they crunched through biscuits and sipped coffee while Freddo Fabian explained about his agency business – Retro Music and Theatre – and that he was fascinated by the cancan troupe.

'Lovely bit of writing, by the way.' He grinned at her through chocolatey crumbs. 'You've got a real talent for stringing words together, duck. You must be professional.'

Blushing, Joss said no, she wasn't, but she'd always enjoyed writing – and that she was delighted that Mr Fabian had liked it.

'Freddo, duck, please. And you are – Jocelyn, did you say?'

She nodded. 'I prefer Joss.'

'Pretty name. Suits you. Right, Joss it'll be then, duck, seeing as we're friends.'

And Joss smiled back at him and felt as though she'd known him all her life.

Freddo rocked back on two legs of his chair. 'So, this dance troupe? Do they have representation? Are you connected to them at all?'

'No.' Joss shook her head regretfully. 'I know several of the dancers – and Topsy – Mrs Turvey who runs them, of course. I do think you'd need to speak to her. They're only local and haven't been going very long. I think they just do fêtes and galas and things like that.'

'But you can introduce me to them and this – Topsy bird, can you, duck? I'd really like to see 'em in action. I could get them a lot of work – in my line of business, the retro stuff is red-hot at the moment. Like I said to you on the phone, I needed to speak to you first to see how the land laid, get a foot in with someone on the shop floor so to speak. Do you think that would be a goer?'

Joss nodded. She wasn't entirely sure she understood at

all, but it was wonderful – simply wonderful – to be having a proper conversation with someone who treated her as an intelligent human being whose opinion not only mattered, but was crucial.

'I'm sure Topsy would be delighted to talk to you. I think they have a few bookings coming up, but she's always saying that she needed more coverage – that's why she was pleased with my article ...' Joss stopped in case this was a toot too far on her own trumpet. 'That is, I mean – not my article as such, but the coverage.'

'Don't you put yourself down, duck,' Freddo Fabian laughed. 'You're a very clever lady with a real talent for putting words together without over-egging the puddin'. I could do with someone like you to do my press releases.' He looked a bit woebegone. 'Mind, anyone I've employed here for anything like that can't write for toffee, can't spell, and wants all the fol-de-rols – computers and e-mail and all that.'

'And you don't have any of those things?'

'Nah, I'm retro through and through. Never got to grips with the techno stuff. I've got a fax machine – and that scares me witless, I can tell you. I've always managed with this old girl ...'

Joss almost clapped her hands in delight as Freddo Fabian pushed a pile of papers aside to reveal a gleaming Remington typewriter.

'Oh, I used to use one of those! Years and years ago. It was lovely! I loved it! I haven't seen one since – well, not for a very long time.'

Freddo's eyes twinkled. 'And you can touch type, can you?'

Joss nodded. 'I used to have about one hundred words a minute – and Pitman's shorthand as well, of course.' She laughed. 'Back in the dark ages.'

Freddo leaned forward. 'Mrs Benson – Jocelyn – Joss ... You haven't been sent by the angels, have you, duck? You wouldn't, couldn't, possibly be looking for a job ...?'

# Chapter Twenty

Joss stared at Freddo across the desk. Had she misheard him? Was he really offering her a job? Was this really happening, or was it simply a figment of her imagination, as the woodland pool had surely been? A result of some strange imbalance in the fragrances she'd inhaled? As she didn't want to leap up punching the air with excited yells if this was all part of her fantasy, she kept quiet.

'No, duck – sorry,' Freddo spread his hands wide. 'Of course not. No sane and sensible person, let alone an intelligent and classy lady like you, would want to hole themselves up in here and work in this pigsty for an old love-and-peace hippie like me. My mistake.'

'No,' Joss shook her head. 'No, I mean, yes – yes – I am looking for a job – but I haven't worked outside the home for years and years. I'm pretty rusty on the old procedures, let alone the new ones. And I know nothing at all about the – er – entertainment industry. I was a sort of secretary – shorthand typist, really – for a builder's merchants before my marriage.'

'A shorthand-typist would suit me down to the ground.' Freddo beamed. 'Especially one who could create order from this chaos, sort out the filing system, get me a bit organised. And you'll easily pick up the agency stuff as you go along, clever lass like you. But,' he looked at her through his tangle of yellow hair, 'it would have to be a sort of partnership, duck. I'm not good at barking orders and expecting people to jump through hoops. I'd hand it all over to you and let you get on with it. You sort out the office, I'll sort out the acts. We'd have to work as a team.'

Oh, Joss thought, how wonderful that would be: working here, using her old skills, creating calm from disorder, having someone as easy-going as Freddo Fabian as her boss. Feeling that she had a purpose, that she was a real person again, that her days would be both filled and fulfilling.

She took a deep breath. 'That sounds perfect to me.'

'You mean – you'd like to give it a try?' Freddo reached across the desk and gripped both her hands in his. 'Blimey, Joss, duck! You've just made my millennium! When can you start?'

Joss returned his grin and the squeeze of his hands. Then reality kicked in. Freeing her hands, she sat back in her chair. 'Before we get too carried away with this – there are some things I think you should know.'

And she told him briefly about Marvin, mentioning the redundancy but leaving out his downward spiral into self-pity and daytime telly. 'I know he's feeling a bit lost,' she finished diplomatically, 'and – er – well, I think he might make this awkward for me.'

'Well, let's play it by ear, then,' Freddo said, pouring more coffee, opening a second packet of biscuits and suggesting an hourly rate for the secretarial post which knocked Big Sava's salary into a cocked hat. 'Let's see how it goes. If you can't, or don't want to, work full-time, then we'll arrange the hours to suit. I'm flexible. Shall we say give it a month either way? If at the end of that time we decide we're not right for one another, or it's causing you more problems than you can deal with, then we'll part company with no hard feelings. Does that sound hunky-dory to you?'

'Very hunky-dory.' Joss smiled, realising with some small alarm that she was, like Freddo, actually dunking her biscuit. Marvin didn't allow dunking. 'Yes, thank you. Thank you so much.'

'No, duck, thank *you*.' Freddo chuckled through his chocolatey crumbs. 'And tell you what – why don't I invite your Marvin along here to meet me, see the place, let him know that I'm not a shyster, set his mind at rest over the whole business?'

'Oh, no – I don't think so,' Joss said quickly, knowing exactly how Marvin would react to the golden-haired, pink-shirted, much-blinged Freddo. 'No, I'll explain it to him – he'll be fine, honestly.'

'Jealous bloke, is he?' Freddo smiled warmly at her. 'A bit protective?'

Joss considered this for a moment. 'Protective? Do you know, I'm not sure . . . No, I don't think he is. I think he used to be, years ago, but not any longer. And jealous? Definitely not.'

'Then he's barking.' Freddo chuckled. 'You'd make any man proud as punch, duck, so don't let your Marvin tell you different.'

Joss smiled. 'Thank you – I think . . . I'm not used to getting compliments. Funny, isn't it? You start out in life with someone and you just assume it'll be roses all the way . . .' she stopped. 'Goodness, sorry! I didn't mean to unburden all my personal problems.'

'Don't mind me,' Freddo handed her another biscuit. 'My wife walked out on me years ago. Ran off with one of my clients – a bleeding conjurer, can you believe that? Spends her life now on stage in seedy clubs in tights and spangles watching him pull rabbits from his hat. Says it was the excitement that did it for her. She always wanted to be on the business side of the footlights.'

Joss bit her lip. 'Oh, I'm sorry. Do you miss her?'

'Not any more, duck – but I miss his fifteen per cent.'

They giggled together.

And after finishing the coffee and the biscuits, Joss filled in an application form, then Freddo gave Joss a quick guided tour of the business. Retro Music and Theatre, he explained, didn't actually represent any of the golden oldies displayed on his walls, they were just for show, but he did have a bulging client list and his agency was not only solvent but extremely healthy.

Joss simply hugged herself and still couldn't quite believe this had happened. Nor could she believe that she hadn't felt nervous or hadn't clammed up at any point. Was it really thanks to the aromatherapy bath that she'd sailed through this with calm competence? Whatever the reason, she'd have to buy Sukie an massive thank-you present for helping to make this possible.

'So,' Freddo said when they'd finished the introductory tour, 'does this all seem okay, duck? Something you'd like to get your teeth into?'

'Oh, yes, please.' Joss was simply itching to sort out the filing system and tidy the two higgledy-piggledy offices and get her hands on the Remington. 'Er – when would you like me to start?'

'Right now,' Freddo grinned at her. 'But seriously – how about a week on Monday? That'll give you ten days or so to square it with your husband, and give me a bit of time to tidy up at least some of the stuff here so it doesn't frighten you off before you've even got started.'

'Lovely.' Joss nodded. 'And in the meantime I'll speak to Topsy about you having a look at the cancan troupe, shall I?'

'If you could, duck. Thanks. And you'd better take one of my cards with the mobile on. Then you can give me a bell and keep me up to speed can't you?'

Joss took the pink and gold Retro Music and Theatre card and slipped in her handbag. 'I don't have a mobile phone but you've got all my contact details on the form there. And are you sure you'd like me to approach Topsy? Wouldn't you rather do it yourself?'

Freddo grinned. 'Look on it as your first bit of work experience. No, you did a sterling job on that write up –

I'll leave the contacting to you. But I'd like to come along and view them soon as. Do you know if they're doing any local gigs or anything?'

'I think,' Joss said, remembering what Valerie Pridmore had told her, 'that they're not appearing in public this year until the beginning of May. At a post-wedding party. In Fiddlesticks.'

'Really?' Freddo pushed his hair untidily away from his face, making his bangles jangle. 'Not for that couple from the pub there? Getting married out on a beach in the Seychelles or somewhere around now, and having the hoolie on the village green when they eventually come home?'

'Yes, I think so,' Joss said, surprised, remembering with pleasure the sheer giddy joy of Fern's hen-night in the Weasel and Bucket. 'Why? Do you know them?'

'Sort of. Indirectly.' Freddo almost jigged with excitement. 'But, more importantly, I've got one of my best acts booked in there, too. The JB Roadshow? Excellent soul band – they're just coming to the end of the Soul Survivors tour at the moment. This Fiddlesticks party'll be their local homecoming gig. Well, well – small world, isn't it?'

Joss nodded. 'And you could kill two birds with one stone. Be there for your – um – soul band, and see the cancan troupe in action?'

'I'd like to see the dancers before that if possible,' Freddo said, leafing through a diary that seemed to be filled with Post-it notes and bits of torn envelopes. 'Do they have a rehearsal night?'

'Tuesdays,' Joss said, knowing how much she'd always envied Val darting off to dance the cancan on Tuesday evenings. 'About seven thirty. In Hazy Hassocks village hall.'

'Tuesday it is, then.' Freddo scribbled something on yet another Post-it note. 'And you'll be there, will you?'

Joss shook her head. 'Oh, no – I'm not really anything to do with them.'

'I'd really like it if you could be there,' Freddo said. 'It'd give you some idea of what I do when I'm looking for acts, and you'd be a sort of intermediary – knowing me and knowing this Topsy bird too. Do you think that's a possible?'

Why not? Well – because Marvin would forbid it for a start.

Joss nodded. 'More than that. It's a definite.'

'See! You're already getting the lingo! And you'll let them know I'll be coming along, will you?'

'Yes, of course. Although I can't guarantee—'

'There's no guarantees in this business – that's something you'll find out soon enough.' Freddo beamed at her. 'It's what makes it so unpredictable – so exciting.'

And Joss beamed back at him.

She was still beaming when she arrived home at The Close.

'Marvin?' she called through the dinette. 'Marvin? Are you there? I've got some wonderful news ...'

Well, she thought, shedding her shoes, handbag and jacket, it was wonderful to her. And even if Marvin had become sniffy over her wanting to work at Big Sava, surely he couldn't object to her working in an office, could he? He couldn't find any reason to denigrate her ancient skills now, could he? Not when she told him they were exactly what Freddo needed and she'd be working in a proper secretarial environment, for a very good salary. It might even spur him on to look for another post himself.

'Marvin?'

The bungalow was empty. The television was silent. The lunch things were still on the table. Where on earth had Marvin gone? He hadn't left the bungalow for – well, since he'd been made redundant.

As she'd floated into the bungalow on a high, Joss now couldn't remember if Marvin's car had been on the drive or not. She peered out of the window – and felt the first twinge of unease.

Marvin's car had gone.

Oh, God. While she'd been laughing and dunking biscuits with Freddo, Marvin had finally snapped. The depression had taken over. He'd driven off – too fast – and . . .

Whoa! Joss tried to rein in her imagination. Maybe he'd simply decided that enough wallowing was enough and he should do as she was doing, and get on his bike – metaphorically, of course.

Going through the mechanics of clearing the kitchen, Joss's earlier euphoria had now all-but evaporated. Of course there was bound to be a simple explanation – but what if Marvin really had driven off in a tearing temper, driven to despair by her sudden new-found confidence, by her new self-assurance? Maybe she hadn't shown him enough sympathy? Enough understanding? How could she understand what the loss of his job had meant to him? She, who'd – as Marvin so often reminded her – simply been a parasite all her married life.

No! She slammed the last plate into the cupboard. She'd been a good wife, mother and homemaker. She'd put up with being put down at every opportunity for years. She'd believed everything Marvin had thrown at her for far too long. Other less loyal or committed women would have left him or at least stood up to him, if they hadn't attempted to murder him, wouldn't they?

Damn it! Joss took a deep breath. She would *not*, under any circumstances, dissolve once more into a wee, timorous, cowering beastie . . .

Wishing, as always, that Val was at home next door so that she could share both the amazing events at Retro Music and Theatre and her concerns over Marvin, she paced restlessly round the bungalow, picking things up and putting them down again, flicking at non-existent dust, straightening already regimented curtains. How awful would it be if Marvin had done something stupid?

Whatever she felt – or didn't – for him, she'd never

226

wanted him dead. But, on the other hand, if Marvin had simply decided to leave her, leave the bungalow, start afresh alone – what would she feel about that?

Shockingly, she realised she really wouldn't mind at all. In fact it would be a lovely satisfying conclusion to the awful sterility of their relationship. It would probably mean the bungalow would have to be sold, and she'd have to rent somewhere – but she could cope with that, couldn't she? It was far easier, she decided, to concentrate on imagining herself being a divorcee, living in a small flat and queuing at the launderette, than as a widow planning Marvin's funeral.

Oh, where the hell was he? And why had he chosen now to disappear – now, when she'd been on top of the world. Typical of Marvin, he'd yet again managed to ruin her happiness – without even trying.

She really should try to ring round and track him down. She knew from watching police dramas on the television that vital hours were always lost by victims' nearest and dearest because they'd always assumed the missing person wasn't one at all until it was too late.

Of course, previously she'd always been able to contact Marvin on his mobile but, as this had been a perk of the job, it had been left at the office with the rest of his life. Joss stared at the phone in the hall, wishing she knew where to start. Would he have gone to see Simon? Perhaps to take up his old golfing skills? Or any of his other friends – their dinner party circle? The ones who Marvin had said would never want to socialise with him again? Or the children? Could he possibly have decided to bare his soul to Ossie and Tilly?

Wherever he was, she was pretty sure he'd be spitting angry that she was trying to find him, but she'd live with that. Taking a deep breath, and with the phone in one hand and their address book in the other, she started her search.

Half an hour later, having drawn a blank and exhausted all possibilities, Joss wandered into the kitchen and switched on the kettle. She wasn't really sure why. She didn't want a drink – but neither did she know what else to do. Marvin's so-called friends hadn't been much help, merely saying they hadn't seen him or heard from him, and seemed pretty off-hand – most of them suggesting he'd simply gone on a job-search and not to worry.

Worrying, Joss took the tea into the garden: the pristine patio leading to a neat oblong of lawn, pollarded rose bushes at each corner, a tub of pansies in the middle – neat and unexciting. The afternoon was turning into a sun-washed evening, the shadows of the bungalows looking like slumbering elephants on the lawn.

She didn't want to stray too far from the bungalow in case the children phoned back. She'd left messages on their answerphones. Casting a hopeful look next door in case Val had come home early – they'd gone for tea, which really meant supper Joss guessed, with their eldest daughter and family in Hazy Hassocks – but which was unlikely, because Valerie and her husband usually ended their soirées in the Barmy Cow, Joss sipped her tea and the worry deepened into quiet panic.

When the phone rang, she spilled the tea dregs over her hands and down her skirt in her haste to answer it.

'Mother?' Tilly's voice sounded disbelieving. 'Are you okay?'

'Fine – well, no I'm not. As I said, I'm worried about your father.'

'How long's he been gone?'

'Well, I went for a job interview at just after one—'

'You did what?' Tilly laughed. 'You? A job? Why?'

'It doesn't matter,' Joss snapped irritably. 'That's not important now – and anyway, I got it and when I came back here your father had gone. And he hasn't left the house since—'

'You've got a job?' Tilly sounded totally incredulous. 'You? What sort of job?'

'Secretarial. Look, Tilly, this isn't important—' Well, it

228

was of course, but not right now. 'What's important is that I'm worried about him. If he turns up at yours or rings you, you'll let me know won't you?'

'Yes, of course, but—' Tilly sounded as though she might be laughing, '—how can you possibly have got a secretarial job? You're not qualified—'

'I'm perfectly qualified for the job in question. I think your father might have become depressed because I was looking for work and he felt he was losing his authority and—'

'Dad'll be okay,' Tilly said. 'Ossie and I understand these things better than you do. If he's gone out, it's probably to network and get himself back into the melting pot. He probably felt the time was right.'

'But why didn't he tell me? Leave a note?'

'Mother ...' Tilly was reproving, 'Think about this. Why would he leave you a note? There's nothing to worry about. He simply needed time to come to terms with the situation and plan his future. I expect that's what he's been doing.'

What he's been doing, Joss thought wearily, has been making my life hell and watching daytime television, but she didn't say so. 'So you don't think I should ring the police or the hospitals?'

'Not unless you want to be a laughing stock – and make dad mad as hell when he comes back, no. He's only been gone for a few hours. He'll be back for supper, you'll see.'

And Tilly hung up. Then the phone rang again and this time it was Ossie who said practically the same thing, word for word.

Joss, who still felt she should report Marvin as a missing person, restlessly watched some television, prepared beans on toast for supper, phoned an irritatingly garrulous Topsy to arrange the meeting with Freddo for the following Tuesday, and was still staring out of the window waiting for Marvin's car to swing into the drive at eleven o'clock.

'Oh, Marvin ...' Joss said wearily to herself, sitting at

her dressing table removing her make-up and brushing her hair. 'Where the hell are you? Why have you done this to me today? I don't want anything to have happened to you – and I'll never forgive myself if you're – well, if you don't come back ... and I have to live the rest of my life knowing that the last words we ever exchanged were angry ones.'

Sighing, she walked into the still-gloriously-essence-perfumed bathroom to clean her teeth.

There was something wrong here, surely? Living as she had, with the bungalow's almost-austere neatness for so long, even something slightly a millimetre out of place jarred on her subconscious. What was it? The bath was clean, the towels neat on the rails, the cabinet doors closed. Frowning, Joss squeezed toothpaste on to her brush and started the mechanics of brushing on autopilot – then stopped.

The three little gemstone-stoppered bottles on the window sill hadn't been there before.

With a foaming mouth, she stared at them. When she'd had her aromatherapy bath she'd replaced them, hadn't she? In her bathrobe pocket? Knowing that they meant she could return to the woodland pool fantasy any time she wanted? She knew she wasn't having a senior moment – she remembered exactly what she'd done.

Which could only mean that someone else had found them? Marvin? Surely not? But what other explanation was there?

Marvin had been infuriated and intrigued about her mid-day bath, hadn't he? Annoyed that she was doing something so out of routine? Cross that she wouldn't tell him what she was doing and why? He must have waited until she left for Winterbrook, then searched everywhere for – what? Some evidence that she was up to no good?

Joss groaned, seeing it all in her head.

And he'd have picked up her discarded bathrobe in the bedroom and the bottles would have rattled together in the

230

pocket, wouldn't they? And he'd have taken them out and looked at them – and been angry because he didn't hold with all that frothy nonsense and he'd thought she'd been wasting money on frivolities ...

Yes, Joss, nodded, she could definitely see him doing that.

And now the bottles sat there in a neat row, as if to accuse her.

Oh, God! Could it even be that Marvin had thought the mid-day bath was for the benefit of another man? Could he – horror of horrors – suspect her of having an affair?

Joss groaned.

It seemed unlikely, given Marvin's constant dismissal of her feminine charms, but as he'd deliberately placed the bottles in such a prominent display, surely there had to be some connection between them and his sudden disappearance? So, what if he'd decided to sniff them? And not knowing what they were, assumed they were some exotic seductive scent for – what? The benefit of a lover?

Did Marvin really suspect her of having another man?

Joss spat out her toothpaste. The whole notion was ludicrous – but Marvin certainly wouldn't have bathed using the essences, would he? No – that would be madness. So, he must have simply sniffed the heady, rich fragrances and then decided that Joss, whose life-long scent of choice was safe and conservative, was being unfaithful, mustn't he?

'Oh, Marvin!' Joss sighed. 'You complete prat!'

So, had he left her because he thought she was committing adultery? Oh, God! And if so – Joss hurried into the bedroom and yanked open the wardrobe's Ikea doors.

'Hell!'

Marvin's side of the wardrobe, where she'd hung and folded his clothes in order and colour coded for years and years, and could do it in her sleep, had several telling gaps.

'Buggering hell!' Joss kicked the wardrobe door. 'Marvin! You stupid, stupid, sod!'

# Chapter Twenty-One

'They're really doing well,' Jennifer Blessing said, smiling maternally at the two Kylies who were carrying out a double-handed nail extension. 'And with you flat-out too, my little empire is flourishing wonderfully. I don't know about you, Sukie, but I think this is going to be one of our best years ever.'

Sukie, trying to escape from Beauty's Blessings with a fresh supply of robes and towels and the next week's massage appointments, nodded. Businesswise, yes, she'd agree wholeheartedly; for her, on the personal front however, it seemed as fraught with pitfalls and heartache as any other year. But she wasn't going to admit it.

'It's all going very well, yes,' she said, trying to edge her way through the door. 'Sorry, Jennifer, must dash – I've got several bookings today, and other stuff to sort out as well and I'm running late. Bye!'

Bundling the towels and robes into the back of her car, Sukie headed off on foot a few yards along Hazy Hassocks High Street to Big Sava. Having dined on an omelette of leftover cheese and a couple of eggs that were probably past their sell-by date the night before, she desperately needed to replenish the freezer with a pile of pierce-and-pings.

April had continued to be a summer rehearsal, and Big Sava was cashing in on the sunshine dreams by displaying pyramids of suntan lotion, sunglasses, and picnic fare. The tannoy blasted with 'Summer Holiday' and 'In the

Summertime'. Sukie, heaping far more than she'd intended into her trolley, almost expected to see the staff divested of their orange tabards and wearing bikinis.

'Sukes!' Chelsea waved from behind her checkout as Sukie emerged from the final aisle. 'Over here!'

Weaving in and out of several chattering groups of women in cardigans and crossover sandals, and elderly people with cheap gin and fish fingers in their baskets, Sukie just beat a man in an expensive suit with two bottles of water and some dried figs to pole position.

'Well,' Chelsea said, whizzing Sukie's month's supply of low-fat, additive-rich, ready meals through the scanner, 'your mumbo jumbo earth magic was a big dud, wasn't it? Not a bloody sniff of Nicky Hambly. Not,' she wrestled with the bar-code on something pseudo-Indonesian, 'that I expected there to be. D'you know I even looked him up on Friends Reunited just to give your stuff a bit of a leg-up, but he wasn't even registered on there. So?'

'So? So what?' Sukie packed her bright orange Big Sava carriers.

The expensive suit, presumably wishing he'd gone to Waitrose as usual, rattled his figs and water together impatiently.

'So what happens now with your plot to get your claws into the delicious Derry? As the magic rubbish is clearly all a big waste of time, you won't be bothering to try and love potion Milla and Bo-Bo back together now, will you?'

'Don't make it sound so calculated.' Sukie frowned. 'I wasn't ever going to try and magic – as you call it – Derry away from Milla. You know that. I only had her best interests at heart.'

'Pshaw!' Chelsea snorted. 'Pull the other one, Sukes. Face it, Derry and Milla will stay together and you'll just have to join the rest of us – single, rushing towards thirty, always destined to be on other people's hen-nights, guests at other people's weddings . . .'

The expensive suit was getting increasingly restive.

'Thanks for making my future sound so irresistible.' Sukie shoved her credit card into the machine and punched in her pin number. 'And anyway, Nicky Hambly might turn up at any time – no one said the distance potion worked instantly.'

Chelsea handed over the receipt, shaking her head. 'Sorry, Sukes – but the whole thing was madness. I never bought all that guff you gave me about Cora's garden being magical anyway. Nice try. See you tomorrow night, then?'

'Cancan rehearsals?' Sukie hefted the last of her carrier bags into her trolley. 'Yes – I'll pick you up as usual. Oh, have you heard from Topsy? About that agent coming to watch us?'

'Yeah – she's rung everyone. Sounds exciting, doesn't it? If he likes us we could get loads of bookings – and we might even get paid for dancing. Imagine that. The extra money will certainly come in handy, won't it? And wasn't it all something to do with that article that Joss Benson wrote?'

'So Topsy said. Do you reckon we'll have to be in full costume?'

'Ooh, I hadn't thought of that. Yes, probably.' Chelsea leaned her elbows chummily on the conveyor belt. 'Mind you—'

The expensive suit screamed and hurled his water and figs on the floor.

'Mrs Allsop!' Chelsea yelled, pushing her alarm button and waving her hand in the air. 'Mrs Allsop! Supervisor needed! Security alert! Code B! Checkout 12!'

Marvin had now been missing from home for a week. Joss, alternating between panic, despair, and occasional guilty joy at the bungalow being a Marvin-free zone, had ignored her children's advice and reported him missing to the police and also left his details with various hospitals. The latter had drawn a fortunate blank, and the former had gently explained to Joss that Marvin leaving home unexpectedly, but without violence and with a packed bag, was very sad but not criminal and that he couldn't be registered as a missing person.

One of the plusses had been that, without Marvin in situ, Valerie Pridmore had been able to call at the bungalow at any time, and had done, night or day, whenever Joss had needed her most. In fact, Joss wasn't sure if she'd have coped at all without Val. Val had been kind and supportive and after her initial amusement at Marvin's defection, had clearly realised how shattered and confused Joss really was and couldn't have been a better friend.

After promising not to breathe a word to anyone she'd helped Joss search for Marvin, taken over some of the daily round of phone calls, had arrived bearing fabulous comforting, carb-filled things which Marvin would have forbidden – like fish and chips and fresh cream cakes – and listened. Oh, bless her, Joss thought, how she'd listened. All through it, Val had remained cheerful and upbeat.

'Why doesn't he just get in touch?' Joss had asked for the millionth time. 'Just to let me know he's all right. Just so I can tell him that I'm not having an affair. Why doesn't he tell me where he is?'

And every time Val had patted her hand and said that he'd be back, or he'd ring, but for someone as, well, powerfully controlling as Marvin had been, the loss of his job must have caused all sorts of problems; problems which had been building up over the last few weeks – and he probably just needed some time to get his head together. Joss would just have to be patient.

And as for Joss's wild conspiracy theory that Marvin had gone because he thought she was fooling around – Valerie had laughed kindly and said that was all nonsense. Marvin had simply gone off 'to find hisself'. Joss would just have to give him time. It'd all be all right in the end, she'd see.

And if Val really thought that Marvin buggering off was the best-ever thing that could happen to Joss – especially now that she'd found herself a lovely little job – she'd wisely said nothing.

Now Joss thought, walking slowly back from Coddles Post Office Stores in the sunshine, she was becoming surprisingly used to her solo life. She missed the presence of another living thing in the bungalow, but she didn't miss the nagging and the censure, or the rigid precision of her previous life. She actually didn't miss Marvin very much at all. And she'd turned relatively easily into a bit of a slob. Of course, it would all change when Marvin came back, but in the meantime, in the moments when she could convince herself that Marvin was still alive and well, she was rather enjoying the restfulness.

She'd phoned Freddo as soon as Topsy had confirmed that he'd be more than welcome at the cancan rehearsal, but had said nothing about her change in circumstances. One, she really didn't know him well enough; two, he probably wouldn't be interested; three, she wanted no one at all to know about Marvin's disappearance; and four, he might even decide to withdraw the job offer if he thought Joss was embroiled in some major domestic upheaval.

So, tomorrow evening, she'd meet up with Freddo at Hazy Hassocks village hall and pretend all was well, and tomorrow, maybe, Marvin might be home.

It really was a glorious morning, Joss thought, taking the long way home to The Close because she had nothing better to do and because Marvin never liked to walk through Bagley in case he had to speak to someone he considered beneath him. Lovely and warm, without a breath of wind, the air filled with birdsong, and blossoms fluttering against the blue of the sky, petals gently swirling around her as she wandered, like pastel confetti.

The lanes, overhung with willow trees heavy with catkins, were almost waist-high with sweet nettles and celandines and daisies, and the cottage gardens were exploding into their springtime best. She wondered if, when

236

Marvin came back, she might suggest they make pretty borders in the front garden of the bungalow, too. It would give such a lift to the spirits to look out each morning on such a riot of colour.

'Joss! Mrs Benson! How are you?'

Joss, startled, peered across the lane. 'Sorry? Oh, Sukie – hello. I didn't realise I'd drifted so far off course.'

Sukie, who seemed to be removing a year's worth of groceries from the boot of her car, straightened up. 'I thought you might be coming to see me. To book another massage?'

'No, I'm afraid not . . .' Joss shook her head, drinking in the tumbled rainbow of Pixies Laughter's traditional cottage garden. 'Sorry – just out on a bit of a constitutional. I've been to Coddles – and it was such a lovely morning, I thought I'd stroll round the village.'

'It is gorgeous, isn't it? I really should have phoned you to find out how your meeting went. Did the essences help?'

Not wanting to say either that the oils had produced a woodland fantasy in the bathroom in case Sukie thought she was insane, and especially not what havoc the essences had wreaked so soon afterwards in her private life, Joss simply nodded. 'Wonderfully, Sukie, thank you so much. I'd really meant to come and say thank you earlier – I-I coped really well – and I got a job.'

'Really?' Sukie grinned. 'Fantastic. With the bloke who wanted to see you? How amazing. Well done.'

Joss continued smiling and explained briefly about Freddo and Retro Music and Theatre and that he was the agent who would be coming to size up the cancanners the following evening. And they both laughed and said 'small world' and laughed again.

'I'm really glad the essences were what you needed and worked so well,' Sukie said, closing her boot lid. 'I did worry a bit afterwards, because although I knew you'd memorised the quantities to use in the bath, I really should have warned you never to use them undiluted. They're very

237

– um – powerful. And sniffing them isn't to be recommended either.'

'Sniffing them? Why on earth not? They were gorgeous ... the scent stayed in the bathroom for days.'

'Oh, yes, diluted they're fine.' Sukie said. 'I just meant to tell you not to open the bottles and inhale them neat.'

'Inhale them?' Joss suddenly felt slightly queasy. 'Straight from the bottles? Why not?'

'Well, as long as you didn't, and don't in the future, that's fine.' Sukie smiled happily. 'It's just that they're very strong, natural extracts. And, as everyone knows, anything inhaled is immediately absorbed straight into the bloodstream. The effect of sniffing the scents from the bottles would be about three trillion times as powerful as anything mixed with gallons of bath water.'

'You mean they're *dangerous*?'

'No, of course not! They certainly wouldn't kill you—' Sukie laughed, picking up her Big Sava carrier bags, '—this is aromatherapy we're talking about – one of the safest, gentlest, most natural therapies around. But that particular combination can have a slightly heady effect even when diluted – neat they'd probably work like some sort of fragrant tipsiness. I'd have hated for you to be too spaced out to even get to Winterbrook. Anyway, it all worked out for the best, didn't it? Ah, well, enjoy your walk – I'd better get this lot into the freezer before it all melts. I'll see you – and your new boss – tomorrow evening. Bye.'

'What? Oh, yes ... Bye Sukie ...'

Joss didn't move. She suddenly suspected that *sniffing* the essences was exactly what Marvin had done. Of course, in his usual nosy way, he'd found the bottles and because he could never, ever leave anything alone, he'd unstoppered them, hadn't he? And inhaled them? And vanished ...

This put a whole new bizarre slant on things. Knowing how vividly real her own fantasy had been, Joss could only imagine what a good whiff of the neat essences had done to

238

Marvin. Oh, sweet heavens above! She almost dropped her shopping basket as the realisation kicked in.

What if he hadn't gone off in a temper because he thought Joss was drenching herself in scent for a lover? What if he'd had an even stronger reaction to Sukie's potions and gone off on some happy hippy trip – high as a kite – experiencing – what? God alone knew! What if under the influence of mind-altering substances, he'd simply thrown some things in a bag, and driven off.

Joss swallowed. Jesus Christ! What on earth was she going to tell the children?

By the time she'd unpacked the groceries, Sukie had convinced herself that there was absolutely no need to have told Joss about the rhyme that went with her calming empowerment bath oils. No need at all. No harm done. And Joss hadn't used them undiluted, and clearly hadn't suffered any sort of ill-effects – she'd have said so, wouldn't she? And as for the other bit of the verse – the bit that could have caused all manner of problems – well, it would be all round the village by now if that had worked, wouldn't it?

Maybe Cora's poem was wrong on this one; maybe wish-fulfillment and love potions simply didn't function together. Unless, of course, Joss had fallen head-over-heels with the abysmal Marvin all over again after her bath? Nah! Not possible . . .

It had probably been a bad idea to make the hawthorn substitution though, given the mind-expanding effect of the perfumes when combined with jasmine and lavender – and not a mistake she'd make in future.

Hmmm, Sukie thought as she slammed the freezer door shut, that could have been a very close call. It would only take one of her mixtures to go wrong for her to have to stop using the garden's plentiful storehouse, which would be an awful shame when everything was going so well, and, worse still, it would have put paid to her ongoing plans for reuniting Milla and Bo-Bo. She hadn't given up on the long distance love spell, despite Chelsea's scepticism; it may not have brought Nicky Hambly slavering to his knees in Big Sava – yet – but there was still time.

Anyway, Sukie smiled happily to herself as she wandered out into the sunlit garden, at least Cora's empowerment essence recipe had worked spectacularly well on Joss, hadn't it, with no disasters? Convinced as she was of the powerful earth magic contained in the cottage's bounty, Joss's stonking success still came as something of a surprise. It gave her quite a glow to think that something she'd concocted had given poor downtrodden Joss enough confidence to find a job – and a really interesting one at that.

Sukie, ducking beneath the arches of burgeoning honeysuckle and budding rambling roses, wondered idly what the appalling Marvin had had to say about Joss's job. She hoped he'd been lovely to Joss and congratulated her both on her new-found confidence and career and taken her out for a slap-up meal to celebrate. Sadly, somehow she doubted it. If she was in Joss's position she'd leave Marvin like a shot. Why on earth did she stay with him? Still, hopefully, the new job would give her a real chance of happiness at last. Joss was such a lovely person, she really deserved something nice to happen in her life.

Pixies Laughter's garden, abundantly overgrown and lush, smelled delightful. Sukie, now able to recognise most of the plants she needed to restock her essence cupboard, quickly forgot about Joss Benson's marital misery as she happily gathered jasmine and buttercups and daises and clover and nettles in the sun.

'Very rustic,' Derry laughed from the garden gate. 'No – don't let me stop you.'

'Blimey!' Sukie straightened up, squinting at him over her armful of plants in the sun. 'You made me jump! Er – Milla's at work – she went in early this morning.'

'I know.' He opened the flaking, creaky gate. 'I've just

been to price up a job a couple of streets away and thought I'd stop by and see if you were in – and if there was any chance of a cup of tea.'

'No chance at all,' Sukie said lightly, hiding her delight and confusion behind a clump of sweet nettles and wild parsley. 'I'm far too busy. Didn't your customer provide one? I thought it was *de rigueur*.'

Derry shook his head. 'Not even as much as a sniff of a tea bag.'

'Tough.' Sukie grinned. 'And if you want a cup of tea here you'll have to earn it. Do you reckon you can put your nan's passed-on expertise to work and tell me where in this lot I'm likely to find chickweed? I think I've got everything else – but I still need chickweed flowers for a new potion.'

'Can we come to some sort of arrangement, then?' Derry asked. 'As I'm just about to die of dehydration I'll go and make tea for both of us, then I'll turn detective. Okay?'

'Okay.'

Sukie watched him walk into the cottage, all faded denim and male beauty, the Spring sunshine spiralling from his blond hair, and exhaled. God – he was sooo gorgeous. And friendly. And why wouldn't he be? After all, he had no idea at all how she felt about him, had he? Thank goodness.

She dumped the armfuls of culled plants into a selection of Cora's ancient trugs by the back door, and stretched. Okay, so Chelsea was probably right, there was something slightly immoral about using the distance love elixir on Milla, but she was still going to do it. Or was she? Oh, damn it – what if Derry really did love Milla? What if reuniting Milla and Bo-Bo broke his heart? Could she live with herself having made him unhappy?

No, she couldn't and wouldn't. Ooooh – bugger!

'Tea, in a pot because it tastes better, milk, sugar, two cups, no saucers or biscuits that I could find ...' Derry appeared in the doorway with a tray. 'And, if you promise not to punch me, chickweed is that ground-hugging stuff

241

which is covering most of the border over there – the one with the little white flowers.'

'Is it? Really? But you could have said that straight away, couldn't you?'

'I could—' Derry set the tray down on a rickety wicker table under the tumbling rose arch and sat gingerly on an equally rickety wicker chair, '—but then you'd have said thanks and goodbye and I wouldn't have got tea, would I?'

'Definitely not.' Sukie smiled, bending down and tugging up armfuls of what she'd always called sweethearts. 'But you might still get a punch for your brass neck.'

They grinned at one another.

'Goodness – this stuff clings, doesn't it? Right, that's got it – I think.' Sukie despatched the sticky mass of chickweed on top of the other plants by the back door and joined Derry at the table. He'd poured the tea. 'Cheers – and thanks. Oh, this is great.'

'The tea, the weather, the garden or the company?'

She met his blue eyes over the rim of her cup, her stomach suddenly dissolving with a delicious mixture of lust and love. 'All of them.'

'Right answer.' Derry smiled at her. 'And do I gather from this – um – harvest, that the home-made potions are still doing the business?'

Relieved to move away from anything personal, Sukie nodded and told him she may need to pick his brains about becoming self-employed before too long, and also about Joss Benson's amazing experience after the empowerment bath.

'So that one wasn't a love potion as such?' Derry asked. 'We didn't find anything in those cross-stitches other than matchmaking stuff, did we? Or was this one you discovered later?'

'Yes, and – well, it did have a bit of the sting in the tail, actually. The blend of essences was exactly what Joss needed for her meeting, but there was a rhyme that went with it – and I was rather worried that it might have caused a few – um – problems, but she didn't say anything.'

'Go on then. What did this mixture promise?'

'Oh, lord,' Sukie stared into her tea, 'are you sure you want to hear this? Okay ...'

*Bathe in jasmine and lavender sweet*
*And love and power will always meet*
*Close your eyes and dream your dream*
*And float away on fragrant steam*
*Everything you wish will be*
*Granted for all eternity.*
 *But mix with hawthorn's sharp desire*
*And lust will rage with burning fire*
*Driving false love from your life*
*Bringing true love to end your strife*

'Not the catchiest thing I've ever heard – but pretty blatant.' Derry grinned. 'And the first bit worked – but not the second? This Mrs Benson didn't leave her husband and take up with the milkman who she'd loved in secret for years, straight from the tub so to speak?'

'No, thank goodness.' Sukie shuddered. 'Hopefully Cora got that last bit very wrong. Poor old Joss has got enough problems with her gruesome husband – although she should leave him in my opinion, but because she wants to, not simply because of the aromatherapy.'

Derry finished his tea and laughed. 'Pretty horny this older generation, weren't they? This village must have been a hotbed of swappers and swingers a couple of generations ago thanks to your great-auntie Cora.'

Sukie giggled. 'Yeah, it makes it seem rather dull now – oh ...'

Derry leaned across the table towards her. 'Sorry – hold still. You've got some chickweed stuck to your jumper. There ...'

Neither of them moved. Neither of them spoke. The

hazily warm garden, sweet-smelling and silent, seemed to enclose them in a magical suspended world. Sukie could hear the thundering of her heart, could see faint freckles smudged across the bridge of Derry's nose and the blond flecks in his long dark lashes, could smell the warm, clean male scent of him.

'Sukie . . . I know—'

'Cooo-eee! Anyone at home?'

They sprang apart as two elderly ladies shuffled in through the garden gate.

'Not too early are we, dear? For our foot rub? Only the ring-a-ride minibus picked us up sooner than we'd expected. Oooh – lovely! Tea! Come on Elsie – get a shift on. Bring yer bunions to the table and grab a cuppa.'

'Er – I'd better be leaving.' Derry stood up, his shoulders shaking with imploding laughter. 'Excuse me, ladies. And Sukie, I'll see you – well, I'll see you.'

'Yes, yes – you will . . .' Sukie said quickly. 'And – um – thanks for the chickweed.'

'My pleasure,' Derry grinned, heading for the gate. 'Enjoy the bunions.'

# Chapter Twenty-Two

Hazy Hassocks village hall was heaving.

'Flip me.' Chelsea gazed around in disbelief. 'Are we on telly?'

'Not television, no—' Topsy, in her best long grey dress and best brown and cream paisley scarf, with her best Alice band scraping her grey hair back from her wizened face, tippy-tapped towards them, '—but there's someone from the local radio here and a reporter from the *Winterbrook Advertiser*.'

'Er – why?' Sukie peered at the noisy throng. 'Have I missed something?'

'It's all to do with Mrs Benson bringing that impresario tonight.' Topsy gave a little on-the-spot pirouette. 'That and the auditions.'

'Well, yes I knew about that – but this is a bit over the top. Have we had loads of applications for Val's place, then?'

'Four,' Topsy waved her hands theatrically, 'but you know what the villages are like – they've brought all their friends and family for support. Quite a nice little crowd, as you see.'

Sukie could see only too well. It was the usual rural turnout for anything free – especially for amateur entertainment, which may well end in the amusing humiliation of the participants. A twenty-first century version of lions and Christians but without quite so much blood.

'We're not doing a dress rehearsal, are we?' Sukie asked while Chelsea skipped off to join Roo, Betty and Trace on the stage. 'I meant to check with you—'

'No,' Topsy shook her head. 'Dorchester and I thought that would be a little intimidating for the new gels.'

*Dorchester and I?* Sukie squinted round the dimly-lit hall – ah, yes, there he was. Holding court in a corner, looking proud as punch in plum velvet and tweed and a Noel Coward cravat.

'Don't you look like that, young Sukie.' Topsy's eyes flashed. 'You and I are the only ones in this room who know the truth about me and Dorchester. Everyone else thinks it's a sweet romance of the third age and we've been biding our time to share our pensions in our twilight years or some such nonsense. You and me both know it was instant and magic and down to the violas, don't we?'

Sukie stared at the dusty floor. 'Yes, well, maybe – but you're happy, aren't you?'

'Happier than I've been for decades.' Topsy's beady eyes twinkled. 'You were very naughty to use one of Cora's potions on me – and to lie about it, saying it were synthetic – but I'm so glad you did.'

Sukie smiled. 'So am I, then. Delighted. Hilton said Dorchester had bought you a boxed set of *Dr Kildare*.'

'He's done more than that.' Topsy's feet *plie*'d merrily. 'He's introduced me to the internet cafe in Winterbrook. He's bought me my very own stethoscope and blood-pressure monitor off e-Bay.'

And greater love hath no man, Sukie said to herself, as Topsy sashayed away to meet and greet, humming the theme tune to *Casualty*.

Among the crowd she could see Valerie Pridmore and her entire extended family, as well as several of her massage clients all holding hands with what looked like newish partners. Oh, and there were Rita and Edie from the card school accompanied by Savoy and Claridge –

presumably poor old Hilton was holding a lone fort at the Barmy Cow again. Tom and Ken certainly looked cosy. Sukie wondered how Cora would have felt about her potions being used to bring out the best in elderly closet gays. She'd have probably been pleased – after all, she'd only wanted everyone's happiness, hadn't she? Oh, and Bert seemed to have found someone too – a stout lady with lilac curls and a sparkly caftan – and was steering her round the throng, making introductions.

Sukie sighed to herself. All in all, the Pixies Laughter potions had worked well – hadn't they? Even if some of the pairings had been a bit doubtful at first. She'd done Cora proud in keeping up the family traditions with no harm caused. And she still had great hopes for the distance potion working for Chelsea – even though she'd decided she couldn't now, in all fairness, use it on Milla. She couldn't break Derry's heart – not even to mend her own.

In The Close, Joss, watching from the dinette window, was as skittery as a kitten. Marvin was still missing, and her new information – that he was possibly suffering from some sort of mental delusion – had not made much impression on the police who'd perked up a bit when they thought they might be on the trail of a drugs baron, but had immediately lost interest when she'd mentioned aromatherapy. The hospitals had assured her again that no one fitting Marvin's description had been treated for anything – especially a fragrance-overdose.

She still hadn't told the children.

Tonight she'd have to put Marvin and his mind-blowing on the back burner, she knew that. Tonight, she'd have to be cool and competent and convince Freddo that he'd picked the right woman for the job. It would be difficult when she was still in a turmoil over her marriage, but when Marvin came back she'd still need to be the breadwinner, wouldn't she? She couldn't possibly let everyone down now.

And, Joss paced the bungalow, she'd had another wood-land bath – to give her the resolve and calm she needed for this evening – and it had been wonderful. Just as magical as the previous one, but not so much of a shock – and, right now, swathed in a fragrant mist of jasmine and lavender, she realised while she should be worrying about Marvin, she simply couldn't wait to get started with her new job – she was even looking forward to seeing Freddo again.

It was all very odd.

Freddo had phoned and said that unless she and Marvin were planning to go to the rehearsals together, he'd be delighted to collect her from The Close if that wouldn't cause any trouble. And Joss had said – truthfully – that Marvin was away from home – so yes, thank you, she'd love Freddo to pick her up.

Now, knowing that he must be on his way, she felt giddy with anticipation like a teenager waiting for her first date.

Valerie Pridmore, who was going to be at Hazy Hassocks village hall like almost everyone else in Bagley-cum-Russet, had been really miffed that she'd miss the collection bit.

'I'd like to give him the once-over,' she'd said, 'just to make sure he looks okay. You're such an innocent, Joss, you really shouldn't go off with strange men in cars.'

And Joss had laughed and said Val sounded like her mother, and that there was nothing remotely strange about Freddo Fabian.

Actually, she thought now, that wasn't really true, was it? Oh, she had absolutely no doubts about Freddo's decency and honesty – but his appearance was sure to raise more than a few eyebrows – probably even Val's.

Joss giggled to herself at the thought, tried to stop, and couldn't. Oh, how wicked she was! Giggling when poor Marvin could be living in a cardboard box or in a hostel for the terminally confused – or anywhere . . .

She hadn't mentioned the aromatherapy bit to Val either – just in case she laughed. Joss couldn't bear the thought of anyone laughing at Marvin. Not now. Poor Marvin – he'd truly been his own worst enemy – and the cause of his own downfall – and she was becoming scarily used to life without him. Since he'd been gone she'd got into the habit of eating cosy nursery meals in front of the television, and had discovered soaps and makeover programmes and comedy shows which in their previous life would have sent Marvin into purple-faced vein-throbbing mode.

And she'd made a bit of a sea-change in her wardrobe, too. Not wanting to touch their bank account because money was even more of an issue than ever and Marvin had always held the purse-strings, Joss had taken several of her more boring cream, beige and taupe outfits to an animal charity shop run by Biff and Hedley Pippin in Winterbrook, and had rather surprised herself by haggling a little for a few replacement items.

She'd emerged with several gypsy skirts which according to Biff were so last year, a couple of almost-new brightly coloured Marks and Spencer tops, a floppy bo-ho shoulder bag and a pair of sequinned sandals – all for practically peanuts.

Tonight, sporting this new look, and with her short fair hair more ruffled than groomed, Joss secretly thought she looked a good twenty years younger. It would all change when Marvin came home, of course, because he'd have a spluttering buggering fit, but for tonight's showbiz venue the outfit seemed absolutely perfect.

Oh, goodness! Joss's heart nearly stopped beating. She could hear a car turning into the drive. In a moment of mental infidelity she prayed and prayed that it wasn't a homeward-bound Marvin. Not tonight. She really wasn't ready for him to return tonight.

With crossed fingers and holding her breath, she peeped round the Ikea curtains and laughed out loud.

A vast, pink and chromium Cadillac convertible was purring on the drive.

Freddo, golden hair flowing, bracelets blinging, a white

shirt over black trousers, leapt out of the car and almost collided with her as she hurled herself out of the front door.

'Sorry, Joss, duck – not late am I? And – my word – you look wonderful. Wonderful. Like a princess. Stunning, duck. I'll be the proudest man in Hazy Hassocks tonight.'

'Thank you.' Joss was fairly sure that simply accepting a compliment was the thing to do. 'You look wonderful, too.'

Well, he did. Different – but wonderful. And that car . . .

'I'll hold the door open for you,' Freddo did so with a flourish, 'but if you just want to leap in to the passenger seat over the top, that's fine by me.'

Joss chuckled. 'No, I'll use the conventional route, thank you. I'll save the leaping for later.' She slid into the dark red leather seat. 'Oh, heavens – this is fabulous. Is it yours?'

Freddo nodded, jumping into the driving seat. 'A bit ostentatious some would say, and one heck of a gas-guzzler, but I love it. I bought it at auction after a boy band went bust and their management had to flog off everything right down to the paper-clips. Right – are we all set?'

Joss nodded, wondering if this was part of her fantasy too, wishing with all her heart that Val could see her now.

Freddo started the car and the feral roar convinced her that this was very, very real indeed.

'Your husband okay with this, is he?' Freddo asked as they left The Close. 'It hasn't caused any problems, I hope.'

'He's still away,' Joss said lightly, loving the warm evening breeze on her face, and the way her hair danced and her skirts billowed. 'But I'm sure he wouldn't mind at all.'

She'd have to come clean about Marvin's disappearance before long, she knew, but not tonight. Nothing was going to spoil tonight.

As the Cadillac swept across the Bagley and Russet intersection, past the Celtic cross and Coddles Stores, several children stood and stared and whooped and waved at them. Feeling as though life could, never, ever get any better than this, Joss smiled and laughed and waved back.

And she was still laughing as Freddo turned up the eight-track and they sang along to Sam and Dave's 'Soul Man', roaring through the Spring countryside towards Hazy Hassocks at dizzying speed.

Outside the village hall, Valerie Pridmore, having a crafty cigarette, was joined by Sukie who wasn't sneaking out for a smoke but who could no longer bear Topsy turning into Arlene Phillips.

'She's driving me mad,' Sukie said, leaning against the pebbledash with Val in the evening sun. 'Because the press are here she's making us do the most ridiculous moves. I hope she'll tone them down for the auditions otherwise she'll have the hopefuls in traction before the night's over. You're well out of this.'

'Tell me about it.' Val blew a plume of smoke into the gentle air. 'Knackering me leg was the best thing I've ever done. Topsy's got far more energy than's good for her at her age. She'll probably kill old Dorchester.'

'Yeah, but he'll die with a smile in his face, won't he?'

'He will that,' Val chuckled. 'Oh – blimey! Look at this!'

Sukie looked.

A long, low, bright pink American open-topped car was cruising into the car park, skittering gravel from beneath its tyres.

'Smart or what? Hell's teeth, Val! It's Joss.'

'Never?' Val choked on her cigarette. 'Never in this world? Oh – bloody hell! Yes, it is! That must belong to the agent bloke she's going to be working for ... Jesus! Lucky cow!'

Sukie laughed to herself. Well, well, well ... And surely the cheerful man behind the wheel, with his flowing yellow hair and tanned skin and air of celebrity, looked familiar.

251

Had she seen him somewhere before? She was sure she had.

'Look at that!' Val breathed in awe as Freddo leapt out and opened the door for Joss. 'Her Marv never did anything like that. And look at him! He's a bit of all right! Oh, wow, Joss – you've fallen right on your size fives, my love. Oh, and look at her clothes! She looks bloody brill, don't she?'

'And she's smiling like she's lit up from inside,' Sukie marvelled at the transformation, hoping that at least some of it was as a result of her potions. 'And so is he. I wonder if they realise . . .'

Val grinned. 'If they don't then they soon will – I hope her Marv never comes back.'

'What?' Sukie frowned. 'Has Marvin gone away, then? She didn't say anything to me when I saw her yesterday.'

'Shit!' Val looked stricken. 'Forget I said anything, Sukie, please. I'm not supposed to have told anyone, and I haven't. Until now. Yes, he's done a runner – best thing that could happen.'

Sukie nodded in agreement. 'I won't breathe a word. No wonder she looks as if she's got a new lease of life. Oh, isn't it funny how life has a way of working things out for everyone?'

Well, life and a few plants from Pixies Laughter's garden . . .

Joss and Mr Fabian walked towards them, not quite touching, still smiling together. Joss, blushing slightly, made introductions. Sukie, still convinced she'd seen Freddo Fabian somewhere before, shook hands to a rattle of bling bracelets. Joss and Val hugged one another word-lessly – words simply not being needed between them now.

'Sukie!' Topsy appeared in the doorway. 'Stop chatter-ing and come along, dear! We're ready to start! Oh – Mrs Benson and Mr—?'

'Fabian. Freddo Fabian.' Freddo pumped Topsy's hand. 'You must be young Topsy. Delighted to meet you, duck. I can't wait for this gig tonight.'

252

Topsy, preening, was almost turning herself inside out with excitement in the presence of a real show-business person as Sukie skipped back into the village hall.

The auditions were truly awful. The four applicants – Sheila, Mary, Loz and Grace – were all good-enough dancers, but Topsy simply terrified them. None of them could remember one step of the routines for more than thirty seconds. Sukie puffed to a halt, yet again, as Topsy screamed for a rerun.

The audience, packed into the body of the hall, was loving every minute. It would have spoiled their enjoyment of the entire evening if things had gone smoothly.

'Frigging hell,' Chelsea muttered as Orpheus retreated into his Underworld and they reformed once more, 'my legs are dropping off.'

'Mine too.' Sukie massaged her calves. 'Topsy – give us a break, please. Let the new girls have a go on their own – just show them a couple of the moves and let them copy you. You can't expect them to know the whole routine.'

Topsy frowned at her. 'When you're good enough to be a choreographer, Sukie, I'll ask for your opinion. But, as we need to put this one to bed as soon as possible, it might be the only way. Gels?' She looked beadily at a quivering Sheila, Mary, Loz and Grace. 'Would you be happier with a solo run? Even in front of this audience?'

Sheila, Mary, Loz and Grace nodded.

'Right,' Topsy sighed, nodding to Dorchester who was in chance of the sound-system, 'off we go again – Sheila first . . .'

Offenbach's rousing music swooped out into the hall, the audience tapped their feet and clapped their hands, Sukie, Chelsea, Trace, Roo and Bet sank gratefully on to the side of the stage, and Topsy put Sheila through her paces.

It was much, much better. Mary, Loz and Grace followed suit with equally vast improvements.

'They're all really good now they're not scared witless,'

Sukie whispered. 'Wonder which one she'll choose?'

'Search me.' Chelsea stretched her legs out in front of her. 'Oh, bugger – here she comes again.'

Topsy, almost skipping out, stood in front of the stage. 'Right, ladies – now I'd like my original troupe to give our celebrity and media guests an idea of what we can do while I come to my decision.'

Joss, sitting beside Freddo in the front row of chairs provided for the special guests, caught Sukie's eye and smiled. Sukie, thinking Joss had never looked happier, smiled back.

Then they were off with their proper routine, and all the aching muscles were forgotten as they swirled and circled and high-kicked and leaped and screamed and flounced and cartwheeled and finally leapt into flourishing splits.

Freddo was on his feet, whooping, applauding loudly, followed by the rest of the village hall.

Topsy climbed on to the stage and beamed at her troupe. 'Super, gels. Absolutely super. Not a step wrong. And Mr Fabian is apparently delighted with us. Delighted. He's going to have us on his books – which is wonderful news. But we do have a bit of a problem – I can't choose between the new ladies. I'd take them all – but then we'd be back with the original problem – an odd number. Oh, dear me – what to do? I don't want to lose any of those new gels. What we need is one more lady to step up on stage to give us ten dancers – then we'd have a proper Moulin Rouge line-up.'

Sukie said nothing for a moment, then she whispered in Topsy's ear.

'Are you sure?' Topsy looked disbelieving. 'Mrs Benson? You're turning into a talent scout as well as a choreographer, are you?'

'Ask her,' Sukie said, hoping the empowerment essences were still working. 'She can only say no. And she is a wonderful dancer – I've seen her in action—'

Shrugging, Topsy squatted on the edge of the stage. 'Mrs

Benson – I wonder if you could help us out here, my dear.'

Joss, looking slightly flustered, nodded, listened intently, shook her head, then smiled. Sukie watched as she whispered something to Freddo and he whispered something back.

Then to the village hall's amazement, Jocelyn Benson from Bagley – sad, frightened, shy, downtrodden Jocelyn Benson – stepped up on to the stage.

Dorchester cranked up Offenbach all over again and Joss, watched Topsy intently, then held her gypsy skirts, tapped her sequinned sandals, counted herself in on the beat and swept across the stage.

'She's a bloody natural,' Chelsea whispered. 'And she must be ancient!'

The village hall was on its feet again, stamping and clapping as Joss simply whirled with the music, prancing and high-kicking. Freddo, Sukie noticed, was standing on his chair, whistling his approval, his eyes fixed on Joss.

Oh, wow – Sukie thought – he's sooo keen on her . . .

The music ended. Joss, panting pulled a face at Topsy. 'Er – sorry – I'm not too good on the kicks and I can't turn cartwheels and I'll never do the splits but—'

'But nothing.' Topsy beamed. 'And I'll let you into a little secret – only Sukie and Chelsea do the splits properly. All my other gels simply slide the front leg forward and bend the other one up behind. No one can tell – and you'll fit in right perfect, my love. So – what do you say?'

'And I'll get to wear one of those gorgeous frocks like Sukie showed me? And all those amazing petticoats?'

'Well, yes,' Topsy frowned, 'of course you will. So – what do you say? Would you like to join us?'

'Yes . . .' Joss said, still out of breath. 'Oh, yes, yes please.'

'Ladies and gentlemen!' Topsy strode to the front of the stage. 'Thank you for all your support tonight – and against all my expectations I'm happy to announce that we're going to be taking all the new ladies to join the Bagley-cum-Russet cancan troupe!'

The village hall, universally as generous in their praise as they were in their condemnation, vociferously showed their appreciation of this democratic decision.

The original dancers hugged all the newcomers.

Joss, hardly able to speak, simply hugged Sukie. 'Thank you – I'm not sure how you did this for me – but thank you so very, very much . . .'

And Sukie, hoping Marvin never came home to spoil this, watched misty-eyed as Joss left the stage and was hugged by a very, very proud Freddo.

It only needed tears and a bit of kissing and a back-flip or two and it'd be just like a football match.

Topsy clapped her hands again. 'So – we now have our troupe – and I'm also delighted to announce that we have an agent – the famous Mr Freddo Fabian from Winterbrook . . .' Topsy indicated Freddo, who was still hugging Joss, but who managed to bow to his audience. 'And I hope you'll come along and see us dance – along with all manner of other entertainments – on Fiddlesticks village green on May Bank Holiday, when we'll be helping to celebrate the marriage of Fern and Timmy Pluckrose.'

The village hall stamped further approval and then began a stampede towards the local hostelry to continue the celebrations.

Having floated through a further delightful hour in the Faery Glen in Hazy Hassocks High Street in the company of new friends and old, Joss now sat in Freddo's car outside the bungalow. The evening had darkened into a chilly night, reminding everyone that summer hadn't quite arrived, and Joss shivered.

'I shouldn't keep you, duck.' Freddo grinned at her. 'Not when it's getting cold – but I've had such a fab evening, I don't want it to end.'

'Neither do I,' Joss said honestly. 'This has been one of the best nights of my life.'

Freddo laughed. 'And mine, duck. Great fun. And even greater company. And you – well, you blew my socks off. You were the star of the show.'

Joss blushed and giggled a bit. 'I surprised myself. I loved it – I've always loved dancing, but Marvin doesn't – didn't – er – well, he doesn't approve . . .'

'Silly sod,' Freddo said cheerfully. 'Ah, well, duck – I suppose all good things have to come to an end, and your husband wouldn't be too happy if he thought we were sitting out here like a couple of teenagers, would he?'

Joss shook her head. Well, he wouldn't. Wherever he was. But, without really understanding why, she really, really didn't want to leave Freddo. 'Yes, I suppose I ought to go. Thank you – for everything. And I'll see you on Monday – at the office.'

Freddo climbed out of the car and opened the door for her. 'It can't come soon enough for me, Joss, and that's the truth. We'll make a great team. Thank you so much.'

And he briefly brushed his lips against her cheek.

Joss, who couldn't remember the last time she'd been kissed, caught her breath. Then with one last smile at Freddo, she fumbled for her keys and let herself into the bungalow.

Leaning against the front door in the darkness, she listened as the Cadillac roared away, then touched her cheek in wonderment. Just one little friendly kiss and she felt as though her world was tumbling upside down. Oh, what a wonderful, wonderful evening it had been . . .

The telephone rang suddenly beside her in the hall, making her jump.

She smiled. Freddo was probably ringing her on his mobile – and he couldn't have got any further than the Celtic cross could he?

Joss lifted the receiver, almost caressing it. 'Hello?'

'Hello?' a woman's voice said coolly. 'I've been trying to ring you all evening – don't you have an answerphone?'

'Er – yes . . . but it's not switched on.' Joss, coming

down to earth with a bump, thought this wasn't the best telephone manner for someone ringing to sell her something at almost midnight. 'Maybe you've got the wrong number. And whatever you're selling, I'm sorry but I don't want it. And it's far too late to—'

'I'm not selling anything. You are Jocelyn? Jocelyn Benson?'

'Yes, but—'

'You don't know me, Mrs Benson, but I feel as though I know you very well. I'm Anneka Lindstrom.'

Joss shook her head, momentarily unable to focus on anything except Freddo and the kiss and the laughter and the cancan. 'Sorry, it's far too late for this—'

'I was your husband's secretary,' the cool voice continued. 'Your husband, Marvin, who in case you haven't noticed, hasn't been with you for sometime. That's because he's now here with me. And very distressed. I think we need to meet, Mrs Benson, as soon as possible, to discuss this situation, don't you?'

# Chapter Twenty-Three

Having caught the early bus to the station, Joss sat on the Paddington-bound train the following morning, listening to office workers yelling to other office workers via their mobile phones that they were just past Reading. This, she thought, must have been the sort of journey Marvin had made every day of his working life; the sort of journey she'd never asked him about and he'd never told her. A stressful journey squeezed in with hundreds of strangers, hurtling though Berkshire, everyone yawning and looking bored.

And when she arrived at Paddington, she'd ...

She sighed. All the rainbow euphoria of the previous day disintegrated into grey mistiness. When she arrived at Paddington, she'd take a cab, as Anneka had instructed given Joss's lack of familiarity with the underground system, and make the journey across London to Battersea and then ...

And then what?

Joss actually had no idea at all. Anneka had said nothing further in the previous night's phone call – simply made sure Joss had the address and phone number and would be there, presumably to claim her brain-fuddled husband who could no longer remember where he really belonged.

So, would Marvin still be as high as a kite? Or angry? Or just Marvin? Joss stared at the countryside flashing past outside, and felt an overwhelming sadness. How cruel it was to have had yesterday's tantalising glimpse of happiness and excitement and *life* only to see it snatched away again so very quickly.

When Marvin was back in the bungalow, he might agree to her working at Retro Music and Theatre, but he'd make it difficult, she knew he would, but she'd fight her corner on that one. She'd come this far – she wasn't prepared to give in entirely. The cancan was a different matter. Marvin certainly wouldn't allow her to dance the cancan – and she knew she wouldn't battle him on this, not even with her new-found assertiveness. They had to live together, and she knew from years and years of experience that it was easier to give in, and if he let her work with Freddo without causing too much trouble, well, one out of two, she thought – paraphrasing Meatloaf – ain't bad.

Freddo . . . Joss exhaled. Could she really work with him now anyway? On a platonic basis? Because, she knew, as she'd known last night, that her feelings for him were far from that.

She smiled sadly to herself: Marvin and Freddo – chalk and cheese.

Freddo was everything she thought a man shouldn't be, but was everything she wanted – and she'd fallen head over heels. What a funny business this love stuff was. And wasn't she far too old to have fallen madly in love for the first time in her life? And with a wild-looking man with dubious dyed hair and spiv jewellery and odd clothes, at that?

And she didn't even have to torture herself wondering if Freddo felt anything for her in return – because she knew he did. And now it would all have to come to an end.

Joss wriggled in her seat and stared momentarily out at the dash of late-Spring countryside, trying not to mind.

The two girls sitting opposite her, young, with their smart office suits and straight glossy hair and blunt French-manicured nails, avoided meeting her eyes. What did they see with the arrogance of their youth? A middle-aged nondescript woman without a life, maybe about to cry, remembering her sad nondescript dreams?

She really wanted to lean forward and wipe the superior looks from their perfect, youthful, unlined faces by telling them that last night she'd begun to fall hopelessly in love with a man whose hair was longer and yellower than hers, and she'd danced the cancan and roared through the Berkshire lanes in an open-topped pink Cadillac singing soul songs.

But if she did, they'd probably think she was mad. Because, Joss thought sadly as the outskirts of London teetered into view outside the carriage's window, if she thought this could ever have a happy ending, she was, wasn't she?

The taxi driver negotiated London with consummate skill. Joss, simply stunned by the volume of vehicles shooting at them from every direction, and the towering buildings, and the teeming mass of people, and the colour and noise, sat back, overwhelmed.

She'd rarely been to London with Marvin; and never alone. Not even on a sight-seeing tour or shopping spree. What an admission! And she'd never met Anneka. Years ago, when Marvin was first climbing his cradle-to-grave job ladder, he'd had a secretary called June – a big, cheerful woman, with big black hair and even bigger earrings. Joss had liked June when they'd met at corporate dinners and functions. Marvin, she knew, didn't. He thought June was common. Joss had always assumed it was because June wasn't afraid of him and held him in no awe whatsoever.

Since Marvin's elevation to managerial levels, he'd never attended the company's social events unless under duress, and if there had been a function he couldn't escape from he'd simply stayed up in town and Joss hadn't joined him. Anneka had been his secretary during these latter years, but she'd simply been a name – a cool, Swedish name who had produced the finished version of the *Bagley*

*Bugle*. Goodness – how long ago it all seemed now ... Joss had admired Anneka's resilience, working with Marvin all day, and had never questioned the relationship, knowing it was strictly business. It would have been laughable to imagine that it could be anything else – it still was.

No, whatever Joss thought she might discover in Battersea, it certainly wasn't going to be a love-nest. She and Marvin would be making the homeward journey to The Close together.

Joss sighed as the south London area signs started to appear at the congested road junctions. She'd always supposed Anneka would be a sort of glamorous cross between the blonde one in Abba and Ulrika Jonnson and would match Marvin's current predilection for Ikea furnishings: blonde, sleek, practical, beautiful and minimalist.

Well, she thought, as the taxi driver turned into a road of elegantly refurbished three-storey houses, she'd soon know.

Feeling strangely bereft as the cab pulled away, Joss stood on the wide white steps and studied the row of glistening brass name-plates. Oh! Oh, how long ago it seemed that she'd looked for Freddo's name-plate in Winterbrook. How long ago when she'd assumed her life was over – and discovered behind that flaking green door that it wasn't.

She rang the bell for 'A Lindstrom'. No one answered. There was no clipped voice telling her to push a button or let herself in or wait or anything at all. Joss stood on the doorstep, the sun beating uncomfortably on her shoulders, waiting, wondering if there was something else she should do to gain access to these imposing-looking apartments.

The white door opened suddenly.

'Oh, good morning—' Joss dredged up a smile and some of her self-confidence. 'Sorry – I think I may have rung the wrong doorbell. I'm looking for Anneka – Anneka Lindstrom.'

'You've found her.'

Joss was momentarily lost for words. The stocky middle-aged woman holding the door open was a Mrs Doubtfire double, with her coiled pepper and salt hair and her thick-rimmed tortoiseshell glasses, no discernible make-up, and her eminently sensible skirt and two-ply oatmeal jumper.

'Ooh – er . . .' Joss took a breath. 'I mean, hello – lovely to meet you. I'm Jocelyn Benson.'

'Mrs Benson.' Anneka held out a very clean square hand. 'Very nice to meet you, too. Please come in.'

After the brief, businesslike handshake, Joss, still trying to equate the real Anneka with her imaginings, followed the sturdy legs up a short flight of gleaming white stairs with gleaming brass fixtures, through a large oak door and into a small square hallway: white-painted, pale wood-floored, uncluttered. Neat – but not as austere as she'd expected.

'Through here, Mrs Benson,' Anneka instructed, almost barking the order.

This was more like it, Joss thought, looking around the living-room – all black and white and starkly expensive, with nothing out of place, no cushions or fripperies of any sort, and obscure angular monochrome things lined in parallel with the edges of other obscure angular monochrome things.

Hercule Poirot would have loved it.

'Can I get you a drink, Mrs Benson? Tea? Coffee?'

'A cup of tea would be lovely, thank you. Um – is Marvin here? Is he well?'

'Very well, now. He was strange and confused when he arrived here, but now he knows what is to happen and is his old self once more. He is out on the balcony reading the morning paper,' Anneka said, still not smiling. 'Maybe we should talk first, Mrs Benson?'

'Joss, please – and yes, of course.' Joss followed Anneka into an equally intimidating starkly ordered white, polished chrome and black granite kitchen, realising that she'd rather delay things by talking to this forbidding woman, who had probably spent more time with Marvin than she had, than face her husband.

Anneka made tea with a ruthless businesslike briskness in businesslike white porcelain cups.

They sat at what Joss considered to be an evilly ugly black and chrome table.

'Your husband,' Anneka said, 'is a truly wonderful man. I want you to know this, Mrs Benson. I've admired him for many, many years. He should not have been treated so badly.'

'I've never treated him badly!'

'By the company, Mrs Benson. They treated him shamefully. You, I feel, simply treated him wrongly. You, sadly, appeared not to know Marvin at all.'

'Sorry?' Joss, wrong-footed, sipped her tea – which was black and too hot – and quickly put the cup down again. 'I've been married to him for over thirty years, given him two children, been by his side—'

'That's not what I mean.' Anneka took a mouthful of the scalding tea without flinching. 'What I mean is that you clearly have never known of his dreams, or his hopes, or encouraged him in any way. Marvin has the mind of a genius when it comes to business. He's a talented and intelligent man who has never been fully appreciated either at work or at home.'

'Excuse me?' Joss, despite everything, felt obliged to defend herself. 'How can you say that? What business is it of yours? I've been a model wife – I've done exactly what Marvin wanted all our life, I've never let him down socially, never argued, never put myself first, never—'

'Never loved him?' Anneka's face twitched into what might pass for a smile. 'Never listened to his heart? Never shared his dreams?'

'I'll thank you not to discuss my personal relationship with my husband! And he didn't have a heart and he certainly didn't share any dreams with me! Look, Anneka, I'm sure you know one side of Marvin very well indeed – but that's simply the work side, and whatever he's chosen to tell you about our home life. You don't know anything

264

about the real man. And I'm very grateful to you for looking after him now while he's obviously unhappy and confused, but—'

Anneka shrugged her large shoulders. 'Marvin said you were a shadow,' she said. 'Someone who didn't have a spark. He was wrong to say that. It isn't true. Do you love him, Mrs Benson?'

'He's my husband.'

'But do you love him?'

'I'm not prepared to discuss this with you. This isn't why you asked me here, surely?' Joss pushed back the spindly chair. 'Please let me speak to Marvin, now. I need to know how he is.'

'Very well – the balcony doors are on the far side of the sitting room.' Anneka didn't move. 'I will not interfere.'

'Good,' Joss said, heading out of the kitchen. 'Please don't.'

The double glass balcony doors were open, and Marvin, looking amazingly fit and relaxed and wearing a pair of beige chinos and a dark red polo shirt, neither of which she'd ever seen before, was reclining on a very trendy chair, reading the paper in the sun. A glass, a jug of orange juice and a crumb-speckled plate was on the table beside him. The city spread mistily away as far as the eye could see.

'Hello, Marvin. How are you?'

'Jocelyn . . .' Marvin folded his paper and squinted up at her. 'Anneka said she'd phoned you. I told her it was a mistake but she – good God!'

Joss, who was wearing another of her gypsy skirts and vivid tops and the sequinned sandals, smiled. 'This is my new look. Second-hand bo-ho. Lovely, isn't it?'

'No.' Marvin eased himself up in the recliner. 'You're far too old for that sort of get-up and your hair is a mess. And I really wish Anneka hadn't contacted you, but she insisted that you should know where I was. I said you wouldn't give a damn.'

265

'How can you possibly have thought that? I was frantic. I've been worried sick. I've phoned the police and the hospitals and all your friends and searched everywhere and – where have you been, for heaven's sake?'

'Here.'

'What? All the time?'

Marvin nodded.

'You bastard! You've put me through hell and—'

'Sit down, Jocelyn. Now you're here, we do need to talk.'

'Too right.' Joss perched on an opposite chair. 'I think you owe me some sort of explanation, don't you? So, talk, Marvin – I'm all ears.'

Marvin, retelling the story, said he had no idea why he'd suddenly felt impelled to leave the bungalow, The Close, Bagley-cum-Russet, with such urgency.

'It was as if my mind had suddenly been cleared of all the turmoil.' He looked at Joss. 'As if I'd been another person, living in some sort of shrouded half-life until that moment – then suddenly, the solution was there. Crystal clear. I didn't stop to question what I was feeling, or why, I just instinctively knew what I had to do.'

'Which was to leave home and come here? To Anneka?'

'Yes. Sorry. Oh, not for coming here – but I suppose for not letting you know. Although, you'd changed so much Jocelyn since I-I lost my job ... I felt you'd probably not even notice I'd gone. Again, I'm sorry.'

'Don't apologise,' Joss said. 'You've never bothered to before – and it's far too late now. But yes, I did notice and yes, I did worry – and I desperately tried to find you – of course I didn't know about this little – er – romantic hide-away, did I?'

Marvin flinched. 'It was never that, Jocelyn. That wasn't why I came here. I've never been unfaithful to you.'

'You mean this and – and Anneka—' Joss swept her hands round the balcony, '—are simply business?'

Marvin shook his head. 'Not now, no. Now it's much,

266

much more – but when I first came here I wasn't aware of that. I just knew that this was where I had to be, that Anneka was the one person I needed to be with, the one person who understood me and what was happening to me. That she was the only person in the world who mattered – and who would know how to make the future bearable. I'm sorry Jocelyn, I have no further explanation – but nor do I have any regrets.'

Joss stared out across the rooftops, where the sun draped itself across the slates and tiles in a shawl of yellow mistiness. How very odd was that? Marvin preferring that huge, scary, self-assured, unfeminine woman to her? Was she insulted? Hurt, even? Joss probed her feelings and realised that what she actually felt was relief.

She looked at Marvin again. 'So was that why you behaved as badly as you did? Oh – I mean – worse than usual, after you'd been made redundant? With all that sniping and griping and watching awful television programmes? Because you were pining for Anneka?'

Marvin sighed. 'Maybe, yes – possibly. Probably. I don't know. All I know is that since I've been here I've felt like me again. I've been happy. Truly happy.'

'Well, bully for you.'

'Jocelyn – I know this is hurting you, but let me try to explain this. When I lost my job I was hurt and confused and frightened. *I* was frightened. I'd always been in control of everything in my life – and suddenly it had all gone. And you – you started to answer back and stand up to me and, for pity's sake, you even wanted to become the breadwinner and suddenly, suddenly I couldn't control you, either.'

They sat and stared at one another in silence for a moment.

Joss traced the pattern of the floor tiles with the toe of her sandals. The sequins danced in the sun. 'The day you left – did you sniff my bath oils?'

'*What?*'

'The bath essences that you found in my bathrobe pocket.

267

Sukie Ambrose told me afterwards they might have – um – strange effects. She didn't know that you'd inhaled them, but I guessed you had and—'

'Tommy-rot and balderdash, Jocelyn! I've never heard such nonsense!'

'But you did sniff my bath stuff? After I'd left for my interview? You nosed around because the mid-day bath was something else I'd done out of routine – and you found those little bottles and opened them and—'

'I can't remember. Maybe I did – I've no idea. Nor do I care. All I know is that until that point I was living a half-life, and you'd walked out on me – saying you were going to find a job – then – yes, I found those stupid little scent bottles ... and immediately I felt free and knew what I wanted.'

Joss stared at him, this man who she'd lived with and slept beside for nearly all her adult life. This man who she now not only didn't love but probably didn't like very much.

'That's fine, Marvin. I'm glad you've found yourself, however you did it. Most people never do. I'll put the bungalow on the market, shall I?'

'What?' Marvin jerked his head round. 'You mean you haven't come here to beg me to come home?'

'No! Why on earth would I?' Joss felt the power surge through her veins. 'You're not the only one to get a life, Marvin. Despite everything you've done to me over the years, I've got a job – a really good job as a PA-cum-secretary – and I'll find a cheap flat to rent or something.' She leaned towards him. 'And last night I drove through Bagley in a pink Cadillac with my new boss and I danced the cancan.'

'Now who's hallucinating?' Marvin went into a toned-down version of the purple vein-throbbing. 'Don't tell such lies, Jocelyn. It's neither becoming nor necessary.'

'I don't tell lies. Last night I found out what I've been missing. And I've enjoyed every minute of being without

268

you. It was like being released from prison after a very, very long sentence.'

'Jocelyn ...' Marvin frowned. 'This isn't what I was expecting—'

'No? Why? Did you think that I'd still be your victim? Marvin, I should have said this, done this, years ago. You've bullied me all our married life – made me miserable and guilty and unhappy. Now, as long as I know you're safe and well, I'm more than happy to live – really live – the rest of my life without you.'

Marvin swallowed and turned his head away from her, staring out over the rooftops.

Oh, God. He wasn't crying was he?

'Marvin ...?'

'You—' he snapped his head round, '—have stolen my buggering thunder! How dare you do this to me, Jocelyn? It was I who was leaving you! I was intending to tell you it was all over – how dare you – what? Jocelyn? Are you buggering laughing – at me?'

'Yes, sorry,' Joss giggled. 'Not very appropriate is it? But beautifully-timed. My moment of glory. I wish I'd caught it on camcorder. Now, what were we saying? Ah, yes – the bungalow – and how about a divorce while we're at it?'

Three hours later, on the Reading train, rattling away from London, Joss leaned back in her seat, smiling. It had all gone so much better than she'd even dared to dream it could.

Anneka had been called out to the balcony, and presumably after years of secretarial nannying, had made fresh orange juice all round and provided warm croissants and cherry jam, and Marvin had said please and thank you in a most unfamiliar way, and they'd smiled at one another almost soppily. And Joss, watching them, had felt no jealously, just a little sadness that they'd all wasted so much time before discovering what it was they really wanted.

And then Marvin had said that she must stay in the bungalow – and he'd be down to collect the remainder of his things, and he'd already drawn up plans for an equity release scheme to give them both a lump sum: Joss's to live on and his to invest in his and Anneka's new corporate head-hunting business.

And Joss had agreed to it all because there was no reason not to, and said she'd sign any papers, deal with any solicitors, do whatever was necessary to finalise everything to do with their marriage – she'd refused to use the word closure as it was one of Marvin's favourites – as long as Marvin made it his business to inform the children.

She'd used Anneka's phone to ring Valerie and tell her briefly what had happened and ask her, if it was at all possible, to find someone to pick her up at Reading station because she didn't want to hang around for the late evening Bagley bus or pay the huge taxi fare across Berkshire. Then she'd said goodbye to Anneka and Marvin, and been brave and happy enough to find her own way back to Paddington on the tube.

And now, she thought, smiling dreamily at the two women opposite her who had clearly been on a shopping spree, she'd go home and invite Val round for the evening – and her big, untidy husband too – and they'd have fish and chips from the paper and cheap wine and play loud music to celebrate.

She was still smiling when she emerged from Reading railway station's concourse into the low, warm late sunshine. What a perfect evening to start her new life . . .

'Joss!' Valerie Pridmore bustled towards her through the throng of coming and going passengers. 'Over here, love! We've found a parking space!'

Joss beamed and they hugged one another and as they chatted at the same time about the wondrous events in Battersea, Joss wondered very briefly which one of Val's offspring's possibly illegal cars she'd be travelling home in – and didn't care. Just as long as she could get home – to

270

her home ... When she got her first pay-packet she'd paint the bungalow's rooms in bright colours, and buy rugs and cushions and big showy plants for the garden and ...

She stopped abruptly.

The pink Cadillac was causing something of a kerfuffle, as was Freddo in his denim and leather and bling.

Joss swallowed her tears, and shook her head at Val who was laughing.

'I didn't have to use much persuasion,' she chuckled. 'Believe me, when I told him what was going on, he was all for driving all the way up to the Smoke to get you. And I came along for the ride – I know three's a crowd and all that – but I ain't going to get many opportunities to ride in a motor like that now, am I?'

And Joss hugged her fiercely, and whispered thank you, and said she was the best friend in the world.

Freddo, spotting them, leapt out of the car and ran towards them through the crowds. With a whoop of glee, he picked Joss up and swirled her round, and then kissed her. And she kissed him back. And it was simply amazing.

'Welcome home, Joss, duck,' he said softly, holding her tightly against him, and looking at her with unconditional love. 'Welcome home.'

# Chapter Twenty-Four

'This is almost like a perfect summer evening.' Milla stretched her long legs, bare beneath her neat linen shirt dress, out in front of her. 'And just what I need after a week of non-stop meetings and frantic buying and selling, relaxing in a peaceful garden. And it's so gloriously warm for April. I'm definitely not a winter person.'

'Nor me.' Sukie, less elegantly dressed in jeans and a T-shirt, slid down in the rickety wicker chair opposite Milla and raised her glass of Chardonnay. 'Here's to May Day tomorrow – and long may this weather continue.'

They chinked glasses, giggling because they were already on their second bottle and the overuse of the word 'may' seemed really funny.

Pixies Laughter's garden was certainly coming into its own. The overgrown jasmine and honeysuckle and clematis formed lush canopied corners, and the orange blossom and lilacs were thrusting glossy leaves into every available nook and cranny. It was a dark green perfumed oasis, away from the world.

'On May Day,' Milla lit a cigarette and blew smoke across the table, 'Bo-Bo and I—'

'Go on . . .'

'No, it's stupid really.'

'Talk about him, Milla – if it helps.'

'Nothing helps, Sukes. The bugger jilted me and

vanished without a trace – nothing can help that, how can it? But I still remember every damn silly little thing that we did together.'

'Like on May Day? Was that special?'

'Very.' Milla nodded dreamily. 'We used to go to Oxford at dawn to see the sun rise. After we'd partied all night, we'd stand on Magdalen bridge with zillions of other people, listening to the choir – which made the hairs on your neck stand on end it was so ethereal – and welcoming in May morning. And then, because it hadn't been banned by the nanny state in those days, we'd stand on the parapet of the bridge and jump into the river!' Milla laughed. 'Hand-in-hand. In full evening regalia! And the police would go mad and fish us out – and then we'd get sort of dry and go to the covered market for a full English ...'

Sukie watched Milla's face, alive, her eyes sparkling. Oh, dear ... The Bo-Bo memories were alive and kicking tonight.

'And, hand on heart, have you seriously never tried to contact him since he – er – defected?'

'Not since the early days, no,' Milla refilled the glasses. 'I guess he didn't want to be found. Big wall of silence from anyone who knew him. Changed his mobile phone and all other mode of contact. Sold his shares, sold his companies, left his flat. Vanished – like he'd never existed. Except, of course, he'll always exist here and here ...' she thumped her head and her heart. 'Sad cow that I am. I hate him so much for what he did to me, and yet—'

Sukie said nothing. It would be the ideal opportunity to raise the issue of the long distance love potion, but she still couldn't do it – not morally or ethically – could she?

'Bo-Bo obviously changed his way of life and forgot about me – and I really think I should be moving on too,' Milla reached to help herself from the bowl of nachos on the rickety wicker table, aiming wildly for the dips. 'Maybe it's time to start anew. Maybe in May?'

They giggled again.

Sukie brushed nacho crumbs from her jeans. 'What – you mean – er – with Derry?'

'Yes – no – God, Sukes, I haven't a clue! I've been thinking though that before long I should bite the bullet and stop running away from everything. It's been great living here, it's done what I always wanted it to do, and you've been a star – but I know I don't belong here. I'm a metro-chick. I need my city-fix. I can't live here for ever, can I?'

'No, I suppose not. But I'd really miss you – even though I never thought it would work out, us sharing.'

'It's been great fun.' Milla chinked her glass against Sukie's with a slightly unsteady hand. 'And of course I wouldn't leave you in the lurch – unlike some. I'd wait until you found another suitable house-mate. But yes, I think I'll have to go sooner rather than later.'

Sukie felt sick – and it had nothing to do with a surfeit of wine and nibbles.

'You mean – you, and Derry, would leave here and—?'

Milla shrugged. 'Derry complicates things, Sukes. We're happy together, I think. But his heart is here, in Berkshire, as is his business – and I wouldn't ask him to give that up for me because I know he couldn't and wouldn't. I suppose we could carry on seeing one another even if I moved back to London, couldn't we?'

'Yes,' Sukie said brightly, stabbing herself in the heart. 'Yes, of course you could. It would probably work out really well Have you told him this yet?'

'No!' Milla rocked back on her chair. 'It's all such a mess, really. I know I need to move on, but even though Derry and I haven't been together for long, he's shown me that there are lovely, funny, kind, decent men around – not to mention his fabulous physical attributes – and I certainly can't imagine him jilting anyone, can you?'

Sukie shook her head. She couldn't. She hoped fervently that this wasn't leading where she thought it might be. 'You mean – you've – um – actually considered marrying him . . .?'

'Why not? He might be persuaded to start a joinery business in London, which would go down a storm in all those up-and-coming reclamation areas – and it would hugely piss off my parents.'

Oh, God ... Sukie buried herself in a handful of nachos she really wasn't sure she'd be able to swallow. Oh, sod morals and ethics! This was self-preservation!

She stared up at the sky, fragmented by the tall bushes, a pastel blur of blue and grey and pink and lilac. 'Okay – what if – just supposing – suspending all disbelief for a moment, it was possible, and you had to choose between them? One man to spend the rest of your life with, to love forever? Which would it be? Derry or Bo-Bo?'

Milla didn't answer. She swirled the Chardonnay in her glass. Sukie couldn't bear it. She'd promised Chelsea she wouldn't try the love potion on Milla without her knowledge – but she simply couldn't stand this any longer.

She balanced her glass on the uneven table and stood up. 'No – don't tell me. Don't answer that question. Please don't. And wait just a minute ...'

And leaving Milla frowning, she rushed back into Pixies Laughter.

This was the only way to sort things out, wasn't it? Well, maybe not anyone's normal way, but it was what Cora would have done, wasn't it? Cora had left Pixies Laughter and its secrets hoping that Sukie might never discover them, but she had – and she'd used them well so far, hadn't she? Would anyone blame her if she now dabbled a bit on her own behalf? Oh, God – where had she put the little phial she'd used on Chelsea? Where? Which bag was it in? Oh, why had she had so many glasses of wine? Why couldn't she think straight? She'd just have to make some more stuff ...

What was the potion rhyme? And the recipe? Could she remember either of them – or would she have to go and raid the work-basket again? Oh, no ... the poem was there, but without the ingredients it was useless – and the ingredients

275

were on that scrap of paper which was – where, exactly? Oh, bugger, bugger, bugger!

Trying to remember, her brain sticking on rosemary and coriander, knowing that Milla would lose interest at any moment, or worse still trot into the kitchen and say the name Sukie knew she didn't want to hear, she resorted to desperate measures. 'Cora,' she muttered out loud, 'if this is even remotely the right thing to do – help me – please.'

And suddenly she was calm. Everything was still. And the words she needed were there, in her brain, on her tongue, as easily remembered again as all her childhood nursery rhymes:

> *So many lonely people*
> *So many broken hearts*
> *So many lovers torn apart*
> *So much loss and so much sorrow*
> *Can be cured maybe tomorrow*
> *No matter how many miles away*
> *Love can be brought home to stay*
> *Belief in the herbal powers*
> *Belief in the scented flowers*
> *Will bring true lovers back together*
> *To be in love for ever and ever*
> *With no more tears and no more pain*
> *Together, never to part again*

Shakily, Sukie rubbed her eyes. The list of ingredients and Cora's dire warning, was also imprinted indelibly in her head now . . .

> *Distance love potions are very effective but are considered powerful earth magic and should only be undertaken as a last resort to bring lovers together.*
> *They should be used only if you are absolutely sure that the outcome is what you want because they may not be reversed.*

*To make: 3 drops ginger, 2 drops rosemary, 2 drops jasmine, 1 drop clove, 1 drop cinnamon, 1 pinch powdered mandrake root, mixed with almond oil. The potion should be rubbed on a pulse point, preferably the left wrist as this will take the infusion straight to the heart of one of the parted lovers while they visualise their beloved. They will, in every case, be united in everlasting love.*

Frantically delving into the kitchen cupboard, Sukie emerged with the essences she needed and a bottle of base oil. Slopping everything everywhere, she rapidly measured and blended and knew that what she was doing was probably wrong, and would probably break her heart for ever.

But she had to know.

Milla blinked lazily as Sukie emerged from the back door. 'I thought you'd gone for good. Left me – like everyone else seems to. Oh, what's that? Something nice to drink?'

Sukie sat down and put the phial on the table between them.

'No, it's part of the game.'

'Oh, fantastic.' Milla leaned forward, pushing her blonde hair behind her ears. 'You mean we have to balance it on our foreheads without spilling it while reciting Shakespeare or something?'

Sukie frowned. 'What sort of weird parties do you go to? No – it's much easier than that. This—' she took a deep breath, '—is a love potion.'

'Oh, I adore it!' Milla screamed with laughter. 'This gets better and better! Go on then, Sukes – what do we have to do?'

'You have to do what you were doing earlier. Imagine just one man, the one man you honestly, truthfully love with all your heart and want to spend the rest of your life with. Don't say anything though. Don't tell me his name. Just think it in your head – and imagine being with him in the most romantic setting possible.'

277

'Okay, that's easy now – I think – and what do you do?'

'I,' Sukie said, shaking the phial and removing the stopper, 'just rub a few drops of this on your left wrist and massage it in – so that the love potion travels straight to your heart, while you're having your fantasy meeting with the love of your life.'

Milla obediently laid her left arm on the wobbly table, wrist up. 'I must remember this for my next board meeting. It'll liven it up no end ... oh, no – sorry – right – I'm closing my eyes and I'm dreaming of—'

'Don't say it!'

'Sorry – okay. Go on then. I'm ready ...'

With her heart thundering, and her mouth dry, Sukie sprinkled the potion on to Milla's slender wrist, massaging it gently into the pulse point at the base of her thumb.

There. It was done. Too late now. And if things didn't work out the way she wanted them to, well, it was better to know now than carry on hoping for the impossible, wasn't it?

'Is that it?' Milla opened her eyes and sniffed her wrist. 'Oh, Sukes – I've no idea what's in this but I think you could give Chanel a bit of a battle. It's absolutely scrummy. So – what happens next? This is fun!'

Sukie smiled. 'Well – now we just wait and see what happens.'

Which, if it was anything like Chelsea and Nicky Hambly, would be precisely nothing.

The garden gate suddenly creaked in the soft twilight, making them both turn their heads.

'Hi.' Derry grinned at them. 'Hope you've left some wine in that bottle. I'm dying for a drink.'

Sukie, knowing that she was going to disgrace herself, managed to haul herself to her feet. 'Er – I'll go and get another glass – and another bottle. Oh, and some more bits to eat. No, you two stay there – I've had more than enough anyway.'

And with stupid tears blurring her eyes, she blundered into the kitchen.

278

Half an hour later, the Barmy Cow offered scant solace. Sukie, huddled on a high stool at the corner of the bar with an untouched pint of shandy, miserably watched the customers laughing and chatting around her, as if they were miles away. The warm evening had somehow managed to penetrate the pub's grey fug, and even the dust had a bit of a sparkle.

Unable to stay in Pixies Laughter while Milla and Derry planned their happy ever after in the garden, she'd escaped as soon as possible, almost running through the darkening village, in the hope that Chelsea, who hadn't answered her mobile, would be in the pub.

Chelsea wasn't.

Everyone else seemed to be though, and all four Berkeley Boys were working like dervishes behind the bar, with Topsy, Edie and Rita sitting together at a corner table watching them avidly like groupies at a gig.

It only took one warm evening to drag the Bagleyites out in force. And tomorrow was a bank holiday, so no one had to worry about having an early night and – Sukie wanted to weep into her shandy. The long distance love potion gamble hadn't paid off – and she only had herself to blame, didn't she?

And this was the worst-ever torture. Not only was she forced to imagine what was happening at home, but she was surrounded by most of the mismatched couples her massage love potions had inadvertently brought together.

Even Joss Benson, looking splendid and carefree and glowing with happiness, was playing darts with Val Pridmore and her family and the glitzy Freddo Fabian. And they were all laughing together – not, Sukie thought, half-heartedly sipping the flat top from her shandy, that she begrudged Joss her happiness. If anyone deserved to be freed from an unsuitable partner, it was Joss – and at least the Pixies Laughter potions had played no part in that little scenario, had they?

279

The cancan rehearsals had been a-buzz with the news that Joss and the vile Marvin had split for good, and that Joss had not only changed her image, but also her man – and was now an item with Freddo. It was the best gossip Bagley-cum-Russet had had for years.

'You all on your own, young Sukie?' Topsy had tip-tapped her way to the bar. 'Nothing amiss, I hope? Nothing medical? Nothing I can help you with?'

'No, I'm fine,' Sukie said quickly, hoping Dorchester hadn't given Topsy a full set of 'Make Your Own Diagnoses For Friends and Family' manuals. 'I thought Chelsea might be here . . .'

'Gorn to Newbury with her family. They was all in here earlier. Some do on at the Watermill.'

Sukie sighed. Everyone was doing something with someone tonight, then. Oh, goody . . .

Topsy, pausing for a quick flirtatious word with Dorchester, peered at Sukie again. 'You sure you're okay? You looks a bit peaky to me? You'll be all right for tomorrow, won't you? The wedding thingy at Fiddlesticks? Only it being our first public performance this year, we don't want to let Mr Fabian down, now do we?'

'I'll be fine, honestly,' Sukie said, wondering if she could really face slapping on the showbiz smile and high-kicking her way across a makeshift stage to celebrate someone else's happy event. 'Looking forward to it. Loads.'

'Good gel. That's the spirit. Going to be another lovely day according to the weather forecast. Should draw in a smashing crowd.'

'Great – I mean – oh, that's great.'

Topsy nodded happily, and carrying three small glasses of something that could be port and lemon but probably wasn't, manoeuvred her way back to Rita and Edie.

Hilton leaned across the bar. 'Something wrong with your shandy, Sukie? You don't seem to have touched it.'

'No, I'm sure it's lovely . . . I'm just not in the mood.'

'Let me add a bit more lemonade for you,' Hilton wheezed across the bar. 'Give it a bit more oomph.'

Too morose to stop him, Sukie sat back as he dripped some flat lemonade into her already torpid glass. Like the other Berkeley Boys, Hilton had paid homage to the warmer weather by wearing an open-necked sports shirt in an unbecoming teal green. Sukie watched with alarm as some sort of medallion escaped from his wrinkly chest and hovered over the shandy.

'Hilton ... your – um – locket thingy – it's dangling – oh, and it's open.'

'Oh,' Hilton seemed momentarily fuddled. 'Right. Thank you. I'll just ...'

Sukie peered at the heart-shaped locket and then at the glimpse of the heart-shaped photo it contained and felt sicker than ever.

God alive! Surely not ...?

'Hilton – I'm not sure I want to know this – but why the hell have you got a picture of me round your neck?'

Hilton blushed and chuckled, and put down the lemonade bottle.

'It ain't you, young Sukie. Oh – what's the harm. Look—' his elderly fingers fumbled with the locket. 'See – yes, it could be you, I'll grant you, but it ain't. It's your Auntie Cora when she was about your age.'

Sukie gazed at the faded sepia picture. Of course, she could see it was Cora now. She'd seen enough early photos of Cora to recognise her great-aunt – but at first glance it really could have been her: same oval face, same thick dark hair, same pale eyes, same determined expression.

Hilton stroked the locket. 'Cora was a beautiful girl, just like you, and I loved her with all my heart. But she never knew – not really. Her heart was broke when her young man was killed in the war and she never got over it. She couldn't care for me or anyone else after that. She never knew I had the photograph, mind. I took that on a village picnic in nineteen thirty-seven – and she gave me the

281

locket, oh years since, when she was clearing out some junk for a village jumble sale. I kept it, probably wrong of me, and put the photo in ...'

'And you've worn it ever since? And you've never looked at anyone else? Or loved anyone else?'

Hilton nodded his elderly cropped head, tenderly closing the locket. 'Ah, that's about it, Sukie. And I'd thank you not to tell anyone if you don't mind. I've kept it a secret from people – except my brothers – for most of my life, and that's the way I'd like it to stay.'

'Yes ...' Sukie patted his hand. 'Yes, of course. Oh, Hilton – why is love so bloody sad?'

'It ain't always, duck. Look at old Claridge and Savoy and Dorchester – they're like puppy dogs these days. And Ken and Tom have found each other – and even Bert's taken up with that Brenda woman from Hassocks what looks like Demis Roussos. And what about Mrs Benson and that there Freddo. Smashing bloke, he is, and makes her really happy. See – it ain't all doom and gloom.'

'But – you're okay. Not being with anyone. Not being in love?'

'Bless your heart, duck, course I am. I've got me health and me pub and me brothers and me friends. And it was enough just to be around Cora and be her chum for all them years.'

Feeling more miserable than ever, Sukie leaned her elbows on the bar, not giving a damn about the stickiness any more, while Hilton bustled off to serve more customers. Would it be enough for her? Being around Derry as his friend? Being able to see him and speak to him and laugh with him, but never, ever being able to love him?

No, she shook her head sadly, it wouldn't.

'Sukie!' Valerie Pridmore was waving from the other end of the bar. 'Sukie!'

Not wanting to make up the numbers in the darts team, Sukie waved lethargically back.

282

'Sukie!' Val was beckoning furiously. 'Come here a moment!'

Sighing, knowing she was going to be dragged into some interminable game of darts which she hated at the best of times, Sukie slid from her stool and forced her way through the Barmy Cow's clientele.

Val grabbed her arm and dragged her into a less-crowded corner. 'Is Milla at home?'

'What? Yes ...' Sukie frowned, not wanting to even think about the subtext. 'Why?'

'Because there's a gentleman over there talking to Joss and Freddo who's looking for her. Says he thinks she lives in this village – not sure where. Says he's been trying to contact her. I didn't want to give him your address just in case he wasn't kosher. What do you think?'

'Probably someone she chatted up in a club and forgot about.' Sukie shrugged. 'Best not to tell him anything. Does he seem like a stalker?'

'He's bloody smashing if you ask me – well, not quite as much of a sex-pot as Derry, but a bit of all right. And posh as they come.'

Oh, God, Sukie thought – it was probably the bald, toothless, much-married baronet who was Milla's mother's son-in-law of choice.

Wearily, she shook her head. 'Don't tell him anything. Anyway, she's with Derry tonight. She wouldn't want a threesome.'

'I wouldn't say no,' Val cackled. 'You have a quick look at him, Sukes. What do you reckon? Kick him out of bed, would you?'

Sukie, not caring one way or the other, peered through the fug.

Jesus!

The man talking to Joss and Freddo was the dead spit of a young Bryan Ferry – all sexy smoulder, with black hair falling over his forehead, and killer cheekbones. The face she'd seen in the photo beside Milla's bed.

He looked up and saw her looking at him. And smiled.

'Er,' Sukie cleared her throat. 'Um – you're looking for Milla, I understand? Would you possibly be—'

'Boswell Borthington.' He grinned, showing a lot of very white teeth. 'Sir Boswell Borthington to my enemies – Bo-Bo to my friends.'

Buggering hell! Sukie closed her eyes. Bo-Bo! At last! And far, far too bloody late!

# Chapter Twenty-Five

Fern and Timmy's wedding party was in full swing. Since midday, Fiddlesticks' vast village green – an anglophile's dream with its criss-crossing sandy pathways, plentiful weeping willow trees, and a rustic bridge over a fat, slow-running, brown-bedded stream – had been like Mardi Gras meets Notting Hill Carnival with extras. Or at least that's how it seemed to the villagers, out in force on May Day, ready to enjoy whatever delectations were offered as long as they were offered for free.

The weather forecast had proved accurate for once, and Fiddlesticks shimmered beneath a clear azure sky and wall-to-wall sunshine. Rafts of people had arrived from Hassocks and Bagley and Winterbrook – and even as far afield as Steeple Fritton, Lesser Fritton and Fritton Magna – to party the day and night away, with free food outside the Weasel and Bucket, and free drinks inside, and Petronella Bradley's Memory Lane Fairground providing traditional rides, and Flynn and Posy Malone's showmen's traction engine adding age-old glamour and excitement to the proceedings.

Joss, who had always dreaded Bank Holidays because they meant Marvin was at home all day and even more snippy than usual, couldn't quite get used to her sense of freedom, of feeling she was somehow bunking off school. Surely, there must be something grown-up she should be doing?

Well, yes, there was: later she'd be up there – she cast another nervous glance at the very professional stage, with its banks of lights and towering speakers and writhing black cables on the far side of the green – dancing the cancan as part of the evening's entertainment, but for now she was simply enjoying every minute of the party.

She was, she admitted to herself, pretty terrified of dancing in public for the first time, although she'd practised and practised the routines, rehearsing each evening until she felt she'd drop, and Sukie and Chelsea had been amazingly patient with her and helped her no end.

She really, really hoped she wouldn't let them down tonight.

Fern and Timmy, blissfully happy, nicely bronzed from their Indian Ocean honeymoon, and wearing full wedding regalia, had been circulating the green for sometime. Joss, her hand firmly in Freddo's, had congratulated them, and wondered, as she did every day since her return from Battersea, how much better life could get.

She'd started work at Retro Music and Theatre and absolutely adored it. She and Freddo were a team in every sense of the word, and however long it took the lawyers to disentangle her previous life, Joss simply didn't care. She felt fulfilled, loved, appreciated and supremely happy.

Before long, she knew, she'd ask Freddo to leave his rather chaotic Winterbrook flat, and move into the bungalow with her, and she knew he would, like a shot – but not just yet. Self-assured she might be – but she'd never be pushy or overconfident. Anyway, there was all the time in the world for that: right now she was simply revelling in her new life; in her independence and the challenge of her job, and, more than anything, being in love and being loved in return.

'I'm just going to sort out a few things for the band,' Freddo said to her, as they skirted the fairground with its old fashioned maroon and gold living wagons and galloping horses circling in the sun. 'They should be here shortly.

Would you like to come with me – or are you okay here, duck?'

Joss nodded. 'I've just seen Val and her family over there. I'm sure she'll keep me entertained.' She touched his face. 'It's okay, Freddo. Really. We don't have to be joined at the hip. I know you have work to do today – and I'm not going anywhere.'

He grinned at her. 'You'd better not. I just don't want you to think – worry – that I don't want to be with you. I do. Always. All the time.'

'Me too.' Joss smiled back at him. 'And we will be, won't we?'

Goodness! Had she really said that? How very forward of her!

Freddo kissed her. 'As soon as it's legally possible to make you Mrs Fabian, yes. Joss Fabian ...' He pondered for a moment. 'Sounds like a rock star, don't it, duck?'

'It sounds wonderful,' Joss said giddily, not sure that she understood. 'And is that – are you—?'

'Asking you to marry me? Yes ...' Freddo laughed. 'Bugger it, Joss – I was planning to do it all romantic like tonight, with moonlight and champagne and roses. Sorry.'

'Don't ever, ever say sorry.' Joss hugged him. 'That's the most romantic proposal anyone could ever have.'

Freddo pulled away slightly, holding her hands in his, and looked at her. 'You – you are going to say yes, aren't you?'

Joss shrugged. 'Oh, I don't know ... Do I really want to marry you? Marry anyone again? The first time round wasn't that great, was it? And as I'm still married anyway, it's probably not legal, so—'

She stared at his face. The tanned leathery lines had practically puckered and his eyes were bleak. He looked totally woebegone. Freddo was absolutely useless at hiding his emotions. Deviousness had passed him by – thank goodness.

She laughed. 'Of course I'm saying yes! Yes! Yes! Yes!'

She practically danced on the spot. 'Er – YES!'

'Jesus!' Freddo exhaled, sweeping her up into his arms and almost dancing with her, kissing her again and again. 'Thank God for that. Blimey, duck – that was the worst moment of my life there. Oh, blimey! We're going to be so blooming happy, aren't we?'

Joss nodded, unable to speak, then she grabbed his hand and shoving through the crowds, hurried him towards the rustic bridge.

Delving into her bag – not the neat and safe bag matching her previous life, but the sloppy, floppy patchwork affair of sequins and glitter – she dragged out her wedding ring and sapphire and diamond engagement ring from Marvin. She'd taken them off on the train home from London, and had intended to dump them in the recycling box but had forgotten.

With an overarm throw that Freddie Flintoff would have been delighted to claim for his own, she hurled them through the air in a glittering arc. They landed several yards away in the fat brown stream with a satisfying splash, hovering on the surface for a nanosecond, before sinking forever into the peaty bed.

'There,' she sighed happily. 'End of an era.'

'You're one heck of a woman.' Freddo grinned at her. 'And that little bauble was pretty sophisticated – which might make this ...' he dragged a box from the back pocket of his tattered Levis, 'look a bit tawdry in comparison. But—' he dropped down on one knee, to the delight of the watching hordes, '—I'll be the proudest man in the world if you'll accept it. Joss – I love you with all my heart – and I always will.'

Joss looked at the massively ostentatious square pink bling ring and squealed with delight. 'Oh! It's gorgeous! Oh, thank you! I love it! And—' she blinked away a tear, '—I love you, too.'

Freddo stood up again, to rousing cheers, and slid the ring on to Joss's finger.

Then, oblivious to the noise and the crowds, they simply melted into one another's arms.

'Hurry up,' Chelsea said crossly. 'I want to get to Fiddlesticks and enjoy at least some of the party before we have to go on stage.'

'You can't dance the cancan bladdered,' Sukie said, looking up from the big theatrical boxes on the living-room floor, 'so the later we are the better. And there'll be plenty of time afterwards for drinking. Now – is that the lot? Ten of dresses, petticoats, stockings, suspenders, garters, knickers, shoes, chokers, gloves, ostrich feathers – what have I forgotten?'

'A sense of humour?' Chelsea squatted beside her. 'Oh, shit Sukes, look, I know how you feel, but—'

'No you don't,' Sukie said quickly, fastening the cases. 'You can't possibly know how I feel – but thanks for trying.'

Chelsea hugged her. 'And you've no idea what happened? What's happening? Where they've gone?'

'No.' Sukie stood up and hauled the boxes across the floor. Ronald, who had been sewing all night like the Tailor of Gloucester's mice on the new dancers' costumes, had delivered them all only half an hour earlier. 'Could you grab one of these, please? If they won't all fit in the boot we can get at least one on the back seat.'

Chelsea, with a final sympathetic look, grabbed the nearest box and dragged it out into the hot May afternoon.

Sukie, checking her make-up in the mirror because she doubted if there'd be any facilities in Fiddlesticks apart from the loos in the pub which was bound to be chock-a-block, was amazed that she managed to look passably human. Surprising, she thought, what a bit of slap can do to hide a terminally broken heart.

Last night, after the mad excitement of discovering Bo-Bo in the Barmy Cow, and deciding that the best thing to do was to ring Milla herself and break the news, life had become a bit of a blur.

Milla, who had probably been romping with Derry, simply hadn't believed her.

Then Sukie had handed her mobile to Bo-Bo and, like the rest of the pub, had eavesdropped as he'd convinced a squawking Milla that it was indeed he, and they needed to meet.

Sukie, who really hadn't thought past the fact that Bo-Bo was there – magically, mysteriously – in Bagley-cum-Russet, had reclaimed her mobile and looked at him.

'So? Does she want to see you?'

'She does,' Bo-Bo had said in his gloriously plummy voice. 'Thank the lord – it's far more than I deserve. She say there's something she needs to tell me, but not, it appears, on her home ground.'

Sukie could understand this. Best not entertain your old lover while your new one was probably swinging naked from the chandeliers.

'We're meeting, in a rather cloak and dagger fashion,' Bo-Bo had said, 'by the Celtic cross in half an hour. Milla informs me that you will give me directions.'

So Sukie had, and then spent the waiting time as any normal house-mate and concerned chum would do, pumping him for every bit of information she could squeeze from him.

Bo-Bo was a good talker. He seemed more than happy to unburden himself.

The jilting, it appeared, was down to Milla's mother. Bo-Bo, already feeling pressurised by the threatened presence of eighteen million wedding guests and exclusive media coverage by *Celeb Watcher* magazine, had finally flunked it after Milla's mother had insisted he must stand up in the family chapel and sing all ninety-three verses of the family song. In Latin. Well – no, he'd admitted, it wasn't quite that bad, but that's what it seemed like.

'She's very scary,' he'd confided over a pint of shandy. 'I'm used to running various companies, and having people jump when I raise my eyebrows, but she absolutely terrified me. So did the wedding. Not, you understand, the

290

marriage. I adored Milla. I always have and always will. I truly wanted to marry her. But I simply couldn't cope with the bloody three ring circus it was turning into.'

'But,' Sukie had had one eye on the clock, wanting to gain as much info as possible in the time, 'surely you told Milla this?'

'Yes. And she understood, I think. But she was just swept along on the whole tidal wave of big, big wedding preparations and operations and military planning – and she didn't want to upset her mother.'

'But – just running away ...?' Sukie had frowned. 'That was the coward's way out, surely?'

'Yes, I suppose it was. But I didn't know what else to do. And I didn't just run away from the wedding.' Bo-Bo had examined several small furry things floating in his shandy with interest. 'Once I knew I couldn't go through with the whole fiasco, and knew Milla simply couldn't face telling her parents that we'd like a quiet affair, I decided to run away from everything.'

Sukie had kindly fished the floating things out of his shandy with the edge of a beer mat.

'No doubt Milla has told you that I sold my companies, sold my shares, sold everything – and vanished. I hated myself for hurting her, loathed myself for leaving her – and maybe I was weak – but she knew how much I wanted her. Will always want her. I just didn't want her family and all the trappings. So – I went to Greece. Not mainland Greece, a small island where no one knew me and—'

'You started working in a bar overlooking the Aegean,' Sukie had sighed, 'and turned into a male version of *Shirley Valentine*. And now you spend your days barefooted in shorts serving retsina to tourists and no one knows you're a Sir and a multi-millionaire.'

Bo-Bo had looked askance over the top of the shandy. 'Good God, no. I bought a couple of hotels, one or two apartment blocks, a restaurant, several villas – I'm a sort of Greek island package holiday king now.'

'Oh.' Sukie had been a bit disillusioned by this. 'And you never wanted to get in touch with Milla and ask her to join you.'

'Of course I did. I never stopped thinking about her, loving her, but how could I expect her to ever forgive me after what I'd done? I'd heaped the worst sort of humiliation on her head. I'd insulted her. Ruined her. I knew she'd hate me. I just tried to live my new life without her – but I couldn't.'

Sukie had leaned forward crossing her fingers. 'So why, after all this time – are you here tonight? How come you're in this backwater village, miles from your Greek idyll? Why?'

'Because—' Bo-Bo pushed his shandy away, '—I had urgent business in the UK for the first time since I left. I told myself I wouldn't try to find Milla because I knew she'd have married someone who really deserved her, and I knew my heart would break even more – but I couldn't let it rest. Everywhere I went I just met a brick wall of silence. No one, even if they knew anything, was prepared to tell me. And then—'

'And then?' Sukie had held her breath.

'And then tonight, I did the decent thing at last. I just had this really, really strange feeling that Milla was close. That she wanted to see me ...'

Ooooh! Sukie had to sit on her hands to stop herself leaping up and punching the air.

'So, I called on her parents.'

'Bloody hell! That was brave.'

'About time I was brave,' Bo-Bo said sadly. 'Anyway, her mother used the worst language I've ever heard in my life. I didn't even understand some of the Anglo-Saxon epithets – but the vitriol was all too clear. Piss off you fucking bastard is much the same in any tongue, isn't it?'

'Yes, I suppose it is. But—'

'Just when I was feeling my absolute worst, and getting into my car, and thinking I'd have to go back to Greece without her and live without her for the rest of my life, her father – who is also terrified of her mother, by the way – scurried out of the orangery and whispered that Milla was living in Berkshire, in Bagley-cum-Russet – but he couldn't remember the address. Then he scuttled off again – and well, here I am . . .'

'Here you are,' Sukie had said happily.

'Do you think she will ever, ever begin to forgive me?'

'She might – if you beg her to. A lot. And grovel your heart out. And if you're going to meet her by the Celtic cross you'd better be going – oh, and tell her absolutely everything that you've told me – but more than that – tell her you love her, okay?'

And Bo-Bo had said okay and thank you and kissed her cheek and left.

And Sukie, feeling on top of the world, had finished her shandy – thanked Cora with all her heart – and skipped all the way back to Pixies Laughter.

Derry, she was sure, would be devastated at Milla's defection – and would need comforting and consoling. He'd probably be sitting sadly in the garden, nursing the wine and the nachos and be in desperate need of a friendly shoulder . . .

He wasn't.

Pixies Laughter was empty. Deserted. There were items of Milla's clothing trailing from her bedroom down the twisty staircase, a suitcase, half-packed, left on the landing and a note:

*Dearest Sukes,*
*You're magic! Thank you! I think I already knew what I was going to do – but in the end the choice was made for me, wasn't it? I'm moving out sooner rather than later – hope that's okay. I'll miss you loads. Will be in touch – and arrange for someone to collect the rest of my stuff. Have left a cheque in my room to cover my rent and then some. Thank you again a googol times for the love potion. You've changed my*

293

*life – and now I'll always be with the right man – the man I love.*

> *Hugs and kisses*
> *Milla xxxx*

'Which one?' Sukie had howled at the dung-heap kitchen, with its mess of potions and essences and empty wine bottles and crushed nachos and curdled sour cream. 'Which bloody one?'

# Chapter Twenty-Six

Topsy was on pins, driving the Bagley-cum-Russet cancan troupe mad. They were nervous enough anyway, fidgeting with their stocking tops, tucking themselves into the big white frilly modesty knickers, fastening ostrich feathers in each other's hair.

As the light faded, the JB Roadshow had already performed for a sensational soul-filled hour, and were now sitting on the edge of the stage, drinking beer, smoking, laughing and relaxing as the cancan troupe prepared for their show.

Sukie, feeling numb, had spent the afternoon scouring the crowd for Derry; had pushed in and out of the Weasel and Bucket, searching; had less-than-casually questioned all the Bagleyites, Fern and Timmy, Amber and Lewis and Jem, the Kylies, both sets of Blessing families, Gwyneth and her dog, Pike, and Big Ida and Val Pridmore and Joss and Freddo – and even Zillah Flanagan, Lewis's mother, who had been on tour with the JB Roadshow after marrying their bass player, the divine Clancy Tavistock, the previous autumn.

None of them it seemed, had set eyes on Derry all day.

And his phone was switched off. And Winterbrook Joinery, closed for the Bank Holiday, simply had his voice on the answerphone. Sukie had rung it innumerable times, just to listen to him, and cry.

Now she leaned against the side of the stage in the falling darkness, staring out at the milling sea of mostly-familiar faces, hundreds and hundreds of them, all crowding though the fairground, and picnicking by the stream, knowing that Derry and Milla must be somewhere, in some small love-nest, celebrating being together forever.

Bo-Bo must have failed in his pursuit, as she'd feared he would. He was probably flying back to his Greek island paradise right now feeling as heartbroken and awful as she did.

Of course she realised now, Milla must have written that note the minute Sukie had dashed off to the Barmy Cow; the moment Derry had arrived in answer to the love potion's magical pull; before Bo-Bo had tracked her down. Even as Bo-Bo and Milla were speaking on the phone, the decision had already been made. Milla must have known she was going to choose Derry; must have known that Bo-Bo had appeared just that bit too late; must have known what she was going to tell him at the meeting by the Celtic cross ...

Sukie sighed.

Ah, well – she'd only got herself to blame. She'd been warned about dabbling with the love potions, hadn't she? She'd taken the risk – and would reap the heartbreaking consequences for the rest of her life.

'Right gels!' Topsy clapped her hands. 'Let's have you backstage. Come along! Quickly! The band is ready to start. They're happy with the Offenbach – and it should be absolutely sensational with live music. Are we all ready?'

'Ready as I'll ever be.' Sukie peeled herself away from the stage. 'Oh, don't frown, Topsy. We'll be brilliant.'

Once behind the canvas backdrop, Chelsea and Sukie exchanged secret doubtful glances. The rehearsals with the ten of them had been very curate's egg. Still, what they lacked in Moulin Rouge expertise, they made up for in whooping, screaming enthusiasm and now – all in their red and black dresses, with the masses of petticoats, and the dancing ostrich feathers in their hair – they certainly looked the part.

'Sukie ...' Joss edged along the line and squeezed her hand. 'Thank you. This is something I've longed to do for – oh, I don't know how long. My life has changed completely because of you. I've no idea what you put in your potions – or even if they really played any part in this – but whatever you did for me, I'll be forever grateful.'

And Sukie had hugged Joss and then the JB Roadshow had roared into the familiar opening bars of Orpheus and the crowd had started screaming encouragement – and they were on.

Running on to the stage to tumultuous applause, they linked arms, and flounced skirts, and flashed their knickers, and kicked and skipped and circled and kicked some more. Almost able to forget her misery, Sukie was swept along by the noisy, dizzying, colourful excitement. Giddily she thought the live band transformed them from some amateur troupe in a village hall into real, live Parisian Bluebell girls – glamorous and talented.

The routines were inch perfect, even with ten of them no one collided with anyone else, and no one missed a beat.

Again, almost able to forget that her heart was broken, Sukie linked with Chelsea, circled, kicked, flounced, screamed and cartwheeled.

The JB Roadshow, playing their socks off, clearly loved every minute of it, and Joss was absolutely amazing. Then they were coming towards the finale, with the final running, and the sexy shimmying of skirts and petticoats over their heads, back, then front, tantalising and teasing, then one final flourish – one last yell – and into the splits.

The applause was astounding. Shakily, out of breath, Sukie could see a blur of faces, all whistling, and calling. It had been mind-blowing. The dancers, way up in the stratosphere, scrambled to their feet and hugged one another with exhausted glee.

297

'Wonderful gels.' Topsy wiped away a tear. 'Wonderful; the band loved it – and they want to do another show in an hour or so. After the Gunpowder Plot have done their firework display. Is that okay with you all?'

And everyone, panting and beaming, nodded.

As the JB Roadshow slammed into another superb soul selection and everyone started dancing on the green, and Joss and Freddo sneaked away into the shadows, Chelsea grabbed Sukie's arm.

'I need a drink,' she puffed. 'Bet there's a queue a mile long in the pub. I'm going to sneak some beer from the band's cool box backstage. Coming?'

Why not? She'd scrumped apples with Chelsea as a child, pinching a can of beer wasn't so different was it?

The music thrummed into her body as she followed Chelsea round the back of the stage, amid cases and boxes and huge rolls of cables. Several couples were hidden in the longer grass and Sukie muttered her apologies as she stumbled over bits of semi-naked flesh in the search for the cool box.

'Here! Got it! Catch!' Chelsea yelled above the band.

Sukie caught.

They'd just opened ice-cold cans of beer with a delicious fizz of froth, just lifted them to their parched mouths, when someone tramped round the side of the stage.

'What are you doing?' a voice barked. 'You two! Yes – you!'

They stopped. A policeman loomed out of the darkness. Shit, Sukie thought, heartbroken and arrested all in the same twenty-four hours. How much better could life get?

His eyes fastened on their jacked-up bosoms and fishnet stockings and gaudy frocks and he grinned – then stopped, looking puzzled. 'Chelsea? Chelsea Hopkins? And Sukie Ambrose? Bloody hell! I'd've thought you'd have been miles away from here by now! Bugger me – were you dancing? Was that really you up there? You were really, really hot!'

Oh, great, Sukie thought, a sex-mad policeman – and one who scarily knew their names.

She peered at him. Tall, thin, dark . . .

He didn't move. 'I don't believe this . . . Chelsea, I doubt if you'll remember me, but I had such a crush on you at school. I was so scared that you'd mess me about, I always blanked you. I was such a prat! I've never found anyone to take your place . . .'

Chelsea was making a gagging noise.

'Jesus Christ!' Sukie shook her head. 'Nicky Hambly! I thought you were in the RAF – still swapping one uniformed job for another must be fairly easy. Chelsea – it's—'

But Chelsea clearly didn't need any introduction. She and Nicky stared dopily at one another for a split-second, then with a whoop of laughter and holding hands, scampered giggling away into the dark shadows.

Sukie, feeling about as unnecessary as it was possible to get, picked up Chelsea's discarded drink, and wandered miserably out to the front of the stage again.

The band, strutting and swaying and belting out a Lee Dorsey classic, had everyone on their feet.

Oh, God, Sukie thought, skirting the enclosure where Amber's Corrie-named goats had been safely penned for the evening, and sitting on a rustic bench in the darkness, how was it possible to feel this lonely in the midst of all this jollity and noise and millions of happy people? How had she managed to magic up romances for her best friends, several acquaintances, and a few for people who didn't even know she'd done it – and feel this bloody awful herself?

She'd just have to concentrate on her career now, immerse herself in work, not give herself time to think about the what-might-have-been with Derry. She'd definitely tell Jennifer as soon as possible that she wanted to break away from Beauty's Blessings and fly solo with the aromatherapy business and work at least twenty hours a day. Jennifer would probably be okay about it – eventually – as long as she could take some commission for any appointments made via the salon or something. Yes, it would be okay.

And whatever the rights and wrongs of the love potions, she knew she'd continue to use the storehouse of garden plants in Pixies Laughter for her massage oils. Cora's legacy would not be wasted. Sukie would carry on the tradition – making people happy in her own earth-magic fashion.

Sukie nodded sadly in the darkness. If only she could be happy, too . . .

'Shove up.'

She turned her head.

Derry grinned at her. 'Budge up a bit. Your petticoats should have a seat all of their own.'

She swallowed, not looking at him, not wanting to see Milla, all glowing, behind him.

'Oh, and beer—' Squeezing on to the bench, Derry removed one of the cans from her fingers. 'How brilliant is that. The most beautiful girl in the world, dressed up in an outfit that would stir a eunuch, and providing cold beer. Thank you God.'

She smiled. He always made her smile.

'You were awesome. On stage. I was so proud of you. And aren't you speaking to me?'

She nodded. 'Yes, of course. And thank you – I-I didn't know you were here.'

'Got here just in time for your show. Stood there, beaming like an idiot, waiting for you to come off so I could tell you how brilliant you were, and then you and Chelsea just vanished.'

She sipped her beer. 'Is Milla here?'

'No, why would she be? She left you a note, didn't she?'

Sukie nodded again. 'It didn't say much . . . It didn't have to.'

'No, I suppose not. Sukie – why are we talking to one

another as though we've only just been introduced?'

'Are we? Oh, sod it, Derry – you know why!'

'No I don't. I got here as soon as I could. I wasn't going to miss your show. I had to leave Bo-Bo's hire car at the airport, and get all Milla's junk in my jeep, and was running backwards and forwards and – what?'

'Milla and Bo-Bo have gone to the airport? Milla and *Bo-Bo*? Together?'

'Yes, that's what I've just said. Milla said she'd left you a note to explain. She wanted to leave her car at Reading station so her company's fleet manager could collect it, and Bo-Bo – bloody stupid name that is, nice bloke though – only had a little two-seater. And Milla had so much stuff – so I volunteered to be an extra driver with the jeep and run everyone everywhere, and make as many journeys as was possible to get them to Heathrow in time for their flight out to Greece. So I eventually left her and Bo-Bo at the airport, which was neat really – sort of full circle – seeing as that's where we'd met. Anyway, it took all night and most of the day and I had to get a couple of hours sleep but—'

Sukie clapped her hand over his mouth. 'Stop! So Milla went with Bo-Bo? Not you?'

'No.' Derry gently removed her hand, but held it, stroking her fingers. 'Not with me. I'm here. With you. Last night, when I came round to the cottage, I'd come to tell Milla it was all over. Which I did. I felt bad about it, but it had to be done. And she was okay about it really, and then you phoned about Bo-Bo. And where I'd been planning to rush to the Barmy Cow and join you in whatever dubious alcoholic beverage the Berkeley Boys could conjure up for the occasion, Milla said she was going to meet Bo-Bo, and she loved him, and she intended to be with him – and would I help her ... So I did.'

'Because you're a nice bloke?'

'Yes, precisely.' Derry grinned. 'And because she said she'd leave you a note. And because I liked her, but mainly because I wanted to get her and bloody Bo-Bo out of the way so that I really could have some space and time to be with you – which is something I've wanted for – oh, God – since the day I woke up in your bed.'

Sukie grinned. 'That sounds wrong, somehow.'

'Sounds pretty good to me.' Derry removed the beer can from her other hand and kissed her. 'And if I've just made one huge mistake – please tell me and I'll go away and quietly hang myself from one of those conveniently placed willow trees.'

'You've just made one huge mistake.'

'What? Bugger – and I haven't got any stout rope.'

They grinned at one another, then Sukie wriggled against him and kissed him again. And again, just in case the first time had been a fantasy.

'I used a love potion on Milla and Bo-Bo,' she said softly. 'And I so wanted to on you – but I didn't.'

'Would have been a complete waste.' Derry traced the outline of her lips with his forefinger. 'I was already way under your spell. However—' he grinned at her, '—I did use one on you – just in case.'

'*What*?' She stared at him. 'When?'

'That afternoon when we were in the garden. When the bunion ladies arrived. I'd made the tea, remember? In a pot?'

She nodded.

'And I thought it might just help things along a bit – so I did the forget-me-not and scarlet pimpernel one – because it was quick and I could find the right essences in the cupboard and I remembered the rhyme.'

Sukie punched him. 'Sneaky sod! Go on then – remind me.'

'*Pimpernel red and forget-me-not blue; Together make love's dreams come true*.' Derry laughed. 'No, sorry – but the poetry's bloody awful, isn't it? The effect, however, hopefully, wasn't.'

'The bunion ladies may have benefited—' Sukie snuggled

302

even closer, '—but it was wasted on me, too. I was already in love.'

'Oh, dear – who's the fortunate bloke? Anyone I know?'

'Nah. Just some gorgeously sexy and very talented joiner from Winterbrook who one day – soon, I hope – might just be moving into Pixies Laughter with me.'

'Lucky sod.' Derry kissed her slowly. 'Bet he can't wait.'

'I hope not.' Sukie bunched her skirts together as he pulled her on to his lap. She slid her arms round his neck. 'And somehow I don't think we'll be needing any of Cora's love potions to help things along, do you?'

'Absolutely, definitely not,' Derry said softly, kissing her again. 'We'll never need any outside influences, Sukes. I reckon we've got more than enough magic of our own ...'

## Seeing Stars
Christina Jones

When city-girl Amber arrives to spend the summer in the village of Fiddlesticks, the only stars she recognises are the ones she reads about in her glossy celeb magazines. So she is stunned to find herself surrounded by new neighbours who organise their entire lives around the astral calendar. More scarily, Amber finds that the villagers actually believe that the stars and moon can make wishes come true.

Even Amber's new boss, Mitzi Blessing, believes in magic. Amber remains loudly sceptical, but she doesn't seem the harm in joining in the odd celebration, especially as they bring her in to contact with the gorgeously enigmatic Lewis. But when, as a result of one of Amber's half-hearted celestial incantations, something totally inexplicable happens, she begins to wonder if maybe, just maybe, there's more to this astral-magic than meets the eye...

## Praise for Christina Jones:

'sexy...unputdownable...a heart-thumping read' Company

'feisty tale of friendship and laughter, loyalty and love...engaging' *The Times*